BOOKS BY RICHARD BARAGER

The Atheist and the Parrotfish

Red Clay, Yellow Grass: A Novel of the 1960s
[Coming 2018]

DEDICATION

To my wife, Gail,
whose artist's soul inspired this story.

"The supreme function of reason is to show man that some things are beyond reason."
~ *Blaise Pascal*

Chapter 1

HIS RESENTMENT LAY LIKE a dragon in slumber, a smoldering, glowing thing unextinguished by the wash of time. And now the drone of an ancient chant, in harmony with the rhythmic flash of an overhead heart monitor, had sparked it anew. Yet if the heavyset, white-haired, walleyed man hunched over the bed rail in front of him had not been a Catholic chaplain, Cullen Brodie might not have loathed him so. Might not have seethed at his simpering piety, his handholding, prayer-mongering intrusion into the intensive care unit. Thomas Lawson hovering bedside, reciting the *Pater Noster* with the parents of a young Latino Cullen had saved the night before. Not with prayer, mind you, but with reason and science—and a crash dialysis treatment, administered by an unflappable gem of a nurse.

He brushed by Lawson and stood at the foot of the bed. A distinctive odor of blood and excrement came from the next room over, where an alcoholic bled into his bowel from esophageal veins made plump and oozing by cirrhosis. The weathered mestizo faces of the boy's diminutive parents lit up at the sight of the *médico* who had rescued their son.

"*Buenos días, Doctor!*" Their hands slipped from Lawson's pink-fingered grasp. They eased away from him.

"*Buenos días,*" Cullen responded. He turned to his patient. Coarse black hair plastered the boy's forehead, begrimed and lank. "*Cómo se siente, Miguel?*"

"Better. Way better. I can move again."

He kicked a leg in the air as proof. Good, Cullen thought. The blood washing of the previous night's dialysis session had completely corrected the life-threatening, muscle-paralyzing excess of potassium caused by unrecognized kidney failure.

Cullen nodded his approval. "Nice. Almost ready for soccer."

Miguel gave a pained look and opened his mouth to speak, but Cullen raised a hand and interrupted him. "I know, I know. *Fútbol*."

Miguel grinned at his parents. Lawson laid a hand on the boy's shoulder and looked at Cullen. "He seems to have responded to your therapy. His parents will be very grateful."

Cullen glared at him. Lawson's eczematous cheeks flushed. "Just doing my job," Cullen said. "The same way I always do." Lawson withdrew his hand from the boy's shoulder and shuffled away from the bed.

An incident barely a month ago had strained their relationship. A patient's husband had complained to the hospital CEO that Cullen refused to acknowledge God's hand in healing his stricken wife. The letter made no mention of his difficult diagnosis that salvaged the woman's kidneys and kept her off dialysis. The CEO turned the matter over to the Quality Assurance Committee, which delegated a hospital chaplain — Lawson — to counsel him about spiritual sensitivity. Cullen's hostile response, telling Lawson to mind his own business and leave the care of ill patients to doctors and nurses, had prompted Lawson to ask if a priest molested him when he was young.

Cullen tensed at the memory of the accusation. As if being made a cornholed catamite by a pedophile priest was the only possible reason an ex-altar boy could have for being hostile to the Catholic Church. Oh, it was worse than that, Cullen told him. He would rather have been molested.

Even that would have been better than living with the nightmare that haunted him still: a small boy drifting face down, his alabaster body immersed in a timeless sea of blue, an image born of an act that could never be undone. A disgraceful night that could never be atoned for, no matter how many patients he helped. No, he wasn't hostile to religion because a man of God molested him; he was hostile because there *was* no God. No loving and omnipotent God would ever have permitted such a thing.

"*Vaya con Dios*," Lawson said to Miguel's parents before leaving. That his pronunciation and accent were laughable compared to Cullen's fluent Castilian was cold solace. Lawson had given them the one succor Cullen was incapable of giving.

Cullen saw his last inpatient by eight and headed to the doctors' lounge off ICU for more coffee. He paused before going in and rubbed his gritty, sleep-starved eyes with the heels of hands that could have belonged to a pipe fitter subduing metal tubes for a living or a chiropractor kneading and twisting spines all day. Instead, they were the huge, corded hands of a 54-year-old nephrologist with thinning hair, dyed brown and swept back, the way he had worn it for thirty-five years. Owing to a strong jaw and sharp chin, his deeply rilled face appeared sure and decisive, save for an elusive sadness in his eyes. Six-foot-five when fully extended, his sinewy frame was as yet unbent by time, though his long spindles of muscle had dimpled of late, become pocked by age.

A nagging vibration prodded his hip. He unholstered his cell phone and stared at the string of digits in the window. He went inside the lounge and dialed the number.

"Dr. Brodie? This is Dawn Price, one of the transplant coordinators at St. Barnabas? We have a donor for one of your patients—Ennis Willoughby. I wanted to make sure he's medically stable for transplant before I bring him in."

"A donor for Ennis? He's at dialysis. I'm headed there now. Your transplant team must be jazzed."

"It's causing quite a buzz. Simultaneous heart-kidney transplants are pretty rare, even for a program the size of ours."

He detected a bittersweet tone to her voice, and what was that about? Coordinators were usually ebullient when they called, the Gift of Life in hand, a miracle in the offing. She should have been wetting her pants over a transplant like this, a landmark win for St. Barnabas in its countywide cage match with the university—and for Logan MacGregor, the medical director of St. Barnabas's renal transplant program and of Cullen's nephrology group. Did she resent such a high-profile, prize set of organs going to an erratic, unkempt cross-dresser whom the transplant committee—on which Dawn Price sat—had initially turned down?

"I'll look him over and call you right back," Cullen told her.

"There's one more thing." She hesitated, a brief, disquieting lull. "Dr. MacGregor's daughter-in-law is the donor. She was in an automobile accident yesterday and was declared brain dead this morning at Bayside Hospital. A procurement team is on standby. He wanted you to know."

Cullen walked unseeing through the hospital lobby and out the front entrance, oblivious to all but the grisly thought of Carla MacGregor being filleted like a pike in the caustic light of an operating room, her heart and liver and kidneys and anything else they could recycle lopped out and plunged into a container of cold saline. Knowing the donor changed things. Especially this donor, the administrative assistant of Nephrology Partners Inc., Cullen's twenty-five-physician medical practice, founded by her father-in-law to provide nephrology services throughout the county, including Beach Park Hospital, where Cullen was based.

He had first met her four years ago, after Cullen fled south from Los Angeles following his divorce—his second failed marriage in as many tries. Carla was at her desk, an elegant swan of a woman with thick brown hair. She glanced up from her pile of papers, small bosomed but full lipped, a minimalist with makeup because she didn't need any. She scanned him from head to toe as if something about him perplexed her.

"I'm Cullen Brodie. I have an interview with Dr. MacGregor."

She rose to her feet and smiled. "I'm Carla MacGregor, his executive assistant. He's been expecting you." She clasped his hand longer than necessary. The gentle pressure of it quivered his shoulders.

He caught her staring at him from time to time thereafter—at office Christmas parties or at social events on the arm of Duncan, MacGregor's underachieving son and their medical group's billing supervisor—with the same quizzical look, the same astonished oval of her mouth. And each time her effect on him was the same. Gooseflesh. An eerie chill fingering his spine. Had she somehow intuited his role in her life, his arrival heralding her fate, the future dispersal of her organs to one of his patients?

He cut across the parking lot to Beach Park Dialysis—thirty yards south of the eight-story main hospital building—and tapped a metal pad that activated a pair of automatic doors leading to a waiting room appointed in mauve and green. An elderly amputee in a wheelchair marked time before the start of his treatment. The floor beneath was tiled instead of carpeted, to accommodate the occasional post-dialysis spill of blood from seeping needle sites of patients in a rush to get home. Cullen entered the code to a keyless lock of a door between the waiting room and treatment area and stepped inside.

Thirty dialysis stations lined the walls of a spacious rectangular room, with a nursing desk in the center. Each station was comprised of an aqua-colored chair resembling a La-Z-Boy and a silver dialysis machine posted next to it. Nurses in blue scrubs moved from station to station, taking blood pressures, responding to machine alarms, and entering vital signs into electronic charts. Patients slept or read or watched flat-screen TVs suspended in front of them by c-arms, paying no mind to the large-bore needles impaled in their arms like harpoons. Given that a patient's entire blood volume circulated through their machine's dialyzer—artificial kidney—every twelve minutes, it was a wonder they weren't all bolt upright, squeezing finger marks into their armrests.

Cullen looked around the room for Ennis, whom St. Barnabas had at first deemed psychologically unfit for transplant due to unresolved gender conflict. At the age of sixty-three, no less, his whole life spent trying to suppress, rather than express, his inner woman. The psychiatrist he was required to see felt that his fragile psychiatric state put him at risk for post-transplant emotional instability and self-destructive behavior—like neglecting to take his medication, the most common cause of transplant failure. Cullen appealed to MacGregor, arguing that Ennis had no *time* to blossom into a fully self-actualized cross-dresser. Without a heart transplant—and, since his kidneys had failed on account of his heart, a renal transplant as well—he would be dead in months. He was melting away before their eyes, growing more gaunt and feeble by the day. He needed a dual-organ transplant, not a personality transplant. MacGregor agreed and reversed the committee's decision, bringing them all to this moment.

He spotted Ennis in a chair along the north wall of the clinic. He had on a snakeskin-print, short-sleeve duster dress and a shiny blonde wig pulled low on his brow to cover his hairline. Loops of blood-filled tubing festooned his chest. On his feet was a pair of black tennis shoes. Hairless legs latticed by thick veins peeked out between the rims of his white socks and the hem of his dress. With caved-in temples and sunken cheeks, a dusky wattle dangling practically to his chest, broken teeth, sallow skin, and a glaze of despair in his eyes, it was hard to imagine a less appealing host for Carla MacGregor's youthful organs. All he lacked was the striped garb of Auschwitz.

Was this really the best they could do for her Gift of Life? A 63-year-old transvestite with gender confusion who bathed once a week? Was this what she envisioned when she signed her donor card? Cullen could stop it, could still prevent the waste of her precious organs. He could call Dawn Price and tell her that Ennis's condition had deteriorated, that he would never survive surgery. No one would question him. Ennis would never know. And the Organ Procurement Agency would reallocate her organs to someone with more potential than an aging, tatterdemalion transgender.

Someone with more potential. He grunted and pursed his lips; he sounded like a social engineer calibrating an individual's worth to society. But what of moral worth? Moral worth wasn't dependent on potential. It was dependent on being human. God created humans in his image, the nuns used to say, and bearing the image of God gives human beings intrinsic moral worth. The nuns: their sanctimonious voices pestered him still. He fingered the lapel of his coat—not the short white jacket of students and trainees, but the long white coat of a fully vested physician—and strode over to Ennis and sat on a roller stool beside him.

"I have something to tell you. Something wonderful. St. Barnabas called. They have a donor for you."

Chapter 2

HIS DOCTOR'S WORDS PINNED him to the back of his chair. He trembled, a fine quiver, then a rampant shaking, what little adrenalin he had left coursing through him like a tonic. His doctor, Dr. Brodie, who hadn't batted an eye the first time Ennis came to dialysis in a dress. A doctor whom, despite his age—not that far behind Ennis—the nurses still had their eyes on, even the young black girl, Sheila. "That man got it goin' on, uh-huh, got it goin' *on*." The doctor who teased him about getting his nails done at the same Vietnamese place their clinic manager, Toni, went to. "They stock one color, Ennis. Harlot red. Don't do it." His used-past-expiration-date of a heart pounded like it hadn't in months. He lurched forward in his chair and thrust his right arm out. His fistula arm, heedless of the needles embedded there, the bloodlines fastened to the hubs.

They have a donor for you.

Transplant was all Ennis Willoughby thought about. At night, when he fell into bed, oxygen prongs stuck up his nose, wondering if he'd last 'til dawn; upon waking, too feeble to shower or shave, no desire to eat, wasting away like a wormy mongrel; throughout the grinding day, a slog just to drive to dialysis or to the store for groceries—let alone slip into a skirt and put a wig and lipstick on, maybe shave his legs and purr like a cat at the silky texture of nylon stockings against his skin.

He came out of the closet in part thanks to the nurses at dialysis and the compliments they gave him, no matter how cheesy he looked, with no strength to gussy up the way he wanted, barely enough to bathe. But now death was bearing down on him like a freight train, and then what? Cross-dresser limbo? Tranny purgatory? He couldn't hold out much longer and had resigned himself to dying without living the life he should have, out of the shadow of shame. The only thing that kept him going was the faint hope of a miracle: a dual-organ transplant, simultaneous heart-kidney, the whole shebang, a brand new pump in his chest and off dialysis in one swoop. If only it could be, he had prayed.

They have a donor for you.

The alarm on his machine sounded, and the blood pump shut down. "Bebe! Be careful," the nearest nurse, Rose, scolded. "You tangled your lines." She straightened his arm and placed it back on the armrest. "Why you so fidgety?"

Bebe. That's what the Filipino nurses in the dialysis clinic called each other. *Beh-bay.* He liked it when Rose called him that too. He pictured a factory somewhere in Manila, scores of little brown women rolling off conveyor belts with California stamped on their foreheads. Not that he cared. By and large, they made good nurses, and if it helped fix the nursing shortage Toni was always carping about, then ship them over by the crate was how he saw it. White American girls weren't interested in nursing anymore. Too much lifting and wiping.

Dr. Brodie stood and moved out of the way, his long, athletic body, his striking, sun-creased face. "Go ahead and disconnect him, Rose. He needs to get down to St. Barnabas. Ennis is getting a transplant!"

Bedlam. Commotion. Nurses clapping, patients cheering. Rose whisked his needles out of his arm and slapped two-by-two gauze pads over his puncture sites. He struggled to his feet and looked Dr. Brodie in the eye but couldn't hold his gaze without tearing up.

"I'm, what you might say, all choked up. Pray for me, Doc."

His doctor gave him a hug, natural and unforced. "Good luck, Ennis. We'll all be rooting for you." He caught the scent of cologne, a tinge of lime. Except for his father, Ennis had never hugged a man before. It felt good. Not queer or anything.

Good.

He wheeled hard into the driveway with his hands slick on the wheel and his mind a jumbled mess. He pressed the door opener clipped to the visor of his Impala and pulled inside the garage. He figured he wouldn't be needing his car for quite some time.

Maybe never.

He hit a button on the wall and ducked beneath the heavy wooden door and stumbled back outside as the rollers grated down their rusty tracks. His breath came in staggered gulps, even this a task for his flabby heart. Either that or he was still hyperventilating over getting called for transplant.

He looked across the street, with a stab of regret, at the red brick elementary school his daughter might have attended had his cross-dressing not driven off his pretty young wife, who took their little girl — five at the time — with her. He turned and faced the butter-yellow rambler he'd bought three years later, in 1984, when his painting business finally took off. He'd lived there a quarter-century now, even paid his mortgage off ten years early. Good thing. A year later viral myocarditis got him and he never worked again. Had to hire a Mexican to paint his own home. Did a pretty fair job, though, did young Jesus. Except for the eaves. Peeling already. Probably weren't scraped good enough. That was the problem nowadays. Everybody was in a big damn rush. Not enough pride in the work they did.

He let himself in to gather his things for the hospital but paused in the entryway. He shook his head at the filth and clutter of the kitchen to his left: food-streaked dishes in the sink, Wheaties box on the counter in a sea of crumbs, travertine creased with dirt. Though his home was small—two bedrooms, a bath, a kitchen, and a living room—most days lately he was too weak for even the most basic of chores. He hired a cleaning service, but the young girls they sent out couldn't speak English and annoyed the shit out of him with the slipshod way they did things.

He kept a packed suitcase in the living room, so it didn't take long to get ready. The nurse coordinator at St. Barnabas said they had only four hours to transplant him once they harvested a donor's heart. The clock would start ticking as soon as he had his blood tested one last time for antibodies. Harvested. It sounded, what you might say, ghoulish.

He added a few final items to his bag—a scarred-up Travel Pro that raised a poof of dust from the couch when he cornered too sharply and banged against it—and went into his bedroom and drew open the closet door. One last decision to make before the cab he had called before leaving dialysis arrived to take him to the hospital.

What to wear?

The psychiatrist the transplant program referred him to—Dr. Rebecca Winthrop; Becky, she said to call her—had told him to concentrate on balancing the masculine and feminine parts of his personality. She made it awfully hard to concentrate on anything the way she crossed her legs and sent her skirt halfway up her thigh. Dr. Winthrop—Becky—gave him a boner. But she wasn't the one doing the transplant today. What if he wore a dress and his transplant surgeon, Dr. Allen, wasn't as open-minded about trannies as Becky was? What if the straitlaced surgeon took one look at him and decided he was too weird to risk a set of organs on

Richard Barager

after all? He wanted to wear women's clothing to his transplant—the first day of his new life, a second bite at the apple—but it wasn't that easy to hush the persistent voice of reproach murmuring in his ear. Though he had made strides with this self-worth thing Becky was so big on— *There's nothing wrong or perverted about it, Ennis; it's who you are*—the part of him that since age nine had come to expect punishment and rejection for wearing a dress was still a force to be reckoned with.

Guilt and shame were seared into him like a branding iron on a steer's hide that summer in Toledo, where his parents settled after the war. His father had been a sailor aboard the USS *Enterprise* during the Battle of Midway. As far as Denton Willoughby was concerned, Midway began and ended with Wade McClusky, the *Enterprise*'s air group commander, whose squadron of scout planes—while running on fumes—located the enemy carrier fleet. Dive-bombers called to the scene by McClusky sank the *Kaga, Akagi,* and *Soryu*, breaking the back of the Imperial Navy and turning the tide in the Pacific.

His father had been obsessed with learning to fly ever since. One of Ennis's earliest and fondest memories was of lying side-by-side with him beneath a brown Philco radio—the one with Bakelite casing and an arched front panel resembling the grille of a car—and listening to *Sky King*. His father smelled of beer and cigarettes. With his dark cowl of hair and New York sneer, he looked like a young Robert De Niro. He put his arm around Ennis and told him that once he got a few flights under his belt, he would take Ennis up with him, so his son would grow up to be like the hero of Midway. Ennis vowed that day to become a Navy pilot—not because he wanted to be like Wade McClusky, but because he loved his father more than anyone in the whole world. Except his mother.

His father saved enough money from his job at the Jeep factory to pay for flying lessons at National Aviation Airport, a small municipal airfield flush against the Ohio-Michigan line. It had an east-west cinder runway and a couple of metal hangars southwest of the airstrip. One Saturday afternoon, while his father was at the airport, Ennis's mother took his two sisters, Sarah and Diane, to a neighbor girl's birthday party. Ennis stayed home to listen to the Cleveland Indians on the radio. He didn't much care for baseball, but his father did, and he wanted to surprise him by telling him the score. Like when his father went for a haircut and Hank the barber told him the score. Hank's face always looked all intense and serious, as if he were reporting something crucial and momentous that no one else knew. But when Ennis saw his sisters in their frilly dresses and patent-leather shoes, something tripped in his brain. He wanted to wear a dress too — the same as when he wanted to play with dolls or have long, girly hair to brush. He never told anyone about these thoughts but having them didn't make him feel bad or ashamed. Only keen to do it, like when you look at a rose and want to sniff it. So he waited until his mother and sisters left, took off his shirt and pants, and slipped into Sarah's yellow smock dress. He daubed on his mother's lipstick in front of the bathroom mirror and puckered and preened like she did, reveling in his reflection — until his father appeared in the doorway, home early from his flying lesson.

His crestfallen look hardened into a gimlet-eyed gaze that nailed Ennis to the wall. "Take the dress off, son. And wipe your lips." His voice was limpid, righteous.

Terrifying.

Ennis did as he was told and stood there in his little green boxer shorts, his heart beating like a snared rabbit's. He snuffled at the sight of his father unfastening his belt and pulling it through the loops of his pants.

"I'm gonna strap your ass, Ennis. You know why?"

"'Cause I put Sarah's dress on?"

"That's right, 'cause you put Sarah's dress on. Now turn around and grab your ankles."

He shuffled his feet and bent over and grasped his ankles.

"This is gonna hurt somethin' fierce, but if you cry, I'll have to keep strappin' you. Navy pilots don't act like women. Not ever."

The lashing he endured on the soft pulp of his ass made his knees buckle but he did not cry. He bit his lip and stared at the tile between his straddled, quivering legs.

Navy pilots don't act like women.

His father's words had their intended effect, even now, at sixty-three. He reached into the closet for a pair of pants and denim work shirt. He put them on and went into the living room and sat on the couch to wait for his cab. The brightness of a mote-filled shaft of light seemed to mock the lie of his existence.

The ride to St. Barnabas took thirty minutes, darting and swerving amidst the high-speed drone of traffic, a white-knuckled game of chicken with freeway-faces wanting their way, forever seeking the advantage, no matter how small, how meaningless. Over a lane change, for God's sake. A fricking lane change.

His grinning cabbie—Joseph Livingston, the license on the visor said—seemed to relish cutting people off, the nicer the car the better, trailing a wake of blaring horns and middle fingers thrust against windshields. The bunched collar of his sheer red shirt lay against his glossy black nape like a red silk hankie nestled in the pocket of a tuxedo.

Ennis moved to the edge of his seat. "Easy there, Livingston. Be just my luck to die on the way to my heart transplant."

Livingston shot him a look in the mirror, all white eyeballs and teeth, the left front one gold. "Heart transplant, mon? Why didn't you say so?"

"That's right, heart transplant. Kidney, too," he added, hoping to knock an additional ten miles an hour off the speedometer. "Where're you from, anyway?"

"Soufrière, on the island of St. Lucia." He let up on the gas. "A heart and a kidney, mon? Who's the donor?"

"Who's the *donor*? My brother-in-law, that's who—said he didn't need his heart any more. How the hell should I know who the donor is? They're dead."

Livingston shook his head. "No good, mon. How can you appease the *ti bon ange* of someone you don't know?"

Appease the T-bone steak of someone he didn't know? "I don't have the foggiest idea what you're talking about. Sounds like voodoo hocus pocus to me."

Livingston waved a long, bony finger in the air. "Voodoo, mon, but not hocus pocus. The soul consists of two parts: an inner core and an outer rim. The inner core is the *gros bon ange*—the great good angel, the energy of life shared by all living things. The outer rim is the *ti bon ange*—the small good angel, the unique traits of a particular human being. At death, the *ti bon ange* must be properly preserved, so the wisdom and knowledge of previous lives can be passed on. A ceremony must be held one year and a day after a person's death to peacefully recycle their *ti bon ange*—and return their *gros bon ange* to the Energy Pool that connects all things. Some of the *houngans* say the *ti bon ange* resides in the heart. If you are going to have someone else's heart inside you, then their *ti bon ange* becomes your responsibility. How can you pay tribute to someone you don't know?"

"Easy. Ever heard of the Tomb of the Unknown Soldier? Tell you what. A year from now, I'll hoist a flute of champagne and throw the glass against a wall. Maybe that'll satisfy your angels."

Livingston gave a look of dismay and fell silent. Soon the steel-and-glass of St. Barnabas Hospital loomed in front of them, the name spelled out in huge orange letters across the top of the seven-story marvel. It had taken Ennis's breath away the first time he saw it: the grand piano in the lobby, with oil paintings of California beach scenes lining the walls; eucalyptus-scented private rooms with floor-to-ceiling windows, flat screen TVs, iPod docking stations, and sleeper-sofas for families (not that he had a family, but still); and outdoor healing gardens, where you could sun yourself with the sweet scent of jasmine swirling up your nose. And a hospital concierge desk. *For what?* he wondered. Snorkeling trips to Malaga Cove? Group visits to Sea World?

Livingston got off the interstate and turned onto an azalea-studded, palm tree-lined drive that could have been the entrance to a Ritz Carlton. He pulled to the front curb and set Ennis's bag on the sidewalk. Ennis handed him forty dollars.

"Thank you, mon. And good luck. May God watch over your souls."

He had already entered the lobby, where a pianist in a lavender dress played *Bolero*—Ennis saw the movie *10* three times, Bo Derek in those cornrow braids; he would have crawled through broken glass for a taste of that—before Livingston's use of the plural registered with him. Souls. As in two. His and his donor's: Voodoo loving, hex placing, Third World bastard.

Try as he might, he headed to registration unable to stop wondering who his donor was.

Things got going once he told the patronizing clerk at admissions—a red-lipped woman wearing a string of pearls—that he was there for a transplant. A kind-faced, overweight nurse with short gray hair and a limp escorted him to a room in ICU, where they fastened an ID bracelet on him, had him sign consent forms, drew half a dozen vials of blood, and had a male orderly shave him from neck to knees. He was then made to shower with Phisohex soap and shampoo to protect against MRSA, some kind of invasive staph infection from hell. The stall had a sliding glass door— the Ritz Carlton touch again. His nurse started a pair of IVs in his arms and he was put into bed to wait. And wait. And wait.

He tried watching TV, but was too anxious to concentrate. His gaze kept drifting to the empty sleeper-sofa, which should have been packed with family by now. It was his father he most wanted there. His strong, handsome father.

Six weeks after he had licked Ennis for wearing Sarah's dress, he carted their whole family up U.S. 25 in a station wagon to watch his first solo flight at National Aviation Airport. They gathered in front of the nearest hanger, basting in the thick July heat. His father snapped off a salute and climbed into an orange and white Cessna 170 and taxied to the end of the airstrip. After waiting for whatever clearance he needed, he rolled down the cinder runway and took off smooth as could be, like McClusky off the *Enterprise*. Ennis thrilled to the sight of his dad's plane climbing the beryl sky and performing a series of flawless banks and dives before skimming off to the south at a cruising speed of 120 mph. He reappeared fifteen minutes later and maneuvered a mile overhead. At the end of his allotted time, he circled into an easterly approach route with the graceful skill of Sky King.

But something wasn't right. The Cessna's wings wobbled and its nose pitched downward. It yawed into a deadly spin. The bottom fell away from Ennis's stomach and a cold, unseen hand clamped itself around his heart. His mother screamed and his sisters cried and his father's plane whistled into the tarmac and exploded.

He ran behind his mother as fast as he could, yelling out, "Daddy! Daddy!" His lungs burned and his eyes poured as he drew near the plane's fiery carcass, to which a ground crew was frantically attending. The father whose approval he so desperately sought to regain—that very morning at breakfast Ennis had promised anew to become a Navy pilot—was entombed in a billow of smoke. The second it cleared, he bolted toward the largest piece of fuselage—the front half of the plane, minus its wings. His father's charred skeleton was melted onto the console. Smoke wafted from his blackened skull, his mouth agape in a ghastly grimace.

"Why the tears, Ennis? Cheer up. You're about to get a new heart and kidney, my friend."

At the foot of his bed stood Dr. Charles Allen, his transplant surgeon, wearing green scrubs and a white lab coat, bald head glistening, black beard shot with silver. A plain-faced slip of a woman in a baggy blue scrub suit stepped forward, syringe in hand.

"This is Doctor Roberts," Allen said. "Your anesthesiologist. She's going to give you something to make you sleep. When you wake up, your new heart will be beating like a drum and you'll be peeing like a racehorse."

She gave a perfunctory smile and jabbed the needle of the syringe into the rubber port of his IV. Her petite thumb depressed the barrel. A delicious, golden warmth worked its way inside his brain, like the tequila he drank at the brothel in Tijuana, where the Mexican girls charged only ten dollars extra when he wore a lace teddy.

He remained vaguely aware of his gurney pushing through a set of double doors. The last thought he had was of how alone he felt.

Then the void.

He was sitting alone at a small table set for two on the deck of an aircraft carrier rolling gently at sea. A faint breeze salted his tongue. It was an old carrier, with the number six stamped on its deck fore and aft. The *Enterprise*, his father's ship! Sailors in service whites lined the deck, standing at ease against a palette of pink and orange, the ocean at sunset.

He was dressed en femme, but with such taste and elegance he passed for a woman, he knew he did. He adjusted his wig, a blonde mane styled and fluffed just so. He hardly recognized himself in the mirror of the compact he pulled from his handbag, the clever application of foundation and concealer, the complex interplay of eye shadow and liner making his eyes wide and mysterious. He fingered a string of pearls at his neck, toyed with a silver earring clipped to his ear, smoothed the long-sleeved, black cashmere turtleneck dress he wore—and checked his L'eggs for runs. Immaculate.

He placed his hands on the table's white linen and admired the rich red gloss of his nails. A moment later, a sailor stepped from the shadow of the bridge, so raffish-looking in his white bell-bottoms and black leather shoes, his tar-flap collar and black neckerchief. He smiled and removed his white Dixie cup hat.

"Mind if I join you?" It was his father at twenty, Seaman First Class Denton Willoughby.

They sat without tension, some sort of accommodation reached. An officer in a high-collared white tunic with gold buttons and black epaulets appeared, bearing two glasses of wine on a tray. He had a round chin, unwavering eyes, and a broad nose. His father stood and saluted. The same salute he gave before climbing into the Cessna that day, sharp and snappy, confident of his place in the scheme of things.

"This here's my son, Ennis, Lieutenant. Come to see the Big E in action."

Why did his father do that, give him away when he was passing for a woman, transgender Nirvana at last?

The officer set the tray on the table, removed his cover, with its black visor and silver eagle in front, and bowed. "Lieutenant Commander C. Wade McClusky, at your service."

The entire crew clapped and cheered. The significance of it dawned on him. Rather than merely passing for a woman, he had been accepted for what he was: a man who chose to dress like a woman. Accepted by the crew and most decorated hero of the most decorated ship of World War II. And, best of all, accepted by his father. For the feminine slice of himself that he could no more deny than could Wade McClusky deny the magnificent uniform he wore. He must have gone to Heaven. How else to explain the strange hymn resounding in his head?

Truth within my conscience reigns
Be my king that I may be firmly bound, forever free.

"Ennis. Open your eyes. Can you hear me? Open your eyes, Ennis." A dream, that's all it had been, a wonderful dream.

A dream dissolved. He tried to move, but couldn't. His hands were lashed to the bed rail. And his chest, oh God, the pain! It felt like he'd been prized apart, crow barred in two. He tried crying out: nothing. Then he remembered. They had warned him not to panic when he came to after surgery, that his hands would be tied to keep him from pulling out a tube in his windpipe to help him breathe. But that meant he was alive! He had made it through surgery. Were his transplants working? Did he even get them?

He opened his eyes. Stabbing white light. Haze. Someone squeezed his hand. He squeezed back. A man bent over him. A man with a beard.

"You did great, Ennis." The man's lips moved in slow motion and his shiny head was the size of a beach ball. Light splattered off the top of it. "Both transplants went off without a hitch. Your kidney is making urine and your heart's pumping like a champ. It fit into your chest with room to spare."

He closed his eyes. He wanted to be back on the *Enterprise*, surrounded by sailors cheering for Denton Willoughby's tranny son. But before he submerged back inside the sheltering chrysalis of his dreams, he grew aware of something inside him. Something foreign. Dwelling there. Inhabiting him.

Whump... whump... whump.

He could feel it pulsing, throbbing, beating, a life force all its own, infusing him with vitality, an unaccustomed torrent of blood rushing through him like a swollen river.

Whump... whump... whump.

His chest rocked, barely capable of restraining the organic generator inside him. And he knew: he had his second bite at the apple. Never again would he submit to shame, be made to play the freak by society's raised brow. Never again. This time, he would embrace his destiny. Openly, brazenly, proudly transgender, thanks to this wondrous gift inside him, this pounding heart that threatened to lift him off the mattress.

Whump... whump... whump.

His donor. Who was she?

Chapter 3

CULLEN SETTLED INTO A tawny leather swivel chair in front of his office workstation and powered up. A giclée of the Grand Canal at sunset hung on a faux-paper gold wall in front of him. Behind him sat a yellow birch wood desk and matching bureau.

A sentimental, slim-shanked junior associate in the design firm MacGregor hired to decorate all of the group's office locations had conceived the entire, color-coordinated scheme. Cullen wound up sleeping with her, another in a passel of outré entanglements with younger women he had little in common with. Tess, her name was: an interior designer with a tramp stamp on her sacrum and schoolmarm chignon she unfurled before sex. Who made him drink Red Bull and go to Adele concerts and eat truffles in bed while reading passages from *The Time Traveler's Wife*—more cloying than the truffles and Tess combined. Tess of the d'Urbervilles, he called her, a not-so-subtle attempt to upgrade the fiction she read. To no avail; Hardy's *Pure Woman Faithfully Presented* was not for her.

He looked at the roguish biceps of the striped-shirted gondolier in the painting and envied the man his age-appropriate wife. He pictured her waiting for him at night with a plate of warm bread and olive oil, her sultry face and thick, creamy thighs. Lately the warm bread and olive oil appealed to him nearly as much as the imaginary woman's legs.

He clicked open Ennis Willoughby's electronic medical record in anticipation of his office visit the following morning, his first with Cullen since Ennis's transplant three months before. The most recent report from St. Barnabas confirmed what Cullen already knew from Logan MacGregor: both organs were working beautifully. He had spoken a number of times by phone with MacGregor since Ennis's surgery, but saw him only once, at their medical group's quarterly business meeting. He pulled Cullen aside for a word in his office a few minutes before it began.

A gold silk settee and maple wing chair with intricate finials occupied one end of the room, a massive cherry wood desk and pair of Continental chairs the other. MacGregor stood beside the desk, a big, barrel-chested man of sixty-four with dazzling blue eyes and a blowsy face. The shock of silver and gray atop his head called to mind the markings of a silverback gorilla, a dominant male. He raised his head slightly to meet Cullen's gaze.

"I know you know this, but since Willoughby will be back under your care soon, I wanted to remind you that donor and recipient identities are confidential. Even Duncan has no idea who got Carla's heart. I'm bound by law to refuse to tell him. The same applies to you if your patient asks."

"I understand. How's Ennis doing?"

"Incredibly well." MacGregor's eyes shimmered. "It's a remarkable gift she gave him. I hope he makes the most of it."

Cullen detected a whiff of regret, and why not? MacGregor and his son and grandchildren were bereft, and the beneficiary was a troubled cross-dresser in his sixties. It was only natural to have wanted Carla's organs to go to someone younger or with an intact family; Cullen had thought the same himself. He put a hand on MacGregor's shoulder. "I'll do all I can to see he does."

He clicked the Patient Communications tab and reread a letter Ennis had sent him the week before. A remarkable letter, in more ways than one. Sometimes virtue thrived in the harshest of soil.

Dear Dr. Brodie:

Now that I've had some time to cogitate on the miracle of my transplant, I wanted to tell you how thankful I am to you for keeping me alive on dialysis and going to bat for me with the transplant committee. It's up to me to make the most of the second life I've been given. I won't let you — or my donor — down.

Having a normal heart and a new kidney is like coming back from the dead. I didn't realize how much of life had been taken from me. Little things people take for granted.

Like food.

I think I must have had a taste bud transplant, too. Spices and flavors I didn't know existed practically explode in my mouth. I crave things I never even liked before. No more renal diet, either. I ate three bananas one day just to prove I could do it. Sat there afraid to move, half-expecting to keel over from too much potassium. Next I went to the movies and had a tub of salty popcorn and a large drink. Instead of swelling up and getting short of breath like I would have on dialysis, all it did was make me have to pee before the movie was over. (I missed the best part.)

Another thing — stairs. Even three of them used to leave me gasping and clinging to the handrail. Now I make a point of taking them. It makes me giggle, like when I was young and got away with something. Energy, that's the difference. Like there's a power plant inside me kicking out kilowatts twenty-four hours a day. Sometimes I'm so charged up it's hard to get to sleep at night.

Other things have changed, too. What you might say, personal things.

My father wanted me to be a Navy pilot when I grew up, but he died in an airplane crash when I was nine. Right before my eyes. I promised his blackened corpse a Navy pilot was what I'd be. But during my senior year of high school, I took one of those pesky eye exams they make you take. The sneaky ones with the numbers hidden in the colored dots? Discovered I was colorblind — red-green color blindness, they told me. Big deal, right? So I had trouble distinguishing reds and greens. Who cared? The U.S. Navy, that's who. Automatic disqualifier.

I was crushed. Felt like I broke my promise to my father. I thought becoming a pilot would show him his little boy had grown up to be a man — not some freak in a dress. Because I loved him and wanted his approval. Even after he was dead.

I was so tore up about it I spent the next ten years drinking and fighting and getting tossed in prison. Kept me out of Vietnam, at least. But I felt guilty over it my whole life. Until now. I had a dream right after transplant that made me realize I never really wanted to be a Navy pilot — that's what he wanted me to be. Just like he wanted me to be all boy and no girl.

I know now that I can love my father more in a dress than I could ever love him in a bomber jacket. Because in a dress I'm living the truth, and from truth comes dignity. And from dignity, love. Fathers and sons — it never ends, does it?

Some other peculiar things happened since transplant, too, but they can keep until my appointment next week.

Your grateful patient,
Ennis Willoughby

❦

He closed the file and leaned back in his chair with the phrase pounding in his head like a ball-peen hammer. Fathers and sons—it never ends, does it? The unwitting reference to Turgenev dug in deep. *Fathers and Sons* was a scorpion's sting of a novel that was Cullen's story, too: the clash of religion and rationalism, of father and son. He closed his eyes and let it sluice over him, beginning as it always did, with Brodie's Tirade, and ending in a calamity he could not outrun, even now, thirty-four years removed. The same punishing image visited upon him over and over and over again, always exactly the same: a boy floating in blue—cold, heartless blue. Pitiless, merciless, immutable blue.

Godless blue.

Cullen had been only twenty-one then, trouble-free and on a glide path to med school. His father couldn't have been prouder of him, but even that gave Cullen no relief from the wrath of Brodie's Tirade. The Tirade was always at DEFCON I—ready for launch without warning. There was no way to see it coming and no way to escape his father's wild-eyed dudgeon once it began. He warmed up by rumbling about Vatican II and the death of the Tridentine Mass, then bellowed and spumed his way to *Roe v. Wade* and Edward Nichols, the city's most prominent abortionist.

Nichols was a charter member of the National Association for the Repeal of Abortion Laws, an obstetrician who opened the first abortion clinic in Minneapolis. Cullen's carpenter father, Chaz—an usher at St. Vincent's, where Cullen had attended grammar school and served as an altar boy—found NARAL and Nichols more repugnant than the Symbionese Liberation Army. It was all Chaz Brodie could do to keep from hurling an ashtray at the screen whenever Nichols appeared on local news.

But on *that* night, the night it all began, the saccharine strains of *The Mary Tyler Moore Show* cut Brodie's Tirade mercifully short. Chaz never missed an episode, not even summer reruns. He claimed the show meant Minneapolis had become an important place.

Cullen bolted out the door of the two-story home Chaz had built twenty years before into a summer downpour to meet Stan Tazinski at Trajan's Bath, a new nightspot on the corner of Fourth and Hennepin. He felt off balance from the moment they paid the three-dollar cover and stepped inside. A silver ball suspended above a transparent floor lit from beneath by colored lights turned slowly overhead, throwing splinters of light onto a farrago of sofas and love seats. Piped in music blasted from every angle, no band in sight. Packs of young males with coiffed hair and open-collared shirts roamed the aisles with giddy faces.

Tazinski ordered two Heinekens from a bartender trickling sweat off his forehead. A fogbank of smoke loitered over the bar's curl of dark wood, stinging Cullen's eyes.

"This place is weird," Tazinski said, blond and bushy and sloth-like. "Dudes keep telling me I'm handsome. I know they're queer, but it kind of makes me feel good. Does that make me homo?"

Cullen took a draft of beer. "They're just being polite. Think about something else."

They pounded brew and checked the scene. Couples gay and straight danced to the addicting sound of a sexy merengue beat, powered by a syncopated bass line and orchestral horn arrangements. Cullen held his water to the point of dribbling before making a bathroom run, leery of what might go on in the men's room. He was surprised to discover that there *was* no men's room — the bathroom was unisex, one stall fits all. He shrugged it off, zipped up, and went back to describe the toilet arrangements to Tazinski.

"This place is outta control!" Tazinski said, above the music.

A narrow-hipped man with bloodshot eyes and a receding hairline and trim moustache pranced down the aisle and shouted back at Tazinski over his shoulder.

"It's Amy, man! She makes the party harder."

Cullen looked at Tazinski. "Who's Amy?"

Tazinski shrugged and ordered another round of beers from the beleaguered bartender. The alcohol and sonic energy of the place launched them on a quest for dance partners. Cullen picked out a platinum blonde in a white jumpsuit who insisted on teaching him a dance called the Hustle. Her name was Twyla, and though she was incredibly patient with him, he had trouble catching on to the assortment of turns and twirls that he was supposed to lead, but which Twyla capably steered them through instead. The Hustle smacked too much of ballrooms and Glen Miller for his taste. He still liked the Bump, knocking hips to a live horn section wailing clean funk. Socially sanctioned dry humping, right on the dance floor. The Bump.

Twyla thanked him and moved on after they danced out the set. "How long have you been into transvestites?" a voice at his elbow asked.

He turned and encountered a long-limbed girl with high cheekbones, a finely tapered nose, and arched eyebrows and painted lips. She filled the space beside him as if conjured from the silver ball above, a fey nymph in designer jeans. Lush raven hair spilled over her shoulders from beneath a cap with *Magnifique* written across it in gold letters. Her elegant line flowed from the graceful curve of her neck to the leonine sweep of her haunch. He lingered on the swell of her turquoise halter before willing himself to make eye contact.

"What are you talking about?"

She pointed at Twyla, by then queued up outside the restroom. "Blondie's a she-male. You know, L-O-L-A Lola?"

It took him a moment to comprehend. "No way. Like I can't tell a dude from a chick."

She threw her arms in the air. "Fine. Check it out if you don't believe me."

He extended his hand in challenge. "Loser buys drinks. You might as well go order now. I'll have a Heineken."

She brushed aside a lock of hair and smiled. "We'll see."

He rounded up Tazinski and trailed Twyla into the restroom. She stepped inside a stall and clicked the lock. They sidled beside it. Cullen wrapped his arms around Tazinski and hoisted him upward with a giant thrust. He strained mightily while Tazinski took a long look before signaling to come down. Tazinski burst out laughing as they cleared the restroom door.

"She undid her jumpsuit and pulled out a big hairy wanger! She's chick-with-a-dick, man. A horse dick!"

Mademoiselle Magnifique came down the aisle and confronted them. "Well? Was I right?"

Cullen nodded. "You were right. She needed both hands to hold it."

She cuffed his shoulder. "I told you! Things aren't always what they seem. Especially around here."

"Since you seem to know so much about this place," Tazinski said, "who's Amy?"

She regarded him as if he were an endearing pet whose antics amused her. "Amy isn't a person, dear. Amy's a drug—amyl nitrate. Gay guys inhale it. It gives a more intense erection."

Tazinski's expression soured. "Sorry I asked."

Cullen flashed a get lost look and he disappeared into the throng, a sloth slinking away to forage. He turned to the girl and offered to pay up on their bet. She waved him off and said she came with a date, but had no idea where he was.

So they kept on talking.

He learned she was an art student named Angie, who, like Cullen, attended the U of M, was twenty-one, and wanted to live somewhere else someday—in her case Paris, to study at the *École des Beaux-Arts.* Cullen said nothing about wanting to be a doctor, but admitted to being an English major—something he wished he *hadn't* told his father, who couldn't understand why he wanted to study a language he already knew.

She raised her brow. "For real? You look like a jock to me. Phys Ed, I would have guessed. What's the last novel you read, mister English major?"

"Gravity's Rainbow."

Her mouth fell open. "You actually read that? I lasted fifty pages. It gave me a headache. I had no idea what it was about."

"Free will and divine predetermination, best I could tell."

She leaned into him and murmured in his ear. "Okay, okay, I believe you. You're an English major." The brush of her lips against his earlobe showered his brain with tiny sparks of delight. "Take me outside."

She huddled against him beneath the front canopy and clung to his arm while rain splattered the street and thrummed the canvas above. A whiff of crushed leaves and leather snaked up his nose, the raunchy scent of her perfume intoxicating him. She talked of *Guernica* and Boo Radley, Monet and Aeschylus, Delacroix and Flaubert, a dark-haired enchantress whose cultured sensibility made him feel like a benighted papist. But the joy cresting inside him from the spell she cast ebbed and died when she reminded him of her date. They went back inside and picked their way through the drunken, milling crowd.

A flailing arm flagged them down. "Angie! I thought you ditched me!"

The black curly hair, cocky grin, and misbegotten swagger of Dempsey Fagan took shape in the aisle—his longtime basketball nemesis. Dempsey jerked to a stop, drunk and wasted and reeking of Pierre Cardin. Cullen felt gut-shot.

"Brodie? I didn't think this was your scene. Missed you at the Attucks yesterday for your weekly ass-kicking."

"In your dreams, Fagan. Can't get over the past, can you?"

Dempsey looked at Angie. "Sorry about disappearing. I got sidetracked. It's like a pharmacy in here." He pointed to a love seat with two tall drinks in front of it. "I got us a spot. I'll meet you there after I take a leak." He gave her a peck on the cheek that might as well have been the *Rape of Lucrece* for the sense of defilement it provoked in Cullen. He would rather have been kicked in the nuts.

"You two know each other?" she asked, after Dempsey headed off to relieve himself.

"We played basketball against each other in high school. He went to Adams and I went to Lourdes. We hated each other from the jump."

She squeezed his arm with more pity than he cared for. "I'm sorry. You must feel awful."

"Well, your phone number *would* keep me from having to commit ritual suicide."

She laughed and fished pen and paper from a small gold purse. She scribbled her name and number and handed it to him. He held it to the light. A cold frisson rattled his spine.

"What's your father's name?" he asked.

"Edward. Edward Nichols. Why?"

The first visit back for a transplant patient was a routinely joyous event, an unrivaled medical happy ending. No less so for Ennis's return. Though the sight of a sixty-three-year-old man in a shoulder-length blonde wig, black capri pants, pink women's Keds, and a pink cotton V-neck framing an angry surgical scar *did* appear to unnerve the patients beside him—a black ex-Marine Cullen saw for hypertension and a senile widow of eighty facing dialysis. Not so much the woman's sympathetic, high school principal daughter, whom he had seen before; her availability to attend her mother's medical appointments seemed unlimited. She smiled and asked Ennis where he bought his capris.

Cullen's redheaded receptionist Bria, her rubicund face bloated by the scourge of youthful obesity, clapped her hands and teared up behind her counter. Ennis beamed and took a bow. Cullen embraced him in the middle of the waiting room—done in soothing pastel green, Tess of the d'Urbervilles again—and congratulated him for so thoroughly cheating death.

He noticed on the way back to the exam room that Ennis's bearing and gait were different, his posture more erect and the swag of his hips languid and dignified. Cullen seated him on a brown leather exam table and considered him more closely. His color held up even beneath the glare of fluorescent tube lights. He looked flush, healthy. Revivified. Yes, partly from the wonder of rouge, but mostly because his anemia had been corrected by a vital young kidney capable of making erythropoietin and his cardiac output had quadrupled thanks to his robust new heart. The sweet scent of violets fumigated the room, rising off his clean-shaven face. Perfume in place of aftershave.

He gestured to Ennis's *dernier cri* ensemble. "Very happening outfit." *For a college coed*, he could have added. "I never knew you were so style-conscious."

Ennis's face lit up like a jack-o'-lantern. "I never cared a lick about fashion before. And that's not the only new preference I seem to have acquired. Just the *thought* of raw fish used to make me gag. Now I eat sashimi twice a week. I like to dip it in that green paste, that hot stuff that makes your nose burn?"

"Wasabi. Japanese horseradish. The toxins in your system when you were on dialysis affected everything, even your taste buds. Quite a few transplant patients tell me that food tastes better."

"It's not just that it tastes better; I crave different *kinds* of food. Like beets. My mother had to practically cram 'em down my throat when I was young. Now I eat 'em like candy."

Cullen extracted a pair of readers from the front pocket of his lab coat and flipped open a laptop that rested on a chest-high countertop. He clicked Ennis's chart open and read his most recent lab results aloud. "Creatinine 1.1, hemoglobin 13.8, tacrolimus level 8.0. Everything right where we want it. The only one out of range is your cholesterol — 278."

"Guess I need to eat sashimi every day."

Cullen put a hand on his shoulder and smiled, paternalistic despite himself, like a father to... a daughter? "Your cholesterol is high because of the prednisone you're on. That's probably why you're craving unusual foods, too — steroids will do that. I'll increase the dose of anti-lipid you're on so you won't clog up your new coronaries. First I need to examine you, though."

He coaxed Ennis's arm out of his sweater and took his blood pressure — 136/78 — and auscultated his heart and lungs: no murmurs or rales. The skin over his anterior thorax was remarkably smooth, not a bristle of chest hair to be found. At least he hadn't done anything weird to his breasts. Not yet, anyway. He pulled the table extension out to accommodate his legs, eased him supine, then palpated over a second surgical scar—far less dramatic than the one carved down the length of his sternum—that slanted across his right iliac fossa, just above the crease of his groin. He flinched at the touch of Cullen's hand, but the transplanted kidney buried beneath felt perfectly normal, about the size and firmness of a ripe avocado.

Ennis frowned. "Why do they put it there?" he asked.

"Because that's where the most accessible blood vessels are to sew into."

"Is it supposed to bulge like that? Sometimes it feels like it's about to fall onto the floor."

Cullen retracted the table extension and helped him to a sitting position. "It's a tight fit in there. That part of your body wasn't intended to accommodate a kidney."

He pumped a dime-sized squirt of sanitizer into his palm from a dispenser next to the sink and rubbed it into his hands. Ennis put himself back together and watched Cullen e-prescribe a 40 mg dose of Lipitor from his laptop to the pharmacy.

"I have a question about something, Doc." Cullen looked up from his screen and over the top of his lenses. "My donor was female, wasn't she?"

"What makes you say that?"

Ennis shrugged. "Some things you just know. But she *was* a she, right?"

Cullen weighed his response. Ennis had been told nothing about his donor—not even the customary information of age, sex, and home state—due to the circumstances of his transplant, with Carla being MacGregor's daughter-in-law. He had to be careful here. "I'm afraid I can't get into that with you, Ennis. You know how strict the new privacy laws are. There's this thing called HIPPA. They can fine or even imprison doctors who violate it."

Ennis tossed his head and fluffed his wig. "I still don't see what harm it would do. It's not like you'd be telling me something I don't already know."

Cullen sniffed and tossed his reading glasses onto the counter. Maybe he heard something when they put him under. It had been reported that up to one percent of surgical patients experienced "unintended intraoperative awareness," resulting in explicit recall of sensory events during surgery. In other words, they felt and remembered their thoracic surgeons sawing through their breastbones and talking about them. Wonderful. A new cause of post-traumatic stress syndrome: insufficient anesthesia during routine surgery. But what if his hunch that his donor was female indicated deepening psychiatric trouble? Maybe this was gender integration gone awry, a pathologic delusion that a heart and kidney *from* a female might somehow make *him* more female. On the other hand, the new clothes he wore and his belief that his donor was female could be positive signs, an accelerated flowering of his transgender identity rather than dysfunction.

Whatever the case, the science part of the visit was over. Now it was time for the art of medicine, the true measure of a physician. It was why he became a doctor, the gritty human engagement of it, eyeball-to-eyeball, no one else in the room. Informed empathy was the coin of the realm here, in this cramped, hushed space, transacting their ancient ritual in digital, their sacrosanct drama, in its own way no less vital than giving birth or having sex or dying.

"What difference does it make if your donor was a woman? Does it really matter?"

Ennis's painted face hardened into a stubborn moue, a petulant woman determined to have her way. "I think about her all the time. I even know her name. It came to me in a dream. Carla."

The soft croon of her name gave Cullen gooseflesh, like hearing the miller's daughter say Rumpelstiltskin.

"I'd give anything to know more about her, Doc."

A tocsin sounded in his head, a premonition of trouble. "Donor families grieve in different ways. Some of them feel that revisiting their grief to satisfy the curiosity of a recipient is asking too much."

Ennis put his hand against his cheek and pleaded, disturbingly female, submissive, appealing to the man of the house to come to his aid. "Can't you help me? Please?"

Cullen fought to remain impassive, to stifle the roiling in his gut. "I'll see what I can do."

Chapter 4

IT HAPPENED TWICE, THE exact same dream each time: a foreign land long ago, sights he had never seen. Uncommon words he somehow knew.

He's lying face down on the cobblestone, too weak to move, nose pressed to the stinking gutter, the stench of pig shit and dog piss and garbage flying up his nostrils like a swarm of putrid flies. Grim towers rise from crenellated walls ringing the town, the medieval town, with its gabled houses of brittle wood and soaring church of polished stone. People walk past him in rough-hewn clothes, their doublets and shawls and woolen tabards. He is cold and dying, too far gone to speak, but they step around him — over him — as if he were not there. His impending death means nothing to them. Less than nothing. Even the priest ignores him on his way toward the church, the grandest building in sight — save for the Norman castle beyond, with its curling river and groaning drawbridge. The hem of his long black gown grazes the back of Ennis's lifeless hand.

And then *she* comes. He feels her presence beneath the gloom of stratus sagging low overhead, young and vital. She bends over his prone body, the only one who stops, the only one who cares. She strokes the top of his head. Her touch is light, her fingers long and slender. He shudders at the goodness of her, the decency. She drapes a luxurious stole over the nape of his neck, silk of such magical quality it slips onto his chest and slithers through his breastbone and undulates inside him until it becomes his heart. He feels it beating: sure, confident, steady. Warm, so warm! Warming every part of him, from his cracked cold lips to his shriveled gelid toes. He rises pink and alive from the squalor and asks her name. Carla, she says, and vanishes in a contrail of mercy and light.

The rumble of a passing garbage truck roused Ennis from his recollection of the dream. He smashed his fist against the dashboard of his Impala. He should have told Dr. Brodie the *details* of his dream. The details about all of it. What it meant. Or what he thought it meant. Instead he glossed over it, minimized things. Becky was right: there was more to cross-dressing than wearing a dress. The way to stop living a lie was to stop holding things in. Full emotional disclosure, she called it.

He hadn't lied so much to Dr. Brodie as failed to tell the truth. About the bizarre, mind-boggling, screwball notion he couldn't get out of his head: that Carla's donated organs were exerting some kind of influence on him beyond their intended bodily functions.

Besides the dream and his new cravings for beets and sashimi, there was the time he turned Elvis off and scanned his car radio for a jazz station instead. He always hated jazz, thought it sounded like a bunch of amateurs tuning their instruments — for the whole song. Now it moved him, the call-and-response of it, the improvisation. Suddenly he *got* jazz.

Another oddity was the resetting of his internal thermostat. He seemed in constant need of a fan or air conditioning. He supposed it could be the steroids, again — sweating and flushing, they had warned him — but shouldn't his body have adjusted by now? His electric bill was up forty percent.

And what about his newfound chattiness? He found himself talking to strangers wherever he went: jawing with the cashier at the supermarket; yapping with the clerk at the video store; telling some young mother in the mall how cute her little boy was. He'd turned into a nattering neighborhood magpie. Very female of him. Effortlessly female.

But none of that held a candle to what happened one night primping to go to dinner at Kuriyama's, a Japanese place near the beach with a crackerjack sushi chef and waitresses too polite to gawk or ask embarrassing questions when he showed up en femme. He was experimenting with some jars of Clinique he bought at the mall that day, his face reflected in the forgiving light of a spanking new vanity mirror. He instinctively began to dab and daub with purpose, some secret technique suddenly at his disposal: makeup artistry for big girls. He brushed different tones of powder over a thin layer of foundation as if some unseen hand were guiding him. He coated his nose and jaw and the hollow of his cheeks with darker shades of powder and dusted his chin and brow a lighter color. Then he ran a faint line of concealer above his lip, causing it to appear plump and full, rather than thin and drawn like it really was, and presto: his old goat of a face transformed into something passably female.

He learned the next day from the makeup artists at the Clinique counter in Bloomingdale's—by far the most transgender friendly in the mall—that the technique he employed was called contouring. Fair enough, except that no one ever demonstrated it to him and he never read about it or even heard it mentioned before.

Becky warned him this might happen, a spurt of pent-up feminine expression that would overshoot before it settled down into a cross-dressing comfort zone. Like the outfit he had on. The sorority girl look was, what you might say, a little over the top. But there were bound to be excesses as the transgender identity he had suppressed all of his life—Elaine, he called her—emerged and took shape. He had given Elaine permission to express herself and she was running with it, that's all. Though there were moments when he feared Elaine might completely overwhelm his masculine personality—which, after sixty-three years, he had grown accustomed to. What if Elaine elbowed Ennis off the stage entirely? He wanted to wear a dress *some* of the time, not *all* the time. What if he became sexually attracted to men instead of women? What if he lost his male sex drive and stopped wanting to hump Becky? He didn't want to cut his weenie off; he just wanted to put it to sleep sometimes, silence its incessant clamor, its non-stop male posturing. Of course Elaine's emergence made him uneasy at times and exhilarated at others. Why wouldn't it?

But the things that had happened since transplant were different—female yes, but distinct from Elaine. He had a growing suspicion something else was at work: foreign tissue remaking him in its image. *Her* image. Carla's image. Was that even possible, to take on the traits and personality of your organ donor? It sounded loony, but what if Carla overpowered them both, Ennis and Elaine? What if Carla's beliefs and tastes and characteristics prevailed, a forced integration of spirit even more wrenching than gender integration? Elaine had been part of him from the beginning. Carla was more like a guest who might never leave. Elaine refined him; Carla inhabited him.

So which inner woman was rising, Elaine or Carla? He had to know. His sanity depended on it. Which was why, after driving home from Dr. Brodie's office in a fugue, he dialed Becky Winthrop's number the minute he walked in the door to request an emergency appointment.

Becky droned on about gender accord while Ennis snuck another gander at her legs, crossed and bare. Her taut black skirt rode halfway up her thigh. A tendril of smoke rose from a stick of sandalwood incense that burned on the desk behind her, perfuming the air with its earthy, mellow scent.

"Ralph Waldo Emerson said, 'Though we may search the world over for the beautiful, we find it within or we find it not.' What you call your inner woman—Carla or Elaine or Tootsie for all I care—is of secondary importance. What's crucial is that you embrace her." She folded her hands on her lap. "Your newfound tastes for sushi and jazz and your increasing skill at applying makeup are wonderful signposts of progress. Celebrate them, don't fear them. Elaine—let's call her Elaine for now, since that's the name you seem most at ease with—is asserting herself. You're worried she'll take over entirely and make you one hundred percent female and leave you stranded in a man's body. She won't. That's not how transgender personality integration works. Eventually your feminine and masculine sides will strike the right balance and you'll be in harmony."

He admired the pearl that dangled in the notch of her neck, then dropped his gaze to her shoes: black suede with round caps, with just enough of a heel to accentuate the sway of her hips when she had walked across the room to start their session—the length of which she tracked to the minute. A committed clock-watcher, the good Dr. Winthrop was. No crisis too dire to carry over to the following appointment. He thought of an old shrink joke—*What do psychiatrists and prostitutes have in common? You feel bad after visiting either one*—and let his gaze wander back to her naked calves.

It was a fashion he had mixed emotions about, this shunning of nylon by women young and old. Some gams were just plain ugly, more like the hock of a pig than the shapely shank of a woman. Flaunting them should be subject to government approval, like movie ratings for children: *These legs are considered offensive to impressionable viewers.* Becky, though, was born to romp barelegged. It was her legs that saved her from being ordinary. Saved her from her limp, mousy hair and long nose—she had kind eyes, though, and a fetching smile. Problem was, Becky's legs were *so* perfectly contoured and supple they distracted him from his therapy sessions. Mostly on days he came drab, as Ennis, rather than en femme, as Elaine. Like today—two weeks after he had called and begged for an urgent appointment. No such thing as integration emergencies at the Center for Sexual and Gender Accord, apparently. But please remember to bring your co-pay.

He shook his head. "It's different from Elaine—female, but with tastes and desires so specific as to come from a separate *person*. I feel like my organ donor is influencing me somehow."

Becky drew a breath and rubbed her temples. Got up and paced the dark wooden floor of her office, surrounded by antiques she had insisted Ennis acquire a working knowledge of, the decorative arts essential for any woman, she claimed. He resisted at first—he figured Elaine was, what you might say, more chambermaid than lady-in-waiting—but now was more than a little proud of his ability to properly identify every piece in the room: the beech wood bergère she had just got out of; the green canapé he occupied, and the velvet wing chair angled beside him; and her Louis XV burled walnut desk, with cabriole legs and matching secretaire. She stopped in front of a large oil of a pirouetting flamenco dancer in a red skirt and folded her arms and glared. He liked it when she broke character instead of sitting there motionless wearing a mask of stone. Her therapy face.

"All transplant patients dream about their donors. It's a subconscious expression of curiosity about a person who gave you an incredible gift. But transplanted organs can't alter a recipient's personality or influence their core desires and tastes. It's unhealthy to attribute the symptoms you're experiencing—and that's what they are, symptoms of psychological turmoil—to something as implausible as transmigration. Your organ transplants restored your health and gave you the energy to nourish your cross-gender identity. But the intensity of Elaine's emergence is frightening you. If you come to one of our group sessions, you'll see firsthand how common transgender emergence anxiety is."

"What do you mean by transmigration?"

She returned to the bergère and sat down and peered at him, unblinking, stolid, back in cyborg mode. "The belief that a deceased person's soul can enter into someone else's body."

A cold thrill crawled across his skin, a quiver of validation. He thought of the cabby who drove him to the hospital the day of his transplant: The *ti bon ange,* the small good angel, the unique traits of a particular human being. Maybe the voodoo bastard was right. The wisdom and knowledge of previous lives must be passed on.

Becky squinted at him and contorted her face, as if pained to talk about it. "There are a handful of rather odd, anecdotal cases about it. Like the man who received the heart of a donor who hanged himself in the bathroom, only to later marry the donor's widow and five years later hang *himself* in the bathroom."

Whoa. And he thought Carla was intrusive. "Sounds like transmigration, if you ask me. What else explains a thing like that?"

"How about a psychological black widow who sucks the life out of whomever she's married to? There are such women you know. I see them all the time."

Too much education was Becky's problem. No wonder her ring finger was bare. What man could stand her? Just as well, too. Poor bastard would probably hang himself in the bathroom. "Maybe there's more to those reports than you think."

"No case of personality or memory transmission from an organ donor to a recipient has ever been published in a peer-reviewed medical journal."

"Not yet, anyway." Typical doctor. If she couldn't find it in a book, it didn't exist. Good thing Columbus didn't think like that. "How do you explain knowing my donor's name, then?"

She set her jaw—the same way he just set his. "We've yet to confirm you *do* know your donor's name."

"Well, it's not for want of trying. I wrote a letter to them through my transplant coordinator. I'm hoping they'll agree to meet me."

Her mouth pinched and she ran a hand through her hair. "You had time to write a letter to your donor's family, but not the letter I asked you to write to Elaine apologizing for keeping her locked in a closet all these years?"

Too much information, that's the mistake he'd made. Shrinks had to be dealt with the way teenagers dealt with parents: strictly on a need-to-know basis. Anything more was asking for trouble.

"Your obsession with your donor is affecting your progress toward gender accord. You're using the imagined presence of Carla to sabotage the emergence of Elaine, because you're fearful of losing your masculine identity altogether. This is a serious issue that needs to be confronted immediately."

She slid the sleeve of her jacket off her wrist and looked at her watch. "I'm afraid we're out of time. Would you like the same hour next week?"

Chapter 5

"HE MUST HAVE OVERHEARD someone on the surgical team," Cullen said, his phone to his ear. "It happens, patients dredging up fragments of indiscreet OR talk. I had one swear he knew how much alimony his surgeon was paying his ex-wife."

"Did he?"

He fashioned an image to match Dawn Price's phone voice. Mid-thirties, forty tops. Straight blonde hair, a dearth of make-up, small breasts. Derisory breasts. And pale. Sun-averse pale. Whatever happened to tan lines? Another outmoded shibboleth he clung to. More evidence he was out of step with the times, like with text messaging. He was incapable of composing grammatically incorrect emails, let alone the perverted syntax of texting. *LOL, r u 4 real?* Phonetic code devised by semi-literate juveniles.

"To the dollar. But that's not why I called. Ennis isn't satisfied with knowing Carla's name. He wants to meet her family and know all about her. Wouldn't you, if you were in his pumps and hose?"

A snort of laughter came over the line. He adjusted his image of her, shagged her hair and swelled her bosom. Now, if only she'd get some sun.

"Of course I would. But it isn't up to me," she said. "Tell him to write a letter to his donor's family. No name, no phone number, no email address or home address, either. He should thank them for their sacrifice and tell them how long he was on the waiting list, what his health was like, and how his life has changed since transplant. He can write about his job, his hobbies, his family — but *no* politics or religion. Have him send the letter to Dawn Price, Transplant Coordinator, St. Barnabas Hospital, 8540 Eucalyptus Street. Once I vet it, I'll forward it to the Organ Procurement Agency and they'll notify the family that they are in receipt of a letter from the recipient. If they choose to write back, the OPA will send their response to me and I'll relay it to Ennis."

A visual of Ennis in his hot pink coed outfit popped into Cullen's mind. "What if he wants to mention being transgender?"

Silence. A long silence. "I don't think that's a good idea."

"Because they might think her organs were wasted on a nutcase?"

"Well... yes."

"I know. I wonder about that myself sometimes."

He said goodbye and slid off the burnt orange leather sectional that squatted like an installation piece in a New York gallery in the middle of his living room. But he didn't live in New York. He lived near a placid cove, with the shimmering Pacific framed by the picture window of his third story condo. The condo he let Tess of the d'Ubervilles redecorate, right down to the furniture, including the leather sofa and matching armchair she talked him into, which were visually appealing, but vexing to sit on. Like greased Teflon, no traction to be had.

That she felt compelled to decorate an ocean view condo in warm Tuscan wall and floor coverings, but then fill it with stark urban furniture — a glass and chrome dining table; a black lacquered platform bed that left him feeling as though he'd had a lumbar fusion when he awakened; and a seven-foot high, verdigris-encrusted bronze sculpture that resembled an extraterrestrial begging for quarters—was only slightly less puzzling than his willingness to finance such mishmash. Another hapless attempt to alter the fateful cycle of all his love affairs: passion, then apathy, then neglect followed by flight.

He turned to his most reliable tonic to fend off the melancholy he sometimes felt about reaching fifty-four without a wife or adoring grandchildren to show for it: a swim in Emerald Cove. He donned a pair of trunks and sandals, grabbed his goggles and a bottle of defogger, looped a towel around his neck, and descended a cascade of foot-worn stairs across the street from his whitewashed condo complex. Nestled between two sandstone cliffs, Emerald Cove enjoyed the protected status of an Underwater Park and Ecological Reserve—meaning abundant marine life and no surfers to cope with. A lifeguard tower straddled the grainy beach, which was half-full with bathers. A small blackboard at the base of the tower gave prevailing weather conditions in white chalk: three-foot surf; sixty-nine degree water temperature; seventy-eight degree air temperature.

He wedged towel and sandals beneath a rock and smeared a thin film of defogger on the inside of his goggles. The afternoon sky ladled a shawl of sunlight onto his shoulders. A pair of lolling gulls and the briny smell of the sea met him at the shoreline. He bent and rinsed his goggles, pulled them on, and sliced into the gently pitching bay. He churned past a flotilla of snorkelers and eased into a slow crawl to enjoy the cove's thirty-foot visibility.

A school of rockfish passed over a pair of skates clouding the bottom in search of a meal. Orange garibaldi strafed the edges of an undulating kelp forest. The stalks grew denser and longer as the cove's bottom fell away. He quickened his pace and broke into open water, cutting through the chop toward a distant white buoy, the splash of his effort the only sound.

He rounded the buoy and made it halfway back before last month's shark attack a mile up the coast barged into his thoughts. A shark estimated by its bite radius at fourteen feet long. A luckless triathlete had been cleaved in half, barely a hundred yards from shore. An expert from the Oceanology Institute attributed the attack to a great white that mistook a human in a wet suit for a seal.

Cullen pulled toward the cove with fraught vigilance, straining into the liquid obscurity beneath him. Though even if he were being hunted by one of the monsters, he would be unlikely to see its lethal rush coming. Great whites ambushed their prey, rising unseen from the bottom to attack from the rear. There would be the initial pain of his pelvis being transected, his blood spewing into the ocean in ribbons of red confetti. His thrashing and screaming would be short-lived, though, soon yielding to the placidity of hemorrhagic shock, blood loss dulling his senses. The end would come quickly enough.

He relaxed only upon reaching the safety of the kelp bed, where he allowed himself to recall the panic he felt the first time a great white stalked his thoughts. He glided across the water and grinned at their terror of it, the mechanical monster and menacing soundtrack that petrified an entire nation.

It was impossible to say how many summer romances *Jaws* spawned that year, but he guessed thousands. Tens of thousands. It was a sure-fire way to get a girl you barely knew to crawl into your lap in the dark and mash her breasts against you. And so it was with Angie. She screamed and shrieked from start to finish and was all over him every time another clueless swimmer got yanked under in a swirl of crimson. He sprang a hard-on each time they cued up the ominous shark music. They fondled and pawed and laughed about how scared they were over drinks at Sadie's Parlor in the Sheraton, and again later on, concealed in a stand of maple trees off a small beach near her home on Lake Harriet. Gratifying their lust beneath a fat, gleaming moon, with frogs croaking and insects chirring and mosquitoes biting his ass. Angie: her fan of lustrous hair, her dark areolae, the sable tuft of her mons.

Cullen had come up the walk of her two-story Colonial on East Lake Harriet Parkway that evening—an enclave of lacustrine wealth and grandeur—more than a little ambivalent about meeting the monster of Brodie's Tirade. No matter what you *called* an abortion—a procedure; a treatment; a fix—there was no denying that suctioning embryos from wombs to snuff out pregnancies was gruesome business. And while Brodie's Tirade failed to arouse any religious objections in Cullen, it had raised questions in his mind about the purveyors of such a service. What kind of doctors *did* that? And why? Out of professional conviction? Or for a place on Lake Harriet among the haut monde?

He paused beneath a swaying lantern in an arched entryway supported by a pair of white columns. Towering elms strewn across their hedged-in yard shaded him from the early evening sun, which dappled the home's façade in a muted patchwork of shadow and light. Wood-mullioned windows with panes unmarred by so much as a finger smear afforded views of Lake Harriet and a looming blue band shell on the far shore.

Cullen sucked a breath and rang the bell. Voices, a flurry of sound. A regal, if somewhat skeletal woman—beyond a doubt the source of Angie's gemstone green eyes—opened the door with a weary smile. Jaded, perhaps, by what Cullen assumed to be a steady parade of eager young males calling on Angie and her sister, Leslie, younger by a year.

"You must be Cullen." She wore a calico sundress with her hair pinned high. "I'm Pam. I know this will come as a shock to you, but Angie's not ready yet." She welcomed him into a black marble foyer. A whiff of fresh-cut posies from a vase on a nearby console tinged the air.

Before he could respond, an apple-cheeked, bow-legged boy burst between them and attached himself to his leg, clinging like a tackler to a running back. Pam Nichols pressed her hands together and laughed.

"That's Grady. He's desperate for a big brother."

"In a home ruled by women," a droll male voice added from the wings.

Even in bare feet and a terry-cloth robe that exposed a mat of salt-and-pepper chest hair, Edward Nichols possessed the gravitas of a three-term senator. He padded across the foyer with the soles of his feet slapping a measured rhythm, reading glasses on the bridge of his nose, cocktail in hand, his black thatch of hair laced with gray. It was hard to believe that this was a man who extirpated fetuses for a living.

He greeted Cullen with a pump of his free hand and exchanged introductions. Nichols plucked his lenses from his face. "Are you the Cullen Brodie who made that incredible shot to win the state title a few years ago?"

Cullen reached down and tousled Grady's hair. It felt soft and velvety against the palm of his hand, like the downy pelt of a puppy. "There were a lot of incredible shots that night. Mine happened to be the last one."

Nichols shot his wife a meaningful glance. "Most famous shot in Minnesota high school basketball history. Adams was undefeated. Nobody gave Lourdes a chance— small, inner city Catholic school against the suburban powerhouse." He shifted his gaze back to Cullen.

"Remarkable duel between you and that Fagan boy. It was a shame either of you had to lose. Though I'll have you know I yelled myself hoarse cheering for Lourdes that night."

"You did? Even though... I mean, I'm surprised that..." His face caught fire. He bent to tickle Grady, hoping to fill the ugly silence with laughter.

Nichols gave the same forbearing smile Cullen had seen countless times on television. "That an abortionist would root for a bunch of Catholics?"

His wife took him by the elbow and steered him toward an open doorway with the aplomb of a high-level diplomat. "Why don't you two get to know each other in the library while I check on Angie?"

Nichols winked at Cullen. "We might be there all night. I'm afraid our daughter has a slight grooming compulsion."

Angie's mother turned him loose at the threshold and bussed his cheek before gliding away. "That's the way *all* young women are, dear. You just don't remember."

They settled across from one another, Nichols in a leather chair beside a roll top desk with a raised tambour, Cullen on a plush love seat, his back to a large picture window. Books of all stripes filled the shelves around them: leather-bound classics, dusty medical tomes, contemporary novels with glossy jackets, and antique collector items that looked as if they might disintegrate at the slightest touch. Nichols took a slug of his drink—a martini, judging by the olive floating in it—and placed the glass on the desk.

"She thinks I don't, but I remember them all. Especially the ones who broke my heart."

He gazed out the window at the lake's dimming refulgence.

"Like Cindy Dietrich. She barely knew I existed, but that didn't stop me from becoming so lovesick over her my parents thought I had mono. I used to wander by her locker just to catch a glimpse of her, the way her mohair sweater clung to her with her head thrown back in laughter at some remark. She had hair like spun silk and the shapeliest legs you could imagine. I pined in secret, a lowly sophomore smitten by a senior goddess."

He drained his glass and chewed the pitted olive and tightened the cincture of his robe.

"I came to school one morning and learned that Cindy had died in a seedy motel in the next county. Some degenerate got a copy of the police photograph and circulated it. It was the most obscene image I ever laid eyes on, the angel I worshipped lying face down and naked on the floor, her knees folded under her with the backs of her thighs collapsed onto her calves and her buttocks angled in the air, bloated by pregnancy. A crude surgical instrument lay on a bloody towel beneath her amongst chunks of tissue. She eviscerated herself trying to terminate an unintended pregnancy. The hooked blade she used to rupture her amniotic sac punctured her uterus and snagged a piece of intestine."

He closed his eyes and shook his head and went on. "I started The Nichols Clinic because of her. And I come to work each day knowing she didn't die in vain."

Angie appeared in the doorway, balanced precariously on a pair of espadrilles, her ankles dainty and laced, her bangs falling appealingly over one eye. "Did you two relive this famous shot I've heard so much about while I was getting ready?"

This time Cullen winked at Nichols. "We relived the entire *game* while you were getting ready."

Cullen worked that summer at Lundino's Pizza Factory, where for five dollars an hour, in a hair net and baker white pants, he ladled topping onto freshly baked crusts, stacked cartons of frozen pizza on wooden pallets, and hosed the plant's shiny assembly line free of stray bits of sausage. Doing his part to help turn Vincent Lundino and his domineering wife, Gina—the creator of Lundino's famous "secret sauce"—into pizza parvenus.

He spent every dollar earned in excess of what he needed for tuition on dates with Angie. Together they danced drunk on wooden tables and wassailed the King with tankards of ale at 1520 A.D., a medieval restaurant on top the Holiday Inn; sat like mobster and moll eating manicotti and drinking Chianti in a red leather booth at Scarpelli's, with its Chicago gangster décor; and took in the latest show at Dudley Riggs, whose ferocious satire left them howling at the absurdity of the adult world they would soon inherit—and no doubt improve. On weekends they sweltered beside her pool, moribund with hangovers, gossiping with Leslie and fending off Grady, for whom Cullen bought an inflatable shark with rows of jagged teeth. Playing Jaws with Grady was one of life's unexpected joys. Cullen pushed him around the pool on his shark float and mimicked the menacing soundtrack—*dunt dunt dunt dunt, dunt dunt dunt dunt*—before submerging with a hand atop his head to simulate a dorsal fin. His sudden rush from below elicited squeals of terrified laughter.

By August he was delirious with love. He stopped going out on Friday night "fox hunts" with Tazinski, wrote poetry—bad poetry, but he wrote it anyway—and threw out his little black book of phone numbers. Undeniable proof of being pussy whipped, Tazinski complained. Cullen didn't care. He made plans to confess to his parents that the girl he'd been seeing was not, as they'd been told, Angela Masters, but rather Angie Nichols, the daughter of the villain of Brodie's Tirade. The use of a pseudonym had been

Cullen's idea. He was hoping that if they first met and liked her — which they did, especially Chaz — without knowing who her father was, it would make it more difficult to object when they learned the truth. Angie called him spineless, but eventually agreed and seemed especially pleased by the alias she chose. She handled his parents' questions about her father tersely — "He's a doctor" — but truthfully in advance of the big reveal.

For a venue they chose Art Rampage, a summer festival sponsored yearly by the university's Department of Art. Cullen issued his parents an invitation to view a piece Angie was showing that day as a pretext to draw them there, hoping the crowd and public place would temper their response.

Cullen arrived a few minutes before one. Moist, suffocating heat draped the day like cheesecloth. Students in jeans and tank tops and middle-aged aficionados in slacks browsed rows of canvases set up on the grass in front of Rarig Center, a modernist structure of gray concrete and dun-colored brick. To Cullen's left, a footbridge spanned the turbid Mississippi, connecting the artsy West Bank with the stately main campus on the other side of the river.

He weaved his way toward Angie, who stood contemplating her work in a spattered cambric smock, brush in hand. Open tubes of paint, a painting knife, and a Mason jar filled with turpentine littered a nearby wooden stand. A shirtless, scrawny man with a greasy ponytail and sandaled feet wrestled with the next easel over. Cullen called out her name and strode past Ponytail to greet her. She dabbed the end of his nose with her brush and kissed him, then stood aside so he could see her large, unframed painting.

A leering boy with shaggy hair and a joint in one hand leaned against the doorway of a murky dwelling, his beckoning finger crooked at two girls in an alleyway — Angie and her sister, Leslie. But the girl the boy wanted was Leslie, who wore tight jeans and stood provocatively akimbo, her face flushed with anticipation. And triumph. Angie stood in the background, spurned in favor of her sister. Humbled, her eyes downcast, her head lowered. Leslie's features were noticeably more dramatic than Angie's, with her lips fuller, her eyes wider, and her hair thicker and shinier — which was not the case in real life. Not the case at all. The coloring and shading of the piece created a mood of profound foreboding, as if the choosing of one over the other would not redound well for either.

"It should be in a gallery," he said. "It's fabulous." Angie tossed her head and preened. A shaft of light glazed her hair, like the glossy plumage of a sun-splattered crow. "It's very flattering of Leslie. And Leslie gets the boy. How come?"

"I have to throw her a bone once in a while. Maybe she'll stop stealing my clothes — and ogling my boyfriend."

"It won't exactly set my parents' minds at ease about your family, though."

Her face narrowed. She plunged her brush into the Mason jar and swirled it around, staining it red. "I never promised to paint a Nichols family *American Gothic*. Maybe inviting them here wasn't such a good idea."

Cullen glanced over his shoulder toward Anderson Hall. "Too late now. Here they come."

He waved to flag them down. Chaz cut a swath through the crowd with Mary trailing, slowed by her need to apologize to whomever he jostled out of the way. They pulled to a stop, his mother tall and bony, Chaz compact and muscular. Perspiration blotted the armpits of his bowling shirt.

"Where's the beer tent?" he asked with a crooked grin. A purple and white Minnesota Vikings cap, pulled low on his brow, covered his flattop.

Cullen's mother mopped her angular face with a hankie, her hair wound in a tight perm. "It's an art festival, Chaz, not a football game." She bunched her hankie and stuffed it into a pocket of the polka dot shift she wore.

Angie showed them her painting. "That's my sister, Leslie," she said.

Mary Brodie recoiled like a vampire confronting a cross. Chaz lifted the visor of his cap and squinted. Cullen looked at Angie, hoping she had sense enough to junk their plan. She forced a smile and thrust her chin in the air. Didn't she feel it, the sense of doom in the air, like Hiroshima while Little Boy fell? This was a Brodie family moment to avoid if ever there was one.

"Cullen and I have something to tell you," she said sweetly. "My name isn't really Angela Masters. It's Nichols. Angie Nichols."

His parents looked confused. Cullen thought of MacBeth. *If it were done when 'tis done, then 'twere well it were done quickly.* "Her father is Edward Nichols. Doctor Edward Nichols. Of the Nichols Clinic."

His mother took a step back. "I don't understand. You lied to us about her name?"

"Yes," Cullen said. "I did. But only to give you a chance to get to know her."

Mary put her hand to her mouth and looked around, as if she were afraid someone might hear them. "We don't *want* to know her."

Chaz took off his Vikings cap and ran his other hand through his hair. "That's a helluva thing, Cullen. A helluva thing." He put the cap back on and draped his arm around his wife to comfort her. She gave an anguished yelp, a *cri de coeur* at her son's treachery. She shook free of Chaz and went over to Cullen, her eyes red and her long face contorted. "How could you *do* this to us?" she cried out.

Angie edged closer to them. "Mr. and Mrs. Brodie, I—"

Chaz halted her with a glare. His eyes bulged. He shook his fist in her face. "Edward Nichols is a baby killer!"

Angie drew her brush from the Mason jar like a sword and jabbed it at him. "My father gives women a choice. Zealots like you would have us barefoot and pregnant forever!"

Chaz lunged at her table and knocked over the Mason jar. A splash of reddened turpentine hit the grass like a spill of blood. He snatched her painting knife and spun toward her canvas.

Cullen reached for his arm. "Dad, no!"

He slashed her canvas with broad strokes, leaving it hanging and shredded, like sheets of sloughed skin.

Chapter 6

NOW ENNIS UNDERSTOOD WHY women were always late. *Four hours* it took him to get ready—and this after a week of laying the groundwork by browsing transgender websites for tips, reading back issues of *Seventeen*, and hanging out at the Lancôme counter picking up pointers on doing face. That's what the salesgirls called it, doing face. Remember, they said: women dress for other women. That the other women it took all afternoon to dress for comprised *other men dressed as women* was beside the point. He intended to show Becky's collection of trannies how a girl with taste put herself together.

He had begun his makeover the day before, by taking a beard groomer to his chest, pits, and arms, hacking away at hairy Ennis to pave the way for fair Elaine. Tweezed his eyebrows, too, arched and delicate, each hair plucked from below rather than above to avoid a shaggy dog look. He iced his brow afterwards to limit the swelling and poured a shot of tequila to dull the pain.

A day later he went at it again with a maple-scented depilatory to dissolve away whatever body hair remained. He ran his hand over his chest and arms when he finished and thrilled at the silkiness of his hairless skin. Next he shaved and moisturized his face with Truth Serum—golden oil that smelled like tangerines and went on like liquid velvet—and engaged in the sacred ritual of powder and paint.

He positioned his circular vanity mirror on the bathroom counter and brandished a concealer pen with a click dispenser. He liked its gold casing, its slim, elegant shape and the way it felt in his hand. He used it to lighten shadows beneath his eyes, fill in facial wrinkles, and contour his lips. He marveled at how plump and full they looked — almost as good as if some waxy-faced plastic surgeon injected them full of fat cells for five grand.

He squeezed a dab of liquid foundation that the Lancôme girls had picked out for him onto a wedge-shaped makeup sponge and squeegeed it across his face. He smoothed it around again and again to make sure the application was even and blended onto his neck, but resisted an urge to layer on some more to cover the nubbins of his freshly shaved beard. *Show me a cross-dresser in pancake makeup and I'll show you a desperate man,* he had read in one of his books. *But show me one with five o'clock shadow peeking through his Estée Lauder and I'll show you a confidant woman.*

That's what he wanted Elaine to be, a confidant woman. He set the tube of foundation aside and dipped the bristles of an extra soft, goat hair makeup brush into a jar of loose powder. He tapped the brush against the rim and dusted beige powder over his foundation. After a few seconds, he repeated the process.

A snuffle of powder tickled his nostrils. He sneezed, a shoulder-rattler that raised a cloud of dust from the jar of makeup. He had to remember to sneeze more like a woman, dainty and suppressed: *achoo,* with a tissue over his face.

He whisked his face clean of excess and traced Pen-silk eyeliner along his lids — careful, so careful, to stay just above his upper lashes and just beneath his lower ones. Next came mascara. Maybelline UltraLash, basic black. To avoid painting his eyelids like he did his first go-around with mascara, he brushed from bottom to top and coated his upper lashes first, wiggling the wand as he pulled it through. He wet his lowers by holding the wand perpendicular and employing a series of gentle sideways swipes.

For lipstick he went with dark cinnamon. He bared his teeth and smeared it on good, then blotted with a Kleenex to thin it out. Last was blush, from yet another of the jars that littered his countertop.

He studied his face in the vanity and mugged, drinking fully from the fountainhead welling inside him.

He sat on the floor to do his toenails, which he trimmed and filed before applying a coat of clear base that smelled like airplane glue. After placing cotton balls between his toes to keep from painting them, he striped each nail, painting first down the center and then along either side, until the entire surface was covered from tip to cuticle with Bogata Blackberry. He repeated the process on his fingernails, moving from pinkie to thumb. He then added a second coat, followed by a topcoat of sealer. The whole process came naturally to him, like painting houses. His nails turned out gorgeous, lacquered to a high sheen with nary a ridge or bubble in sight. Now, if only they weren't so *stubby*.

He grew festive and felt the way he did while hanging bulbs on a Christmas tree after the lights were strung. He pulled on an underwire bra with silicone breast forms; slipped on a damask blouse, gray pants, and black bolero jacket—minus the pads, to minimize his shoulders—and added jewelry. Quality stuff, not the gimcrack discounters sold, a pair of gold hoop earrings and matching necklace, big and bulky to offset his thick male neck and large face.

For hair he chose a lush brown wig made of artificial fiber. He bought it at a transgender-friendly wig shop that cut and styled it for him. All he had to do was shampoo it, let it dry, and put it on. He shoehorned into a pair of women's ten-and-a-halfs — compared to his usual men's nines — and minced around the house to get used to their block heels before preening in front of the mirror one last time.

The reflection he saw drew a whistle from his painted lips: Elaine in all her glory. The sad tranny that stumbled slapdash and frowzy from the closet had transformed into a regular Cosmo girl. It wasn't pride he felt so much as fulfillment, doing what he was meant to do. Embracing who he was meant to be. He fluffed his wig, donned a black leather purse and was off, Elaine out and about.

With Ennis nowhere in sight.

The Center for Sexual and Gender Accord's group therapy room had mood lights, soft gold carpeting, and chairs made of molded plastic and chrome legs. They drew into a circle in front of a dark, heavily varnished desk — oak, Ennis figured, by the deepness of the stain. Large-pore wood like oak took pigment better than dense wood.

It wasn't much of a group, just Becky and three others besides Ennis, two en femme and one drab. Becky insisted they use their femme names to introduce themselves: Vanessa, Rachel, Elaine, and Sondra. Drab Sondra, wearing brogans, dungarees, and an Oakland Raiders jersey, with a two-day growth of beard. They overcame their initial wariness and fell with surprising ease into girly patter about nails and makeup and the hazards of depilation, like housewives at a coffee klatch.

Becky waited until their excitement subsided before instructing them to share their fears about cross-dressing, beginning with Rachel, a fine-boned brunette in a long sleeve madras top and faded jeans. Ennis admired her wig —

it *must* be human hair — with a stab of envy: she was the only one among them capable of passing for a woman.

"I'm fearful of attention I get from men," she said. "I like it, but I don't know how to respond."

Ennis wanted to reassure her that she wouldn't have to worry about it once they got a load of her voice, like a cement mixer in need of oil, but he held his tongue. The others gushed over her looks until Becky made them all squirm.

"Have you ever wanted to be with a man?"

Ennis's stomach rolled over. Wasn't gender identity enough to sink her teeth into for one night? Did Becky have to put *that* in play too? Her desire for psychodrama was insatiable, week after week, month after month, dysfunction without end. Until their insurance ran out. Then it was a pat on the ass and out the door they went.

"No, I haven't," Rachel calmly replied.

Becky twirled her hair and crossed her legs — did the little show-off ever wear slacks? — and trained her sights on Vanessa, who was the farthest thing from a Vanessa Ennis could imagine. Her wig was absolutely hideous, too shiny and red. Couldn't she have spent a few extra bucks and got something that didn't look like it was part of a Halloween costume? And her makeup, holy moly — like Vincent Price in drag.

"I'm afraid my wife is going to leave me," she said.

It's a miracle she hasn't already, if that's how you looked when you came out of the closet, Ennis thought. He stroked his wig and smoothed the velour of his jacket and wondered what the others thought of how he was dressed?

Becky's face softened. She would never be beautiful, but when the light caught her right and she gave that shy smile, there was a coziness to her that made you take notice, like the girl in biology class you ignored all year, then asked to prom on the spur of the moment.

"Be careful not to expect too much from her," Becky said. "Remember: she married a man, not a man and sometimes a woman. She'll need time to get to know how wonderful Vanessa is. But if you're patient, you'll be rewarded with a girlfriend like no other."

That was Becky for you. One minute a merciless shrink and the next so wise and sweet it made all her cajoling and scab picking worthwhile. Women: unpredictable as the weather, and wasn't it grand to be one of them? Sitting in the sisterly circle, feeling less and less alone each passing minute.

A wave of relief swept him, followed by a surge of determination to build on the self-confidence the group inspired in him. He toyed with an earring and vowed to make Elaine a fully-realized woman: one who kept her knees together when getting out of a car, who remembered to place her dinner napkin on her lap folded points out and end in, who took small bites of steak and chewed slowly, and who drank wine only when her mouth was empty, to avoid smearing the rim like Ennis did. It had never felt so good to *be* Elaine. So right to let the female in him soar, both parts of him fiercely alive, the one masculine and penetrating, the other feminine and receptive. Distinctly Ennis *and* distinctly Elaine.

Sondra, whose male name was Ed, confessed her cross-dressing fears next. "I'm afraid of losing my job. I'm a fireman. Life would be unbearable if my co-workers found out about me."

Ennis was about to offer some words of encouragement, but Ed's thick chest and broad shoulders and silver and black jersey that hung like a gladiator's cape caught him off guard. Something inside him swooned: butterflies, warmth, a marshmallow giddiness. He suffered a moment of apprehension about being a fag, a latent homo, but even while banging prostitutes in his negligee, he had never once wanted a man in bed with him.

It must have come from Elaine. Except that the men he, Ennis, had always found handsome—not in a queer way, just men whose looks he admired—were clean-shaven, rangy types, like Charlton Heston or Clint Eastwood. Not a burly fireman in need of a shave. Why would Elaine's taste be any different?

And then he knew. Knew as sure as the sun rose in the east, as sure as death and taxes why Ed the Fireman had given him such a jolt.

Whump-whump-whump.

"That brings us to you, Elaine. Tell us your fears."

His hands shook. His head pounded. He tried to control himself, but couldn't. It wasn't Elaine that Ed appealed to. He tapped his chest with his finger. "I'm afraid another woman's soul entered my body after she died."

Becky's seething glare said it all: He'd gone off the reservation again and this time he wasn't going to get away with it.

Cullen told the hostess, a blonde with ivory skin, wearing a gold armlet above her elbow, that he was there to meet Dr. Winthrop. She led him past an empty bar that come five-thirty would be jammed with très chic seekers and strivers. A swarthy, white-shirted bartender placed two goblets of wine near the server's station and winked at her as they passed by.

Rebecca Winthrop had called him earlier that week to discuss Ennis. Ennis's gender identity therapy, it seemed, had fallen hostage to something called emergence anxiety— "cross-dresser stage fright," she explained it. Cullen had little time to talk the day she called, but since her psychiatric center was not far from Nephrology Partners' flagship office near St. Barnabas, he proposed stopping by that Friday on his way there. She countered by suggesting they meet over lunch, so here he was, at a tony Chinese bistro to meet Ennis's psychiatrist.

She rose to greet him, a straight-shouldered woman with the homely face of a French peasant, one of the beggars at the feast in *Les Misérables*, the dishrag hair and vulpine nose, the slight overbite. Yet oddly coquettish, her coy smile and teasing tilt of her head the mannerisms of a confident female, secure in her desirability. To whom? he wondered.

She held out her hand. "Becky Winthrop. Thanks for coming."

"Cullen Brodie. My pleasure."

She glanced down at their clasped hands — the disappearance of hers beneath the enormity of his — and gave a short laugh. "I wasn't expecting someone so — big. My visual of a nephrologist is a little bald guy with glasses." She withdrew her hand and recovered her poise. "Ennis thinks the world of you."

"He thinks you're all that, too."

"Lately not so much, I'm afraid. We'll talk."

She ordered Moo Goo Gai Pan and green tea to his Spicy Honey Shrimp and Pellegrino. An elfin Asian waitress delivered a tray of steaming food to their table. She spun away in a pour of shiny black hair that twitched like a horse's tail across the small of her back.

"Did you notice those Terra Cotta Warrior replicas in the entryway?" Cullen asked, waiting for his food to cool. "The National Geographic Museum has some originals on loan from China. Wouldn't the actual burial site be something to see?"

"It's breathtaking."

He searched her placid face. "You've been there? To Xian?"

She nodded. "Ten years ago. Rows and rows of life-size clay soldiers in battle formation, thousands of them, each with a unique face. They were supposed to accompany the first Emperor to the afterlife to protect him from rivals. Such magnificence from such an ignorant, primitive belief."

"You could say the same about the Sistine Chapel." He caught himself and gave her a rueful smile. "Sorry. I'm a recovering Catholic. I hope I didn't offend you."

"Hardly. I'm agnostic."

"Ah, hedging your bets, huh? Afraid to commit."

She poked at the teabag steeping in her cup. A woodsy, citrus scent drifted across the table. "To what?"

"Atheism. Either there's a God or there isn't. I say there isn't."

"Don't you have even the slightest niggling of doubt?"

"About what? Adam and Eve? Immaculate conceptions? Jesus turning water into wine and rising from the dead?"

She took a sip of tea and shook her head. "That's all low hanging fruit, easily dismissed by science. What about human consciousness? Morality? Altruism? I'm not saying they're proof of a divine being, but they are things that science has yet to account for."

He waved his fork in the air and felt his cheeks flush with conviction. "Not yet, maybe. But look at all that natural selection cleared up and the mysteries Watson and Crick put to bed. The failure of science to explain human consciousness isn't proof of God. It's proof of persistent human ignorance, which only science can keep from becoming permanent."

She tipped her head to the side and gazed at him with admiration. The corners of her mouth turned seductively up and she fluttered her lashes, a plain-faced woman making a run at him—though he was but a shell of the man he'd been in his prime, more husk than hunk these days. Hotties in their twenties looked right through him now. But Becky Winthrop wasn't in her twenties; late thirties, he guessed. And he doubted that she ever looked through anyone. She seemed intelligent and worldly and even had the God thing right—or nearly so—but he needed to *feel* something, a spark of arousal to kindle the flame, inspire the ancient dance. He scoured her face, but felt nothing. Even though he tried.

She seemed to sense his failure to launch. The ardor left her eyes. "Ennis thinks the soul of his deceased organ donor is taking over his personality." She was all business now, a doctor in spite of herself. "He's attributing typical signs of female gender emergence to the imagined influence of his donor. Things like preferences for refined types of food and music and skill at applying makeup."

He savored the sweet, pungent sauce dripping off his shrimp while she argued that Ennis's belief in transmigration was a defense mechanism formed in reaction to an intense fear: that the *true* female inside him—Elaine—would overwhelm his residual male, Ennis.

"Anxiety over gender emergence is perfectly normal. But Ennis has developed an unhealthy *idée fixe* about a figment named Carla. It would make all the difference if you were to intervene. You're an enormous figure in his life."

Cullen put his fork down and shrugged. "Except that she's not a figment."

She gave a dumbfounded stare. "Surely you don't believe...?"

"That his donor's soul is communing with him through her transplanted heart and kidney? Of course not. But her name *was* Carla. It turns out she was the daughter-in-law of one of my partners, Logan MacGregor."

Her eyebrows arched like rainbows. "The director of the transplant program?"

Cullen nodded. "She died in a car accident the day before. Most heart transplants come from local donors, and Ennis was at the top of the waiting list. He must have heard her name mentioned during surgery—incomplete anesthesia. It happens more often than you think."

She put a hand to her mouth. "Oh, how awful! That sounds terrifying." She collected herself and went on. "Unfortunately, that will only harden his illusions about his donor. He's already attempted to contact her family. So far, they haven't responded. You should make sure they never do. I'm concerned that Ennis is beginning to envision himself as a channel between his donor and her grieving family. The longer he indulges this fantasy, the more irrational and destructive it will become."

"I disagree. I hope they do respond. Recipients of organs from deceased donors often feel they aren't deserving of such altruism. Communicating with the donor's family sometimes helps relieve their guilt. Maybe they'll make him see that she *wanted* him to have her organs."

They went back and forth, points scored on either side. She warned that Ennis's pursuit of Carla ran the risk of unhinging him altogether and that he might stop taking his transplant medications because of it, to silence the troublesome spirit he imagined inside him. Cullen argued exactly the opposite, that until Ennis satisfied his curiosity about his donor, his magical thinking would continue.

They went at it all until their plates were empty and she excused herself to use the restroom. She dabbed her mouth with her napkin, pushed her chair back, and flounced off. Cullen did a double take at the sight of her calves disappearing down the aisle in a sculpted sweep of rich, brown muscle. A gold bracelet dangled from her ankle, a sexy bangle he imagined unfastening. Slowly.

He waited for her to return. Her legs were even more heavenly from the front. The hem of her black dress fell just above her knees, revealing a tantalizing glimpse of sleek, curvy thigh. They took over his brain like a virus commandeering a hard drive. It was all he could think about: her thighs quivering at his touch. Squirming beneath him. His head between them.

"Would you like to have dinner with me this weekend?" he asked.

Cullen went straight from the restaurant to his medical group's corporate headquarters for their monthly financials review. The dimmed conference room and his full belly from lunch with Becky Winthrop left him prone to musing. Duncan MacGregor's PowerPoint talk on revenue-enhancing ancillaries like renal dietician visits, vascular access centers, and erythropoietin injections failed to hold his attention. His gaze drifted from the screen to Duncan, his mop of red hair, the sorrow limned on his fleshy face by the loss of his wife. Preceded by that of his mother, Catherine, two years before, to multiple sclerosis. A once-vibrant woman reduced to dribbling Ensure onto her lap.

Duncan's casual Friday attire of canvas lace-ups, chinos, and an open-collar shirt looked typically inapt amongst the white-coated physicians ringing the mahogany conference table. His puerile use of animation to enliven his talk revealed him for what he was: a maturation-arrested scion doing distaff work—medical billing. Kind and generous to a fault, he was forever writing off their delinquent accounts, his golden eyes full of gullible compassion. He lived on the margins of MacGregor's empire, their charismatic doyen's only son.

Cullen yawned and stretched his legs. Reimbursement codes didn't interest him. Patients did. It was only on account of Ennis that he attended Duncan's anesthetizing talk in the first place. He had approached MacGregor about him while everyone else was still filing into the room. MacGregor motioned toward his sumptuous office, the grouping of fine furniture at the end of the room. Cullen sat on the sofa; MacGregor settled into the chair. He crossed his thick legs and smiled, his ruddy face, his gleaming hair, a lead silverback indulging an underling.

"We were touched by his gratitude," he said, in response to Cullen's inquiry about the letter Ennis sent through the Organ Procurement Agency. "Some recipients never think twice about their donors, as if their organs came off a shelf at Costco. But meeting Carla's organ recipient is not something Duncan is ready to do. Willoughby might try thanking God instead. It helps me cope with my feelings of unworthiness. It might help him, too."

Try thanking God instead? Not MacGregor, too. Cullen felt like the doctor in *Invasion of the Body Snatchers* who learned his friend had turned into one of the pod people. The nuns were right after all. Jesus *was* everywhere. Cullen thanked him for his time. MacGregor rose from his chair with a wince and trailed him back into the conference room.

He waited until after the presentation to seek out Duncan, whose face was still blotched with nervousness over his talk. He clutched his indispensable codebook— *Current Procedural Terminology, 2007 Edition*—like a bible. Just looking at it made Cullen grind his teeth.

CPT was a registered trademark of the American Medical Association, to which he had faithfully paid dues for more than two decades. The AMA made seventy *million* dollars a year off sales and royalties from their monopoly on creating and maintaining the procedural codes used to numerically define medical services doctors provided to patients. And who granted this monopoly? The United States government, via the Health Care Financing Administration (HCFA), which just happened to set the ever-declining fees doctors were paid for these very codes. In other words, the government gave the AMA a lucrative monopoly to create a coding system the government then used to limit physician income—which, when adjusted for inflation, had been going down for over a decade. While the income of the AMA's trustees and officers soared, funded by a codebook used to bludgeon its rank-and-file. No wonder AMA membership had collapsed. Another once-venerable institution made venal by power and money. Along with the Catholic Church. It was a wonder anyone had faith in anything, secular or spiritual. Only children remained unsullied by it all—and then not for long.

Duncan at least had that to cleave to. Wives came and went, but a child was different, the best shot at immortality one could expect. Far superior to what religion promised: eternal life that was at best delusional, if not a cruel lie. But immortality achieved by the transmission of chromosomes alone was woefully unsatisfying—the sperm bank donations Cullen traded for pocket money during med school were evidence enough of that. A phrase came to him, an ancient phrase full of beauty and meaning, despite its origin: *Begotten, not made*. It was from the Nicene Creed and was intended to describe Jesus—the Son equal to the Father, yet distinct. Cullen liked it for what it implied about earthly fathers and sons: *Begotten, not made*. He had made babies, but he had not yet begotten one. Unlike Duncan, whose grief over Carla would diminish, but whose eternal wonder at his children would not.

He cuffed Duncan's shoulder, a good-natured thump born of sudden tenderness. "Good job. You almost sounded like you knew what you were talking about."

Duncan's blotches evanesced from red to pink to a cinnamon splatter of freckles again. He grinned. "What parallel universe were you in? At least your head didn't pitch forward like Dr. Windemere's did, though. I thought she stroked."

"Did you know that during a typical classroom lecture, the average male college student has a sexual fantasy every ninety seconds? You're lucky I'm getting old. Mine only came every five minutes." He turned serious and squeezed his forearm. "How are you holding up?"

Duncan's eyes darted away and back, glistening. "I'm okay. My children keep me from feeling sorry for myself."

"The hurt will stop one day," Cullen said, though he knew it wouldn't, that at best it would diminish to a dull throb, instead of the lancinating grief that cracked your heart and made you scream the silent scream of lunacy. He stepped back and put some distance between them. "Would you mind if I asked you something about Carla? It's strange, the things we become curious about when people die. Regret over not having known them better, I suppose."

Duncan licked his lips. "Sure, go ahead."

"What was her favorite kind of music?"

A wry smile crossed his face. "Jazz. We fought about it all the time. I'm a pop rock guy."

Cullen beat back the jolt he felt and kept his expression blank. "I once heard her say she liked beets, too. Was that true? That she liked beets?"

Duncan threw his head back and laughed, straight from the belly. "Ate 'em like candy. I never understood it."

The same claxon that sounded when Ennis first mouthed Carla's name wailed in his head again. "There's something else I've wondered about, too. Has Carla's recipient tried to contact you?"

Duncan fussed with his watch. "Yes, he has. Through the Organ Procurement Agency. As you can imagine, he was extremely grateful for Carla's donation. The privacy laws are pretty strict, so all he could say was that he was a retired painter and that heart failure and dialysis were pretty rough on him. He couldn't even say what city he lives in. I was curious to know more, but in the end my father and I decided against it. Like you said, one day the hurt will stop. Maybe then."

Cullen cast his gaze across the room, to where MacGregor was doling out advice to a colleague. Their eyes met.

MacGregor looked away.

Chapter 7

ANGELA MASTERS HUNG A "CLOSED FOR LUNCH" sign on the door of her gallery and loped west down Te Ara Marie Nui on a torpid afternoon swaddled in Tropic of Capricorn heat. She passed the Seven-In-One Coconut Tree—one spindly, frond-topped trunk surrounded by six more, all twisting like magic beanstalks into the sky—and paused at the traffic circle in the heart of downtown Avarua. She was flanked on her left by the jagged green thrust of Mount Ikurangi, and on her right by the wash of the old harbor, formed by a V-shaped break in Rarotonga's necklacing reef. A half-dozen skiffs trimmed in orange and pink and lime lay at anchor beside the wharf, rocked by the lave of the harbor. A procession of motorbikes and cars and yellow tourist buses streamed through the roundabout. She turned right and stopped in front of a block building made of coral and stone next to the quay: the Black Pearl Bar, once the most notorious watering hole in the South Pacific.

A boy with smooth cocoa skin and dark, prowling eyes sat on a white motorbike parked outside the entrance, one foot braced on the pavement, the other on his bike. He wore a green knit polo over black baggy shorts. She returned his smile—was that desire she detected, her appeal enduring, even at fifty-four?—and pushed through the Black Pearl's slatted red saloon doors with five minutes to spare.

She waved at Lonnie, a wizened, tattooed, frizzy-haired Kiwi toper who tended bar until nine, and ordered two

Export Golds before traipsing through a layer of fresh sawdust, a tradition passed down from the Black Pearl's glory days, when rum-crazed sailors on shore leave spilled beer and puke and blood onto the floor in equal parts. She inhaled its woodsy scent, organic and clean, and made her way to a booth in back to wait for Ty.

Lonnie ferried the beers and a plate of oysters to her table. Ty showed up a few minutes later, sweaty and exhilarated from another of the cross-island treks he advertised to unsuspecting tourists as "Ty's Nature Walks"—grueling hikes into Rarotonga's fecund, rugged interior. He wore what he always wore on the hikes: a floppy orange hat, the latest sunglasses, a white tee over faded gym shorts, and low-cut Adidas with no socks. He carved five treks a week into the rain forest and swam two miles a day in the lagoon, leaving his body marmoreal and brown, like Myron's *Discus Thrower*.

One of his favorite rituals was to make an exhausted, traumatized group of tenderfoot hikers—most of whom could barely put one foot in front of the other without groaning in pain from their shredded leg muscles—guess his age. The closest anyone came was fifty-two, and then only because a tree branch snagged his hat and exposed his perfectly smooth coconut of a skull. Most often they took him to be in his forties. Ty turned sixty-eight the previous fall.

He flashed a broad smile of white teeth, one chipped, and wrinkled his blunt-featured face. "*Kia orana.*"

"So, old man, did you leave any tourists on the mountain today? Or did you bring them all back to brag to their friends that they survived a morning in the woods with Tuti Okatai?"

He sat across from her and took a long pull of lager. His Adam's apple bobbed three times. He clapped the bottle back on the table with a crack. "I showed them the Truth today! Like I showed you the Truth when you came to Rarotonga, all those years ago."

She first learned of the Cook Islands as a little girl, when her mother told her of the Marsters family of Palmerston Atoll—as had her grandmother told her mother, and so on and so on, five generations back. The story began not in the South Pacific, but in England, with a young boy named William Marsters, who was said to have had a recurring dream of owning an island full of women. At the age of forty-two, William chased his phantasmagoria to the Cook Islands, where he took a Maori woman named Sara for his wife. He soon moved Sara—and her sister—to a tiny island northwest of Rarotonga: uninhabited Palmerston Atoll. William declared himself an official Anglican minister and proceeded to marry Sara's sister and cousin as well, leaving him with one island and three bickering Maori wives. He made up for his dearth of islands and surfeit of women by having his second and third wives live on opposite ends of Palmerston, with Sara occupying the middle third. Said in later years to resemble Moses, William Marsters died in 1899 at the age of seventy-eight, having sired seventeen children and fifty-four grandchildren. Thousands of his descendants—Angela's mother among them—were scattered all over the globe, though only fifty remained on Palmerston Atoll, where the clan's surname had long since morphed from Marsters to Masters.

That she was descended from a polygamist was of no interest to Angela. What had enthralled her about the story as a child was the exotic island in the South Pacific she dreamed of escaping to in the frozen nadir of winter. She had no way of knowing then that when she finally did flee to Rarotonga, it would be to keep from going insane.

She swallowed the oyster she had been working on—the slick, rubbery texture of it, its ocean taste—and washed it down with a sip of golden lager. "You showed me more than the Truth when I came to Rarotonga." That was what Ty called the forest—the Truth. "You showed me *aroa*."

He speared a gray blob of shellfish with his fork and nodded. "You were eager to be one of us."

More like desperate. Within a week of arriving, she rented a room in Avarua, got a job at a downtown gallery, learned to snorkel, took Cook Island Maori lessons—with eight consonants and five vowels, it wasn't hard to learn—and went on one of his cross-island treks, which she survived only because of the indestructible nature of youth. Ty, as inquisitive as the rest of Rarotonga about the young American girl claiming to be a Marsters, invited her home to meet his wife Kura and their four children. She stayed for dinner and, despite failing to satisfy their curiosity about her past, was instantly accepted into the Okatais's wide circle of family and friends.

More hikes followed. Under Ty's tutelage, she learned about *kuru*, the globular green fruit known as breadfruit; learned how to recognize the soft trill of a *kukupa*, the Cook Islands fruit dove, with its green wings and white breast and yellow underbelly; and learned how to spot the thick trunk and poisonous seeds of the *Utu* tree. She learned, too, that Rarotonga was divided into humid slope forest at lower levels and cooler cloud forest at upper levels, where the exotic *Sclerotheca* thrived, an endemic fern with pale green flowers and a garish purple center.

In return, Ty expected to be included in every facet of her life. During one arduous climb to *Te Rua Manga*—The Needle—a precipice of sheer rock said to be among the five most sacred energy spots on Earth, he stopped in a small clearing along the densely wooded trail and voiced frustration over her reluctance to give the details of her improbable migration to Rarotonga. A blotch of perspiration soaked the front of his tee, but his breathing was as unaffected as hers was labored.

"Kura and I are your Maori family. You know much about us—how we met, the death of our daughter, which son-in-law is alcoholic. But we know little about why you came here. This hurts us."

He kicked at a network of roots. She stared at a stand of frangipani behind him, its brindled branches and fragrant pink and yellow blossoms, its crisp green leaves. He looked up and went on.

"The greatest word in our Maori language is *aroa*. *Aroa* is all aspects of love. Generosity, mercy, kindness—the things we do for one another. *Aroa* is the foundation of Cook Island life. I want you to have a greater *aroa* with my family. The forest reveals the Truth. So should you. Sharing the past deepens the bond between friends."

Later that day, in the shadow of *Te Rua Manga*, with the sough of the forest whispering in her ear, she told him her story of heartbreak and shame. He would never be critical of her again, saying only of her early tourist-humping years on the island that she seemed to be taking Cook Island hospitality to an extreme, and later holding his tongue like a forbearing father during her ill-advised marriage to Avarua's wastrel, Vicodin-popping, Belgian doctor.

Her introduction to *aroa* that day on the Mountain of Good Energy launched her on a life of spiritual inquiry, steeped in Rarotongan myth and ritual. The wisdom *aroa* blessed her with—the wisdom to know that pride, not temptation, was Eve's sin, and humility her salvation—had given her the courage to revisit the fall from grace her own pride had caused, hauntingly rendered in a nearly completed painting in her atelier.

"How much longer before I see it?" Ty asked, after they finished their beers.

"Soon. Very soon."

He studied her face, the sorrow in her eyes. "It still hurts, doesn't it?"

"Like it was yesterday. I thought I could light the fire and still control the flame, but I was wrong. I underestimated the terrible passion of male rivalry."

Her first real glimpse of the hostility between them came a few weeks before Chaz Brodie slashed her canvas at Art Rampage. Cullen had invited her to watch him play basketball at a place called the Attucks—short for Crispus Attucks—in a neighborhood where a fireman bent over a hydrant had been shot and killed during the race riots of '68.

Hers was the only white face in the crowd. Her cheeks stung from the scowls and snickers she got on her way to a seat in some worm-eaten bleachers alongside an asphalt court enclosed by a fifteen-foot chain link fence with a padlocked gate. The moment she sat down, a fierce-looking street warrior in a purple muscle shirt, with veins the size of garden hoses lining his biceps, stood over her and grinned. He had a huge Afro and skin that gleamed like polished obsidian.

"I'm Slade. Cullen axed me to sit wit you." One front tooth was made of gold and his lower lip was massive and puffed, as if swollen from a bee sting. He scanned the bleachers around them with a menacing expression and raised his big bass voice for all to hear. "If you Cullen's lady, you cool wit Slade."

The glowering looks withered and the susurrus of snide remarks died an instant death. He sat next to her and, in ghetto patois she struggled to follow, explained his connection to Cullen. As best she could make out, no white player had ever set foot on the Attucks until the summer of 1971, when Slade happened by one day and noticed a tall white boy with slim calves and big thighs practicing jump shots.

"I tole him to boogie, fo I kicked his honky ass back across the Lowry Bridge. So what do the crazy mothafucka do? Axes me, do I wanna play one-on-one? White boy comes to the Attucks—*alone*—an calls out the baddest nigger on the block. I was gonna fuck him up, but there was sumpin 'bout him, standin' there all calm, socks 'round his ankles like he was Pete Maravich. 'Less git it on,' I tells him. Beats me ten-fo, throws down two nasty dunks 'long the way. In mah *face!*"

He bellowed a deep, rolling laugh that shook his shoulders.

"'Whas yo name?' I axed him later on, after he done whupped my ass again. 'Cullen,' he say. 'Cullen Brodie.' He been playin' the Attucks ever since."

He leaned back against the bleacher seat behind them and stretched his legs out on the one in front and pointed toward the court. "He the second white to play the Attucks. An only then 'cause Cullen agitated fo it. Which made *no* damn sense to me."

Angie looked to one end of the asphalt court, where two teams of five, shirts and skins, had squared off to play. Lined up chest-to-chest opposite Cullen was Dempsey Fagan, his curly black hair falling over his ears and nape. He extended one arm to deny Cullen the ball, his face intense. Too intense, as if preventing Cullen from receiving a pass might save the world from nuclear holocaust. Cullen swatted his hand away and maneuvered to free himself. They jostled and hand-checked from one end of the court to the other that way, the one trying to score, the other straining to stop him. And why exactly, she wondered, did it matter?

The muscles of Cullen's bare torso tensed and flickered in the light of the sinking sun, and she liked that. She liked, too, the fluid way his body moved, like a ballet dancer, only stronger, with more raw virility. And she liked that his hands, his Pantagruelian hands, could grind her bones to dust, and that even at five-foot-nine she had to look up at him. What was absolutely lethal about him, though, was when he went cockeyed, his left eye the least little bit lopsided when he had too much to drink. A tiny flaw that made her want to hold him. How many times, she fretted, had Cullen Brodie gotten laid on account of having strabismus?

She found herself unexpectedly taken by the elemental rhythm of the game, the power and grace of the athletes, sinewy bodies flying to the rim in defiance of gravity. And she understood why Cullen brought her there. Basketball—the way it was played at the Attucks—was a game of joyous physical expression, and the players artists, painting brushstrokes onto an asphalt canvas while seeking to impose their will on one another. But for all the striving and pushing and street smack she witnessed that night, nothing came close to matching what went on between Cullen and Dempsey. "They gettin' it *on!*" Slade growled, nodding his great head when they collided like rams on a mountainside while chasing down a loose ball. Only then, at that precise moment, did she truly understand how horribly vulnerable male pride could make a man.

But in the days following Art Rampage, after Chaz Brodie left her painting tattered and ruined, Angie's infatuation with Cullen gave way to an unslakeable fury. It had taken her months to complete what Chaz wrecked in seconds. How dare an uneducated, reactionary bigot sit in judgment of her progressive, courageous father? She should never have agreed to lie about her name in the first place, as if she, rather than Cullen's fatuous, philistine parents, had something to be ashamed of. Cullen had no backbone. He was contemptible, despicable, a callow boy afraid to stand up to his parents. What had she ever seen in him? She had men waiting in line to take her out who would never dream of insulting her that way, demanding she use a pseudonym. Who did he think he was? Her despoiled painting was beyond salvage, but her pride was not.

She refused to take Cullen's calls and waited barely a week before going out with Dempsey. She met him at the downtown apartment his parents paid for. That much, at least, the two of them had in common: rich kids unaccustomed to being denied. From there they walked to the Gopher Theater to see Warren Beatty in *Shampoo*, then went drinking at Sadie's Parlor, where Angie had way too many tequila sunrises. On the way back to Dempsey's apartment, walking down Hennepin past topless bars and leering bums and skanky whores selling comfort to suburban men pulling cars haltingly to the curb, the booze hit her full force.

Cullen had humiliated her. He hadn't loved her enough, that was the problem. Hadn't *desired* her enough. She needed to get his attention, concentrate his mind. And nothing concentrated the mind like pain. Oh, yes, she would bring the pain to Cullen Brodie. Pain like he'd never felt before. Pain to make him want to pluck his eyes out.

It was only while lying flat on her back in Dempsey's bedroom, his window raised to a racket of horns and sirens and shouts from the street below, that she realized it was *false* pride that brought her to this. To Dempsey's grunting and sweating and rough talk, grimly trying to undo what could never be undone: the winning shot of a state championship game three years before. The sound of a basketball being dribbled adagio forever in Dempsey's head, Cullen the winner, Dempsey the loser, no matter how many do-overs Cullen gave him at the Attucks. No matter how hard Dempsey plowed away at her now.

When it was over, when the room stopped spinning long enough for her to totter to her car, she hung her head beneath the spangled sky and wept. Like a rape victim left smeared and dripping, before the vileness could be wiped away.

Before the fight for dignity began.

⟨ ⁂ ⟩

Ennis opened his wardrobe door and stared at the rack of dresses and tops and slacks that took months to accumulate. He reached out and fondled an off-white blouse, the silky texture of it bliss in his hand. It had come to this. Again.

His chest rocked and his throat grew thick. A tsunami of grief steamrolled him, black and viscous, like when his father's plane corkscrewed out of the sky and landed in a charred and smoking heap. How fast the circle had closed, the terrible circle he was so sure he had finally squared.

It began three weeks before, with a message on his answering machine, his heart surgeon's reedy voice made all the more whiney by the poor quality of Ennis's recorder.

"Ennis? Dr. Allen here. Please call me at the office as soon as possible. I need to discuss the results of your biopsy with you."

His kidney could be monitored for rejection with blood tests, but his heart required an actual hunk of tissue. He had undergone surveillance EMBs—endomyocardial biopsies— ever since transplant, but had never quite gotten used to the procedure. The puncturing of his right jugular vein and threading of an instrument called a cardiac bioptome—a long, pliable tube with small metal forceps on the end—into his right ventricle to snag a piece of heart. He imagined the bioptome getting out of control, its snapping metal jaws eating away an entire wall of his heart, like in a science fiction movie with Sigourney Weaver. It gave him jitters only Ativan could squelch.

"Your biopsy showed some rejection," Dr. Allen told him, when he called back. "Grade two R, moderate. Nothing to be concerned about. We'll snuff it out with a course of steroids."

He pictured his immune system attacking his transplant, sheets of pissed off white corpuscles—T cells, Dr. Allen called them—invading the muscle of his heart. Bathing it in all kinds of destructive proteins and chemicals. Swelling it. Harming it. Until it failed.

But it didn't fail. Dr. Allen increased his dose of prednisone to 300 mg a day for five days, and then tapered him back to his previous dose. Within a week his biopsy was back to normal, his episode of rejection, what you might say, nipped in the bud. But he couldn't stop asking the dreaded question all transplant patients asked in his shoes.

Why?

Why had his body attempted to reject his heart *now*, rather than the week before or the week before that? What was different this time from all the other times, when his surveillance biopsies had been pristine? Dr. Allen's answer—that three-quarters of all heart transplant recipients experienced a bout of rejection during the first year of transplant, but hardly any in later years—failed to satisfy him. Doctors knew what they read in books. But the stuff that wasn't in books for them to read was what worried him. The stuff they hadn't figured out yet.

He went over everything he had done since his last EMB and the one that showed rejection, searching for something that could have upset the delicate ceasefire between his immune system and his transplanted heart— his kidney was fine, unfazed by it all. Tough little bastards, beans were.

Maybe he'd inadvertently gotten into some St. John's wort, which, he'd been warned, could lower his Prograf level and make him susceptible to rejection. But he hadn't taken any herbs or eaten any crazy health foods. Nor gotten drunk and missed his medication, or mixed up his pill bottles or traveled to Mexico and got diarrhea—or clap. He hadn't taken too much or too little of anything. Not a single thing different from any other week.

Except one: Elaine. Elaine was what was different.

He went en femme five days in a row before his bout of rejection, all Elaine all the time, morning to night, nails to nightie. Run with it, Becky had urged. Loosen the reins. Elaine needed to stretch her legs. Harmony would be his reward, sweet harmony, the Holy Grail of gender accord.

What he got was anything but harmony. Minor disturbances at first—second thoughts about a dress making him look dumpy; regret over a pair of shoes that looked darling in the store, but that made his feet look big once he got home; disappointment at his reflection in a store window—then a full-blown panic attack, a tear-your-face-off meltdown. But only while dressed as Elaine, never as Ennis. He felt as if someone were watching him, watching *Elaine*— what she wore, where she shopped, how she did her hair. Someone disapproving. "A man in drag, that's all you'll ever be, and an old one at that."

That's when he had, what you might say, an epiphany: two was company, three was a crowd. His bout of rejection was caused by Elaine trying to rid herself of Carla, a near-lethal hissy fit over female primacy. One or the other had to go—and it couldn't be Carla, or they all would die.

He began yanking clothes off hangers and hurling them into a gray, fifty-gallon Rubbermaid container he wheeled into the bedroom beside him. Hurling and howling, howling and hurling, yelling as if he'd been stabbed. His wigs went and then his shoes and bras and panties and make-up, his closet purged of all feminine vestures. Like countless times before, 'til all that remained was a meager collection of man clothes. Drab clothes.

He pushed the Rubbermaid down the hall and out the door to the end of the drive and sat down on the curb with his face in his hands. A plump and lambent moon rose over the hillocks behind him and climbed high into the cold, black firmament before he went inside.

Sooner or later, a singular moment of clarity strikes all love affairs, an ineluctable flash of truth revealing, for better or worse, how things really are. Cullen's and Becky's came in front of the gorilla exhibit at the African Animal Park. It was their third date and they had yet to sleep together, which for now was fine with Cullen. Sex complicated things. Madcap relationships tended to ensue. Sometimes marriage. None of which had ended well.

Becky stood pigeon-toed in green cargo shorts and white tennis shoes, her thighs pressed against a three-foot-high orange railing, her legs smooth and supple and brown. Cullen trailed ten feet behind, Becky having run ahead like a child to secure a spot in front. Sunlight spilled unfiltered onto her hair. The white muslin top she wore hung like lingerie on her shoulders.

She peered across a thirty-foot cement chasm at a troop of Western Lowland Gorillas, housed in a grassy, steep-walled enclosure studded by granite boulders, tree stumps, and eucalyptus. A female whose belly spilled onto her thighs munched ficus leaves in the center of the exhibit, with a waterfall and grotto behind her. Her face brimmed with pathos, her mournful, deep-set eyes and flattened nose, her small ears and thrusting jaw. A silverback knuckle-walked behind her, a magnificent, scowling beast with black shaggy fur over his massive arms and chest and a sleek, canescent coat of hair down his back.

Becky turned, searching for him. In a moment he would see her rustic face, her long nose and pointed chin. Would his stomach sink at her plainness? A tender swell crested inside him. It was not her too-long nose or detracting overbite he saw, but her demure smile and intelligent eyes, the graceful cords of her neck and taut ripple of muscle above her knees. He gazed at her and grinned.

She ran a hand through her hair. "What?"

He gestured to the gorilla enclosure. "Did you know that the dominant male gets exclusive mating rights to all females?" He tattooed his chest with three quick fist beats, like in an old Tarzan movie.

She gave a sly smile, a seductive one that made her nose smaller and her overbite imperceptible. She walked over and jabbed his chest with a forefinger. "Until he gets old and some young ape pushes him out of the troop. Then he gets nothing. Nada. While all the females keep right on mating. Is that what you want to be some day, a celibate silverback alone in the forest? How sad you'd be."

He liked her like this, all spunk and raillery. He looped his hands around the small of her back and pulled her against him. "Alpha dominance has its downside. The trick is to get out while you still have some juice left—and take your favorite female with you."

She thumped his shoulder with her fist and squirmed away, but couldn't mask her satisfaction. "I'm surprised you haven't jumped into the exhibit to challenge King Kong over there for his harem. Take me on the tram ride."

The centerpiece of the African Animal Park experience was a wheeled tram ride, in powder blue cars with white vinyl roofs and open-air windows. The thirty-minute, narrated excursion snaked through hundreds of acres of grassy hills, dusty plains, and lush oases teeming with wildlife. Giraffe, white rhinos, springbok, cape buffalo, zebras, wildebeests and more roved a meticulously planned habitat intended to simulate their native environment—

frequent stands of palm and oak notwithstanding. Cullen listened to the mike-aided commentary of their twenty-something guide as they pulled alongside a herd of antelope.

"Springbok are capable of an escape speed of fifty-five miles per hour," she said, from her perch in the cab.

He fixed on a vigilant buck forty yards away and admired his two-tone coat—tan on top, white on the belly, a dark brown racing stripe in between—and muscled flanks, his innocent white face and floppy, finger-marked ears.

"But there's always something faster—like cheetahs. Try *seventy* miles an hour. You know what we guides call springbok when we're being evil? Cheetos!"

The visual of a streaking cheetah taking down and snacking on an adorable springbok elicited a groan of revulsion from the bevy of tourists wedged shoulder-to-shoulder in the tramcars, but a trill of wonderment, too. Seventy miles an hour, was that even possible without an internal combustion engine?

He nudged Becky and said in her ear, "Cheetahs are proof there's no God."

She looked at him as if he were one of her most impaired patients. "You lost me."

"What kind of Intelligent Designer would create an animal to run down and butcher a springbok? Natural selection has no sensibilities. A Divine Creator would."

She smiled and nodded. "Ah, I see. And besides, who designed the Designer, right?"

He stuck out a hand and fist-bumped her. "Exactly. If you've heard one teleological argument, you've heard them all."

They set out to see the lions with the sun in their faces the entire way. Joyous children darted in and out of a swirling crowd parted by islands of hobbled, arthritic seniors pushing gamely forward with walkers and canes.

They paused near the Congo Cafe to view a pair of squawking, raucous macaws fastened to a tree branch by powerful talons, one a flame of red plumage, the other a spray of ocean blue.

For some unfathomable reason, they inspired Becky to update him on Ennis. Only a psychiatrist could be moved to shop talk by a couple of cackling macaws.

"You know that episode of cardiac rejection he had? He thinks his feminine personality tried to reject the feminine soul of his donor. Because there isn't room for two of them in one male body. He's afraid that if he cross-dresses again, his transgender female will provoke another rejection and he'll die. He threw out every article of women's clothing he owned and stopped coming to group. It couldn't be more obvious: His transmigration delusion is about guilt over cross-dressing."

Cullen didn't see why it couldn't be guilt over cross-dressing *and* guilt over Carla's altruism. And that's what he should have said. But he didn't.

"So he doesn't cross-dress for a while. He'll survive."

She lit into him like a third macaw, her shrill voice adding to the jungle din. "I can't believe you said that! Dressing like a woman is the only way a transgender can *be* transgender. It's like telling you to stop seeing patients for a while. You'd still have your medical license, but you wouldn't really *be* much of a doctor, would you?"

The thick scent of corndogs from a nearby food cart wafted up his nose. There was a weakness to her analogy, he was sure of it, but the means of articulating it escaped him. "All I'm saying is that gender accord isn't the only thing on his plate. He had a dual organ transplant, for God's sake. He has more important issues."

Her eyes bugged. Veins bulged. She balled her fists and shook. Vibrated, almost.

"More important than what? Living an authentic life? Let me tell you something: gender discord makes people ill in ways you can't even imagine. Most of them would rather pass a kidney stone a day for the rest of their lives than suffer such anguish."

A sudden ruction shrilled from the bird enclosure, a feathered fracas that bought Cullen time to compose himself and avoid saying something he might regret. He feigned interest in the quarreling pair of exotic birds at first, but then considered them with genuine curiosity. Macaws mated for life, the Plexiglas display tacked to the trunk beneath the two squalling parrots said. How did they do it? How did they keep from cracking open their mate's skull with their sharp, strong beaks? He sighed and held his tongue. De-escalated. Like a good macaw.

"Look, he's hit a rough patch emotionally. Just like you said he would. The next time he sees me, I'll tell him we talked. I'll try to get him to release Carla's soul and resume gender therapy."

This seemed to mollify her — along with the corndogs he bought, slathered in mustard and piping hot. They ate and talked and patched things up enough to move on to the lion exhibit, where they encountered a mob six deep at the top of a bluff overlooking a hollow bounded by cyclone fencing. The crowd converged on a mounted telescope that required a quarter per minute of viewing time. Cullen asked the couple in front of them, two young Hispanics with three children in tow, what everyone was so worked up about.

The man, short and compact and no more than thirty, smoothed the bristles of his sleek moustache and pointed toward the hollow. *"Los leónes están apareandose!"* His voice was edgy, expectant, like at a prizefight or soccer match.

Behind them, a corn-fed woman with harsh yellow hair and puckered thighs informed her Jack Spratt of a husband that African lions mated twenty to forty times a day without hunting or eating. For three days running. Cullen glanced at Becky. She extended four fingers of one hand and curled the forefinger and thumb of the other into a circle. *Forty?* she mouthed with a sexy grin.

It took fifteen minutes to nudge their way to a clear view line. A lioness and a male lion with a lush, dark mane were lying on the ground beneath a tree in the center of the hollow. The female was on her back, paws lolling in the air; the male lay couchant, gazing in the opposite direction. After a while, the female righted herself and went over to him. She nuzzled his neck and rubbed her shoulder against his chest and gave a low, guttural purr that carried across the valley and up the bluff. Cullen felt his dick stir, half-ashamed it did.

He slugged the telescope with a quarter and adjusted the focus. The male rose and licked the lioness's rump. She bolted ten yards away and crouched with her tail beating the air. The male tongued her nape and mounted her. His haunches pumped in short thrusts, his tawny hide like glazed caramel. He shook his head and climaxed with a ragged roar, earning a nip to his muzzle from the lioness when he dismounted. She collapsed as if shot with a tranquilizer and rolled onto her back, all four paws in the air. The male fell on his side and shut his eyes—all this before the minute Cullen's quarter bought had expired.

Half an hour later they repeated their coupling, this time with Becky's eye pressed to the glass. She stepped away from the telescope tense and flushed, appearing slightly out of breath.

"Well?" Cullen asked. "What did you think?"

She walked over and clutched the front of his shirt and bit his lower lip. He grabbed her buttocks with both hands and squeezed.

That evening she stayed overnight at his condo.

Chapter 8

CULLEN TAPPED A FINAL keystroke and sent his consultation note—a diabetic with Stage IV Chronic Kidney Disease—into cyberspace to the woman's referring physician, the digital wonder of Nephrology Partners' fifty-thousand-dollar-per-doctor electronic medical record fully manifest. Why such an ominous classification system, though? It smacked of oncology's lexicon, where the higher the stage the closer the patient to death. For oncologists, Stage IV was time to call hospice, society's sub rosa euthanasia squad. Stage IV kidney disease signified fifteen to thirty per cent kidney function remaining—not a good thing, but hardly a death sentence.

"Dr. Brodie?"

Bria filled—*occluded*—the threshold of his office, mouth agape and drawing air. She looked as if she'd just stepped off a treadmill, though the distance from her desk to his door was no more than fifty feet. The presenting face of his practice, afflicted with morbid obesity; she might as well greet patients with a burning cigarette dangling between her lips, no less unhealthy a first impression would it make. Yet she wasn't without appeal. Her creamy complexion and strawberry hair and the sensuous smile of her round, stippled face had attracted more than a few young males willing to overlook her ponderousness.

"We have a situation in the waiting room. His appointment isn't until eleven, but you need to see Ennis Willoughby *now*."

"Why?"

She pinched her nose between her thumb and forefinger. "Because he stinks. He's going to clear out the waiting room. One patient rescheduled already."

Cullen squeezed past her and strode down the hallway. Ennis sat reading the swimsuit issue of *Sports Illustrated* with three empty chairs to his left and three to his right. The rest of the patients shrank in opposite corners of the room, squeamish and fidgety and eyeing him with varying degrees of revulsion, as if he had TB. Bria was right. They were moments from a mass exodus.

He called out Ennis's name. His head snapped up, but he didn't smile. He wore a begrimed sweatshirt and paint-spattered beige pants. His face was wan and grizzled, his hair greasy and unkempt.

The stench hit him before Ennis made it halfway across the room, the warm, yeasty reek of the unwashed. He choked back an urge to gag and led him to an examination room—quickly, to spare the others from suffering a second more of the miasma infiltrating the waiting area. His ripe, squalid odor fouled the air of the small exam room so thoroughly Cullen soon ceased to even notice it.

He seated him on the table and took a step back to appraise him, the pasty wattle flopping from his neck, his lugubrious, wasted face. "You look pretty rough. Is everything okay?"

He hung his head. "I'm, what you might say, in a quandary."

"How come?"

"I'm afraid if I cross-dress again it'll cause another rejection."

He looked up and searched for Cullen's reaction. Cullen checked an impulse to ask if he thought bathing would cause a bout of rejection, too. "What makes you think that?"

He listened patiently while Ennis explained. It was just as Becky said. He believed that his feminine transgender personality, Elaine, refused to accept the soul of his female donor, Carla.

"What makes you so sure a piece of Carla's soul is inside you?"

His pewter eyes brightened. He leaned forward, a wraith turned human again. "I like things I never liked before. See things I've never seen before. Places and images that belong to her, not me." He said his visions were preceded by a flutter and swell in his chest, as if something inside him wanted to emerge.

Cullen jumped all over the buzzword he'd used. "Are you sure it isn't Elaine that's trying to emerge?"

Ennis scowled at him. "You been talkin' to Becky too much."

Cullen tried to conceal the ripple of pleasure he felt at the sound of her name, but something in his eyes must have betrayed him. A look of suspicion darkened Ennis's face.

"Are you sweet on my shrink?"

Amazing, how he'd found them out. Intuition, perhaps. Female intuition. Other than lying—which was out of the question, since trust was by far the healing arts' most precious asset, more so than lasers and robots and dialysis machines combined—there was no good way to skirt the question. Besides, he *wanted* to tell someone he was falling for Becky Winthrop. He gave a raffish grin.

"Yes, I am sweet on her. She and I are dating."

Ennis bared a mouthful of broken yellow teeth. "Shitfuck! You're bonin' her, aren't you?" The expression he wore wasn't a grin. More of a grimace. Of pain; no, envy.

The possibility of Ennis having a crush on Becky had never occurred to him, but it made perfect sense. Transference, projection, the intimacy of psychotherapy: all in play. And the short skirts she wore, the crossing and uncrossing of her magnificent legs. He felt as if he'd been caught dating his best friend's girl.

"I'm sorry. I had no idea you felt that way about her."

"Aw, hell's bells. Trannies have feelings too, you know. I'm attracted to a sexy woman same as you are."

He gave a helpless shrug and turned his attention to the care of Ennis's kidney transplant, which Cullen was able to proclaim unaffected by the episode of cardiac rejection he suffered. His creatinine of 1.0 mg/dl remained normal.

But for how long? How long before his unnatural belief in some nebulous residue of soul persisting inside him unnerved him completely? Becky could talk to him about fear of gender emergence until her lips fell off and it wouldn't matter. It wasn't Elaine that Ennis needed to come to terms with. It was Carla; jazz-loving, beet-eating, vision-visiting Carla. And he doubted MacGregor's suggestion that Ennis thank God instead of his donor's family would help, either.

The certainty of what would come to pass if Ennis didn't resolve his guilt over Carla's organ donation tore at Cullen like the serrated teeth of a piranha. There would be missed doses of medication, followed by a second bout of rejection and then a third, Ennis's stern belief in his unworthiness leading to the fate he was convinced he, instead of his donor, deserved: death. Self-inflicted death, caused by the unshackling of his immune system, freeing it to attack the organs Carla bequeathed him, T-cells liberated from pharmacologic immurement swarming to the task like a hive of angry bees.

Oh, they would try to save him by blasting away with corticosteroids and anti-thymocyte globulin and monoclonal antibodies. But the damage would already be done. His cardiac ejection fraction would steadily decline, until his left ventricle barely twitched. His kidney, starved of blood by his enfeebled heart and swelled by waves of cytokine-secreting T-cells, would begin to fail as well. Fluid and waste his transplant had so effortlessly eliminated would turn his skin sallow, swell his legs with edema, and leave his lungs sopping and stiff. He would be unable to lie flat without drowning in his own body water, his breath reeking of the ammonia-laced stench of uremic fetor. And in his mouth, the bitter taste of metal, his taste buds ruined again.

He would agree, under pressure from Cullen, to return to dialysis, where his noncompliance would continue. Because he would not want to be there, back on a machine thrice weekly, suffering the needles and rigors of his treatments again, the dehydration and muscle cramps and passing out. One day he would stop coming and lapse into a coma, his skin purpled by uremic coagulopathy, his hair broken and thin, his body and face wasted and sunken, as if his underpinning had dissolved away.

Cullen would stipulate uremic poisoning as the cause of death, but in truth it would be terminal lack of self-worth that killed Ennis Willoughby. Pigheaded refusal to accept without guilt the beneficence of another human being, who, if she were able, would tell him she *wanted* him to have her organs, cross-dresser or not. But how would he ever know? Who speaks for the dead?

The answer came to him from across the centuries, from Orestes and Hamlet and Jean Valjean: the living speak for the dead.

He bored into Ennis's hopeless gray eyes and tried to give him what he needed, without betraying the confidentiality he was sworn to. "I imagine you'd like to know the identity of your donor. Every transplant patient does. All I can tell you is this: heart transplants are different from kidney transplants. Hearts don't keep as well—four to six hours at best. That's why heart transplants usually come from local donors."

He looked for the flash of comprehension that would relieve him from saying more than he had already. Nothing. Only a frown and twitch of his jaw.

"What I'm saying is, you might try checking the local obituaries from the week you got your transplant."

He had second thoughts the minute Ennis left the office. He had all but given Duncan MacGregor's name and number to the recipient of his wife's heart and kidney. A recipient Duncan had declined to meet—though Cullen sensed some ambivalence there, a chance Duncan might reconsider if approached about it again. But that was beside the point. Duncan was entitled to his privacy and Cullen had violated it. And yet, it was the right thing to do. Ennis was coming apart at the seams with guilt. The only way he would ever believe he deserved Carla's organs was if her husband told him he did.

Cullen had regret over betraying Duncan to Ennis for another reason, though, too: fear. Crazy, irrational fear, but fear nonetheless. What if meeting with Duncan revealed that Ennis's personality change and coincidental penchant for beets and jazz and eerie knowledge of Carla's name were only the tip of the iceberg? What if he possessed other traits and behaviors and knowledge of his donor, too, things so specific to Carla as to be impossible to attribute to happenstance? What if Ennis's outrageous claim of being influenced by both a transgender female and a transmigrated female was true?

An adage that served Cullen well during residency and guided him still came to mind: When all else fails, listen to your patient. Meaning your patient will tell you the correct diagnosis, if you give him the chance. But the implications of what Ennis was trying to tell him threatened his most fundamental conviction: disbelief in God.

It shamed him to admit it, but maybe his religious skepticism wasn't as mature and impervious as he thought. Maybe his atheism, like that of Ivan Karamazov, had not yet truly been tested. And maybe Ennis's bewitching contention that Carla MacGregor's soul inhabited his body was such a test.

In which case he should welcome, not fear, a rendezvous between Ennis and his donor's family. Duncan would surely repudiate Ennis's transmigration fantasy and Cullen's atheism would be confirmed. There was beauty and satisfaction and wonder enough in the natural world, without having to invent a supernatural one.

He struggled to keep his thoughts from distracting him from the patients he saw after Ennis left—three with chronic kidney disease, one with resistant hypertension, one with a transplant—and then drove to the hospital to admit Oscar Walton, who had come in through the ER with abdominal pain. He took the elevator to Four South and found Oscar sitting in bed reading, a pale blue hospital gown bunched around his tumid middle. His buzz cut of black and gray bristles made his oblong head appear even larger than it was. He looked up at the sound of Cullen's voice and set aside the page-worn Bible he held.

"Praise Jesus, I'm feeling a lot better, thanks to you and the man upstairs." He jerked a thumb toward the ceiling and smiled with the certitude of the already saved, as if in possession of a divine salvation voucher.

Oscar's bumptious fundamentalism was trying even without a load of narcotic in him to goose his rapture. Cullen wanted to tell him that he felt better because of the morphine and IV Levaquin he prescribed to treat his case of diverticulitis, not because of the man upstairs. And upstairs *where*, exactly? Mars? Pluto? Some unnamed star in the Andromeda galaxy? As if some alleged deity had decided, out of the hundreds of millions of demands made daily by the planet's faithful, to answer Oscar Walton's quotidian prayer. Weren't there more weighty matters for almighty God to attend to than evangelical belly pain?

He ached to have a little confab with Oscar, talk exegesis with him: rail against God's existence. Did he truly believe Moses conversed with a burning bush, turned his staff into a serpent, and lived to one hundred and ten? With no detectable decline in vigor or health? And what about the murderous, misogynistic rhetoric of the bloodthirsty old coot? Not to mention the New Testament. Now there was a piece of work: anodyne falsehood to pacify the masses. Matthew, Mark, Luke, and John, the Four Horsemen of the apocryphal, fabulists all. No serious person could possibly regard the New Testament as a meaningful historical document.

But he said none of these things. No doctor worth a damn bickered with patients over religion. He thumped Oscar's huge, round shoulder and gave his best doctor's smile.

"We should have you out of here in time for Sunday services."

He left Oscar's room and caught sight of Thomas Lawson lumbering along in front of him. A piece of white tissue paper clung to the heel of his shoe. Cullen slowed down, intending to let Lawson board one of the elevators at the end of the hall while he took the stairs. But his timing was off. He rounded the corner with Lawson staring at him from an open car, his blowsy cheeks and rumpled white hair, his suit jacket speckled by dandruff. Their eyes met.

Lawson cast his gaze to the floor, anticipating the usual shunning Cullen gave him.

Cullen stuck his hand between the doors and prevented them from closing. He pointed at Lawson's foot. "There's a piece of tissue stuck to your shoe."

Lawson bent to remove it. He looked up, dumbfounded, his scaly cheeks bright red. "Thank you."

Like a curtain on a stage, the doors drew together on Lawson's conflicted face, strangely like his mother's on that awful night, all those years before, as he drove away: her futile gesture, the rage in Cullen's heart, a fateful beat in time and space that spawned an incubus that tormented him still.

Chapter 9

CULLEN PULLED AWAY FROM the curb with Earth, Wind & Fire wide open on the car radio and his mother waving at him from the front stoop. Only later would he learn that she had been trying to get his attention to tell him Angie was on the phone.

Singing in the car on his way to the Attucks was the high water mark of his night. He clanked his first three shots and was a step slow in defending Dempsey Fagan, who hit everything he threw up and played with brazen confidence, his black curls flying all the way to the rim. He hazed Cullen with trash talk, a constant contumely emboldened by— what? Had Dempsey forgotten whose shot went down that night at Williams Arena? Had he forgotten ABA Left?

ABA Left was the name Slade had given to the move Cullen used to win the 1972 Minnesota State High School Basketball Championship. With eight seconds left in overtime, Lourdes had trailed Adams by a single point. A ceaseless roar cascaded onto the court. Cullen posted up on the left side of the lane, Dempsey on his hip, even with the free throw line. He took an entry pass and began a move that came from a place deep inside him. A place that made him love basketball in a way he could not explain.

He ball faked to the middle, causing Dempsey to lean in, then spun and dribbled down the lane with his left hand, using his body to shield the ball. Dempsey recovered and slid after him with one hand held high to disrupt his shot.

Their sweat-slicked bodies skimmed off one another. A concussion of sound hammered Cullen's eardrums until it became white noise. Until he heard nothing. Until he was a boy with a ball, alone. In his world, not theirs.

He came to a jump stop with two seconds left on the clock and exploded out of his stance. *Away* from the basket, the ball cocked in his left hand, inches beyond Dempsey's lunging reach. His ten-foot, off-hand, fade-away jumper banked cleanly through the net as the horn wailed and the arena erupted. The photo in the paper the following morning of Cullen hanging in the air with the ball a fraction above Dempsey's anguished fingertips cast a bright nimbus around his image and a grainy penumbra onto Dempsey's, the difference between winning and losing as infinitesimal as consequences were eternal.

The shot was the icing on the cake of a dream year that had landed him a partial scholarship at the U of M: the Big Ten, college prime time. Dempsey followed him there—stalked him—as a walk-on. Neither one lasted a year. Dempsey got cut and Cullen tore up his knee. All he was fit for now was playground ball, his lateral movement too impeded to compete against elite college players.

He called for the ball next time down the cracked blacktop of the Attucks. His side needed a basket to win. Time to jog Dempsey's memory. He took a pass in the high post from Jinx, a squirt of a point guard with circle vision and thighs like black oak. By the time Dempsey recognized what was happening, it was too late. Cullen spun down the lane, flew into his jump-stop, and launched a left-handed jumper from the top of his fade. The ball caromed off the backboard and through the chain mesh net with a metallic sigh.

Cullen pumped his fist. Jinx screamed at Dempsey. "ABA Left, mothafucka, ABA Left! In yo' face!"

Dempsey heaved the ball to the opposite end of the court and rushed toward Cullen. "That's bullshit, man! I kicked your ass up one side and down the other and you throw up a prayer and act like you're fucking Dr. J. That shot was playground slop then and it's playground slop now!"

Cullen smirked, the natural order between them restored. "Kiss my ass, Fagan. Second best is your middle name."

Dempsey shambled closer and spoke in a baiting lilt loud enough for all to hear. "You think so, Brodie? Why don't you ask Angie her opinion? She didn't seem to think I was second best last Saturday after I took her to see *Shampoo*. 'Fuck me harder, Dempsey, fuck me harder!'" he mimicked in crude falsetto.

A peculiar thing about mortal enemies is that they come to know each other like brothers. How far the other one will go in order to win, how he reacts to the taste of his own blood—how he looks and sounds when he's lying. Dempsey Fagan, Cullen could tell, was not lying.

He clamped his hands around Dempsey's throat and forced him to his knees. Dempsey clawed at his fingers; it was like trying to peel away welded iron. Cullen kept throttling him. Dempsey's face turned purple and then like cold ash. His eyes roved. Cullen let go only because Slade hit him with a pulverizing shot to the head that buckled his knees.

"Das enough, man! Dude can't breave!"

Dempsey gagged and sprayed a crimson mist into the still, crepuscular air. Slade wrapped Cullen's arms and hustled him to the edge of the playground.

"Go on back to yo crib an chill." Slade planted his feet and glared like a bouncer denying entry to a club. His biceps kissed his forearms and the veins of his neck filled to his jaw line. There would be no getting past him, but it didn't matter.

Cullen walked away. It was Angie he wanted now.

He charged up the front walk of her home and stood beneath the lantern in the archway in Attucks raiment: scuffed Adidas, faded gym shorts, brine-soaked tank top. He banged on the door as if his fist were a battering ram. A mosquito sank its beak into his shoulder. He reached to squash it and glimpsed Lake Harriet in the gloaming, placid and grey, the silhouette of the band shell on the far shore already indistinct. The nightly view from her father's library, his shelves crowded with Plato and Aristotle, Homer and Virgil, Tolstoy and Hugo, Shakespeare and Euripides. What good had such treasures done Angie? All she'd gleaned from their genius was how to dishonor your lover.

Visions of her betrayal flashed across his mind like a porno flick. He clamped a hand to his forehead to make it stop. The best he could hope for was that it had been a loveless coupling, a grim chore to wound him. But why was he being punished for Brodie's Tirade? As if his father's religious fanaticism were his fault?

The door swung open. Leslie appeared, wearing a gray Panama Jack bikini like the one in the commercial. "Cullen, what a surprise! Grady and I were about to go for a swim." She searched his face and took a step back into the foyer. "Are you okay?" Grady peeked around her hip, shirtless in red swim trunks that billowed to his knees.

"Where's Angie?"

"She's not here. She's with my parents at White Bear Lake. They're spending the week at our Uncle Monty's to celebrate his birthday."

Cullen fought to dim the bloodlust in his eyes, to draw strength from the unsullied goodness of Grady's cheeks. Leslie's shoulders relaxed. Grady wagered a grin.

"I didn't feel like going until tomorrow," she said. "Grady stayed behind to keep me company, because he's my Oompa Loompa, aren't you?" She lunged and sank her fingers into his belly. He squealed and wriggled free from her tickles and wrapped himself around Cullen's leg.

"Play Jaws with us!"

Cullen fingered the knot Slade raised behind his ear, which throbbed more by the minute. "I don't know...."

Leslie poked his shoulder. "Oh, come on, don't be so uptight. I don't want to have to look at Grady's pouty face all night if you turn him down."

He considered her more closely and realized he had never really paid much attention to her. Angie was a cynosure who burned too brightly for anyone else to be noticed. Alongside her sister, Leslie was like a daisy to a rose, like green quartz to emerald. Her hair lacked the luster and volume of Angie's, and whereas Angie was voluptuous, Leslie was like a greyhound, with small breasts and narrow hips. Even her cheeks were less prominent. But away from Angie, he was surprised at how appealing she was, how intelligent and aware her eyes were—and no less striking than Angie's. How many times, he wondered, had Leslie been overlooked on account of Angie's freakish beauty? It was odd that only now, in the encroaching darkness, did he really see her.

He shrugged and agreed to a quick swim. Grady took him by the hand and dragged him into the kitchen and up to the sliding glass door that led to their backyard pool. Cullen unlatched it and drew it open. Grady looked up, guileless and sincere.

"I wisn't sure you'd stay."

Cullen bent low at the waist and spoke sotto voce. "I only stayed to play Jaws with you. Don't tell Leslie. It might hurt her feelings."

Grady beamed and swelled his chest. "I wiln't."

He scampered off to fetch his Jaws float and then shot through the open doorway with Cullen and Leslie trailing. Cullen peeled off his tank top, discarded his socks and shoes and dove in. He chased Grady's shark float around the pool with his hand on his head, an imaginary fin, and dove underwater to attack from below, grabbing squiggly toes and chubby legs to screams of delight. But Angie's infidelity paraded across his mind like the trailer of a triple-X movie, 'til he could stand it no longer. He moored Grady's float in the deep end and instructed him to wait there. Cullen returned to the shallows and told Leslie about Angie and Dempsey.

He chopped his hand into the water and sent a wave curling through the air. His whisper became a growl. "Thinking of them together makes me insane! I can't get it out of my mind."

Leslie waded over and put a hand on his shoulder. "Not so loud! Grady might hear you." She glanced behind her, to where Grady lolled beneath the diving board, then back at Cullen. "Angie used sex as a weapon to settle a score. Women do that sometimes. It meant nothing."

She turned the pool lights off and started a new game. Grady paddled after them in the dark and tried to tag them, being awarded a free dunk in the middle of the pool when he did. After a round in the shallows, they swam to the deep end and treaded water. Grady churned their way, splashing and giggling and vowing to catch them.

Leslie drifted next to him. "Sink to the bottom."

She reached for him early in their descent. The slick pleasure of her legs and belly against his skin stifled any urge to resist. They embraced and sank through liquid silence, through time and space, concealed from the hurtful world above. He understood before their toes scraped cement that it was a reckoning for each of them, two willing bodies using sex to settle a score, him motivated by jealousy, her by envy, jealousy's calculating cousin.

They lingered on the bottom to kiss and grope, handfuls of buttocks and breast that made him stiff in an instant. He shot after her like a seal pup hungry for mother's milk when she broke free and scissored to the surface for air.

They convinced Grady to call it quits by reminding him that *The Incredible Hulk* was on. Leslie slid the kitchen door shut behind them. Grady called out from the family room.

"Leslie, what channel? Hurry!"

She put her hands on Cullen's shoulders. Drops of water beaded her cleavage. "We can count on Lou Ferrigno for an hour. Wait for me in the library."

He stared at the backs of her legs and the way her bikini clung to her as she padded across the floor and disappeared. He walked through the kitchen and down a hallway to the library, which lay tenebrous and silent at the other end of the house. He sat down on the floor. Streetlight filtered through the picture window, its soft glow barely enough to make out the names of famous cheaters all around him: Emma Bovary, Anna Karenina, Willy Loman, and Horatio Hornblower, too, not even eighteenth-century superheroes immune to such sin. But a girlfriend's sister? Only Stanley Kowalski sank that low.

Leslie joined him moments later, carrying a woolen blanket and wearing a loosely sashed silk robe. Pool-damp hair fell onto her shoulders and about her face. She unfurled the blanket and knelt down on it and undid the sash of her robe.

Angie's presence hung over them like a third person standing in the room. A person they wanted to hurt. Everything they did was choreographed for her, as if she were standing there, forced to watch. It charged their coupling with the force of retribution. Of vengeance. Ferocious, was how Cullen would remember it. Together they rode the wave, surfed its steep, canted face for all they were worth.

Until the wipeout came.

He awakened alone on the library floor with the ripe scent of sex investing the air. A spectral glow sifted through the windowpanes as he stood to pull his briefs on. A large stain spread like a Rorschach on the blanket beneath him. He scrambled into his clothes and fled the room as if it were the very fountainhead of evil.

He found Leslie beside Grady on the couch in their wainscoted family room, *The Incredible Hulk* nearly over and done, the monster back in the bottle again.

If only it were that easy to put monsters back in bottles.

She sensed his presence and turned with her robe drawn tightly around her and her hair matted in a morning kind-of-way. The expression she wore relieved him, her eyes narrow and weary, her mouth set in grim acceptance of what they'd done. It was a look mercifully free of expectation.

"I should be going," he said.

She told Grady she'd be right back. He ignored her and stared at the television, savoring every last second of his show.

They walked to his car in silence. They had used each other to satisfy their nasty lust for revenge, but if she felt the remorse and self-loathing over it that he did, she didn't let on. She brushed a lock of hair from her brow and took his face in her hands.

"No one has to ever know."

He clasped her wrist. "No one ever will. It's awful enough that we do."

He drove off as quickly as he could, anxious to get home and shut the door against the foul, rotting night. Against a trespass that had so exceeded Angie's, he lay beneath the sheets and quaked at what it might bring next.

Chapter 10

ENNIS DRAGGED A YELLOW Magic Marker across the name in the obituary and read the whole piece again to make sure he wasn't hallucinating. Or drunk, even though he'd downed barely half his Coors Light, which tasted like watered-down piss, but had only 102 calories. Just because Elaine was in hibernation didn't mean she was dead. A girl still had to watch her figure.

MACGREGOR, CARLA: May 18, 1976 to July 19, 2009. Carla left us without warning the morning of July 19, 2009. She was born in Laguna Beach, California and raised in San Francisco. She is survived by her loving husband Duncan and three beautiful children, Loni, Cassidy, and Lucas. She was the executive assistant to Dr. Logan MacGregor, her father-in-law and CEO of Nephrology Partners medical group. Carla was a dedicated employee and devoted wife and mother. She loved jazz, her family, and helping people with kidney disease. Her beauty, elegance, and loving heart will be sorely missed. A private memorial service celebrating her life was held on July 23, 2009.

Son of a fucking bitch. His donor worked for his doctor's medical group. Dr. Brodie must have known all along, but couldn't say so. No wonder she donated her body parts. Considering who employed her, how could she *not* have checked the *Yes, I want to be an organ and tissue donor!* box on her driver's license? Carla: he'd been right about her name from the beginning. From the moment she came to him in that medieval dream, her female spirit communing with him from inside his puny tranny chest.

His only hope of cross-dressing again without rejecting her organs was by knowing all about her: who she was, where she came from, what she liked and disliked. Everything. To make her more familiar to Elaine. So Elaine wouldn't feel so threatened by her. It sounded crazy, but things were what they were. Carla MacGregor's transmigrated soul—or a piece of it, anyway—came to him at the precise time Elaine's transgender personality was trying to emerge. And since Elaine was there first, she resented Carla's uninvited arrival. Two was company. Three was, what you might say, a crowd.

The only solution was for Carla and Elaine to become friends, gal pals instead of hissing hussies. And the only way that was going to happen was if he, Ennis, got to know Carla first, by meeting her family. Once Ennis knew her, Elaine would know her. And accept her. Then Elaine could be Elaine again without rejecting Carla's heart and kidney. The three of them would be in harmony. A little more complicated than Becky's idea of harmony, but harmony all the same.

That was the difference between the two doctors in his life, Becky and Dr. Brodie—who were now humping each other, and wasn't that a pair to draw to? Becky refused to even consider the *possibility* that the soul of his donor might have somehow come to him with her organs. She demanded that he, the patient, conform to her reality—not a good thing for a shrink to do. Dr. Brodie cut his patients some slack— even though he didn't believe in transmigration any more than Becky did. "If all else fails, ask the patient," he preached to the nurses at dialysis. "Patients will tell you the diagnosis if you give them a chance." Dr. Brodie was the best — even if he was poking Becky.

He laid the obituary page on the kitchen table and reached for his Coors. Next would come the delicate matter of contacting the MacGregors. Seeing as how writing letters had gotten him nowhere, a more direct approach was called for. Something they couldn't ignore.

The beer tasted thin and weak as it slid down his gullet.

"Mr. Carlton is here," the woman behind the reception desk said. *Her* desk. Carla's desk. She placed the phone back in the cradle and smiled. "Dr. MacGregor is expecting you. This way, please." She was a mulatto with tight kinky hair who looked to be in her late forties, fleshy and carnal and crammed into a red knit dress. He looked to her nametag: Estella Price.

He stood and fiddled with the knot of his black and yellow checked tie; smoothed the lapels of his charcoal gray Men's Wearhouse suit; glanced approvingly at the sheen of his black wing tips: Mac Carlton, philanthropist owner of a local contracting company, dressed to the nines and reeking of Old Spice.

The pretense for his appointment was not strictly speaking a lie. He *was* there to talk about a donation to the St. Barnabas transplant program: Carla's. He never said he wanted to talk about a financial donation. And he did own a contracting company — Ennis Willoughby Painting. His only real fib was the name he'd given: Mac Carlton. A little play on words — Carla MacGregor, Mac Carlton? Not too shabby for a painter.

He tried to picture Carla instead of the woman in front of him: she would be young and slender, with brown hair and creamy skin. The rest remained vague. But that's why he was there. To search out the woman whose two hunks of spiritually endowed tissue had saved his life—and then commandeered it.

He strode around her desk and followed Estella Price into Logan MacGregor's inner sanctum with his eye on her fanny and cocoa butter calves. The smile she flashed when he first arrived—was she flirting with him? Women were suckers for starched shirts and pressed slacks. Or maybe it was his cologne. He wondered what it was like, to slip it to a black woman? All that rhythm squirming beneath you—and blues.

A stout, imposing man with a presidential face stepped forward and shook his hand. "Mr. Carlton? Dr. MacGregor. It's a pleasure to meet you. Please, have a seat." His grip was sure and firm.

Ennis dropped his bottom into a gold-braided chair that looked like it could have been in Philadelphia for the signing of the Constitution. MacGregor sat across from him at a cluttered cherry wood desk. His bountiful head of silver hair caused Ennis to fidget and run a hand across his denuded scalp. But MacGregor's smile put him at ease and made him feel special, as if he had never given that particular smile to anyone else in the world.

"I understand you're interested in a donation to the transplant program at St. Barnabas. That's very generous of you." He had a voice like a stage actor, deep and clear.

Ennis felt puny, tiny: unworthy. This man oversaw a group of kidney specialists—*twenty* Dr. Brodies—and a kidney transplant program that did two hundred transplants a year. And his daughter-in-law not only helped administer this kidney empire, this kingdom of piss—

actually of no piss, since that's what kidney failure was: no piss—but had coughed up her own heart and kidney to boot. Because it was the humane thing to do.

So how did her grateful recipient express his thanks? By tricking her father-in-law into seeing him after her husband had already made it clear that he preferred to remain anonymous. He was a worm, undeserving of anyone's organs, let alone a family like this.

He forced himself to look into the inviting pools of MacGregor's eyes. "My name isn't Mac Carlton. It's Ennis Willoughby. Your daughter-in-law, Carla, gave her heart and kidney to me. I'm sorry for lying to you, but I wanted her family to know how thankful I am." He wanted to tell him how much love he had for Carla and her family, but he thought he might cry, so he didn't. Navy pilots never cried.

MacGregor's charming silver veneer peeled away. His smile broke apart and his eyes hardened into winnowing blue lasers that raked Ennis from stem to stern. "My son would be deeply touched by your gratitude. As am I. How did you find us?"

Ennis told him about his recurring dream, about lying in the gutter of a medieval town until a faceless young woman rescued him from death. "The woman in my dream was named Carla. Dr. Brodie thinks I overheard the surgical team in the OR say it, but he's wrong. I checked the obituary pages from the week of my transplant. There was only one Carla."

"What made you so sure your donor was local?"

A photo on the desk with a shiny, filigreed frame stole his attention. It was of a young couple and three children—a boy and two girls. The children stood in front of the couple, who knelt side by side behind them. The woman wore a gauzy shirt, unbuttoned to below the notch of her fetching neck. She had brown flowing hair, high prominent cheeks, and a knowing smile on her face. What did she know? That she would die soon? That, in death, the grace of her generosity would make her spirit holy? Anoint it with power to touch the living?

His heart—her heart—fluttered, and his breath came in quick, shallow drafts. He pointed at the photo. "That's her, isn't it?"

MacGregor nodded. "Yes, it is." His eyes melted at the edges and turned to water again, blue puddles Ennis fell into. "Part of me didn't want her dissected. Eviscerated. Though I of all people knew how much good it would do. How many lives she would save."

Ennis knew in that moment how Carla had catered to him, understood how overpowering a boss he could be. And how rewarding her job was, the satisfaction she had at the end of the day, working for a doctor—an entire *group* of doctors—like Dr. Brodie, so smart and tireless and devoted to saving lives from the certain death of kidney failure. He had no idea *how* he knew these things, but he did. All in that moment. And he said so.

"She truly cared about helping people, I can tell. I bet for her, working for doctors was the next best thing to being one."

MacGregor blanched. He picked up the picture with both hands and fastened his gaze on it. Even the hair on his fingers was silver. "What did you say?"

Ennis shrugged. "I said I bet she liked working for you, because—"

"Because working for doctors was the closest thing to being one," MacGregor recited. The tremor in his voice matched the tremble of his hand as he reached to set the photo down. "That's what she used to say, time and again. 'Working for doctors is the closest thing to being one.' You took the words out of her mouth."

Ennis studied the grieving man's face. Better to call a spade a spade. "This isn't the first time her thoughts have come into my head. I can't explain it, other than to say she puts 'em there, if you get my drift."

MacGregor pursed his lips and shook his head. "I think what we've just witnessed, Mr. Willoughby, is female intuition. And I don't mean Carla's—if you get my drift."

Disillusion clenched his stomach. MacGregor had whet his shiv and stuck it between his ribs, like all the rest. "You think the déjà vu I just had is female intuition on the part of my transgender personality."

"I do indeed."

"That's what my psychiatrist thinks, too. But I think she's wrong. I think your daughter-in-law's soul came to me with her organs. A piece of it, anyway."

MacGregor grimaced, as if what Ennis said caused great physical pain. "In all my years of caring for transplant patients, only a handful have ever claimed to experience anything remotely like this. And every one of them had a psychiatric problem. What you are suggesting is not possible."

"Why? Don't you believe in the human soul?"

"What I believe is that there is an impassable wall between life and death, and that it permits one-way traffic only. Souls inhabit a realm on the other side of this wall. Not human bodies."

Ennis thought again of Livingston, the cabbie that drove him to his transplant. "Some people believe souls are a little more, what you might say, interactive."

"If you came here expecting me to invite you into my son's living room to tell his children that their dead mother's organs talk to you, then you are sorely mistaken. My son lost his wife, his children lost their mother, and I lost my daughter-in-law and coworker. We are in pain, Mr. Willoughby, great pain, and you make it worse. It is professionally fulfilling to me to know that Carla's organs have rejuvenated your life, and I wish you nothing but the best, but you are too unstable to be around my son and grandchildren."

His voice shook and his eyes were red. Ennis couldn't tell if anger or grief had the upper hand, but he was certain of one thing: Logan MacGregor loathed the sight of him.

"You probably wish they never put me on the transplant list. So that someone else could have had her organs. Someone normal."

MacGregor stood, towering over him, knuckles pressed to his desk, his scowling face a mask of righteous anger. "I'm the one who put you *on* the list. What I wish is that Carla were still alive."

This he was not expecting. That it was MacGregor who green-lighted his transplant, personally approved the tranny his daughter-in-law willed her organs to. The worthlessness he felt before was nothing compared to the shame that convulsed him now. What an asshole he was: what an ungrateful, insensitive, selfish asshole.

"I think maybe I was wrong to come here today. I'm sorry."

MacGregor picked up the phone. "Estella? Would you be so kind as to show Mr. Carlton out?"

She opened the door and pinned it behind her plump, chocolate ass while ushering him out. Ever so graciously. He halted beneath the transom and turned around to face MacGregor.

"You got it wrong about souls. Their world might not be accessible to us, but ours is to them." He tapped his chest. "Trust me on that one."

He paused in the reception area and withdrew one of Duncan MacGregor's business cards from a brown plastic holder on Estella Price's desk.

Chapter 11

ANGELA STOOD AT A small sink in her cluttered atelier and rinsed turpentine from her hands. She dried them with a frayed bath towel and reached for a bottle of Mauke Miracle Oil, a local balm made from the island of Mauke's rare *pi* plant. A billow of gardenia and coconut swelled the air when she rubbed the secret concoction between her palms and smoothed the backs of her chafed hands with it, luxuriating in its rich, oleaginous texture. She wiped the excess on the front of her paint-spattered gray shorts and let her gaze wander to her legs.

More varicose veins. They grew like kudzu, peculiar blue worms of age ruining her once-flawless calves. Time for another trip to the vein clinic in Auckland. She gathered up her hair and let it fall down her back. It felt thin and meager. What remained of her beauty vanished monthly it seemed, like sand between her fingers, no matter how desperately she cupped one hand beneath the other to preserve it. But her mind was on other things. One thing.

The only thing.

She turned to the painting behind her that she had finally finished and sat on a wooden stool in front of it. Getting it right had consumed her, reducing her usual prolific output—and gallery profits—by half. She had wanted to evoke what Delaroche evoked in his underappreciated gem in the Louvre—a painting that made her tremble whenever she viewed it on one of her frequent trips to Paris. Sometimes with no purpose for going other than to visit that one painting, the pathos it provoked, the sorrow and transcendence: the fine line between life and death, senseless tragedy unaverted. It was, in her opinion, the best of all his paintings, the highest achievement of Delaroche's life and underrated career.

Delaroche—a brilliant, but neglected and forgotten painter. Rating barely a paragraph in art history books and hardly a minute or two in lectures. Yet in his day, a celebrated triumvir—alongside Delacroix and Géricault—of the French Romantic School: feeling over thought, emotion over logic, a counterrevolution to the Enlightenment. Reappraisal of the Age of Reason.

The Romantic Period was her favorite artistic era, and Romanticism— which arose from the ashes of the French Revolution and from the German *Sturm und Drang* phenomenon of intuition and emotion—was her favorite cultural and intellectual movement. And no wonder. For as far back as she could remember, her most intense satisfactions and insights had been emotional and intuitive in origin. It wasn't that she was unable to think logically or to appreciate the basic precepts of mathematics and science, but she had always been instinctively aware of their limitations. Like when, as a young girl, she saw the movie version of *The Sound of Music* and listened to "Climb Ev'ry Mountain" for the first time and realized that feelings revealed greater truths than facts. Later, in college, it was not in biology and physics and chemistry that she found meaning, but rather in the music of Chopin and Schubert and the works of Austen and Byron and the paintings of Delacroix and Delaroche, Romantics all. Logic and reason explained how things worked; intuition and emotion revealed what they meant. And it was emotion and meaning that she wanted on the canvas in front of her.

Had she succeeded? Had she dug deep enough into her wounded heart to spill her emotions the way Delaroche did in that most ethereal yet grisly of all his paintings? Was she true to his dramatic use of light and composition, to his prominent use of impasto? Did she capture the heartache and despair of that terrible night so long ago?

Yes. She did.

How could she not have? Guilt had a way of wringing the truth from people. By the way it diminished them. Reamed them hollow until they would do anything to make it go away. Like guilt had reamed her hollow, ever since the visitation depicted on her canvas.

She had waited until the last possible moment that evening before calling Cullen, in advance of the fanfaronade Dempsey Fagan was sure to unleash at the Attucks. The sexual bragging he would do. Better—far better—that Cullen hear it from her first. Cullen's mother, who surprised Angie by not hanging up on her, tried to flag him down, but couldn't. She had made her call a minute too late. He was on his way to the Attucks.

She fell into an edgy funk. Now Cullen would hear the uncensored version of things. Nothing elided, no merciful omissions to cushion the blow. All she could do was wait for his call and brace for the worst.

She and her parents—to be joined the next day by Grady and Leslie—were staying the week with her aunt and uncle in their New England style two-story on White Bear Lake. But when their phone jangled later that night, it wasn't Cullen. It was a nurse from General Hospital informing them that Grady had suffered some kind of accident. The three of them sped off toward downtown, taking a freeway that was so new there were hardly any cars on it. The crunch and smear of bugs on the windshield of her father's Fleetwood pattered their grim silence. She studied him in the mirror, the evening stubble on his face, the worry etched in his thick brow. Angie reached around the seat and grasped her mother's arm. Her mother's hand closed over hers.

They hurtled down the highway.

The emergency room at Hennepin County Medical Center—still General Hospital to Angie, the name only recently changed from Minneapolis General—strained and yowled beneath the evening yoke of pain and suffering. Ambulances delivered payloads of human misery to the hospital's crumbling unloading docks: stuporous drunks found down in alleys, vagrant epileptics convulsing on transport gurneys, the usual road carnage, mangled bodies that would never be the same.

An overweight nurse with greasy hair met them at the registration window and led them to a dingy waiting room. She seated them on a thin-cushioned sofa and excused herself to fetch the doctor assigned to Grady's case. Moments later, an exhausted-looking, bewhiskered young doctor in blue scrubs and a kind-faced social worker with short gray hair appeared.

Angie and her parents rose to greet them. The doctor introduced himself as Jerry Beathard, the social worker as Evelyn Peters. Beathard's lids drooped and his narrow shoulders sagged, but his handshake was firm and substantial. He reminded Angie of photos of Confederate soldiers toward the end of the war, bedraggled and beaten. Their elegiac faces and hollow eyes.

He told them Grady drowned that evening in the family swimming pool.

Angie screamed and covered her mouth with her hands. Her mother keened a broken ululation, the unhinged grief of a woman who had lost her only son. Her little boy. Their darling Grady. Tears stained her father's mortally wounded face. He put his arms around the two of them, but Angie found neither strength nor hope in his grasp.

Beathard hung his head, then looked up and went on. "Your daughter Leslie was babysitting. She went downstairs to do a load of wash a few minutes past nine. When she returned, Grady was gone. She thinks he might have gone after a float he left in the pool when they went swimming earlier. He evidently got out through an unlatched sliding door. She dove in after him, but was too late. I'm sorry. I can't imagine anything worse."

Angie's grief sloshed inside her like hot tar, coating her heart—sealing it—in despair. She raked her knuckles across her eyes and snuffled. A kernel of outrage formed beneath her breastbone. How could this happen? Why didn't Leslie watch him more closely?

"Where's my sister?"

Her voice had an edge to it. Beathard stiffened. "She's in one of the treatment rooms. We had to sedate her. She blames herself for your brother's death."

Evelyn Peters stepped forward and squeezed Angie's shoulder. "Leslie needs forgiveness, and the sooner the better. The death of a child can destroy a family."

She was right about that.

The sight of Grady's corpse lying on a gurney in the netherworld of the ER nearly finished them all off. A morbid viewing her parents insisted on, Grady's face and neck congested and swollen, the front of his chest marred by splotches of brown rimmed with green. The rest of him ghostly translucent.

Leslie lay slumped against the car door in drugged despondency during the short ride to their home on Lake Harriet, wearing a silk robe Angie gave her on her last birthday. And in the front seat, amidst jagged weeping, her mother averred over and over that she never wanted their swimming pool in the first place. Her father hewed to the road, hands frozen to the wheel, jaw clamped shut, offering no defense for the symbol of affluence he had long coveted. Angie drilled a cold, condemning stare into the side of her sister's face, unable to fathom her carelessness.

She and her father dragged Leslie upstairs and put her to bed in a fresh nightie without the help of her mother, who wandered in and out of Grady's room to grasp at his things: his stuffed tiger; the pair of pajamas he would have slept in that night, which she fondled and smelled; his piggy bank, half-filled with change he was saving to buy Christmas presents for the big sisters who loved him so.

They put her to sleep with one of the Valiums Dr. Beathard prescribed for Leslie and changed into their pajamas and met downstairs in the living room. The living room: it was hardly that. They rarely entered it, let alone lived in it. It was fake, a replica, full of furniture they weren't allowed to sit on and antiques they weren't allowed to touch. What had her mother been saving it for? Better to have let Grady romp in it, roll around in it, spill and soil it. Live in it. She sat beside her father on the forbidden sofa. New rules were in play. Rules they would need to make up as they went along. A floor lamp illuminated his bereaved face, the cracked corners of his eyes, the thin grimace of his lips. His surgeon's hands rested on his thighs.

She collapsed onto his chest, choking on her sorrow.

"It hurts, Daddy! It hurts so much. I want Grady back!"

He held her and stroked her hair. "What will we do?" His voice was distant, strained, as if talking to someone who wasn't there. "What will we do?" He sounded shattered, weak, destroyed. It frightened her.

She felt ashamed of herself. Of course he was shattered. She had no right to expect him to be strong. His only son lay livid and wrinkled on a coroner's table, blotted from their lives. The risk of parental love—the instinct to propagate, to beget offspring to feed and shelter and protect, no matter the personal cost—was that children could be taken from you in an instant. She understood now why couples had big families—to hedge their bets. Against this.

She sat erect with her chin in the air and put her hands on his shoulders. "You still have us. Your girls."

Leslie lurched into her room later that night. She grabbed hold of the bedpost to steady herself and sat down at the end of the mattress, her hair matted and wild. Her torso swayed from side to side in the murky glow of a nightlight on the far wall. Angie strained to make out her face: anguished, forlorn. Riven. She sat to comfort her, but thought better of it and drew her knees to her chest.

"Tell me what happened."

Leslie bowed her head and spoke in a ragged voice.

"It was right around sunset. Grady asked me to take him swimming. We changed into our swimsuits, but before we made it outside, someone rapped on the door. It was Cullen, looking for you."

Angie flinched on learning that Cullen had been at their home. Leslie swayed back and forth, back and forth, her cycle maddeningly constant.

"Grady talked him into playing Jaws. He told me in the pool that he found out you slept with Dempsey. Because of Art Rampage. He was insane with jealousy. Insane. I tried to calm him down and told him that sometimes women use sex as a weapon."

Her body ceased swaying. She looked up. "I knew then that I was going to do the very thing with him that you did with Dempsey. And that nothing would stop me."

The lurid hand of treachery reached out and seized Angie's throat. She sat up straight and twirled an end of her hair. Leslie went on.

"I kissed him underwater in the pool. We went inside and put Grady in front of the television. We did it in the library, on a blanket on the floor. When it was over, I walked him to his car and told him no one ever had to know. I knew he still loved you. Not me.

"I went back in the house to make popcorn for Grady and remembered the blanket. It had a huge stain on it, so I set the tin of popcorn on the counter and took the blanket downstairs and put it in the wash. When I came back upstairs, Grady was gone."

Angie put a hand to her head. And whimpered. "Oh my God. My sweet, sweet brother."

Her sister's shoulders slumped. "I went room-to-room, but he didn't answer. I doubled back through the kitchen and noticed that the sliding door was open. I switched on the yard lights and ran to the pool. He was in the deep end, floating above the drain." She paused and hung her head. "I tried to save him, but it was too late."

Grady was gone. Angie would never touch him again. Never kiss him. Because of her wretched sister. She rose up on her knees. "Grady is never coming back because you decided to fuck *my* boyfriend. Why? What did I ever do to you?"

Leslie stared at her with a far-away look in her eyes. Stricken. Befuddled. "If only I hadn't gone back to wash the blanket."

Angie slapped her, a loud thwack that snapped her head to one side. "Answer me! What did I ever do to you?"

She reached out and grasped the straps of Angie's nightie. "You made me feel plain. Forgive me. Please!"

A stab of guilt knifed Angie's chest. She thought of her ruined painting that had portrayed Leslie as the more desirable sister. Maybe if she had done more than paint an imaginary scene to make Leslie feel less plain this would never have happened—or maybe Leslie would always be envious of her, no matter what Angie did.

She swatted her sister's hands away. "You washed that blanket in Grady's blood." She pointed to the door. "Get out! Out! I hate you!"

Angie dressed before dawn. She pulled on a pair of jeans and open-toed sandals and slipped a white organdy top over her head and scribbled a note explaining that she needed to sort things out, but would be back before dinner.

She set out on foot around Lake Harriet's eastern shore and walked to a pancake house at Lyndale and Lake, where she picked at a plate of waffles and bacon. Few families in all of Minneapolis would awaken that day to greater wealth than her family—or greater sorrow. What good were worldly possessions compared to the flesh and blood of her brother? Grady was little-boy kisses and giggling laughter, like a puppy full of joy and wonder. But now his lifeless body would decompose in a box in the dirt, his arms and legs never to lengthen into the limbs of a man, his voice never to deepen, his face never to whisker. Her darling brother, dead. Because of a wet spot on a blanket.

The treacherous little whore. The conniving slut. It made her head pound, the hatred inside.

She paid her bill and went to where she always went to make sense of things. To a place where she would *feel* the truth. The Minneapolis Institute of Arts was on Third Avenue, about two miles from her home. She sat down on the front staircase and waited beneath the six-pillar colonnade and pediment that graced the white granite façade of the Beaux-Arts building. A pair of marble Chinese guardian lions mounted on plinths flanked her on either side.

The museum's twelve-foot doors opened beneath a blue sky stuffed with heaps of cumulus. She flashed her member's card to a dour woman with big shoulders and wandered all morning in search of something that would call out to her. It was nearly one by the time she reached the Impressionist galleries. What she sought whispered from a Van Gogh: *Olive Trees with Yellow Sky and Sun*. A canvas of an olive grove near Saint-Rémy, as it appeared to Van Gogh in the heat of his insanity. One of a series of olive tree paintings at Saint-Rémy that reflected Van Gogh's emotions about the Agony in the Garden—without the image of Christ. She scrutinized the short, thick brushstrokes of agitated genius, the maniacal chiaroscuro that made Van Gogh's olive groves unlike any other: a numinous sun sitting like a halo in a radiant yellow sky; rich, brown soil undulating across the canvas like a great river in motion; gnarled trunks and branches of olive trees, ancient and mystical; explosions of green foliage; shadows bleeding across sacred ground in a spill of purple; a gray, looming ridgeline, cold and uncompromising.

Van Gogh the zealot, showing all there was to know about Gesthemane in a single painting: Divine Light; Power; Wisdom; Sorrow; Redemption; and God's Preeminence. It pulled her in, until she felt as if she were there, the olive grove convulsing around her, filling her with thick, molten sorrow.

But it was not only sorrow that she felt. There was moral agony, too. She was wracked by it, torn by whether or not to tell her parents that Grady died because of Leslie's need to bed Angie's boyfriend? That he drowned while she washed their sex-stained blanket.

Telling them served no purpose. The moral thing—the merciful thing—was to forgive Leslie and keep her tryst with Cullen a secret. Why tear the family apart any more than it already was? It was enough that Leslie told *someone*; she didn't need to tell everyone.

She contemplated the painting more deeply and shook her head. She wasn't trying to spare Leslie by withholding the truth from her parents; she was protecting herself. Never once had she made herself ordinary so that Leslie could shine. Instead, she flaunted her appeal at every turn, played for blood all the time. It was no surprise that Leslie laid her boyfriend; the wonder was it took so long. The moral thing to do was the hard thing to do: tell her parents everything.

"Young lady, are you all right?" A docent stood over her, wearing a blue blazer and slacks. She was a small, elderly woman with heavy mascara and dark lipstick. She thrust a Kleenex at Angie. "You were sobbing out loud, for goodness gracious. Is something troubling you?"

She took the Kleenex and blotted her eyes and blew her nose and pointed at the painting. "It overwhelmed me. The glory of it."

The woman squeezed her shoulder. "Van Gogh does that. He's unpredictable that way." She turned heel and returned to her post in the doorway.

Angie stopped beside her on her way out of the gallery and bent over and whispered in her ear. "God bless you, ma'am."

Outside, the sun slid off its zenith amidst billows of clouds shot with splinters of light. She walked home in awe of the redemptive power a madman's olive trees could hold.

The house was still. Morbidly still. Leftover gloom hung from the walls like funeral crepe. Death was in the air. Grady's death. Her little brother.

The smell of burnt toast came from the kitchen, but her parents weren't there, only their blackened crumbs on a plate. Her heart was full of forgiveness, but her mind was resolute, committed to telling them the truth. She walked through the house in silence and descried them in the living room, like characters in a play. Her mother sat hollow-faced on the sofa, still in her nightgown. Her father knelt in front of her, administering halting, desperate touches of reassurance. She had hoped to find them in better shape. Were they strong enough to withstand what she was about to tell them? She hesitated, fearful they weren't.

"Mom? Dad?"

Her mother registered a blank stare, no hint of recognition. Her mouth moved, but no words came out. She picked at the air. Her hair lay thin and lank on her shoulders, rinsed of color. She looked frail, ravaged, senile, someone you would put in a nursing home.

Her father shuffled his knees and turned his shoulders to face her. He was unshaven and grim and the white tee he wore was stained with coffee. He bowed his head like a condemned prisoner before an executioner.

This was worse, far worse, than she had anticipated. They were altogether broken people, her distinguished, self-confident father as deeply in thrall to grief as her mother. She started toward them. Her father raised his head to speak. His body shook and he listed to one side, as if the effort might topple him over.

"Leslie jumped off the Cedar Avenue Bridge and drowned today. She left a note saying she deserved to die the way Grady did."

Chapter 12

THE JANGLE OF THE telephone on the nightstand beside his head—the minatory jolt it gave him, the churn of his stomach and dread he might have to go in—yanked him from the pitiless dream that had tormented him for over three decades. It wasn't a dream so much as an image: the still, glowing body of Grady Nichols, submerged and drifting face down in a sea of viscous blue. He fumbled for the phone and put it to his ear, grateful for the intrusion. Even being rousted from bed in the middle of the night to dialyze the most objectionable patient imaginable was better than one second more of that.

"Dr. Brodie? This is Heather Gilbert on Four South. Remember me? You were my preceptor when I was a nursing student. I'm working nights at Beach Park now. Sorry to bother you, but Mr. Wilcox, your dialysis patient in Room 483? He has a blood pressure of 194/90 and doesn't have any meds ordered. Would you like to give him something?"

It took him a moment to adjust, to throw off the yoke of Grady and comprehend what he heard. "Dr. Brodie?" she said again. An image of her coalesced in his mind, her short blonde hair and earnest face. Young Heather, a full-fledged nurse working the night shift. A sudden treacle welled inside him. The sweet timidity in her voice, the respect she had for him—like a daughter for a father. He cleared his throat and hoped it passed for a cough.

"Of course I remember you. I would have been nicer to you if I'd known you'd be working nights someday. Now I'm at your mercy. He can have clonidine, 0.1 mg po every four hours, prn BP systolic greater than 180."

"Thanks, Dr. Brodie. Good night."

He hung up, but the memory of her lingered. Her round chin and full cheeks, her bright, eager eyes and honey brown hair: so wholesome and kind and smart. His smile faded and the warm lump inside him turned bittersweet.

Heather Gilbert made him sad. Why?

Because he had no daughter of his own to send to nursing school or med school, that's why. Or even law school—if she were a cold, heartless bitch. Someone to dote on him in his... dotage. Once an adult, twice a child, that's what was coming. Dependency. It was always the daughters who brought their elderly parents to the office, daughters who laid out their pills and cooked their food and dressed them. And on rare occasions, feckless sons angling for an inheritance. Not that he would have turned his nose up at a son. But he had neither. Was his childlessness karma for his hand in Grady's death?

He had first learned of it in the newspaper, two days after it happened. The article said Grady Nichols accidentally drowned in the family pool after slipping undetected past his twenty-year-old sister, Leslie, who was babysitting at the time. Overcome by guilt, she took her own life the following day by jumping off the Cedar Avenue Bridge. Brother and sister, both drowned.

Their deaths stupefied him, horrified him: left him catatonic. He had been there that night with them, Grady ecstatic with fright when Cullen pulled at his toes from underwater, Leslie opening beneath him like slick velvet, her pool-damp hair, the catch in her throat when she came. So vital and human—with only hours to live. His propinquity to it made him shudder.

He agonized for a week over how to confess to Angie, but her letter beat him to it. He learned that Grady drowned while Leslie was downstairs washing the sex-stained blanket they had lain on. Angie called his death the end product of a chain reaction— started by Chaz—that her phone call to Cullen's home that night came a minute too late to stop. She blamed herself for Leslie's death, her refusal to forgive her. The guilt was unbearable, she said, and if she stayed, a bridge would soon beckon to her, too. She closed by saying that she was already far away, but if Cullen loved her, he would keep the cause of Grady's death secret and never go near her parents again. They had suffered enough. At least this way they could die loving all their children—instead of wishing their daughters had been aborted.

So he never made the call to Edward Nichols that he should have. But the devastation he wreaked on Angie's family left him poisoned, toxic, corrupted—like Hamlet after striking down Claudius. The difference was that Hamlet was allowed to die. Cullen, rather than joining the dead, envied them, his days full of self-recrimination, his nights void of all repose, the ghost of Grady Nichols already haunting his dreams. He took up smoking, quit playing basketball, gained ten pounds, and grew a mangy beard. He grew so bitter even Tazinski avoided him.

The *Star and Tribune* ran a follow-up piece a month later, reporting that the sole surviving Nichols child, Angela, had fled and disappeared, her whereabouts unknown. The story parenthetically added that in child drownings, the marriage of the involved parents ended more than half the time.

The news of the Nichols family's epic misfortune affected Chaz in a manner inversely proportional to Cullen. He cut back on beer, lost ten pounds, and bought a pair of plaid pants and a leisure suit. As for Brodie's Tirade, it never launched again. He even told Cullen that he was sorry about "that Nichols girl" and her painting. Cullen could tell, though, that Chaz was certain beyond all doubt that God had punished Nichols for the abortions he did.

Cullen yearned to tell his father what his defilement of her painting had set in motion—though Chaz would probably feel vindicated, as though he and his son were agents of God striking down an infanticidal monster. But Cullen didn't care. What Angie asked was too much. He would tell him anyway.

He came into the living room one night during *Mary Tyler Moore*. His father sat in his easy chair, his feet on the hassock and a sweating bottle of Pabst in his hand, his crew cut steely gray. Chaz stared at the screen with a whipped smile on his face, his crush on Mary Richards ridiculous to see. Waiting for her to throw that hat. Just waiting. Cullen opened his mouth to speak, but didn't. He spun and walked away. For Angie. Because he loved her still, and always would.

He glanced at the red numbers on the face of the digital alarm next to his bed: 1:30. Plenty of sack time left, despite Nurse Heather's call. He drifted back asleep with a telling thought in mind.

Becky Winthrop still had a few good years left before the last of her eggs went bad.

With each of his ex-wives, Cullen had simply fallen in love. More or less. Practical considerations never entered into it. This time would be different.

He began to appraise Becky with the detached eye of a trainer evaluating a broodmare. After all, this was about choosing a mate to give him the one thing that would make his life complete and bestow it with meaning: a precious foal of his own. A child. It seemed only prudent to consider whether the mare he'd been trail riding was suited for breeding, what kind of horseflesh they were talking about here.

So he decided to apply the same time-honored criteria to Becky, the prospective mother of his children, that elite trainers used to assess prospective broodmares: pedigree, competitive performance, physical symmetry, age, overall health, and maternal instinct.

At thirty-eight, Becky had a still-youthful body, took no medications, didn't smoke, wasn't obese, didn't have diabetes, drank moderately, and exercised regularly. In short, she was healthy as a horse—so to speak.

But pregnancy past the age of thirty-five was less than ideal no matter how healthy the mother was. He had talked to a colleague in high-risk obstetrics and done some reading on his own. There were issues. Women past thirty-five were not as fecund as younger women: their conception rate was barely fifty percent, and declined steadily to an infertility rate of ninety percent by age forty-five. And there were heightened risks during pregnancy. The miscarriage rate in women under thirty was five percent; in women thirty-five to thirty-nine it was thirteen percent. The cause? Declining oocyte quality—bad eggs. The rate of ectopic pregnancy in women over thirty-five was six times higher than that of younger women and the risk of fetal chromosomal defects— Down syndrome and others—rose steadily with maternal age. Not to mention stillbirths. Two to four times as likely past the age of thirty-five. None of which was a deal breaker, but her biologic clock was ticking. Like his wasn't. If they were going to do this, they needed to get on with it.

Becky had acquired the animal beauty of her legs on the tennis court—tennis being the vehicle her surgeon father chose to mold her, classical piano her pathologist mother's choice. Each of these activities was subordinate to school in the well-ordered Milwaukee home she described growing up in with her two younger brothers—one a trial lawyer, the other a commodities trader, both now living in Chicago. "They might as well have become marines, for all the daily combat they engage in," she said of them. As for her? Phi Beta Kappa as an undergrad, Alpha Omega Alpha in med school at Northwestern, and a psych residency at UCLA capped off as Chief resident.

Last on the list was maternal instinct. Becky was affectionate to a fault with her cat Siggie—short for Sigmund, of course. But it was hard to know what that meant. Cullen was amazed at the number of people who loved their pets like children, yet treated other human beings like dogs. The movement afoot to value equally the life of an animal—or frog or minnow or nematode—with a human made no sense. Yes, they all came from dust and would all molder and return to dust, but Da Vinci and a worm of equal value? Really? Human beings were sui generis, distinct from animals by virtue of human consciousness. Did anyone ever refer to the conundrum of *animal* consciousness? No, they did not, because it was human consciousness—the mind—that made humans distinct from animals.

Though human consciousness was not, as apologists liked to argue, proof of God. The human mind did not require God to explain its existence: only the wonders of neurobiology, the firing of specific neuronal circuits that kindled emotion, desire, purpose, movement, and complex thought. Research on the biology of empathy suggested that defined areas of the brain—the amygdala and anterior cingulate cortex—were responsible for creating feelings of sympathy toward other human beings. Synapses accounted for human compassion, not God.

But back to Becky.

She lived in a split-level home thirty minutes south of Cullen's condo, a mile from the coast, with a backyard pool and view of the ocean from the upper story. She tackled Rachmaninoff the first time she played piano for him, on a Yamaha black baby grand in her living room, surrounded by family photos and one of an old boyfriend—left out to send a message, perhaps. That she had options. That she wasn't desperate.

"His name is Adam," she said, after Cullen inquired about the photo when she sat down behind the piano to play. "Why do you ask?"

That was a good question. Why was he asking? The answer was far more complicated—and reprehensible—than she imagined. He shrugged and gave her the narrowest of explanations. "I want to know who the competition is." Even if the competition was a smirking metrosexual with a weak jaw.

"We broke up three months ago," she said. "He's a dermatologist I met through a friend."

"Why did you stop seeing him?"

"I never really fell in love with him. You know, like in fairytales?"

"Well, as far as I'm concerned, he's still competition. I already don't like him."

He wasn't really threatened by young Adam, but it would make her feel good to think he was. It made Cullen feel good, too, no matter how remote a threat her dermatologist ex-boyfriend was. Dermatology: please. He'd sooner be an accountant than look at rashes all day. Where was the drama? The high stakes? Cullen had gone into medicine to save lives, not to scrape barnacles off geriatrics in order to avoid night call and weekends. But none of that mattered. It was enough that there *was* competition. Someone to vanquish.

Becky reached for her sheet music. Cullen was pretty certain from the flush of her cheeks and the self-conscious, adoring look she gave him that she had that old fairytale feeling now, but that wasn't necessarily a good thing. Falling in love with him had not turned out well for a single woman who had. Especially Angie. And wasn't competition at the heart of things then, too? After all, Dempsey had dated Angie first, until Cullen stole her away from him at Trajan's Bath—behind Dempsey's back. Having Cullen Brodie compete over you might feel good at first, but it tended to turn ugly later.

Her piano playing was determined to the point of being obsessive, almost as if her mother—stoic and uncompromising, according to Becky, descended from Polish aristocracy with a maiden name of Korzenowski—were standing behind her, waiting to pounce on her slightest mistake. Her head remained fixed at a thirty-degree tilt the entire time and her hands savaged the keys in a driving, merciless rhythm. He detected no errors—not that he would have recognized any—but her pianism failed to move him. It was constricted and tense, her lips pressed tight in a moue of intensity born more of a need to play flawlessly than a need to play. It made him sad, that somewhere during childhood her passion for music had been wrung out of her.

He stood and clapped. "Bravo! Bravo!"

Her tension melted and her body language relaxed. "Thank you, but I'm afraid you're not a very demanding critic. I made three mistakes." Cullen had failed to notice even one, and wouldn't have mentioned it if he had.

She went into the kitchen and returned with two glasses and a bottle of chilled Pinot Grigio and took him onto a balcony that looked out over the pool to the ocean. The sun had already set. Its sunken hue tinged the horizon red.

"Do you enjoy playing piano?" he asked. "Or is it just another box to check on your list of achievements?"

She dropped her jaw in mock indignation. "You make me sound like some joyless Type A that's a slave to success."

He ticked off her résumé. "It's not exactly the profile of a slacker." He refrained from pointing out that the clothes in her closets were organized by color and the books in her library alphabetized by author.

She curled her knees to her chest and stared at the darkening sea. "I like playing for myself, but I don't like playing in front of an audience. Even of one. I let my mother down in music competitions. Always a couple notes away from perfection. I couldn't help it. I wasn't good enough. I understood music theory and could read sheet music well enough, but I didn't *feel* the music. I could never seem to relax and let it take me."

But she had played piano for him. He had been elevated, in the short time he had been seeing her, to special status. She was showing herself to him, one telling revelation at a time. "It must have been difficult to play in front of me. It makes me feel good that you did." The more time he spent with her, the more he liked her. Not in a crazy, fall deeply in love sort of way, but in a way that might actually last.

She stretched out on the chaise and turned on her side to face him. "What about you? What scars of youth do you bear?"

He had never told either of his ex-wives about Grady and had mentioned Angie only in passing, a summer girlfriend from college. Perhaps it was the psychiatrist in her that enticed him to do it, her skill at prying dirty secrets from people with her non-judgmental, disarming face. The promise of unburdening she offered, someone to understand what he had done without hating him for it. He wouldn't blame her if she did, though. If she despised him for the disgrace he carried like Lord Jim. Maybe it would take a bullet in the chest to put things right for him, too. Nothing else had worked.

The night air cooled. Crickets chirped an indolent song. He told her everything, from the state championship game against Dempsey to the night he and Angie met to the day Grady died, all of it, Chaz and Edward Nichols and Brodie's Tirade, too.

"Grady went back outside through the kitchen door while Leslie was downstairs washing the cum off the blanket we laid on. He drowned before she found him. The next day, Leslie jumped off a bridge into the Mississippi River and drowned, too. None of it would have happened if I had just gone home from the playground that night. Instead I went looking for Angie. To hurt her."

Becky sat up. A complex visage of horror and pity and dismay marked her face. Not the stylized, professional pity of a psychiatrist, but of a conflicted human being, a woman who cared about him and was anguished for him, but who was not about to condone what he had done, because his turpitude dispirited her. She reached for him, but he waved her off.

"It's not pity I want."

She hesitated. "What then? If not pity, what?"

"I want you to know why I did it. Why I was incapable of going home from the Attucks. I want you to know how flawed I am."

She nodded. "Okay." She went inside and came back with another bottle of wine. He filled their glasses. Her neighbor's irrigation system started up, showering precious California water on her lawn to keep it green. How absurd human beings could be. And how cruel.

"When I first met Angie, I knew that I wanted to see her again. But when I found out she was on a date with Dempsey, I *had* to see her again."

"Why?"

He could tell by her voice that Angie had got to her, the way Angie got to most women. The way she made them insecure. Though Becky had never met her. She smoothed her hair and crossed her legs. And Cullen had held back. Hadn't told her how unnaturally gorgeous and sentient Angie really was. Nor would he. Ever.

"It triggered something in me. Something bad."

Becky frowned. "Well, yeah. You were rivals." She sounded impatient, dismissive, as if he were attaching too much importance to a self-evident, commonplace thing.

"The summer after we graduated from high school, I asked Slade to let Dempsey play the Attucks. It was my idea. I'm the one who got him in there."

She drank her wine with an inquisitive look on her face. "Were you trying to give him another chance to compete against you?" She so wanted to see him in an admirable light, giving poor Dempsey another shot at him. It would have been an honorable thing to do, if that had been his motivation. But it wasn't.

"I invited him there to give *me* another chance—to dominate him. When I drove down the lane with the crowd roaring and the state title on the line, there was nothing he could do to stop me. Domination of a worthy foe is an intoxicating drug. I didn't want it to end. I brought Dempsey to the Attucks to *keep* dominating him. When Angie came to the club with him that night, I wanted to take her from him. To dominate him."

She tried to keep her poker face on, as she had been trained to do, but it was a mean, self-aggrandizing impulse he'd confessed to. She reacted the way he wanted her to: with a look of condemnation. Good girl. Now they were getting somewhere.

"When he told me he slept with her, I went berserk. Off the charts berserk. She was mine, and he had taken her from me. For the first time, he was the dominant one. I would have killed him, but Slade stopped me. So you see, it wasn't only about Angie that night. It was about Dempsey, too."

She put her hand on his leg. "I can help you work through this, but I'm going to sound like a psychiatrist."

Fine. Why not? She could be his girlfriend later on. "You won't charge me, will you?"

She gave a seductive smile and winked. "I'll give you HMO rates." He didn't really like winkers, but that was a pretty witty line. She was a good girl, from a good family. As he had once been a good boy from a good family.

He refilled their glasses. They were drunk now, careening toward an accommodation of what he had done and what she needed. A pardon for him and feminine validation for her. Human beings made him sad. So very sad. He sat back and listened to what she had to say. Listened to her spin. Her justification for loving him, loathsome though he was.

"Your relationship with Dempsey was a proving ground. You wanted to dominate an alpha male you respected—and at some level probably feared—in order to prove your masculinity. Angie would have known this—any woman would have. So when your father ruined her painting, she got even by attacking you where you were most vulnerable. Her infidelity confronted you with a loss of power over Dempsey, which threatened your masculinity, and a loss of your most treasured possession, Angie. So you went insane and would have killed them both. What you did was hateful and destructive, but you need to understand that there were powerful forces in play. Jealousy is a biologically based emotion, an ancient adaptive response that seeks to guarantee that your genes are the ones that get passed on through the female you couple with. It's not easily extinguished, no matter how maladaptive it becomes."

None of this was news to him. He had thought it through a thousand times and saw it much the way she described it, though perhaps not in such a clinically logical way. His reason for telling her wasn't so that he could understand what he had done; it was to be understood for what he had done. And for this he was grateful. He had reasons. Not excuses, but reasons.

"It's very merciful of you to blame it on biology."

"There's one more thing that might help. A villain that might surprise you."

"You mean my father, for what he did to Angie."

"No. I mean your mother, for what she did to you."

"My mother? She didn't do anything that day, other than make the sign of the cross."

"Oh, but she did. She carried you inside her and gave birth to you. You were born from a gender different than your own. All men are. Your need to dominate other men comes from your need to separate from your mother. Camile Paglia said it best: 'A woman simply is, but a man must become. Masculinity is achieved by a revolt from woman, and confirmed by other men.'"

Her words hit him in the stomach. It was almost incest she was implying, Jocasta and Oedipus type stuff. But she was right. It was his mother who had read to him as a child and who had nurtured his love of literature. His mother who had encouraged him to choose a career devoted to helping other human beings. He had always credited his father for his drive and competitiveness, but maybe the credit was due to his mother. And maybe his need to dominate Dempsey—his need to be male—wasn't so pathologic after all.

He took Becky from behind that night. She didn't particularly like it, he could tell, but she let him do it anyway.

Becky's passion for music might have been extinguished, but not for tennis. He found that out one afternoon at the tony club she belonged to. The locker rooms had plush carpet and piped-in music and there was a loggia with a swanky restaurant and bar. Outside, lighted courts fronted a small grandstand used for tournament play. They had plans that same evening for dinner and a movie. Cullen had sacrificed his choice, *District Nine*, in favor of hers, *Julie & Julia*. It could have been worse. *The Time Traveler's Wife* opened that month, too.

He had toyed with the idea of suggesting they play each other as a way to check out her game, but after watching her first few rallies against a rangy blonde at least ten years her junior, he was relieved to be in the stands watching rather than opposing her. Becky proved to be a top-flight club player who would have tromped him the way Billie Jean King embarrassed Bobby Riggs.

She crouched like a graceful jungle cat when waiting to return serve, sprayed forehands with vicious abandon, and blasted two-fisted backhands to the baseline with the thew of a man. All while emitting primal grunts Cullen found more than a little arousing. She ran like a deer, her range incredible, no ball she couldn't get to. He drank in the contour of her calves and the play of muscle beneath her lime green tennis skirt—a surpassingly *short* skirt, riding barely below the curve of her buttocks—and admired the athletic figure she cut in her black tank top, her tan, sinewy arms and petite rise of bosom.

Toward the end of the first set, with Becky ahead five games to two and returning serve at break point, the blonde girl hit a slicing serve that struck the forecourt and skittered so far left Becky was several feet out of bounds when she reached it. The safe play would have been a controlled return to her opponent's forehand. Instead, she scorched an impossibly difficult forehand of her own down the line, a kill shot if ever there was one. It clipped the line and sailed past the lunge of her overmatched rival. Becky pumped her fist. The blonde girl shook her head and talked to her racket.

"Great shot, babe!" he yelled through cupped hands. She played tennis the way he played basketball: with passion and joy and a fierce competitive edge.

After the match, won by Becky in straight sets, he kissed her flushed, sweaty face and grinned from ear to ear. "I like you in that skirt. Maybe you'll model it for me tonight."

She rubbed against him and curled her hand around his neck. "With nothing underneath."

"I'll pick you up at seven. We have a lot to talk about." The broodmare appraisal was over. Becky wasn't getting any younger.

And neither was he.

He stopped at the office on his way home to sort through mail and lab results from the day before, which he had taken off to have a long weekend. After finishing up, he armed the office alarm and was on his way out the door when he noticed a large, thin, cardboard package—marked Fragile—that Bria had set aside for him to open on Monday. He gathered it up and carried it to his car and stowed it in his trunk.

The winter sun had already plunged into the Pacific by the time he showered and dressed. The ocean looked mournful and gray. He glanced at his watch; plenty of time before he was due at Becky's. He brandished a pair of scissors and knelt on the carpet in front of the cardboard package and scanned the sender's address before going to work with the scissors: Avarua, wherever that was. Avarua Fine Arts. Inside was a framed painting packed in excelsior. He slid it out of the box and leaned it against the couch.

It was his incubus come calling, Grady Nichols floating face up in a swimming pool.

A pair of red trunks billowed about his waist and legs like a parachute. Dark thongs of leather crisscrossed his wrists, binding his hands in front of him. Like a martyr. A halo hovered over his head, a thin gold circle of empyreal light that illuminated his small white torso and face—his holy, martyred face, eyes closed, lips thin and blue. The lambency of the halo colored everything beneath it soft and yellow, even the dark, lapping water. The background of the painting was obscure and foreboding, the pool at night, its coving barely discernible. The lower right hand corner bore a signature.

Angela Masters.

He sat on the floor in front of it and ignored the incessant ringing of his telephone all through the bottle of Makers Mark he drank. Ringing and ringing, over and over, first his landline, then his cell. Until finally it ceased, as if it had spent itself. The way Grady spent himself. Thrashing in the pool. Coughing, gagging, choking, sucking more and more water into his sodden lungs until they weighed him down and sank him. Wondering all the while where Leslie was? Why she wasn't there to save him?

What kind of God drowned a four-year-old boy in his backyard pool? And compelled his sister to leap from a trestle into the Mississippi the very next day? The God of Exodus and Genesis, that's who. A God who demanded that retribution be eye for eye, tooth for tooth. A God who urged Joshua's ethnic cleansing of Jericho. A God who turned Lot's wife into a block of salt. What use had he for a God like this? What use had he for any God? For it was his father's belief in God and, as a God-fearing man, his requisite hatred of the town abortionist, Edward Nichols, that set things in motion. There was no God. Only untold misery on account of humanity's belief in one.

Reclaiming his honor back then had proved a stubborn thing to do, the deaths of Grady and Leslie graven onto his conscience. To what end had they perished and he lived? What warranted his survival and not theirs? He searched for some redeeming purpose to his life, some ennobling reason for it to continue. The best way to make restitution to the dead, he decided, was to minister to the ruck of the living. Improve the human condition. So he put himself through med school with the aid of student loans—beaucoup student loans—and odd shifts at Lundino's. He took not a dime from his father, whom he viewed as the catalyst of it all, though he never told him so. After med school he fled Minneapolis for Atlanta and a three-year internal medicine residency. Grady's ghost came along, thickening the fog of sleep deprivation that was a rite of passage of medical training to begin with.

To service his debt—fifty thousand dollars of it, equivalent to four times that now—he began moonlighting in Atlanta ERs the day he got a Georgia medical license. Between residency and ER work he spent more nights in hospital call rooms than his Virginia Highlands apartment, but somehow still found time to date an anesthesiology resident from Boston named Liz Warden. By the end of their stay in Atlanta, they convinced themselves they should be married. The thought that Liz might have chosen anesthesia because she didn't like listening to patients never occurred to him.

They headed to Los Angeles for his nephrology fellowship at USC a week after the wedding, but that fall, Cullen's younger brothers started college. As part of his self-imposed atonement for Grady and Leslie, he had promised to pay for the twins' tuition at the best school they got into, which turned out to be Notre Dame—the cruelest of ironies, sacrificing what was left of his youth so his brothers could attend a Catholic university, when it was Catholicism, and Chaz's unstinting belief in it, that caused his troubles in the first place.

It was an expense that even constant moonlighting at Kaiser could not cover—and one that Liz, who had taken a job as a junior faculty member at LA County, wanted no part of. Cullen made up the difference by borrowing more money, but the mushrooming debt and long hours away from home strained their relationship. Liz rebelled, complaining that putting Michael and Bryan through college was a higher priority for Cullen than she was. And since he had chosen to leave the story of Grady and Leslie untold—a pledge to silence only the vanished Angie could release him from—he had no justification for his extraordinary commitment other than family loyalty. Which was a lie. He and his parents rarely spoke. Cullen never forgave them for Art Rampage.

His personal burden weighed heavily on their marriage. Liz divorced him a few months before he finished his fellowship and joined a nephrology group that practiced out of St. Vincent's. His self-identity and even self-worth came to depend wholly on patient care. More than a means of atonement, medicine became his reason for living. A daily fix he could not do without.

Another addiction grabbed hold of him, too—a taste for younger women. Los Angeles teemed with attractive females in their twenties in search of fame, most with only subsistence living to show for it. Being single with MD after his name afforded easy access to a bottomless pool of bimbos. By day he ministered to the human condition; by night he was a sybarite, indulging himself in all the delights eighties LA had to offer. He bought a gold Jaguar XJS convertible, wore Armani suits, and spent countless evenings at Laker games and clubbing on Sunset with hot twenty-somethings on his arm. He had season tickets at the Forum, met Magic Johnson and Chick Hearn, never waited in line at Nicky Blair's, and traded bons mots with bouncers at the Rainbow and Roxy, who knew him by name.

But none of it kept his incubus at bay. The only thing that did—and this imperfectly so, with many a night still haunted by the specter of Grady suspended in cobalt-colored water thicker than honey, like blue amniotic fluid— was the gratitude of patients for the care he gave them. One such encounter banished Grady from his dreams for a full month before its salubrious effect waned.

He was at St. Vincent's one morning when he got a stat page from a nurse two floors down about one of his dialysis patients, Matt Shipley. Shipley was a sullen, deaf, nearly dumb man of thirty who communicated—when at all—by unintelligible grunts and groans. The day before he had undergone a radical orchiectomy—surgical removal of his testes and related structures—for testicular cancer, a seminoma that had metastasized to his lymph nodes. A course of cisplatin-based chemotherapy was next. The good news was that this particular kind of tumor had a ninety-five per cent five-year survival rate.

Allie, the nurse who paged him, spoke in a low, stunned voice. "Dr. Brodie? Mr. Shipley suddenly started screaming and pointing at his buttocks. There's some kind of... *growth* coming out of his rectum. I've never seen anything like it. It's getting bigger by the minute."

He drew a blank. He had no idea what she might be describing. "I'll be right there."

He tore down the stairwell and burst into Shipley's room to find him writhing on his right side and bellowing like a bull pierced by a matador's spear. Shipley spotted him and pointed to his behind.

"Oh! Oh! Oh!" he yelled.

Cullen squeezed his shoulder and pulled back the sheet and lifted his gown. A distended, striated, glistening mass of tissue the size of a beach ball protruded from his anus, inflating before Cullen's very eyes, growing like a soap bubble off the end of a blow-wand. Shipley thrashed his left hand up and down and pounded his hip. "Oh! Oh! Oh!" He wanted the thing gone.

Cullen pulled on a pair of gloves and told Allie, a sleek brunette with a shaken look on her face, to hold Shipley's arm down. He cupped his hands around the mass of tissue—the circumference of it dwarfed even his oversized mitts—and gently pushed against the extrusion. Like magic it began to shrink, steadily receding back inside Shipley's anus. Cullen glanced at Allie. Her mouth was open and her pretty eyes were wide with horrid fascination. He kept stuffing the slick organic beach ball back into Shipley's rectum.

"It's an intussusception," he said, without looking up again. "He has so much tumor bulk in his lymph nodes that it raised the pressure in his peritoneal cavity and pushed his sigmoid colon through his rectum and out his anus. Once outside his body, it became entrapped and began to swell. I'm reducing it, like you'd reduce a hernia."

A moment later, there was a short sucking sound and the mass snapped back inside Shipley's anus and disappeared. Shipley's head nodded furiously.

"Ahh! Ahh! Ahh!" He reached back and took Cullen's hand. Held it. Squeezed it. *Crushed* it. "Tnk U! Tnk U! Tnk U!"

For as long as he was Cullen's patient—another three years—Shipley never failed to make eye contact and give him a glorious smile when Cullen came by to see him on weekly dialysis rounds. Stuffing a man's swollen, strangulated intestines back through his asshole with your bare—okay, gloved—hands. Now *that* was ministering to the human condition.

But it was not Matt Shipley who visited the stupor he fell into in front of Angie's painting that night. It was Grady, a martyr bathed in hallowed light.

He awakened on the floor the following morning in much the same condition he had awakened on the floor of the Nichols library the night Grady drowned: enervated by shame. He rubbed his swollen eyes and held his throbbing temples and squinted at the exquisite, ghastly painting that rested against his living room couch. Even his Makers Mark-addled brain comprehended what must come next.

He fired up the iMac in his study and, after visiting the website of Avarua Fine Arts, began pricing airline tickets to Rarotonga.

Chapter 13

ENNIS SAT IN HIS usual spot on the green canapé with Becky across from him in the beech wood bergère, her hair pinned in a chignon—just because he'd stopped dressing like a woman didn't mean he'd forgotten all he'd learned about being one. He glanced at the oil painting hanging on the wall to his right, the flamenco gal whose poppy red skirt was the color of Becky's blouse. Becky's elbow sleeve, hooker-sheer, cropped red blouse. With a little imagination, he could almost make out a lacy black bra underneath. And that skirt she had on—had her legs gotten longer? Or maybe her dry cleaners shrank it. Korean, no doubt. It used to be the Greeks who had a lock on the dry cleaning business. At least they spoke English and didn't have stinky breath. What did those people eat to smell like that so early in the morning? He sniffed the sandalwood incense burning on the desk behind Becky to neutralize his brain's remembered odor of it.

She leaned forward with her knees together and palms pressed to her thighs. "Since your bout of rejection, you've purged your wardrobe, haven't been to group, and haven't gone out en femme a single time."

He looked down at the dark hardwood floor between them, studied the lines and whorls of its grain.

"Throwing Elaine's clothes out and putting her back in the closet will not rid you of the need to wear a dress. You know that."

He raised his head and suffered her frustrated glare. He liked her chignon. Pulling her hair into a bun kept it from looking so limp. "I'm scared to death to put one on."

Her left toe began to tap. "Because you think your transgender personality Elaine resents your organ donor, Carla, whose soul you believe inhabits you. And you're fearful that the next time you cross-dress, Elaine will cause another episode of rejection, this time involving your kidney, too. Perhaps severe enough to put you back on dialysis. Or worse."

He nodded. "But only until she gets to know Carla better and accepts her. Then she won't."

Her expression hardened. "You're confounding your fear of society's rejection of you for being transgender with fear of transplant rejection, projecting one onto the other. Projection is a defense mechanism we use to avoid facing painful truths about ourselves. You're blaming Elaine for rejecting Carla instead of blaming yourself for failing to accept what you are—a man with a woman inside you. You're suffering from a transmigration delusion caused by unresolved guilt over cross-dressing."

He felt like a skinned animal, a mink stripped of its pelt or a whale flensed of its blubber, left raw and bleeding on the shore. Like when his father strapped his ass. *Navy pilots don't act like women.* He squirmed and wanted her to stop, but she didn't.

"Let go of your guilt. It's preventing you from fulfilling your need to be feminine. What are you going to do? Never dress in women's clothing again? How likely is that? You won't be at peace until you once and for all own being transgender."

He bit his lip and fought to keep it together. Emotions frothed inside him. He felt like a blender about to blow its lid and spew milkshake all over the floor.

"Accept the satisfaction and exhilaration you get from cross-dressing. The relief. You deserve it. Elaine deserves it."

Something gushed inside him, a gutful of shame and joy and hope and love. He put his head in his hands and sobbed. Becky came over and sat beside him on the couch and held him, stroked him like a child in her arms. Her gossamer blouse grazed his cheek, the fine texture of it, the thrill of silk against his skin. He inhaled her perfume, a subtle blend of orchids and oranges. What he had so foolishly denied roused inside him, a feminine glow of nurturance and empathy and curiosity.

He snuffled and rubbed his eyes. Opened them. The most shapely, sexy, tantalizing inner thigh he had ever seen lay before him like a page out of *Playboy*, sloping like a superhighway to the promised land. He sprang a boner a cat couldn't scratch, the hardest he'd had in years, maybe ever, the kind he used to wake up with at sixteen and have to jerk off to relieve. He moaned, overcome with desire. He reached over and ran his hand up her skirt, smoothed his palm over the soft flesh of her thigh.

And came in his pants.

She grabbed his arm and flung it with a look of revulsion on her face, as if it were a rotten carcass crawling with maggots. "Stop it!" She clambered to her feet and tugged the hem of her skirt with both hands and cracked the side of his face with a thunderous slap that rattled his teeth.

"I tried to comfort you and you molested me! I should call the police and have you..."

Her eyes fell to the huge stain wetting the front of his trousers. He threw his hands in the air.

"I'm sorry, Becky, I'm sorry! I'm so sorry! Oh, God, what have I done?"

She staggered back and fell into her chair and gaped. "You ejaculated into your pants from touching my leg." She clutched a fistful of blouse with one hand. "Do you understand how wrong that is?"

"I know, I know! I lost control. I'm sorry."

She let go of her blouse and repositioned herself in the bergère with a flash of comprehension. "When I held you and you cried, was that Elaine or Ennis crying?"

"Elaine."

"And when you became sexually aroused, who was that?"

"Ennis."

The outrage drained from her face. "How often do you masturbate while dressed in women's clothes?"

He hung his head. "A lot."

"Have you ever had sex in women's clothing?"

He looked up. Her face was stern, but non-judgmental. He thought of the Mexican whorehouse in Tijuana, the lace teddy he wore. The jolt it gave him, like a testosterone-and-Viagra-laced cocktail. "As often as I can afford it."

"Do you see what's happened? You've linked sexual gratification to cross-dressing. That's a fetish, not gender accord. If you don't decouple sex from wearing female clothing, you'll never rid yourself of guilt and shame."

He scowled, a baleful look that made her shrink in her chair. "Being a woman comes easy to you." He pointed to his soaked britches, to the humiliation of his orgasm. "It doesn't to me. It's not fair!"

She held his gaze. "No, it isn't fair. I know it's not. I can't imagine how hard it would be to have to learn to be a man. But we are who we are. Some of us are born without arms. Some are born deaf. Others inherit genes programmed to cause leukemia."

She twisted in her chair and pointed to the painting of the flamenco dancer across the room. "She's lovely, isn't she? The dark, Spanish beauty of her?" She turned back around. "Being beautiful comes easy to her. It doesn't to me. I wear short skirts because I have a homely face, but nice legs. That's what I was born with—a homely face. And I will have a homely face for the rest of my life. You were born transgender. And you will be transgender for the rest of your life. Cross-gender expression is not a choice for you; it is a need. A basic need. But you do get to choose between dignity and shame. Between self-worth and self-loathing. I want to help you choose dignity, by fully embracing who you are."

She smiled, warm and open and humble. "The inconvenience of my homely face is pitifully insignificant compared to the burden of being transgender, but I've let it affect my role as your psychiatrist and that must not happen again. From now on, I'll wear slacks to our sessions, and check what little sexiness I have at the door. Together we will choose self-worth and dignity over shame and self-loathing. That's why the Center for Sexual and Gender Accord exists. That's its mission."

He cocked his head at the flamenco painting and grinned. "She's okay, but I'm, what you might say, partial to California girls. Like you."

She rolled her eyes and motioned toward the restroom. "Go clean up before the vice squad comes and takes us both away."

The pressure inside him was like a volcano about to blow. All he could do when Elaine came crashing out of the closet was make sure it was a controlled eruption. But things would get ugly in a hurry if Saturday rolled around with nothing for her to wear. He would get desperate and grab anything off the rack at the nearest discount store. Elaine deserved better. Besides, he had a particular look in mind this go around. That was the silver lining to purging; it guaranteed the pleasure and thrill of shopping for female clothing. Except now that he was retired and living on a fixed income, it was too damn expensive to build a wardrobe from scratch. He'd said it a dozen times before, but this time he meant it: no more purges.

He ventured that Friday to a swanky three-story mall with a Victoria's Secret on the second level. His trembling, sweaty hand gripped the rail of the up escalator with his heart pounding—technically Carla's heart, but come tomorrow maybe he'd stop thinking of it that way. Gender accord wasn't the only thing he lacked. A little spiritual accord would be nice, too.

The mall had already started to fill with the after-work crowd, enticing young women with boob jobs and short skirts and lean-faced, hungry-eyed lawyers and stockbrokers heading to a bar on ground level to get liquored up, before following one another home for a night of mindless sex that might even lead to a first date. Youth was wasted on the young, that's what Toni used to say, whenever one of her young nurses came to work hung over.

Toni Fortier: now *there* was a piece of work. A feisty Italian with wide hips and big knockers and pretty hands that flashed lacquered nails and bejeweled fingers. Haute couture hands, dangling from a pair of stevedore arms. Toni knew every patient in her clinic. *Really* knew them: how many children or grandchildren they had; what their jobs were or once had been; who used drugs and who quit; what religion they were; who was hiding assets from MediCal; who was willing to go on life support and who wasn't; whose NFL team made the playoffs.

The first time Ennis laid eyes on her was a week after he started dialysis, right before Christmas. A thick-legged woman with dark eyes, a plume of black hair, and a proud, smiling face marched a dozen or so children in white shirts and ties and fancy dresses into the center of the dialysis clinic and lined them up two deep. One of the dialysis techs, Nua—a Samoan kid who looked like he could have played nose tackle for the Raiders—told Ennis that it was Toni, their clinic manager, with the children's choir from her church. They were there to sing for the patients, a clinic Christmas tradition Toni started two years before, when her son and daughter sang in the choir.

Ennis squinted at the passel of children forming rank behind her. Judging by their brown faces, the Fortiers must have been the only white family in the parish. He shivered and pulled his ratty woolen blanket to his neck and drew his arms beneath it and closed his eyes. The last thing he needed was to be serenaded by grade schoolers singing "Jingle Bells." He was full of kidney toxins and felt like crap. *And* he was cold. For that he blamed the nurses, who had gotten the upper hand in the daily thermostat war. Dialysis nurses were in constant motion and wore scrubs and gowns and masks and gloves that made them hot, so they liked the room cool. Dialysis patients, on the other hand, sat still as stones for hours and were anemic and cold to begin with, so they liked the room warm. That particular day, probably because Toni—whose clinic credo was *Patients First*—was preoccupied with her warbling brood of Mexicans and Filipinos, her staff had turned the place into an igloo.

He opened his eyes halfway through their first song, "Joy to the World." The little twerps were pretty good. Really good, their sweet soprano voices in perfect harmony. The next number, "Silent Night," sounded as good as the first, if not better. He glanced around the room. Thirty of the sickest people imaginable, sallow and wasted from end stage renal disease, had forgotten they were ill. Not a lick of distress on a single face. Only delight, as if their dialysis water had been spiked with Christmas cheer. They kept it up for fifteen minutes without missing a note before coming to a song that sent Ennis straight back to Toledo, when he was no older than the carolers in front of him and the ground outside was white with snow and the tree his father had cut and trimmed was redolent of pine and sticky with sap. It was his father's favorite Christmas song.

> *Hark! the herald angels sing*
> *Glory to the newborn King.*

He jerked upright in his chair to get a better look at the choir, which by now he was so admiring of, they might as well have been the Mormon Tabernacle Choir. The rapture inside him grew with every bar. He felt light and airy, as if gliding along beside the herald angels themselves — whatever herald angels were. Like town criers, maybe. Or news anchors.

> *Peace on earth and mercy mild,*
> *God and sinners reconciled.*

He grew wistful and longed to see his father again, the way he was when Ennis was little. Before he put on a dress and broke his father's heart.

> *Joyful all ye nations rise,*
> *Join the triumph of the skies.*

He had never felt so transported before. So mystical and... unmoored. As if he were up in the sky looking down, triumphant and glorious. But something was wrong. The children fell out of focus and stopped singing. Toni, whom he had yet to even meet, was coming over to him. Fast, like Flash in the comic books, one minute leading the choir, the next at his side, yanking his blanket off and talking in tongues.

"Shut off his blood pump," she said, "and put him in Trendelenberg!"

A pond of blood covered his trousers, enough to swim in. One of his needles lay floating in it, spewing blood out the tip. He must have dislodged it from his fistula when he sat up, but no one saw it because of his blanket.

Toni saw it now. She pointed to his lap, her face taut and flushed. "It's his venous needle, that's why his machine didn't alarm! Reverse his lines and return his blood through his arterial needle!"

Commotion all around, nurses and techs gawking and shouting and scrambling to carry out her orders. Toni reached for his arm to stanch the flow of blood spurting from the puncture site in his fistula left by the dislodged needle. His hand flapped into the lake of blood and splashed her face and the front of her green Christmas dress, matted her hair and coated her brow and glazed her cheeks. She barely blinked, so focused was she, so intent on plugging the hole in his hemorrhaging arm. So single-minded she scared him.

She clamped his forearm between her thumb and fingers and applied such pressure he thought it might snap in two. He'd never met a woman this strong. Was she a nurse or a woman wrestler?

They cranked his chair back until he was head down at a thirty-degree angle. He drifted in and out of consciousness, but in the ambulance on the way to the hospital he wept at the overwhelming goodness he encountered that day: the children in the choir; the terrifying nurse-angel who saved his life; the nobility of purpose of the dialysis clinic. He never again failed to keep his fistula arm visible during dialysis, and never again came to dialysis without a special-made button pinned to his shirt—and later his dress: *Dialysis Nurses Rock!*

He breezed into Victoria's Secret in search of a bra, panties, and hose. The proximity of so much frill and lace gave him gooseflesh, so much gorgeous lingerie to fondle. His sales associate was a bubbly Mexican girl in a silver miniskirt named Jessica Calderon. She had shoulder-length black hair, brown slender legs, and a svelte figure made top-heavy by synthetic boobage. A girl did what she had to do: Jessica stuffed silicon into her breasts; he stuffed his unwieldy male body into clothes intended for Jessica.

He junked his usual charade of shopping for a wife— "Oddly enough, she's exactly the size I am"—and instead leveled with her. "I need a bra, some panties, and thigh-high hose. For me, if you get my drift."

Her smile never cracked. She gave him a quick onceover while he inhaled the musky scent of her perfume. "Do you know your sizes?"

"Thirty-six B on the bra, with padded cups, fourteen on the panties, and a D-size for the stockings."

"Okay. Let's do the bra first. I have just the one in mind."

She discreetly helped him pick out the items he wanted, then hung them in a fitting room to try on when he was ready—meaning whenever he could slip in unobserved. Once inside, he stripped naked and climbed into a banded, lace trim bra with underwire cups and adjustable straps; black cotton panties that, if worn backwards, gave his weenie room to breathe—a trick he learned in trannie group that took advantage of the fact that women's panties were cut larger in back than in front; and a decadent pair of thigh-high, black nylon stockings, with a sexy back seam and lace band on top. He thrilled at the feel of silk and lace against his skin and fantasized about wearing the ensemble with Jessica Calderon, her black pubes and chocolate nipples, but Becky's warning about sexual gratification from cross-dressing short-circuited the stiffie it gave him.

Next he went to the women's shoe department at Macy's. A blond clerk in patent leather shoes and a gray suit with a peach hankie in the breast pocket asked if he needed anything.

"I'd like two pairs of size twelve flats, please, one black and one brown, with no straps and no more than an inch heel."

He had learned the hard way to avoid stiletto heels and ankle straps. Their pointy tips mashed his toes together and his foot slid with each step and gave him blisters. Plus it was hard to find shoes like that in his size—a man's ten, equivalent to a twelve for women.

The clerk swirled his arms and looked perplexed. "For whom are you buying these?"

"For me, that's *whom*." He stuck out his hand. "Ennis Willoughby. I'm a cross-dresser."

A fraternal look lit up the man's face. He gave Ennis's hand an over-exuberant shake. "I'm Troy. Troy Blankenship. I'll take good care of you."

Ennis found the fitting surprisingly enjoyable, thanks to his squeaky clean feet—which left him blissfully free of self-consciousness—and Troy's patience and professionalism. He learned from Troy that the front of a shoe was called a vamp, which Ennis had thought was a sexy woman who snookered men.

Troy sat across from him on a leather stool, with Ennis's bare foot propped on a slant board between them. Troy paused with a shoe in his hand and gave a bashful smile. "I hope you don't mind my asking, but I'm dying of curiosity about something."

"Shoot," Ennis said.

Troy glanced over his shoulder, then leaned forward and spoke in a hushed voice. "When did you know you were transgender? I knew I was gay when I was twelve. I, uh, thought about penises when I jerked off."

Ennis flushed and looked around to see if anyone had heard him. "That's what you might say, too much information there, Troy. I guess I knew the first time I put on a dress. I didn't really think about it like that, though. I just knew I liked it."

Troy put down the shoe and sat upright on the slantboard, his voice no longer hushed. "But *why* did you like it? What's the payoff?"

For some reason, Ennis had expected gays to be more knowledgeable about cross-dressing than most people, but that didn't seem to be the case with Troy. "Wearing a dress *is* the payoff."

Troy frowned and fussed with his hankie. "When you wear a dress, do you want sex with a man?"

The intense look on Troy's face made him uncomfortable. He put his hands up, as if motioning a car going in reverse to stop. "Whoa, whoa, Bucko. It's all women for me, no matter what I'm wearing, blue jeans or a blue bonnet."

Troy got it, eventually, the difference between a man dressing like a woman and a man wanting to be with another man. He apologized for being so nosy by knocking forty percent off the bill. Ennis left with two pairs of Nine West peep-toe flats, one black and one tan, with a three-quarter inch rubber heel and a leather flower at the vamp.

He moved on to women's apparel for a dress. A middle-aged woman with tired eyes and wide hips who called herself Persian—like that was going to fool him into thinking she came from someplace besides Iran—walked him through a number of fittings without so much as raising a waxed eyebrow. Sales commissions worked wonders when it came to tolerance. He settled on an Ann Klein long sleeve with a high collar and smashing pink-and-black pattern, size 16 L: snug at his broad male shoulders, but billowing at the waist, with plenty of slack to conceal his dearth of womanly curves.

He stripped to his briefs inside the fitting room and pulled the dress over his head. It was a lot of money, but he never before had the confidence to choose such a refined, tasteful, elegant piece of clothing. Becky's influence, for sure. He pictured himself at dinner at Kuriyama's, and couldn't resist seeing how the dress looked on him in the three-way mirror outside the fitting room. He tiptoed out and eased barefoot onto the riser in front of the mirror. It hung just right on him. The only other item required would be wads of tissue paper to stuff into his bra to give Elaine some bosom. He exhaled with relief and twirled in front of the mirror.

A sour-faced woman with two little boys in tow wandered by. She wore a green-and-white button on her blouse that said Peace Now and black leggings that were too tight for her heavy thighs. Probably ate arugula and did Pilates, then snuck over to In-N-Out Burger on the way home. One of the boys pointed at him with a wide-eyed look on his face.

"Mommy, mommy! That man is wearing a dress! Is he a clown?"

The woman seemed unaware that Ennis was watching in the mirror and listening to every word. The other boy broke free from her grasp.

"I want to see the clown!"

He took two steps before she caught hold of him and wrenched him back under her wing. "Never, ever go near men who dress like women! They steal little children and hurt them. They're bad, bad men!"

She dragged them away, but the taller one looked over his shoulder and waved. Ennis made eye contact in the mirror and waved back—like a sad clown in the circus. He watched them disappear and looked at himself again. The confident woman of moments before was gone. In her place was a clown in a dress. He felt his old demon self-hatred slip his chains, but this time he was ready for him, with that prayer the alchies used.

God grant me the serenity to accept the things I cannot change, the courage to change the things I can, and the wisdom to know the difference.

Society would never accept him the way he wanted. But it didn't matter. He stepped off the riser mouthing aloud the words Becky had taught him. "Though we may search the world over for the beautiful, we find it within or we find it not."

The Persian woman appeared at his elbow. "Is anything the matter, sir? Are you upset about something?"

He smiled and told her to ring up the dress.

The next day, Ennis rolled his Impala to a stop in front of a handsome home in a neighborhood of gargantuan houses on undersized lots. His heart—her heart—beat a furious rhythm. A mishmash of feelings surged inside him, like a swollen river breaching its banks. For an instant he experienced things inside out, from Carla's perspective: the shock of her youthful organs landing in an old, battered body; her yearning for her children; her regret. Of what? Dying prematurely? Or her heart and kidney going to a cross-dresser? It made him anxious. Powerful anxious.

Logan MacGregor had warned him to stay away from Carla's family, but there was no way that was going to happen. Ennis had called Duncan MacGregor anyway, and now here he was, at Duncan's invitation. He headed up an Italian Cypress-lined walk to a French Mediterranean with cream-colored stucco, a clay tile roof, and a pair of mature Robellinis guarding the entry. A six-foot stucco wall latticed by climbing espaliers bounded the back and side yards. The home and surrounding area struck him as a little rich for a secretary and a bill collector. He paused on the stoop with his gut in a knot and the heady smell of jasmine in his nostrils. The gift he brought, a Seiko quartz clock in a glass case, shook in his hand, his trembling made all the worse by the Prograf he was on. A minor drug side effect, transplant had told him. Doctor Brodie said a side effect was minor when somebody else had it; when you had it, it was major.

He rang the bell and tried to slow his breathing. A chubby redhead with freckled cheeks and a warm, vulnerable face opened the door. "Are you Ennis?"

His stomach fluttered. He stuck out his hand. The man stepped forward and hugged him instead. "I'm Duncan. I'm glad you found us. This is special for us. Really special."

Ennis had been called many things in his life, but special wasn't one of them. He embraced Duncan with his free arm and closed his eyes to the plangent hum of a mower next door. He felt like he was falling down a mineshaft.

"I'm sorry," he said. "I'm really sorry."

Duncan took a step back, puzzled. "For what?"

"Because I lived and your wife didn't."

Duncan shook his head. "She wanted you to live. That's why she was an organ donor." He wrapped an arm around Ennis's shoulder. "Come inside. I want you to meet our children."

They passed through a small foyer into a living room packed with furniture Becky would have liked. Duncan seated him on a thick-cushioned mauve chair with three-quarter arms and caster legs and excused himself to fetch the children. He returned with two well-behaved girls, Loni and Cassidy, ages six and seven, and one rambunctious boy — Luke, five. Loni had her father's red hair; the other two took after their mother. The girls were dressed in ruffled dresses, one pink and one blue. Luke wore khakis and a green and white plaid shirt. Duncan and his children sat across from Ennis on a plush white couch, Luke on his right, the girls on his left. A glass coffee table cluttered with porcelain figurines fronted the sofa. Duncan eased a leather-bound photo album onto one corner of it.

The children eyed him. Luke fidgeted and looked over at Ennis. "My mom gave you her heart," he said, in the trusting way of a child, but not completely so. More like, *My mom gave you her heart, so what are you gonna do about it?*

Loni put an index finger to her lips and shushed him. Cassidy told him he was rude. Duncan tousled his head and grinned. "That's Luke for you."

Ennis felt warm inside. "She sure did, little fella. And her kidney, too. Your mama saved my life. And I'm here to thank you for sharing her with me." He looked at each girl, then Duncan. "All of you."

Luke stuck his chest out. Loni stroked her hair and smiled. Duncan nudged her. "You're welcome," she said. "You're welcome," Cassidy echoed, after a look from Duncan, who nodded, but said nothing.

He didn't have to. The relief on his face made Ennis realize that in his small, pathetic way, he had given something important to Carla's bereaved children. Because of him, Ennis Willoughby, a no-account, cross-dressing, retired painter, their mother's sudden, unexpected death would never be a cruel, random thing, the fickle indifference of God. His mere presence gave her death meaning—she died so another could live. Meaning: the only thing that made life bearable, made all the pain and misery and loss and humiliation worthwhile.

One by one they came to him, touched him, sat on his lap and told him things: her pet names for them; the games they played together; favorite places she took them; the prayers they said for her at night.

How much they missed her.

Something inside him whispered. *I love you, my darlings. I love you.* But there was a whisper of regret, too, her stubborn lingering in the human world. She wanted to be with them. It was as simple as that.

A slant of light filtered through a nearby alcove's stained glass window as if raining down the nave of a church. He opened his shirt and let them finger his scar. They had the most generous, selfless, kind mother in the whole world, he told them, and she lived inside him now. They believed him, and it filled him with joy. With meaning.

They visited with him a while longer before heading off to play. Luke cleared the room last, with an odd waddle to his gait.

"I see Luke has a little hitch in his giddy-up, there."

Worry lines creased Duncan's face. "It showed up about a month ago. His pediatrician says it's from a lack of blood to the ball of his hip. She prescribed a course of physical therapy that seems to be helping. They're doing some more tests, but she thinks he'll eventually outgrow it."

He disappeared into the kitchen and returned with two glasses of chilled white wine and a bowl of loquats. Ennis took a sip of wine and told Duncan about dreaming Carla's name and the taste for beets and sushi he'd acquired.

"Doc Brodie is, what you might say, a skeptic about it. He says taste buds change after transplant and patients can develop new food cravings from steroids. As for knowing her name, it turns out there are quite a few cases of patients remembering conversations during surgery, because they're not all the way under from anesthesia. He thinks the surgical team inadvertently mentioned Carla's name in the OR. None of that explains why I like jazz, though. It used to annoy me. Now I listen to it all the time."

Duncan sagged against the cushions and softly whistled. "Carla loved beets and sushi—and jazz. What are the odds of liking three specific things your donor liked that you didn't like before transplant? *And* of overhearing your donor's name in the OR from insufficient anesthesia? I know millions of people like beets and sushi and jazz, but it seems like a lot of coincidence to me."

It occurred to Ennis—because it would have occurred to Becky—that Duncan might be as desperate for contact with Carla as he was. Projection, Becky would call it, the grieving husband projecting his desire to be reunited with his dead wife onto Ennis, making him into a vessel to channel her spirit. No different than going to a séance or fooling with a Ouija Board. Ennis Willoughby, medium extraordinaire. But Becky was an atheist and Dr. Brodie, too, he suspected. Human afterlife to them was about on par with the afterlife of a pair of Goodyears. Dead tire people, Ennis called them. That was the problem with being overeducated—all knowledge, no wisdom.

He plucked a loquat from the bowl and held it aloft. "All this talk about taste buds has got me hankering to bite into one of these." A silky explosion of peach and mango rinsed his mouth. Doc was right: your taste buds did change after transplant. Everything changed. He spit the seed into a napkin and pointed at the photo album.

"Are those pictures of her?"

Duncan reached for it and nodded. "Come over and have a look."

His heart took off and his hand tremor kicked up again. He stood and made his way around the coffee table—carefully. All he needed was to knock over one of the porcelain fairies and break it. They had to be hers, Lladros collected piece by piece, each of deep personal significance. His head thrummed from the eagerness he felt to lay eyes on her—the real Carla, candid Carla, revealed the way only family photos could.

He sat next to Duncan and drank his wine and stared transfixed at a slowly turning compendium of Carla

MacGregor's life: wedding photos; their honeymoon in Tahiti; profiles of her swollen, pregnant belly; holding a baby in her arms; dressed as a witch on Halloween, her skin green, her lips black, her snarl adorably wicked; at her desk at Nephrology Partners, cool and efficient in navy blue; standing over the stove in sweatpants, a lock of hair in her eyes; with her children and Goofy in front of Sleeping Beauty Castle at Disneyland. Telling pictures that made him want to shout with joy. This woman inside him, he knew her now, was part of her family!

He peeked at Duncan, who had gone silent with the album open in his hands.

"She got up early that day to drop the children off at my father's while I slept in. We were going to spend the day together, have lunch at the beach, walk along the ocean. Hold hands. She never made it back. I never kissed her goodbye."

Ennis bowed his head and picked at the cushion beneath him. A stab of shame pierced him. His joy was this man's grief. He struggled to quell his guilt.

"I want you to know that a piece of your wife's soul is inside me." He thumped his chest. "Here. Right here."

Duncan pressed his ear over Ennis's heart and kept it there. Ennis's chest rose and fell, rose and fell, a whistle in his nostrils the only sound. Until Duncan began to cry. He felt as if his new heart might break in half. He cried, too, a real chest-rattler Becky would have been proud of. Oh, he was in touch with his emotions now. He was authentic now.

Duncan collected himself and gathered their empty glasses and went into the kitchen. Ennis blew his nose and wiped his eyes and stood in the middle of the room. Duncan returned with refills and they separated to neutral corners, Duncan on the edge of the couch, Ennis slouched in the chair. The wine in his glass pitched back and forth, kissing the rim.

"You wouldn't know it from the photos," Duncan said, "but we had our share of troubles. Everyone does."

Ennis liked looking at Carla and imagining things about her—good things, perfect things. She was his donor, his hero, the woman of his dreams. He didn't really want to hear about her marital problems.

"I wanted to quit working for my father and go to culinary school in San Francisco, where Carla was from. She refused to even consider it. She was too attached to our lifestyle—our home, the children's private school, the predictable incomes we had." He waved his hand in a grand swirl. "All of it thanks to my father."

He confessed that he resented his dependence on his father, who had given them their jobs with Nephrology Partners, paid their children's tuition, and made a sizable down payment on their home. He called his family Clan MacGregor, because it functioned like a fifteenth-century Scottish tribe—a well-intentioned but stifling patriarchy, made worse by the death of his mother, Catherine, seven years before, from multiple sclerosis.

"Carla and I fought over it all the time. 'I want to go to culinary school,' I told her one night after dinner.' She clenched her jaw and kept on swabbing the countertops. 'And what will you do after culinary school?' she asked me. 'Open my own restaurant,' I said. She looked at me the way she did Luke when he said something stupid. 'Our children go to private school. We own a home in a good neighborhood. Why would we risk all that on a restaurant?'"

The peeved wife expression on his face was comical, but the way he imitated Carla's voice irked Ennis.

"I tried to tell her that Clan MacGregor wasn't all it was cracked up to be, that the MacGregors were known in Scotland as Children of the Mist for the way they disappeared into the Highland fog after a night of mayhem and thievery, but she didn't think I was funny. Her mind was made up."

He assumed her persona again, the nattering voice and affected feminine manner. "'How would you have us live? With the smell of burnt cooking coming under the door of our rent-controlled apartment? With our children in public schools run by teachers that can't be found past two in the afternoon? You should be grateful your father helps us.'"

It was beginning to tick Ennis off, this sullying of his angel. He shouldn't have drunk so much wine.

Duncan snorted a sarcastic laugh, the wine getting to him, too, it seemed. "She conveniently forgot that my father initially opposed our marriage. She didn't have the pedigree he was hoping for. But it finally dawned on him that Carla meant more MacGregors, and since I wasn't exactly a babe magnet, in the end he was relieved I found someone to marry me."

He raised his glass and toasted her vapors. "You buried my dream of being a chef, but I love you. God how I love you."

Was this Carla's regret? Snuffing out Duncan's dreams in exchange for material wealth? Was this the reason she couldn't move on, couldn't recycle her *ti bon ange* the way it was meant to be recycled?

Their conversation lightened and wound down and they ended the afternoon on the best of terms. Ennis swagged down the front walk a half hour later in high spirits, dead bang certain that Elaine would never again mount a rejection of Carla's organs. Not after what she learned today. Carla was like she was: flawed, but magnificent, in the way all women were magnificent. They were sisters now. Gal pals.

It was time to celebrate. The drab days were over.

That night at Kuriyama's, Ennis refreshed his lipstick before ordering dessert. He rolled a new application of Red Revival Maybelline onto each lip, stuck his index finger into his mouth, and puckered on it before slowly withdrawing. Transferring the excess from lips to finger and keeping it off his teeth. Details mattered.

His waiter returned to take his dessert order and complimented him on his pink-and-black speckled dress. He fluttered his lashes and thanked him.

He had never felt like such a lady.

Chapter 14

THE WHITE AND BLUE game ball arced cleanly through the white net of the goal. Angela clapped and yelled for Kelani, who sank the shot from the shooting circle on the left end of the court. Makea Taputu squeezed Angela's elbow and grinned. His burnished face was worry-free and he wore no hat, despite the fierce sun beating down on Avatiu's weathered netball court.

"My daughter is having a good day. A good day! Someday she be like Angela Maote in '95. Make Cook Island people proud!"

Angela returned his grin and pounded her fist against the mound of his shoulder. "Make her daddy proud!"

She leaned around the tee-shirted barrel of his chest and looked beneath the brim of her straw hat at Ritua, standing to the right of her husband in a blue mu'mu with green palm fronds on it. Clouds swirled like the breath of gods over the green cordillera jutting behind her in backdrop. Ritua thrust her fist thrust in the air and shouted, *"Ae! Ae!"*

Angela cupped a hand to her mouth. "I'm so proud of her!"

Ritua looked at her and gave a restrained nod. *"Meitaki. Meitaki ma'ata."* Thank you. Thank you very much. She exaggerated the Maori glottal stop between vowel sounds even more than usual. Gracious, but cool. Mistrusting.

Angela had walked from her gallery to take in the Saturday club match between Kelani's Titikaveka side and Avatiu at the netball court alongside Avatiu Harbor. A dozen or so sailboats lay at anchor, their naked masts stark and white. Brightly colored skiffs moored along the western jetty swayed to the lazy rhythm of the tide, while on the port's eastern side, beneath a pair of white terns banking toward the reef, a hulking green-and-white inter-island trading vessel was lashed to the bollards of the harbor's sun-bleached wharf.

The Titikaveka girls wore red skirts with white tops, the Avatiu side navy skirts and gold tops. Kelani's position bib lay across her chest with the letters GA emblazoned in red, identifying her position as Goal Attack, one of two primary scorers—along with Goal Shooter—on her seven-player team. She flashed a mouthful of straight white teeth at her cheering section. Pure Polynesian joy graced her classic *tama'ine* face, her broad nose and round cheeks, her long eyebrows and dark eyes. Her hair fell to mid-spine, a flow of black lava restrained by a red Nike headband. She had thick, powerful legs like her father, but her arms and torso were long and slender, like her mother. She was the best shot on the team and had wonderful ball skills, with the superb hand-eye coordination all Cook Islanders seemed to have.

Angela had never heard of netball until she came to Rarotonga. Invented in the 1890s as an English offshoot of basketball, it caught on in the Cook Islands about the time she arrived. Netball, she had been surprised to learn, was the world's most popular team game for women. And no wonder: it demanded female skills, cooperation and teamwork, all passing and no dribbling, a non-contact sport where defenders stood three feet from the player they were guarding—in contrast to the chest-bumping belligerence of basketball, netball's male progenitor. Basketball was an American game, full of brash pride—as she had once been an American girl, full of conceit. Fatal conceit.

Ritua was jealous of Angela's relationship with Kelani, whom Angela met nine years before, when Kelani was a precocious eight-year-old in the art class she volunteered to teach at the local school in Titikaveka. Angela was drawn to her from the start, an instant maternal attraction to her trusting Polynesian face. It was a vulnerable time for Angela, her mid-forties, with her sexual desirability on the wane and her last viable eggs shriveled like raisins. She grasped at Kelani to fill the void, reached out to her—seduced her—to ease her remorse over the one thing in life she regretted more than Dempsey Fagan: relinquishing her only child for adoption.

She didn't know it, but by the time she slept with Dempsey, she was already pregnant with Cullen's baby. The abortionist's daughter had become careless with her birth control pills. She at first paid little heed to the period she missed, but after Planned Parenthood in Laguna Beach—where she fled after Leslie's suicide, drawn by its burgeoning art colony—confirmed she was pregnant, she declined their offer to "take care of her problem" and carried her fetus to term instead. Because it wasn't a problem, she decided. It was a life. A precious, miraculous, human life.

But not one she could provide for. She knew the grim statistics that awaited children from single-parent families by rote: her father cited them all the time. Her child deserved a stable, two-parent home, not a déclassé young mother trying to outrun her shame. So she surrendered her daughter to the county adoption agency without laying eyes on her and left for the Cook Islands a week later, a shattered twenty-one-year old who couldn't bear to *be* Angie Nichols anymore. Two years would pass before she found the wherewithal to even call her parents to let them know she was alive. By then her father was a hopeless drunk and her mother lay dying of breast cancer. She went back for the funeral, but didn't stay.

She waved at Kelani and smiled reassuringly at Ritua. The older woman had nothing to fear from Angela. Kelani was giving them both the slip, leaving childhood and adolescence behind—and Rarotonga, too—for the University of Auckland, courtesy of a netball scholarship. But it made her sad and more than a little afraid. Her years with Kelani had been a liniment to her soul. Their cross-island treks and picnic lunches; languid afternoons snorkeling near Angela's home; intimate hours spent in her atelier, teaching Kelani to limn and color a landscape—and sketch her imaginary trousseau chest. Kelani helped her through the worst of her depression and anxiety, sleepless nights wracked by compunction and regret over forfeiting the joy of motherhood. A joy Angela partially reclaimed by poaching on another woman's family.

Ritua's mistrust of her began on the first Ash Wednesday after Angela converted to Catholicism. She attended Mass early that day at St. Joseph's Cathedral, a single-level stone building with a white-pillared portico on Ara Tapu, halfway between Avatiu Harbor and the traffic circle. Angela advanced through the queue at the end of the service and presented herself to Bishop O'Connell, a gaunt, gray-haired man standing at the foot of the altar in vestment and miter. He dipped his bony right thumb into a silver urn filled with a slurry of holy water-and-ash and imposed the Sign of the Cross on her forehead.

The ashes he smudged there—made of burnt palms from the previous year's Palm Sunday—remained all day, during which she fasted and abstained from meat as a sign of repentance. Ritua stopped by her gallery that afternoon with Kelani, their foreheads similarly marked with ash by the Cook Islands Christian Church, the dominant congregation of Rarotonga. Angela's previous indifference to religion had been a sore point with Ritua, so when she saw Angela's forehead, her rough-hewn face opened into a broken-toothed smile. Angela told them she joined the

Catholic Church. Ritua clasped her by the elbow and congratulated her; Kelani asked if she could attend mass at St. Joseph's with her to see what Catholic services were like. Ritua turned Angela loose and crossed her arms and scowled. *"Ko taku tama`ine teia.* This is my daughter." Her dark, smoldering eyes never left Angela's. "She go to my church." Art lessons were one thing. Sampling Angela's religion was quite another.

Angela's spiritual journey to even get to that day had not been an easy one. The Nichols household was a religion-free zone by the time she and Leslie hit adolescence. She held her father responsible for their de facto atheism—and the annus horribilis that came later. Yes, Chaz Brodie started things off when he slashed her painting, but he did it in a towering rage over her father's chosen line of work: extinguishing the unborn. Her father's choice to abort fetuses had consequences: her vengeful sex with Dempsey, Cullen's retaliatory sex with Leslie, Grady's death, Leslie's suicide, Angela's relinquishment of her baby, her father's collapse into alcoholism. That's the way it worked. Immoral choices led to devastating consequences. Because that's what morality was: the way human beings treated one another. The capacity to make moral choices was what made humans different from animals.

A distinction she unfortunately spent years learning. Soon after arriving on Rarotonga, she indulged in a prolonged bout of youthful hedonism that numbed her for a while, but later yielded to an infatuation with the ancient concept of *aroa* and a pre-Christian god named *Tangaroa-o-Avaiki*—Tangaroa, the mythical father of Polynesia and only Polynesian god to have persisted in any meaningful way in the lives of contemporary Rarotongans. She found much to admire in ancient Rarotongan theology and culture: reverence for the sea, respect for the forest and mountains, liberal sexual mores, appreciation of human beauty, the wearing of scented flowers, the use of coconut oil to give sheen and luster to skin, sensual dancing, and the drinking of *kava*, a mild narcotic prepared from pepper shrub roots. But the less savory aspects of the Code of Tangaroa—idolatry, cannibalism, polygamy, and tribal warfare—left her disenchanted. Her spiritual inquiry led next to pantheism and nature-worship, an easy transition to make in the South Pacific. But nature was neither moral nor immoral; it was amoral. The rules of morality had to come from something that was not only moral, but good. Goodness itself: God. God and the Ten Commandments. What Angela craved was absolution—from someone with the chops to give it. Her need to be shriven drove her to Catholicism and months of catechism under the direction of Bishop O'Connell, who heard her first confession, confirmed her, administered her first communion, and dusted her forehead that first Ash Wednesday.

"Angela! Angela!"

A voice behind her startled her. She turned away from the netball court and spun around to see who was calling her.

It was Ty's fourteen-year-old granddaughter, Taira, wide-eyed and beaded with sweat. Dark stains dampened the neck of the blue and orange cotton dress she wore. She put her hands on her knees and panted, appearing to have run the entire half-mile from Avarua Fine Arts, where she worked for Angela part-time, to Avatiu Harbor. She caught her breath and straightened up and told Angela that an American named Cullen Brodie was in the gallery demanding to see her.

Angela put her hands to her mouth and gasped.

The Air New Zealand flight bearing Cullen to the Cook Islands announced its final approach into Rarotonga

International Airport. Jet-lagged flight attendants with morning-face and plumeria petals in their hair passed through the cabin collecting empty coffee cups. He raised the back of his seat to upright and popped his ears as the plane banked and descended. A solid mass of blue loomed out the window, a confluence of sky and sea, no land yet visible.

He pulled a worn piece of paper from his shirt pocket and stared at the name in the contact box he printed off the website.

Avarua Fine Arts
Angela Masters, Proprietor

Angela Masters, the pseudonym she used at Art Rampage the day his antinomian father went berserk and cut her painting to ribbons. Chaz was in his eighties now, only a few gray bristles of crew cut remaining, but his zeal for God and beer intact.

What did it mean? That she was single? Divorced? Or married and painting under a different name? And why *that* name, the one she used the day Chaz's zealotry launched the fatal cascade that undid them all? Except Chaz, who got away more or less scot-free. And why, after all these years, had Angie contacted him in such a morbid way, Grady bound and floating like a martyr? A Christian martyr.

He scripted what he would say when he saw her, searching for a clever *mot juste* to set them both at ease. A sudden hum of conversation interrupted his thoughts, a caffeinated murmur sweeping the cabin. He looked out his window, shocked by what he saw, the primal beauty of the real thing superior in every way to the Eden he had imagined.

Rarotonga rose out of the sea like cut emerald, its jutting ridges and plunging slopes tufted dark green, like a head of broccoli. Waves of blue spumed over an encircling reef, drawing a white lasso around an aquamarine lagoon that girded the entire island. Whitewashed homes and villages stippled a narrow coastal plain, a glorious diorama that made him grateful such a place even existed. A reverent hush fell over the cabin, like an awed crowd in front of a famous painting.

They descended onto a dun-colored airstrip cut into the island's northern piedmont, west of a diamond-shaped harbor. Cullen weathered their uneven landing and a short, bumpy cab ride into Avarua, capital city of the Cook Islands. It seemed barely a town, several blocks of haphazard shops and restaurants and bars on either side of a traffic circle next to a small harbor. Swarms of motorbikes and a congeries of tinny-looking cars flowed British-style over well-maintained asphalt streets, driving on the left-hand side of the road.

His first concern was getting a driver's license, at the Cook Islands Police National Headquarters, west of the traffic circle. It was the most contemporary structure in town, a two-story building of gray stone and smoked glass, with the national flag waving from a pole outside the entrance — a blue ensign with the Union Jack in the upper left corner, and a circle of fifteen white stars — one for each island — in the upper right. The license cost him ten New Zealand dollars and was good for one year. A polite clerk with curly strawberry hair and a freckled face and smeared lipstick — who called him mate — wrote out directions to Avarua Fine Arts, located two blocks east of the traffic circle on Ara Maire Nui, the main drag that became on either end of town the circle-island road known as Ara Tapu. He stuffed the directions into his jeans and went outside and inhaled a fragrant blast of Polynesia, exotic scents of unknown flowers and fruits riding currents of warm tropical air.

He rented a car at a Budget kiosk—a small, four-door red manual with the steering column on the right—and drove tense and flinching to his hotel on the east side of the island, unable to shake the fear that he was driving down the wrong side of the road. He somehow avoided a crash and pulled into a lush compound with manicured grounds and heavy vegetation. Cook Islanders wearing orange and purple tropical print dresses and orchids in their hair—or, if male, Bermuda shorts and printed shirts of the same coloring—helped at every step of the lengthy check-in process. Each young girl seemed prettier than the next, like fashion models at a luau, graceful and smiling and possessed of an understated sensuality.

A porter with a black moustache and brown calves packed with muscle led him to a beachfront studio overlooking the white sands of Muri Beach and the pale green waters of Muri Lagoon. Two small motus, or mini-islands, sat in the middle of the lagoon, halfway between shore and reef. The blue Pacific lay beyond. His garden-level room was done in burnt orange floor tiles, gold walls, and bamboo furniture. A sliding glass door led to a tree-shrouded veranda, where a white lounge chair with oversized cushions overlooked the beach. He tipped the porter and drew aside the glass door and stepped outside. Combers boomed on the reef and tropical smells a hundred times more pungent and fresh than in Avarua gushed up his nostrils.

He stifled an urge to change into his swimsuit and plunge into the beckoning lagoon and instead unpacked and showered and drove back into town, more comfortable by the minute with left-hand traffic. He parked near the traffic circle and went into a nearby shop to look for a gift for Becky to make amends for jilting her and abruptly leaving for the South Pacific. She could have been more understanding, though. She knew the whole Angie saga and the chance for closure it gave him; the catty way she called Angie his *old* girlfriend was unnecessary.

The gift shop was located inside a crumbling, coral-block building. Variations of the same wooden tiki occupied shelf after shelf: a squat, stern-looking warrior with a high forehead, etched brow, pinned back ears, protuberant belly, wide tread, and enormous phallus, hanging nearly to the ground. Cullen had noticed a statue of the same well-endowed figure in front of a shopping center on his way into town: interesting, but touristy. Not a gift to send to your psychiatrist lover.

A smiling, heavy-set woman with thin blonde hair came out from behind a glass display of pearl earrings and necklaces. She had the face of a fisherwoman, but wore a black sundress with spaghetti straps and a décolletage cut below the tan line of her heavy bosom. A black pearl pendant floated beneath the notch of her neck. She spoke with an Australian accent and introduced herself as Cammie. Her beefy arms and thick middle were too much for her petite-size dress, but the pearl dangling from her neck was of such lustrous beauty it made her look elegant.

"Something particular I might help you find?"

On impulse, he pointed to her pendant. "One of those. It looks wonderful on you."

She fluttered her lids and gave a demure smile, like a debutante being complimented on her gown. "*Poe-parau.* Black pearl. From the black-lipped oyster." She fingered it with a slow, loving touch. "A grain of sand embedded in its flesh provokes the secretion of layers and layers of nacre, until a pearl is formed. The pearls in my shop are cultured in Manihiki, one of our northern islands. They come in many different hues."

She was right. Each of the half-dozen pendants she pulled from the display case bore a different colored pearl:

black, brownish-black, dark brown, peacock green, and green. Cullen settled on a fifteen millimeter, greenish-black beauty that was as close to round as he could find, offset by eighteen-carat gold in a necklace of black neoprene. He had no idea what it cost, but he wasn't buying a whole string— only a bead. How much could it be? Five or six hundred, he guessed. Eight tops. It turned out to be more. Much more: one thousand, nine hundred fifty New Zealand dollars.

He gave her his credit card and noticed a dramatic painting on the wall behind her, a massive cloudbank hovering over a lagoon, with a shock of pink illuminating a strip of horizon visible between the roiled waters of the lagoon and black swirl of the storm above. His throat tightened at the brushwork and shading of the water, the *jamais vu* it provoked. His eyes fell to the artist's signature: Angela Masters, in the same flowery hand as the painting she had sent to him. "*Ohh,*" he uttered.

"Magnificent, isn't it?" Cammie asked. "It's called *Storm over Titikaveka at Sunset.* One of our locals painted it. You should stop by and see her gallery. It's only a short walk from here. She's one of the most beloved artists in the South Pacific."

She put the box containing the necklace into a gold gift bag with white handles and a string of black pearls embossed on its sides. A jolt ran through him as he took it, decades of pent-up emotion. He held the bag aloft and waggled it.

"I hope she likes black pearls."

Avarua Fine Arts occupied all of a one-level, chalk-white building with a thatched roof, arched windows, and pair of wooden doors with iron knockers. Cullen would learn later that it was one of several historic coral-block buildings erected by the London Missionary Society. It took him fifteen minutes of pleading and cajoling to persuade the skeptical teenager minding the gallery—a stubborn island girl named Taira—that she needed to get her employer on the premises as soon as possible. She scrutinized with wrinkled brow his newly issued Cook Island driver's license, his passport, and even his medical license before she entrusted the gallery to him and hurried off to fetch her boss.

Dozens of oils and acrylics illuminated by track lighting lined the gallery's textured walls; several brightly upholstered armchairs were scattered across its glossy wooden floor. A sleek computer screen and black keyboard sat on a glass counter opposite the front entrance. Behind the counter, an open doorway led to a cluttered studio.

Cullen paced the gallery with his gift bag in hand, scanning first one wall and then another. All of the pieces were Polynesian in theme and of the highest quality. There were landscapes of Rarotonga's verdant mountains and flaming vegetation, colorful abstracts evoking the South Pacific, young women in pareos, wizened fisherman trolling the sea, a breaching whale, children at play in a lagoon, and shimmering fish hovering over spectacular formations of coral.

He lingered at a canvas that drew him in, hoping to descry the artist through her work. It was a treatment of feminine mystique, island style, a topless girl on all fours at the edge of a transparent lagoon, her shoulders squared to sea. Her full, round backside was clothed in a wet sarong that clung to her buttocks. Her hands sifted for shells to put in a hemp bag beside her. Finely pebbled sand marked the foreground of the painting, a caramel strip of shoreline. Her straight dark hair hung almost to the water, and her right breast was three-quarters visible: an island goddess of surpassing beauty, captured by an artist once possessed of the same. The last time he saw her was at Art Rampage. His vision of what he lost that day remained vivid and true: Angie in a painter's smock and jeans, holding a brush in one hand and smoothing her swirl of raven hair with the other, a black panther of a girl whose every unfurling movement enthralled him. She was like a rare Bordeaux, the product of a freakish harvest producing a once in a lifetime varietal that left all who came after wanting by comparison.

The gallery doors flew open. Sunlight stabbed the floor. His old lover ploughed across the threshold and stopped ten feet in front of him. She blinked at him, open-mouthed, as if seeing a long-lost Greek monument, dumbstruck it had withstood the ravages of time. The gift bag fell from his hand. His eyes locked onto her in an unslakable stare. Cullen, too, found words incapable of expressing the shock he felt.

A white sunhat with a green band at the crown dipped low on her face. Black hair washed over her bare, elegant shoulders, its volume half of the luxurious mane he remembered. She wore a strapless, black print dress patterned with white and green plumeria that fell to her knees and flattered her body, her full bosom, her arresting sweep of hip. Loose folds of flesh hung from her arms and veins lined her calves. Her pedicured feet, clad in black rubber thongs, looked oddly younger than her legs.

He peered at her in wonder. The gorgeous young art student he had fallen in love with had found an artist of her own, a plastic surgeon whose gifted hand had somehow preserved the natural structure of her face—the sculpted cheekbones and delicately tapered nose—even while etching a timeless veneer. Tiny webs of wrinkles at the corners of her eyes added a touch of realism to her canvas, the look of an aging queen who has known great sorrow.

He walked over to her and got down on his knees and took her sun-spotted hand and kissed it. He felt a surge of ruthless joy at the bareness of her tanned, arthritic fingers that wore no ring. The silence between them persisted, neither daring to disrespect it.

She pulled him to his feet and studied his face as if it held the answer to an ancient riddle, the vivid green brilliance of her eyes undiminished by time. After a moment—a long, fraught moment—she rubbed her palm against the two-day stubble of his cheek and took his hand and led him across the room, the slapping of her thongs and squeaking of his shoes the only sounds. He stooped and snatched his fallen gift bag along the way.

They walked around the glass counter and through the doorway behind it into her atelier. Open shelves filled with tubes and bottles and cans of solvent were stacked above countertops littered with wooden boxes and plastic containers. A small sink with a mirror above it sat beside an array of cleaning supplies: a can of turpentine, a sponge, a pumice stone, and a stack of hand towels. On his left, a high-backed maroon swivel chair was pulled up to a wooden drafting table sloped at an angle. A square of thick white paper secured at the corners with masking tape covered most of the table. There was a back door—her secret exit?—and two sliding glass windows for ventilation. The wooden floor beneath him was unvarnished and scuffed. An artist's stool stationed in front of an easel occupied one corner of the room, with a trove of paints and brushes and canvases in easy reach.

She closed the door and opened the windows. A change of clothes hung from a hook on the door, a pair of shorts and a gray sweatshirt spattered with paint. She opened the hot water tap and rolled the chair in front of the sink and nudged him into it. Had she gone mute? Maybe there was too much to say.

He put the gift bag next to him and watched in the mirror as she gathered some things from a cabinet and laid them beside the sink. She wet a towel beneath the spigot and gently wrung it out, then eased him back in the chair and applied it to his face. Its soothing warmth briefly distracted him from the peculiarity of the moment. He turned his head. She had a black, straightedge razor in her hand, poised in the air.

She grabbed a leather strop chained to a towel bar near the sink and pulled it taut. She pressed the razor flat against it and ran the razor down the length of the strop, then flipped it over and reversed motion the other way. The razor emitted a crisp, metallic swoosh with each practiced stroke of her hand.

After twenty or so strokes, the strop fell from her hand and she plucked a hair from her head and drew it over the blade of the razor. It split with a faint popping noise. She set the blade down and removed her hat and shook her hair over her face, messy and sultry. The towel came off of him and she reached for a blue bottle with green lettering on it: Mauke Miracle Oil. She inverted it and squeezed a gout of oil onto her palm and worked it into his beard with both hands, an oil slick in place of shave cream. She saturated his cheeks and neck with long, sensuous strokes, an enchantress prepping him for sacrifice with an unctuous, fragrant potion of gardenias and coconut. He quivered beneath the satin touch of her hand.

She bent over him with the straightedge. Her lips were red and slightly parted, but he could not read her inscrutable face. Somewhere in the room, a clock ticked. He closed his eyes.

She stretched his skin and took the razor to him. It made a gritty sound as she pulled it across his face in short, sure strokes, then in longer ones. A rush of adrenalin hit him. What they were doing felt dangerous, exhilarating, his throat exposed to the brandished blade of a woman whose life he had ruined. He felt manly, aroused, the love of his youth servicing him in this raw and intimate way, a test of his courage to see if he trusted her to forego her revenge. All conveyed without a word. Through feeling. Emotion. It was brilliant. Inspired.

Poetic.

He opened his eyes. A freshet of tears wet her face and dripped onto his shoulders and chest, three decades of anguish, the crushing sorrow of ill-fated love. She scraped away every last patch of stubble before setting the razor aside and tenderly wiped him with a towel. The great gash in his heart opened anew. He took hold of her arm.

"I never stopped thinking about you."

She pulled away. "You've been thinking about someone who no longer exists."

Angie—he still called her that, but she didn't seem to mind—closed her gallery for the day and took him down the street toward the harbor. Motorbikes and cars and yellow tour buses chugged through the traffic circle. A green spire she called Mount Ikurangi stood watch in the background.

They stopped at another historic coral-block building alongside the wharf, a place called the Black Pearl Bar. It had red saloon doors and sawdust on the floor. Angie waved at the bartender, a leather-faced man with tattoos on both arms and hair that looked like it had been burned by a curling iron. He nodded and pointed to an open booth, where Angie ordered Mai Tais—served the way Cullen liked them, with a garnish of pineapple and an oil spill of dark rum swirling the bottom—and a plate of coconut shrimp. They circled one another like boxers in a ring before tacitly agreeing to avoid for now a brutal rehash of Grady and Leslie, and to instead unpeel the lives they had forged since. At this Cullen was relieved. He was sleep-deprived and jetlagged and would soon be drunk—too combustible a mix for confronting bêtes noires.

They traded his and hers memoirs writ brief. Angie's recounting took them through the shrimp and into an order of fish and chips, accompanied by an indeterminate number of Mai Tais. Cullen's rum-soaked brain struggled to keep it all straight: her Polynesian heritage and the story of the Marsters family of Palmerston Atoll; her decision to run away to the island paradise her mother told her about when she was young; and her early days on Rarotonga, under the protection of a local who befriended her, Ty— short for a Maori name Cullen didn't catch, because he kept falling into her eyes and trying to get over Angie being a woman in her fifties. A strikingly attractive woman in her fifties—albeit with the slightly frozen look of a Botox addict. He heard every word, though, about her father's long demise from alcoholism, which Cullen instantly felt responsible for, the death of her mother, Angie's marriage to a Belgian GP with a nasty prescription narcotic addiction, and her growing acclaim as an artist. He drew more satisfaction than he should have from her divorce and failure to remarry.

They took a bathroom break and reconvened with fresh drinks at an outside table on the wharf. A scrim of stars lit the austral sky and the rhythmic slosh of the harbor lapped the quay beneath them. The warm night air hung thick and still. Angie gave an arch smile from beneath the brim of her hat and talked over a bunch of sunburned, roistering tourists at the table beside them.

"Your turn. By now you should have enough rum in you to tell the truth."

He hoisted his glass and gave a deferential nod. "To truth."

He told her about his promise to make restitution to the dead by ministering to the living; about borrowing and working his way through med school; about keeping the pledge to secrecy she bound him to in her letter; about his residency in Atlanta and marriage to Liz, the resentful anesthesiologist; their move to California to do his nephrology fellowship ("Dialysis and transplantation: serious shit, shit to atone by"); his commitment to send his brothers to Notre Dame ("Trust me, it had nothing to do with Catholicism"); his single years in LA; and the failure of his second marriage.

"What was her name?"

Even his sleep-starved, sodden brain registered her forced smile and feigned cheerfulness—and choice to skip over a quarter century of his life in order to sweetly inquire about wife number two. This was not benign female curiosity at work, oh no. Claws had been unsheathed.

"Janet Winston. It was her second time to the altar, too. We lasted three years. She owned an upscale home-furnishing company with two mega-stores, one in West LA and another in the Valley. She was a natural saleswoman, but driven? I thought I was bad. She lived for business. We entered into a merger, not a marriage." He declined to add that at least she had been his age, though—unlike the decade of bimbos before her.

Angie stirred her glass as if exorcising it. "Maybe you didn't give her enough support. Was she pretty?"

Why had his second marriage set her off so, when mention of his first barely fazed her? A clout of drunken insight knocked him upside the head—drunken insights came no other way. Angie's marriage hadn't bothered him either, but a second one, closer in time to their reunion, would have. He, like Angie, wanted the field clear of competition. In case their old magic could be conjured up again. The intensity. The heat. The ache: their impatience to get at one another, to consume each other. The high it brought, euphoria-inducing catecholamines flooding their limbic systems. The rush of love. He remembered it more than felt it, a love affair three decades and change in abeyance no easy thing to rekindle. Age blunted love's language. Where once his heart bounded at the sight of her, now it merely twitched. It did twitch, though, and with feeling.

"She was handsome, but not beautiful. Not like you."

Her lashes beat a sultry rhythm and a siren's smile crossed her face. The goddess of his youth, calling to him across the years.

He reached inside the gift bag. "I have something for you."

He withdrew the necklace and unclasped it and stretched its black neoprene with either hand. Flanked by stunted ribbons of gold, the huge, globular pearl swung like the clapper of a bell. It mesmerized her, like a hypnotist's watch. "It's beautiful! But it's too extravagant. I can't..."

He cut her off with a fierce look of—what? Insult? Reparation? Love? Whatever, it subdued her. She gathered her hair behind her and raised her chin, exposing her throat—her sleek, smooth, wrinkle-free throat.

She chemical-peeled that, too? What else had she glazed and augmented and lifted? Was there a single part of her left unaltered by a surgeon's knife or dermatologist's potions? For whom was she trying to stay so young? Herself, perhaps, to preserve a vestige of what she had been before Grady died. Before her favored life ended and her haunted one began.

Grady. There would always be that between them. Shared visions of shame, his in a recurring dream, hers in a painting. He laid his palm against her cheek. Lightly, reverently, with compassion for the suffering she had surely endured. The same suffering visited on him. Over a death so cruel and unjust it refuted the God of Abraham's very existence.

He leaned across the table and slipped the pendant around her neck. A glint of silver flashed beneath it, a crucifix on a delicate chain. He took it between his thumb and forefinger.

"Why are you wearing this?"

"Because I converted to Catholicism. Four years ago."

He fell back against his chair and thought of the painting that called him to her, across the Pacific, Grady as a hands-bound martyr, the halo and numinous use of light. It was a religious painting, harking back to the early days of Christian Europe, depicting Grady as a witness of God, an intercessor whose death was a validation of faith. Angie's faith.

Her cross-on-a-chain was a definite mood-killer. Religion had ruined their lives—didn't she see that? The elation and anticipation he had felt only moments ago ebbed away. Now he wanted the night to end, so he pled jetlag and asked for the check from a big-boned waiter in shorts and a print shirt. He paid it and sifted through his change. An image on the back of a Cook Island silver dollar caught his eye, the same well hung character that inspired all the tikis at the gift shop.

He thrust the coin at Angie. "Who is this guy? He's everywhere."

She pulled at her hat and smiled. "That's Tangaroa. I'll tell you about him tomorrow. I'll pick you up at seven-thirty. Eat a good breakfast. I have a little hike planned for us."

Chapter 15

ANGELA AWOKE AT SIX A.M. with a faint, nearly subliminal headache. It could have been worse; she had a lot to drink the night before. But Cullen was out on his feet from the time change, so they had called it a night early and she was in bed by half-past nine. Plenty of time to sleep off the industrial-strength Mai Tais Lonnie had kept serving them.

"Lighten up on the rum," she had scolded him, during a return trip from the women's room. "Are you trying to get me drunk?"

He flashed a lewd grin and rasped in his Kiwi lilt. "I'm hoping your Yank friend over there gets lucky tonight. Purely vicarious, since there's no chance of me ever getting in your pants." He pushed another Mai Tai at her. "Is there?"

The tattoo on his forearm of a parrot drinking a beer was blue and green and red, with intricate line drawing and layers of brilliant coloring. Angela loved tattoo art and she loved Lonnie's tattoos, but not enough to love Lonnie. His crush on her was legendary. She lifted her drink off the bar and blew him a kiss.

"Not with all the VD you've had. But it's nice to know *someone* still thinks about jumping my osteoporotic bones."

"I'd climb Te Rua Manga in the buff for a roll in the sack with you."

She had grinned at Lonnie and nodded her head toward Cullen. "He doesn't know it, but that's exactly what he's going to do tomorrow. Not in the buff, though. And no roll in the sack at the end, either."

Angela tittered at her fuzzy memories of the night before. She sprang out of bed, showered, and dressed in black cycling shorts, a yellow and black tank top, high-top hiking boots, and a black cap. A quick onceover in the bedroom mirror made her shake her head. She had been aiming for pert and sexy, but her old-lady chicken wings and varicose veins scotched that, so she lowered the bar to healthy and fit and headed to the kitchen for a bowl of oatmeal, half a pawpaw, and two cups of Atiu coffee.

The driver she hired to ferry them to their departure point in the Avatiu Valley—Keu Narayan, a friend of Ty's— beeped in her drive twenty minutes later. She grabbed her backpack and locked the front door, something she'd only recently started doing. It made her sad each time she did.

Keu called out from a white jeep as she came across the lawn. "*Kia orana!*" He had sturdy legs and a big belly and a morning smile that made her feel as happy as having to lock her door did sad. She sat in the front seat and thought about Cullen on the way to his hotel on Muri Beach, a short drive on Ara Tapu from Titikaveka, where Angela lived. Gray clouds hung low overhead. A refreshing mist spritzed her face—Keu liked driving with the top down. The wipers squeegeed a languid rhythm.

When Taira first told her that Cullen was in her gallery, Angela had prayed that the daughter she relinquished in Laguna Beach might be with him, even though the purpose of prayer was to commune with God, not ask favors of him. But pray she did, with the sincerity of a nun making vows, in hopes that her abandoned child had somehow found Cullen. But all Cullen brought was the sorrow of their past etched upon his face. A sorrow even her straightedge couldn't scrape away. Sorrow that would deepen immeasurably when she told him about the daughter she had given away — his daughter. All these years, and she was still bringing the pain to Cullen Brodie. Sometimes she truly did hate herself.

The physical changes in him were more than she had expected. His hair had thinned and his face had a hunted look to it, as if under duress. Altered, too, were his magnificent hands, his long, pleasing fingers now crooked and thick — from cracking his knuckles too often, if last night was any indication. Every doctor she'd ever known, including her father and dissolute ex-husband, had been afflicted with one sort of tic or another. Theirs was a twitching, convulsing profession. And though his eyes were the same dreamy hazel — the left one unruly when he drank, like last night, when it veered all over the place — there was a hint of anguish to them. The cause of which she understood all too well.

She pitied him for it, the years of suffering he'd done for the sins they committed — with no relief in sight, because he didn't believe in sin. That much was clear from the way he recoiled at her crucifix, like a vampire in an old movie. (She saw his reflection in the mirror when she shaved him, though, so that was good.) He couldn't say goodnight fast enough after she told him she had become a Catholic, as if she were the apostate, not him.

He was outside waiting for them, leaning against the trunk of a palm in front of the hotel. He wore a white tank top and black shorts, a white USC cap, and a pair of battered high tops. His biceps spooled in long bunches of dimpled muscle.

Keu pulled to a stop. Cullen bounded to the jeep with the grace of a natural athlete. His big frame had a look of raw power to it that gave Angela a thrill, as if she'd leaned too far back in a chair. She let it pass and appraised his legs, judging how they would hold up under the strain of the steep, awkward climb ahead—a climb she made twice a week without difficulty. His big thighs would handle the rugged grade just fine, she decided, but those slim calves were another matter. Cullen was a thoroughbred, not a packhorse.

He drew alongside her and gave an embarrassed grin. "Those Mai Tais last night packed a wallop. I passed out and didn't move until my wake-up call."

Deep wrinkle lines and the sharp cut of his chin gave him a handsome cragginess she had failed to appreciate the night before. The unintended radiance of the smile that escaped her seemed to fluster him. He hesitated, his hand on the door, his eyes on her face.

"At least you didn't have to shave," she quipped, to put him at ease. He laughed and climbed into the back seat.

They arrived at their drop-off point by eight, in the steep ravine of the Avatiu valley, surrounded by lush orchards and bountiful gardens and pens straining with domestic pigs. The sky lightened and it stopped misting. She instructed Keu to meet them in five hours on the other side of the island and struck out toward the spot she hoped to reach before the heat became intolerable: the base of Mount Te Rua Manga.

They hiked south from the headwaters of Avatiu stream and came quickly to slope forest dominated by white-flowering *mato* trees. A meshwork of roots covered the fast-rising trail, making for precarious footing, but offering good handholds. Patches of blue sky appeared through holes in the green canopy above them, which glistened from an overnight rain.

The path and stream coextended and the grade steepened. Sunlight soon mottled the trail, heating the rainforest like a greenhouse. A break in the foliage yielded their first peek of the sheer, stony face of the Needle—Te Rua Manga, rising a quarter mile high and lying four kilometers due south.

She stopped to look back at Cullen. A patina of sweat coated his brow and soaked his shirt, the humidity of the young day already smothering. He swatted at the squadrons of mosquitoes that strafed him, the repellant she doused him with already ineffective, diluted by sweat.

He caught up to her near a stand of green-stalked plants that resembled cobs of red corn growing on sticks in the ground. She bent over and broke one off and rubbed its knurled pods between her palms. Suds appeared and the scent of ginger wafted through the air.

She held it out to him. "Shampoo plant. The little red cones hold moisture and become soapy."

He took it from her and rolled it in his massive hands. She marveled that they didn't pulverize it and grind it to seed. His face lit up like a child's at the fragrant lather the pods produced. He took his cap off and rubbed some into his hair.

"I could shower with this!"

Angela crossed the trail to a small tree laden with green, globular fruit, another of the forest's comestible delights. "You think that's great? Try this." She plucked one off a slender branch with big-veined leaves. "Rarotongan guava. We eat them like apples, rind and all."

He put his cap back on and chomped into it. Juice drenched the corners of his mouth and chin. He swiped the back of his hand across his face and finished it in two huge bites, its pink, juicy pulp and piquant green rind, its clustered seeds. "That's unbelievably good. It just grows here like this, with no one to tend it?"

She pointed at the vista afforded by a bend in the trail behind them, the turquoise lagoon and foam-flecked reef lying beyond the coastal plain and sparkling harbor of Avarua. "You're in God's orchard, dear. Paradise."

He wiped his hands on his shorts and gazed at her with a lovelorn look. She chided herself for calling him dear, but at least now she knew: he still cared for her. Still wanted her. And oh, God, it felt good to be wanted! To be desired, a woman of fifty-four the object of male ardor. *This* male. This man: this big, hunky, man. Please don't let him go cockeyed, she thought. There was no telling what she'd do.

He squatted in a catcher's stance and picked at the trail. The stream burbled by. "If Eden were real, this is how I would imagine it. But there's no need to credit God for it." He rose and looked for her reaction.

She pressed a finger to her lips and pointed to the bough of a nearby tree. A bird with a white breast and parrot-green wings and a lemon-yellow belly and scarlet forehead sat serenely perched on a reed-thin branch, beside a pair of similarly colored chicks, save for their brown, downy heads.

"*Kukupa.* Cook Islands fruit doves. Magical, aren't they? Whose hand do you see in their making? God's? Or Darwin's?"

A smug look crossed his face, as if he were privy to recondite secrets he now deigned to share. "I'll let you speak for God, but here's what Darwin had to say about it. 'It is interesting to contemplate a tangled bank, clothed with many plants of many kinds... and to reflect that these elaborately constructed forms... have all been produced by laws acting around us.' That's my condensed version of the last paragraph of *On the Origin of Species.*"

She moved closer to him. "But evolution came late to the game. A lot went on before natural selection came on the scene: the birth of the Milky Way, the formation of our planets, the appearance of oxygen in our atmosphere. All of it governed by laws so precise that the slightest deviation would make the whole thing incapable of supporting even a single galaxy. Do you really think such perfection just happened? That a complex planetary system came out of nothing from a cosmic accident? And that another equally improbable accident then gave rise to life? That's an awful lot of statistical improbability, isn't it? A lot of chance."

He put his hands up, as if to stop her from coming closer. "The odds aren't as daunting as you think. Read about the multiverse—multiple universes. Some scientists think there could be billions of them, trillions even, each governed by different mathematical laws. One of them was bound to look like ours. But when all of the universes in the multiverse are considered together, the natural laws of any particular one aren't so mind-boggling."

"Is there any tangible evidence these other universes exist? Any mathematical proof?"

"It's a theory. A very elegant theory. Advanced by one of the great physicists of our time."

She crossed her arms and pursed her lips. "I see. A theory." Typical atheist sophistry is what it was. "In other words, this multiverse is a belief. Something to be taken on faith. Like God."

He smiled and came over and kissed her cheek, tenderly, which completely flummoxed her and made her legs weak. He stepped back, forbearing and unruffled and thicker-skinned than she had expected.

"Is this what they're teaching in catechism nowadays? How to skewer a skeptic?"

She adjusted her backpack and shrugged. "We'd best get going. We have a lot of ground to cover."

He walked over to the guava tree and picked a fruit off a branch and threw it into the forest. It landed with a splat. He turned to her.

"This is going to be a long hike, isn't it?"

She led him higher, toward the summit, where primordial rainforest with garlands of dripping vines yielded to coarse, hardy ferns, the pale green flowers and purpled center of the beautiful endemic *Sclerotheca*. Cullen made it a point of honor to keep up. He forged after her like a quadruped, grasping for handholds and scrambling for purchase on the trail's lattice of wet roots. He grunted and panted and sweat twirled off him as if flung from a sprinkler head, but the distance between them never widened. He stayed even by sheer force of will, thrusting upward, ever upward, a tyro tourist paired with a veteran local hiker. The play of his muscles enthralled her, his long, spindled triceps, his powerful thighs and cabled wrists, the way she remembered him when he flew to the rim at the Attucks. The young boy she loved, drenched with sweat on hot summer nights: nights beside the lake, hidden in a grove of maples, murmuring of love while deep inside her. She gave her head a shake and pushed on, disconcerted by the tactile memory of it.

Te Manga flared high above them to the east, the tallest peak on the island; the rich red umber of Avarua's coastal plain lay behind them, back the way they came. They reached the base of the Needle and rested beside one another on a broad, flat rock in the shadow of its precipice, one hundred meters of volcanic formation rising straight up on the perpendicular. Similar in shape to the columns of Stonehenge, Te Rua Manga—the Mountain of Good Energy—was said to be among the five most sacred energy spots on Earth. An inland breeze soughed around them. The sun burned hot and yellow overhead.

She slid her backpack to the ground and fished a bottle of water from it and passed it to Cullen. He drank half and gave it back. She swilled the rest and blotted her face with a towel. Cullen removed his hat.

"The way you painted him tore my heart out."

She looped the towel around her neck and twisted to face him. "It's the motif Delaroche used in *Le Jeune Martyre*. He called it the most sad and most holy of all his paintings. It's true. I've seen it. It evokes the presence of God. That's what I wanted to do."

His jaw tensed and he cracked the knuckles of his great hands. "What kind of God permits an innocent child to drown in his own swimming pool? Tell me! What kind of divine, benevolent being would do such a thing? If God is the source of all good, and if God is omnipotent, and yet God allowed that sweet boy to die, then Grady's death is proof there *is* no God."

She shook her head. "You're wrong. Grady's death was like Delaroche's painting: holy, consecrated. Death has no meaning in the absence of God."

His eyes flashed. He took her wrist in his stonecutter's hand. How easily he could have snapped it.

"When my father slashed your painting, he lit a fuse that blew up our lives. He did it in the name of religion, the Church's stand against abortion. And not one of us had the strength of character to resist the destructive passions he unleashed. Religion kills, that's the meaning of Grady's death. And it has always been so, from the Emperor Constantine to the Crusades to the *conquistadores* — and to my father."

An image of Chaz Brodie's contorted face, full of fury, came to her — along with a flood of memories. She eased out of his grasp. He hated the very thing that had been her salvation.

"Maddening, isn't it? How two people can look at the same thing and one sees a circle and the other a square? You blame religion for Grady's death; I blame godlessness, my atheist father's choice to destroy the unborn. That's what evil is—an immoral choice. The same as goodness is a moral choice." She folded her hands in her lap. The Truth was all around her, in the trees and streams and soaring peaks of the island she loved. "The presence of evil in the world does not disprove the existence of God. To the contrary: the presence of evil is proof of God. That's the lesson of Original Sin."

He put his hands to his head as if it might explode. A network of veins lined the backs of them. The blue worms of aging, like her legs. His gaze bored into her, full of contempt.

"Original Sin, the Fall, corrupting serpents and forbidden fruit, all of mankind descending from a single couple.... It's preposterous. What did the two sons of Adam and Eve do to propagate, marry their sisters? Is that the kind of moral choice you mean? Is that your idea of goodness?"

"The banishment isn't meant to be taken literally. It's meant to show why evil exists."

He frowned. "How so?"

She let the spiritual power of the Mountain of Good Energy—which ancient Rarotongans and, for a while, Angela had mistaken for the pantheistic energy of Nature, but which she knew now was God's goodness—fill her with grace.

"Adam and Eve ate from the Tree of Knowledge of Good and Evil. They chose knowledge *of* good and evil over remaining *free* of evil in the Garden of Eden. But what they really chose was freedom of will over freedom from suffering. The story of Adam and Eve is meant to show that God gave humans the capacity for free will, knowing full well they would sometimes choose evil over good. The capacity to make moral or immoral choices is uniquely human. Among all God's creatures—among all Darwin's species—we are the only ones to possess it. But the laws that define morality came from God. That's why Grady's death affirms God's existence. Your father exercised his free will by destroying my painting. Then you and I exercised ours. We made choices. Immoral choices."

She put her arms around him and murmured in his ear. "We chose evil."

He shuddered. She pulled him against her and held him. "The stain," he said, in a cracked and hollow voice. "If only there had been no stain on the blanket."

They picked their way around the sacred worshiping rocks of Te Rua Manga and down the south slope of the summit, the most difficult part of the trek behind them. Angela stopped for lunch at the Pool of Rejuvenation, an inky black, freshwater swimming hole bounded by thick bushes and *mato* trees, redolent of wet bark and dripping leaves.

"Ancient warriors swam here to restore their health. Go ahead and cool off. We'll eat when you're finished."

She unpacked the lunch she had prepared the night before and discreetly watched him peel off his tank top and slip out of his trunks. Remnants of his once-splendid body lingered like ruins of ancient Rome or Greece, crumbled by time, but refusing to surrender completely their classic lines and form: his long cylinders of muscle and slab of chest, his narrow hips and wide shoulders. His penis swung into view during his plunge into the pond. Her schoolgirl fascination with it surprised her.

She waited until he emerged and pulled his trunks on before she yanked aside the overgrowth of bushes that concealed the sign informing prospective bathers of the huge fresh water eels that lurked in the pool's ebony waters—black and evil and ravenous- looking in the picture on the signpost. He stepped away from the water's edge with a hand pressed to his crotch.

"Very funny. What's their favorite food—mainlander testicle? I'm surprised you didn't scatter a little chum in the water before I dove in."

Angela burst out laughing and so did he. She had forgotten how they used to make each other laugh, sidesplitting, stomach-aching crack-ups over the silliest things.

"They look fierce, but they don't have any teeth. Lunch is ready. Are you hungry?"

"Famished. Like I haven't eaten in days."

He put his tank top on and sat on the ground across from her with his back against the trunk of a fallen tree. She made amends for the eels by serving ahi sandwiches and fresh pawpaw, washed down with spring water. He didn't look up until the last traces of sandwich had been licked from his fingers. That was another thing about doctors—they had the table manners of feral dogs.

He noticed her critical expression and reached for a napkin. "Sorry. It's a survival skill from residency that never got extinguished." He wiped a smear of ahi from his chin and shrugged. "We learned to bolt our food before our pagers went off and pulled us from our meal. Anyway, that was the best sandwich I've ever had."

She smiled. "Everyone says that after a morning climb to Te Rua Manga."

Still, his gratitude pleased her. She wondered, for a brief, giddy moment, what life with Cullen Brodie would be like? But only for a moment. Loving Cullen again was not an option, his face a daily reminder of the daughter she gave away. The *aroa* she had achieved in her solitary island life was far from perfect, but at least she was at peace with herself. And with God.

She sat cross-legged alongside her open backpack. "Last night you asked me about Tangaroa. He was a major god of pre-European Rarotonga—God of Fertility *and* God of the Sea. The standard composition of his carved image was a thickset body, a large head with specialized eyes, and a penis that dragged in the dirt."

Cullen gave a wicked grin. "A god's God. Judging from the gift shops and silver dollars, the guy's a rock star again."

She withheld her smile. She hated that Tangaroa had become a tiki god, hated the commercialization of him, the exploitation of his prominent sex organ to titillate tourists in search of an erotic paradise.

"The most important word in Maori," she said, "is *aroa*. Modern day Rarotongans will tell you it means love, but in ancient times, *aroa* was a state of peace achieved by following the Code of Tangaroa. For the ancients, the Code of Tangaroa was their Ten Commandments and *aroa* was their grace. But because they believed that man's separation from nature was divine punishment, they were seduced by pantheism— seeking spiritual meaning in rocks and trees and the sea. Christianity taught them that morality was all that mattered, how human beings treated one another: the choice between good and evil. And that guidance on good and evil came not from nature, but from one true God who was above nature."

He fidgeted and pawed the ground with his hand. "They abandoned one myth for another."

"Yes, they did."

He sat up and raised his brow. "So you agree that the Bible is totally irrational? That it can't possibly be true?"

She stuffed their soiled napkins and empty water bottles into her pack and zipped it. Kitchen closed. "Faith and religion *are* irrational. But that doesn't make them wrong."

"Of course it does. Reason leads to truth. Faith leads to delusion."

She set the backpack aside. "Reason allows us to understand and manipulate the physical world in wonderful ways, but there are limits to reason. That's why there was a reaction to the Enlightenment—Romanticism, the Counter-Enlightenment, the celebration of emotion and feeling rather than rational thought."

He shifted onto his elbow. "But music and art intended to provoke only feeling is self-indulgent. It has no higher purpose."

"The painting I sent you was adapted from a Romantic masterpiece that hangs in the Louvre. When you saw it, how did it affect you?"

He stared over her shoulder into the understory encircling the clearing, the dense bushes and shrubs that thrived beneath the canopy of majestic *mato* trees. "I drank myself into a stupor over it. It filled me with sorrow and shame."

"Precisely. Some truths must be felt rather than deduced. The Enlightenment was a glorious age, but not without, as they say in your profession, certain side effects. The Enlightenment gave rise to extremes of reason, an unhealthy worship of literalism that led to religious fundamentalism on the one hand, and atheism on the other. Europe's intoxication with reason ruined the concept of myth."

She had him on his heels, she could sense it, had him reeling from her assault on his hallowed Age of Reason. A shadow of doubt crept across his face. She finished in a bright, quivering rush, a burning evangelism not unlike that of Chaz Brodie at the height of *his* rapture, the day he defaced her painting.

"Science explains how. Myth reveals why. Science will never discover God. God is knowable only through myth, and myths are made known by ritual. Like in the Catholic

Liturgy. Scientific method is the tool of reason; myth is the tool of faith. Each leads to truth, but they are different truths."

She pitied the sudden anguish on his face, as if he were in crisis: spiritual crisis. She must have struck a chord, made him understand in a single afternoon what had eluded him for years. He looked miserable, wretched, really suffering. Had she been that effective, spoken so eloquently and persuasively that it shattered his skepticism? His religious doubt? Were they still so connected that she could reach him this way?

"What's wrong?" she asked, prepared to clasp him to her bosom and seal his conversion.

He rolled onto his back and gripped his calves and groaned. "Cramps! I'm having terrible leg cramps!"

Chapter 16

CULLEN SPENT THE REST of the afternoon at the hotel, his legs trashed and aching, his body welted with bites. The walk from the jeep to his room after their driver dropped him off—with Angie enthused and waving from the front seat, looking as if the Bataan Death March she put him through had been a walk in the park for her—was excruciating. His calves cramped with each step, each contraction, each flicker of muscle. He could barely put one foot in front of the other without wincing. The only thing that helped was a massage in the spa, the strong hands of a middle-age masseuse in white shorts and a navy top kneading his shredded legs until he thought he might cry with gratitude. The aromatic attar she slicked on in deep, healing strokes calmed the incessant itch of his mosquito bites—as did the two Mai Tais he had with dinner and the nightcap he nursed on his veranda.

He lay with Courvoisier in hand on the plush white cushions of his chaise, wearing a hotel robe and nothing else. He stared at the darkening lagoon in the softening ebb of day. Gulls cawed. Waves lapped. His mind wandered.

He was thankful to have tomorrow to recover, to loll about the beach and swim. Angie was busy at the gallery and unavailable until the day after, when she had invited him to go snorkeling. She wouldn't have the advantage over him in the water that she did on the mountain—he was embarrassed by how hard it had been to keep up with her.

He'd check out a mask and fins at the hotel and test them out and be ready this time.

He'd be ready for her religious beliefs, too. Angie, a Catholic: life truly was stranger than fiction. She had ambushed him in the forest, caught him unprepared for the intensity and hermeneutic sophistication of her faith. A faith steeped in myth: the Creation myth, the myth of the Annunciation, the Resurrection myth, the myth of Ascension—all of it, myth. Religious myth.

Entire civilizations had been perverted by it. Had she never listened to that madman Ahmadinejad, his religious rants and fantasies about the return of the Twelfth Imam? His dreams of apocalypse? The religious insanity that had spawned crushing unemployment, misogyny beyond belief—honor killings, stonings, sanctioned rapes—and a diaspora of Iranian intellectuals? Soon the lunatic clerics would have a thermonuclear weapon in their grasp, the means to commit genocide in the name of God: faith on the verge of destroying reason. And Angie was willing to ignore all this to impugn the Enlightenment for *too much* rational thinking?

The world needed more reason, not less, a second Enlightenment, not an unthinking, visceral retreat from the first. She thought morality came from God by way of free will? A nine-peptide molecule, that's where morality came from, Zak's research showing that blood levels of oxytocin were correlated with acts of generosity and compassion. Good and evil resided in the brain's empathy centers, the anterior cingulate cortex and amygdala. And free will? Free will was an elegant symphony of one hundred trillion discharging synapses.

He looked out past Taakoka motu, the southernmost of Muri lagoon's mini-islands, into a swirl of purple and orange painting the horizon. A geyser of water erupted and a mammoth shape framed in a shock of puce heaved into the air, a breaching humpback whale silhouetted against the western sky. It hung suspended for a moment before crashing beyond the reef in a detonation of spray.

He glanced up at the blackening sky, the first shimmering glimpse of Alpha and Beta Centauri pointing towards the Southern Cross, then back to the roiled water of the whale's magnificent breach, the raw beauty of nature and the sublime wonder of the cosmos, all in one night. One moment. He drew great satisfaction that such sights gave no less pleasure to him, viewed through the prism of logic and reason, than to Angie, who attributed them to God. But if the thin gruel of religious belief gave her comfort, so be it. Who was he to begrudge her relief from the sorrow and shame of their past? Religious coping worked: he'd seen it himself, many times. By and large, the faithful died at peace—deluded, but at peace. And he respected their delusion.

A few of them, though—spouses, usually— sniffed out his skepticism, no matter how hard he tried to conceal it. And they could not resist asking what all believers wanted to ask of skeptics.

"What would it take to make you believe in God?"

He had never yet answered truthfully: that not even a woman turning into a pillar of salt or a rod into a serpent could make him believe in God.

He parked his car on Ara Tapu, the circle island road, next to a cemetery full of graves marked by rudimentary crosses and gray headstones. FRUITS OF RAROTONGA, a rectangular sign tacked to a post on the curb said, in blue lettering trimmed with yellow. The fruit stand's doors were drawn open and a pair of motorbikes were parked out front, one red and one white. Two tourists in shorts—a man with thick white legs and a woman with a long ponytail—stood at the counter, in quest of the homemade jams and tropical-flavored chutneys and fruit smoothies the stand was noted for. Pigs and goats and chickens ran free in the yard of an adjacent home.

He toted his snorkeling gear past the cemetery toward Tikioki Beach, where Angie was waiting for him. He stopped to read the epitaph inscribed on one of the tombstones.

IN LOVING MEMORY OF MY HUSBAND,
AITEINA TAURARII
10th JULY 1888 — 25th AUG 1946
TOO DEARLY LOVED, TOO SADLY MISSED
GOD'S GREATEST GIFT IS REMEMBRANCE

Greatest gift or greatest curse? It depended on the remembrance. Memories could not be outrun. They were graven onto us, until the final heartbeat. The most that could be hoped for was that the snatches of love and joy and triumph that came our way might nullify the shame and failure and grief that found us. Was it all happenstance and luck? Or did we get the memories we deserved? Aiteina Taurarii, it seemed, had been a good man.

He followed a dirt path through a grove of palms and over a small dune onto a spectacular tongue of sand licked by the green waters of Tikioki Beach. The muffled crash of surf on the distant reef loitered beneath the rustle of fronds and high pitch of birdsong.

Angie waved from the shade of a nearby tree, in the midst of a score of other beachgoers. She wore a black swim top with white straps and the same black cycling shorts she'd worn on the hike. The declivity of smooth, round breast that spilled from her top was too full to be real: the wonders of silicone. But the cycling shorts frustrated him. She once had the most delectable inner thighs imaginable, like silk and butter against the palm of his hand. He wanted to see them, wanted to see all of her, as close to naked as he could. He smiled to himself. Life had come full-circle, hoping to get Angie out of her shorts again.

But it wasn't to be; the shorts stayed on. They smeared defogger on the insides of their masks and rinsed them in the lagoon, then donned their fins and entered eighty-degree water that was as pristine as cut crystal. They snorkeled in lazy figure eights, floating over coral that pullulated with life. The lagoon was deeper there than anywhere else on the island, making for a more dramatic perspective of the wonders beneath.

She directed his attention to a school of lemon-colored fish fluttering below them like a stand of azaleas. At her signal, they dove to a depth of about nine feet and gently propelled themselves toward the school's glistening yellow mass. She took his hand, binding them together in rays of bent sunlight. That he was again submerged in nine feet of water while clasped to a daughter of Edward Nichols was not lost on Cullen. But this time he was holding the hand of the daughter he *should* have been with that night.

Later, during one of their periodic rests at the surface, Angie educated him about the various fish they had seen: trevally, parrotfish, rainbow fish, angelfish and more. They lolled on their backs with the tips of their fins breaking water. The teal blue sky was the same color as the ocean beyond the reef.

"Parrotfish were once considered royal food," she said. "Ambrosia, practically. You can't tell their sex because they start off as one and change into the other and their coloring varies along the way. It bothers marine biologists to no end, but the fish seem to like it just fine. Being both male and female, I mean. God made them the most beautiful fish in the lagoon."

They had lunch at her home in Titikavaka, five minutes away. He followed her red Jeep onto the macadam of a one-level, saffron yellow home with green trim. She stationed her Jeep under a carport; he parked his rental behind her. They rinsed the brine of the ocean off themselves beneath an outdoor shower in back, where a deep yard with an orchard and well-tended lawn sloped to a picket line of elegant palms, bounding the sugar white sand and pale green water of the lagoon.

Cullen toweled off and pulled his shirt over his head while she went inside to change, leaving a bi-fold door to the interior open behind her. He dropped onto a rattan couch with blue and white cushions. A teak dining table sat to the right, with a decorative bowl of the same wood as a centerpiece. He put his feet up on an ottoman upholstered like the couch and took in the view: an orchard studded with fruit trees bearing paw paw and passion fruit; a pair of wooden trellises laced with purple bougainvillea; the vitreous lagoon and sapphire sea beyond. She must have sold a lot of paintings to afford beachfront property like this: a *lot* of paintings.

He thought of Becky while waiting for Angie to reappear. Thought of her for the first time, he realized, since he had walked into the gift store to buy a necklace for her — which he'd impulsively given to Angie instead. What an asshole he was. He should call her. But there was the time zone difference, and what, exactly, would he say? Better to deal with Becky when he got home. It was all about Angie, now. Where things would go between them.

She fetched him for a tour with her hair tangled and wild, wearing white sandals and a green, hibiscus-print pareo that draped her from bosom to knee with no fastening loop. She wore nothing underneath, it appeared, no undergarments between skin and sarong. He imagined her nipples and dark thatch grazing the pareo's inner fabric. He trailed her like a hound on spoor into a pale yellow great room with brown floor tiles and a Polynesian abstract dominating one wall. With each step she took, his desire to see her fully unclothed became more intense. If only the knot drawing her pareo around her were to loosen....

He found the silver cross dangling in her cleavage oddly arousing — her Catholicism, that's what it was. There was no sex like forbidden sex, the repressed desire of a Catholic girl in the back seat of his car in high school, her greedy tongue and dry-humping pelvis, her pent-up lust slipping its chains and breaching the levee: like a dam breaking.

He let an erection die stillborn in his pants and focused instead on the island panache of her home, the colorful oils that covered the walls, the bronzes of Polynesian royalty that loomed in every corner, the eclectic mix of antique and contemporary furniture, with an abundance of windows and skylights bathing every room in thick sunlight. Style and beauty and grace: like her. And he lost it all to a fit of jealous rage. Maybe coming to her home wasn't such a good idea.

A brief stop in her bedroom made his misgivings even worse. Paintings of nude island goddesses adorned the wall above her bed, a queen-sized platform with a slatted headboard and frilly pillows. It was a bed they should have shared, a bed that children and later grandchildren should have bounced on in the bright, clear light of dawn. *Grandpa, wake up, you promised to take us to the zoo!* Instead she slept alone and so did he, childless, both of them.

She served lunch on the veranda: homemade lime salad dressing, spiced with turmeric; seared tuna on fresh bread; and mango ice cream for dessert. They sipped chilled Australian chardonnay and talked deep into the afternoon, with her hand on his wrist more than once, and what did that mean? That she wanted more than talk? Or that she was still an inveterate flirt? The latter, probably, as they spoke mostly about their careers, a merciful rest from the sadness of their past. He let the wine and languor of the day sedate him, the fragrant scent of honeysuckle and orange blossoms, the susurrus of wind-rustled palms and sparkling turquoise of the lagoon.

His trance dissolved when she rose to clear the table. The loveliness of her long neck and fullness of her buttocks beneath her pareo were too much to resist. He tailed her into her brown-tiled, yellow-walled kitchen, with its stainless steel refrigerator and gleaming dishwasher and full ocean view. She stood at the sink, running water over their dirty dishes. Sunlight glossed her hair. His heart caught in his throat. He put his hands on her shoulders, tentative, hesitant, hoping she'd melt against him.

Instead she wriggled from beneath his touch and spun to face him, her hair falling over one eye, looking hurt and confused and defiant all at once, though she said nothing. She didn't have to. He understood. She had worn a garment that covered her from top to bottom and denied his eyes the pleasure of her body because he was there for lunch.

And nothing more.

It might have been the moon that set him off. Waxing all week, more luminous by the day, culminating in this, a full and golden orb climbing the eastern sky. Moonrise over

Rarotonga, lovers' beams of moonlight raining down and stabbing the sea, even as the setting sun purpled the sky and turned Muri Lagoon lavender, like stained glass, a riot of color from west to east as day gave way to night.

Or it could have been the rum, flowing through him like hot lava and setting his brain on fire. But mostly it was the look she had given him, her wounded face. He drained his glass and stood on the veranda outside his room. He clenched his fist. His chest heaved.

He threw his head back and howled.

Oh, the humiliation of it, the disgrace! His manhood at stake and he responded like a shuddering boy afraid of his first kiss. His shrinking, hesitant hand on her shoulder, his feeble and inconstant grasp, wrong, all wrong. What a fool he had been! It wasn't that his hands had gone too far; it was that his hands had not gone far enough. She wanted to know if he desired her, truly desired her, as she was, older, in the autumn of life. And to leave no doubt about it, one way or the other. She wanted a man who knew his heart and was willing to show it, and he showed her nothing. No heart. Only indecisiveness.

He slipped his room key beneath the chaise and went down to the lagoon and looked out across the water to Titikaveka, where she lived, a mile and a half distant. What about his heart? For whom did it ache? Angie Nichols, the flawless girl of his youth? Or Angela Masters, the woman she'd become?

He stepped out of his sandals and shed his robe. He loved her then and he loved her now, the girl and the woman. He would always love her. She was his goddess, his Venus, and on this night, if she would have him, he would be her mortal lover.

He plunged naked into the lagoon and cut through its silvered waters toward Titikaveka.

Angela put her brush down and looked at herself in the bathroom mirror, the fleshiness of her arms in the black nightie she wore, her brittle hair and anile pinch of her face. Time leaching away her color, the queen of the ball fading like a pair of stonewashed jeans. She longed for her halcyon years, when the more disinterested she was, the more her phone rang.

She had first discovered the intoxicating power of playing hard-to-get in high school. *If thou thinkest I am too quickly won, I'll frown, and be perverse.* Rivals accused her of being a bitch, but what they didn't understand was that playing hard-to-get had nothing to do with bitchiness, and everything to do with being wanted. Yes, her looks made it easier, but there were scads of attractive girls who graduated without ever comprehending what she learned as a jejune sophomore, when she road tested hard-to-get on Doug Reynolds, that year's Homecoming King. She noticed him behind her in line one day in the cafeteria, his big shoulders and jaunty sideburns, his Mick Jagger lips and thick brow. She shook her bangs over her eyes, pulled her mohair sweater snug over her budding breasts, and corkscrewed to wave at an imaginary friend at the back of the line. She felt his eyes all over her, like the hands of a blind man caressing a sculpture. He introduced himself—like she didn't know who he was—and asked if she'd like to sit at his table, inhabited by the usual foxes and hunks. Though she was dying to, she smiled demurely and said, "No, thank you, I like to read during lunch." She tossed her head and went to a desolate corner of the cafeteria and pulled out a paperback copy of *Pride and Prejudice*. She did, in fact, like to read during lunch, but she'd just blown off the Homecoming King, and what was she thinking? She struggled to focus on

Mr. Darcy's unwitting attraction to Elizabeth, but five minutes later Doug Reynolds was at her table asking her out. Within a week, his class ring dangled from her neck on a lanyard of gold yarn.

Playing hard-to-get worked, but it spoiled her. She became accustomed to being wanted and began to expect it, to demand it. But as with Mr. Darcy, pride became a problem, for it was pride that caused her to bring the pain to Cullen by sleeping with Dempsey. Which loosed God's wrath on them all.

Cullen.

She thought of his face when she pulled away from him that afternoon after he put his hands on her shoulders. So hurt and confused. But what did he expect for such ambivalence? For his halting touch, his timid trial balloon to see how she would respond? Bloodless, is what it was. Torpid. Insulting. Did he want her or didn't he?

She went into the kitchen for a slug of guava juice to wash down her evening dose of calcium. The big white tablet sometimes stuck in her throat, capping her glottis like a manhole cover until she blasted it free in a paroxysm of coughing. A foreshadowing of senescence, no doubt, choking on pills in a nursing home. The juice's thick consistency guided the tablet down the right pipe.

A sound came through an open window, an urgent voice carrying across the lagoon. A man's voice. She hurried to the great room and flung open the bi-folds and tilted her head.

"Angie! Angie!"

She bounded across the veranda and peered into the night. Cullen stood fierce and naked in the shallows, his torso bathed in moonlight, his genitals dangling above the water line.

"Angie! Angie!"

An astonished gurgle died in her throat. She pulled her nightie over her head and cast it aside and ran like a young Rarotongan princess, her feet slapping the sand, her breasts gyrating. Faster, faster, her arms pumping, her lungs sucking great gulps of air, frantic to cover the scant strip of beach and water between them. She wasn't playing hard to get now, was she? *If thou thinkest I am too quickly won, too goddamn bad.* He stood there calling her. Summoning her.

"Angie! Angie!"

She hit the water and high-stepped into his arms. The force of her charge knocked him over. They spun into the lagoon in a desperate embrace. She smashed her lips against his and moaned and grunted at the impaling swell inside her. She did not care about the cross around her neck, or if Cullen believed in God. She did not care about anything.

Only that her man wanted her.

They showered in her back yard, transfixed by one another's nakedness. The light of the new moon painted their wet bodies a translucent shade of silver. They touched each other with cupped and tender hands, in silence, as if to confirm the other was real and not illusory, a chimera from the past. Satisfied that Cullen, at least, wasn't—about herself she wasn't so sure, not of anything, not even who she was, Angela Masters or Angie Nichols—she pressed her index finger to his lips and scampered inside for a pair of towels. He patted himself dry, the whole time devouring her with his eyes, the way he used to, as if she were in her twenties again rather than her fifties. His arm and shoulder muscles undulated in a pleasing way when he toweled his back.

She led him inside and laid a sheet on the great room floor. He knotted a fresh towel around his waist and sprawled on the floor, propped up on one elbow. He had no clothes, no car, and no plan for getting back to his hotel. Angela went into her bedroom and changed out her cross for the black pearl necklace he had bought her and put another nightie on—silk, red, sheer, like wearing nothing. She detoured to the kitchen and uncorked a bottle of Aussie Pinot noir and filled two crystal glasses with wine. She brought them into the great room and bent to light a vanilla-scented candle. Cullen reached for her. The whorls of gray that streaked his chest saddened her. She thought of him with Leslie that night, this same way, on a blanket on a floor, but for the first time felt no resentment over it. Instead it made her smile, that her beautiful sister made love to this man, too. That they shared him, as sisters sometimes did. She kissed the back of his hand and broke away to load the CD player.

They drank the wine and listened to all the old songs and fell through a wormhole in time, transported by the dripping candle's stuttering light and the sensual funk of Earth, Wind & Fire, Philip Bailey's pure falsetto cresting like a flute, telling them reasons had no pride. Angela knew it was true, because for a thousand reasons, all of them selfish and weak, she whispered that she loved him when he came inside her.

He waited until morning before asking about her scars. They sat side-by-side on the veranda, Cullen with one of her pareos wrapped around him. They sipped coffee and watched the ocean swallow the spent, pale moon as tongues of pink and yellow licked up out of the east.

"What happened to your legs?"

The compassion in his voice nearly broke her, his bewildered pathos at the disfiguring heaps of leathery tissue that marred her once-exquisite inner thighs. The grotesque fibrotic swirls he had obsessively traced with fingers and tongue the night before, in horrid fascination of it.

She stood and tightened her robe. "I need to take you back to your hotel now."

It began soon after she arrived on Rarotonga, in the gallery where she worked. The owners, a New Zealand couple in their sixties, the wife kind and generous with curly white hair, the husband bald and reedy, encouraged her to use their small atelier to paint after hours. They said her work showed great promise.

She soon discovered that she could use a modified palette knife to contour her work—the top side of a drop handle with a trowel blade honed to a fine edge, the bottom side left untouched. The modification allowed her to slice away layers of caked paint that distorted her shading without damaging the canvas beneath. And it could still be used on the occasions she chose to apply her paint with a knife rather than a brush.

One evening, though, she became careless with it. She forgot that her previously blunt knife was now razor-sharp on top. When she wiped it free of paint with a towel, the honed edge cut through the rag and into the meat of her hand.

She stared dumbstruck at the blood seeping from the slice in her hand, unprepared for the release she felt, the sudden melioration of the agony in her heart. Shame and guilt hissed out of her like steam from the radiator of an overheated car. She had been brought up to express her emotions, not hold them in, but her terrible sins—sleeping with Dempsey, refusing to forgive Leslie, relinquishing her child—had festered inside her. Devalued her. Made her less than human.

She was amazed at the sense of calmness that descended over her, the disappearance of her knot of anguish. It was mystical, an exorcism in crimson of emotional tension so excruciating she would do anything to alleviate it. Anything.

A week later she tried it again. At her apartment this time, the palette knife beside her on the bed. She sat in bra and underpants on a towel with a plastic garbage bag beneath it, to keep from staining her bedding. She picked up the knife and took the blade to her thigh, her silky inner thigh that was catnip for lovers' hands. She sliced her unblemished skin just inside the long sweep of muscle and tendon that attached high up on her groin.

Oh, the sweet relief! The peace it brought, the euphoria. And something else, too, something just as satisfying as relief. Control. Control over the unbearable sorrow and rage that buffeted and battered her without mercy, the blackest of passions she had until now been helpless to resist.

It was a quid pro quo forged in blood, self-injury in exchange for relief from the disgrace that haunted her. It didn't last, of course. The relief was only temporary. But she began to crave it, to fantasize about cutting herself. So she did, regularly, until she was addicted to it, always on her inner thighs, where she could conceal the hideous ridges of scar that formed. She abandoned her palette knife in favor of a straightedge razor that she sometimes used to shave her legs and sometimes used to cut them, depending on her mood. It was only after converting to Catholicism that she finally stopped cutting herself—though she continued to use the straightedge to shave her legs. It made her feel sexy and alive; *this* she was not willing to give up. Cutting herself, she later realized, had been the equivalent of mortification of the flesh, her version of sackcloth and ashes: "For if you live according to the flesh you will die, but if by the Spirit you put to death the deeds of the body you will live."

Angela pulled her white linen, v-neck cocktail dress on and fastened Cullen's pearl necklace over her silver crucifix.

She would tell him that evening over dinner at The Flame Tree—not five minutes from his hotel—about the scars he discovered two nights before, when he had emerged like a sea-god from the lagoon and made love to her.

And she would tell him about their daughter, too.

Cullen splashed on some cologne and checked the bathroom mirror. He liked the way his black chambray shirt hung on his frame, and the sharp crease of his cream slacks. Rarotonga agreed with him. He looked tan, fit—younger. A brigand's smile crossed his face. The touch and smell of Angie on his brain, two nights removed from making love to his island queen. He couldn't wait to see her, to inhale her scent and brush his lips against her cheek. He became aroused, semi-erect: the wonders of Cialis. For when the moment was right. Like tonight.

The short walk to the restaurant took him down a winding, sylvan path, with the fragrant smell of frangipani and musk of the jungle in his nostrils. The air was thick and warm. Birds sang. He felt alive, virile: in love.

Though, yes, the scars on her thighs that she refused to explain when she drove him back to his hotel were disturbing—Cullen feeling like a fool in one of her pareos, like Ennis in a dress, sneaking from her car to his room to avoid being seen. But then she called and invited him to dinner his last night on the island and sent his hopes soaring again. He was already planning to fly her to California as soon as she could take time away from her gallery. Becky would be furious, but with Angie back in his life, there would be choices to make.

The Flame Tree Restaurant was nestled in a grove of trees at the end of a long gravel driveway—though he didn't see any flame trees, the exploding canopies of red that made his jaw drop every time he saw one. He stepped across a covered wooden patio with a creek running beneath it and tables set with white linen, and continued on to the main building, a single-story structure of white wood with a vaulted ceiling. A dozen fans suspended by long metal down rods churned the air. Two men in loud shirts and a pair of women in flimsy dresses sat at a bar made of rich wood — *tamanu*, a waiter told him later. Local mahogany.

He gave his name to the hostess, an island girl in a clinging yellow pareo embossed with palm fronds. She led him back the way he came, to an outside table for two in the corner, past a young couple holding hands and staring into each other's eyes. She lit a large white candle in the center of the table and gave him a quizzical smile.

"Don't worry. She'll be here," Cullen said.

She bent low and blew out the match she used to light the candle with an exaggerated O of her lips. "Oh, I have no doubt of that. Enjoy your evening." She headed back inside in that distinctive way island girls walked, every move a dance, the South Pacific oozing from every pore. He followed the sway of her hips until she disappeared from view.

Angie arrived a few moments after the New Zealand Viogneir he ordered came to their table. She shimmied across the creek and onto the slatted boards of the outdoor deck in a white linen dress cut above the knee, a vision in the gloaming. Heads turned. Conversations stalled. A gardenia graced her dark sheet of hair and the pearl necklace he had bought her flared from the low v of her dress, dangling beneath the ridgeline of her dainty clavicles. The *curves* she had for a woman her age, the Hollywood hips and bosom.

The waiter who brought their wine pulled her chair out from the table as if he were seating a royal subject. The hostess stopped by and remarked on what a pretty pair they made. Cullen grinned. "A decaying vestige of the grandeur of our youth," he said. She snapped a photo of them with his pocket-sized Sony.

He started off with a paw paw and coconut salad garnished with grilled haloumi, then parrotfish in vanilla sauce for the main event. Angie countered with a smoked marlin mousse and pan seared yellow fin tuna. Waves of solicitous staff hovered around their table wearing concerned faces. "Ms. Masters, is everything to your liking?" they asked repeatedly.

Cullen learned the reason for the fawning service they enjoyed on a sojourn to the restroom—the first of several such visits, thanks to his enlarged prostate. A half-dozen of Angie's paintings lined the walls of the main dining room: beryl seascapes, jutting green landscapes, and a magnificent canvas of the Cook Islands Christian Church, with its walls of white coral and slanted red roof and crumbling tombstones in the graveyard. The pieces were on indefinite loan, Angie told him, an act of goodwill for her favorite restaurant.

She told him about her scars after their waiter uncorked a second bottle of Viogneir. He dropped his fork on the table and slumped back in his chair. Her tale of self-mutilation was hard to take, the despoiling of her heavenly thighs. The depth of shame she professed made his seem insignificant by comparison. Trivial. Was her emotional pain really that much greater than his? Her conscience that much keener? It probably was. Fear of God was a powerful thing. Even so, he should have been the one doing the self-mutilating, not her. She wasn't even there that night.

"Your sister and I betrayed you. *We* were responsible for Grady. Not you." He leaned forward and took her hands in his, entombed them in a cavern of bone and gristle. "I don't care about your scars. I want you to come to California with me. I love you."

She smiled and gently withdrew her hands from his. It was a weak smile, sympathetic almost... no, not sympathetic — apologetic. An apologetic smile. Not exactly the response he'd been hoping for.

"I'm sorry," she said. "It's upsetting to talk about. But I'm afraid you *do* need to care about my scars."

"Well, it's not that I don't care about them. I just meant it doesn't make me think less of you."

She took a gulp of wine and fidgeted in her chair. "That's the problem. You should." She looked suddenly older, her face anguished and drawn.

"I *should* think less of you? Why? I don't get it. Didn't you hear me just now? I said I love you."

A moue of frustration crossed her face. "Why do men think 'I love you' is such a mic drop? A wrap. Curtain call, that's it folks, show's over. He loves her, you can all go home now. It isn't that easy, Cullen."

He frowned. "Look, I know there are things to work through, but unless I was drunker last night than I thought, I could have sworn you said you loved me, too. It's still there between us, Angie. It always will be."

She stood up and set her napkin on the table. "Excuse me," she said. "I'm sorry. I'll be right back."

Their waiter escorted her to the restroom. Cullen drank more wine and shook his head. "She's a bigger mess than I am," he muttered to himself.

She returned no more composed; if anything, she seemed more unsettled than before. She rearranged the silverware, clenched her fists, and then leaned over her plate and spoke in a low, growling voice. "I was pregnant when I got to Laguna Beach. Pregnant, do you understand? We had a daughter, you and I. A beautiful girl. And I gave her away." Her voice rose. "To the county adoption agency." And burst into an urgent cry. "I gave our daughter away!"

Waiters froze in their tracks. The pretty young hostess gawked. She was yelling now, a stricken howl that turned every head in the place. "Do you love me now, Cullen? Do you? Do my scars matter now?" Her black spill of hair lashed this way and that. Her eyes blazed: bright, virescent.

Possessed.

He stared at her maniacal face, astounded. A child. He had a child! A daughter. Somewhere in the world there was a person with half his genes, her mannerisms and proclivities and personality predetermined by him. A bolt of pride rattled his shoulders. He was a father—would always be a father. He had fulfilled that most essential of male instincts after all. His bloodline lived!

But a rising tide of anger swamped his swell of joy. She had no right to conceal the birth of their child from him. They could have talked it over, figured things out. Kept her. He would have worked himself to the bone for her. Hadn't he done as much for his brothers? How much more would he have done for his own daughter?

Instead she had robbed him of his only natural purpose. Banished his child from his life. It felt no different than an abortion, an involuntary loss of a child, his role as father over before it began. What could have been, had Angie not deprived him of it? Had not emasculated him so.

Fury seized him. His hands shook. He couldn't breathe. He reached for his wine and knocked it onto the table. Its fimbriated stain on the white tablecloth reminded him of deliveries he attended in med school, the bloodstained sheets and groaning, straining mothers and anxious, waiting fathers. He should have been there at Angie's delivery. Ready to stand astride his daughter and roar, to dare someone to even think of harming her.

"You had no right!" he howled.

He steadied his hand and glared. She ignored his spill of wine. So did their waiter; only a fool would come near their table now. She searched his face and saw what he could not hide. His rage at having no say in the matter. No voice. An ugly sneer distorted her expression, a merciless snarl.

"I brought you to Rarotonga to tell you the truth, but I knew it would end this way. How could it not? This is what life together would be for us. Spending the rest of our days ripping open the wounds of Grady and Leslie and our baby girl. I can't do it. That's why I cut myself. And if not for the grace of God, I would keep on cutting myself. Deeper. More often. It was spiritual pain that drove me to it and spiritual salvation that made me stop. May God forgive me."

She stood and pressed a hand to her damp forehead. The other clutched her stomach. She whirled across the deck and over the bridge without him moving so much as a muscle to chase her down.

He walked back to his hotel in the dark. Bereft. Adrift. Cloaked in silence, the primeval forest around him void of sound. Starlight leaked through from the firmament above, mocking his insignificance. His meaninglessness. An anxious dread crept over him, the feeling he had each year as a boy, when in the first weeks of September a cool, colorless day of autumnal gloom came calling, its steely sky herald to the death of summer and portent to the long, bleak winter ahead.

His stay in Paradise was over. Tomorrow he would return home doubly bereaved: once for Angie, nevermore his, once for the daughter she deleted from his life. He wished she had never sent him her exquisite painting of the martyred Grady, had never lured him to Rarotonga to tell him about their child. It would have been kinder that way. Less cruel. Now, for the rest of his life, he would be left to wonder. Wonder, but never know: what she looked like, where she lived, if she had children. If she were even alive. Already he fretted over her childhood, the sorrow she must have endured while longing for what every child desired: her own flesh and blood to love and protect her.

It kept him awake all night. But by daybreak, with Muri Lagoon still and perse in the pale light of dawn, a new set of images replaced the dreams of Angie he had nursed for so long. Dreams of his daughter. His child.

His only child.

Chapter 17

ENNIS HAD LOOKED FORWARD to an evening of fun watching Duncan's three children cut loose in a pizza parlor-cum-amusement park for kids. That was the kind of place the tag line on Chuck E. Cheese's website boasted it was: a friendly, welcoming place Where A Kid Can Be A Kid. So why, standing on the walk beneath a neon sign of a smiling mouse in a purple baseball cap with a big yellow C on it, did he feel like he was about to do something sleazy? Like going into a XXX movie or a peep show? It was the seedy curb appearance of the place, he decided, the stucco strip mall it was in and bright red doors and black tinted storefront windows.

He paced back and forth, refusing to go in. He had dressed drab instead of en femme, in baggy jeans and a knit shirt, his hair neat and combed, but even so, an old man coming stag into Chuck E. Cheese's would be about as welcome as a keffiyeh on a 747. Not that loitering outside like Chester the Molester with no foot traffic to give him cover was much better, but unless he wanted to sit in his car like a pedophile, he'd have to make do out front until Duncan and his brood arrived to make him look respectable.

All the same, he was feeling much better about gender accord these days. His male and female selves were coming into harmony and he no longer feared Elaine rejecting Carla's organs. He cross-dressed freely and didn't give a rat's ass what anyone thought about him. All that mattered was self-respect. Personal dignity.

Now, if only he knew what to do about Carla.

He was growing weary of her presence. Three had become a crowd. It was exhausting, the premonitions and dreams, the strange new tastes and personality changes: her constant agitation. Gender confusion was trauma enough. How long would it take to sort out spiritual confusion—being confused by another spirit? How long before her *ti bon ange* recycled itself, so he could enjoy what years of gender accord he had left? He didn't want her to think he was ungrateful—it was no easy task to dismiss someone who had saved your life—but it was time for Carla to move on.

He thought at first it was maternal regret that kept her rooted inside him, refusing to leave his body until she had a chance to say goodbye to her children. But she had her chance the day he visited her home, and again the time they all went to a movie together. No, it was something else that held her there, something to do with Luke and his limp, the bone condition with the hyphenated name: Legg-Perthes disease, the ball of his hip starved for blood. Duncan told him that some of the time, as with Luke, it was caused by a genetic defect that resulted in a tendency to form blood clots in veins—in this case, veins around the ball of the hip. Either Duncan or Carla had transmitted the faulty gene to him—and maybe to Loni and Cassidy, too. Duncan and the girls had been tested for it, but their results weren't back yet.

Ennis was betting Duncan's test would be negative. That was why Carla couldn't move on, he figured. Because Luke got the defective gene from her. She felt guilty over passing it to him and making him limp. But Luke's case wasn't that bad, Duncan said. Milder than most. Maybe if Carla saw that he could still run and play, that life went on and he would outgrow it soon like the doctors said, she would stop beating herself up over it and do what she needed to do: go to heaven. Split. Recycle her *ti bon ange*. And stop making Ennis a wreck.

So he hit on the idea of taking them all to Chuck E. Cheese's. Yes, it would feel good to do something nice for his donor's family, something to relieve his guilt, but his, what you might say, ulterior motive was to show Carla that Luke was going to be okay. Calm her jangled nerves about it. So she could move on to the next world where she belonged. And leave him in peace. Grateful and loving her always, but at peace.

Duncan arrived ten minutes late. Not bad, considering that rounding up children for an outing was like herding cats. They hit the ground with the focused energy of an amphibious landing, an all-out assault on the entrance, with Duncan—wearing jeans and sandals and a long sleeve white pullover stamped with a red lion posed rampant on a yellow Royal Standard of Scotland banner—struggling to keep them in check. The admission routine impressed Ennis with its concern for child safety. A young woman in the Kid Check Area, a processing station inside the doorway that made him think of Ellis Island, stamped the back of each child's hand with the same number she stamped onto the hands of Duncan and Ennis. No child was allowed to leave unaccompanied by an adult bearing the same number on his or her hand as the child. NOT A SUBSTITUTION FOR ADULT SUPERVISION, a square red sign warned about the process. Ennis liked that. It was thoughtful and—well, motherly. Which, though he hadn't dressed that way, was precisely how he felt after clearing the Kid Check Area. He nodded at another smiling young female employee in a red blouse and black slacks and passed into the thumping, whirling, dizzying chaos of Chuck E. Cheese's.

The blat and clatter and junk food smell of the place hit him full force, children of all ages running and pushing and climbing and yelling. And eating, long rows of identical wooden tables bearing pizzas tallowed with pale, gooey cheese. A bewildering array of rides and amusements and video games and an overhead network of brightly colored plastic crawling tunnels called Skytubes—like a maze of ducts in an old hotel—competed for the mercurial attention of scores of sauce-stained, snot-nosed, running, shoving, frantic children. It was genius, pure genius: a playground, amusement park, video arcade, and school lunchroom under one roof, with only a modicum of adult supervision.

They bypassed the Toddler Zone—four and under—and steered Luke and the girls into the Kiddie Area. Ennis bought a fistful of brass tokens with Chuck E. Cheese's image engraved in the center and the company slogan, Where A Kid Can Be A Kid, inscribed around the rim. He doled them out and helped Luke slug a machine that dispersed a token certificate that functioned like a debit card when swiped to play an arcade game or participate in an activity. Duncan did the same with the girls, who wore matching tops and jeans and Keds and reminded Ennis of his own sisters in Toledo, long ago. Some of the games were familiar to him—Skee Ball, Air Hockey, Tic Tac Toe—but most were not: Smash A Munch, Ticketblaster, Drop & Pop, Snowboard Run! and countless more. He played Skee Ball with Luke to help him win some of the redeemable tickets that could be used to trade for items in the Chuck E. Cheese's store. Ten dollars of tickets got you a twenty-five cent prize—though you would have thought they were lifetime passes to Disneyland by the way Luke squealed and pressed them against his chest.

They broke for lunch a half-hour later. Ennis was surprised and more than a little thankful to learn that Chuck E. Cheese's served beer and wine to sedate the adults and keep them from running for the exits with blood trickling from their ears from the constant, piercing screams that were like daggers to his eardrums. They ordered two medium pizzas, one Canadian bacon and one pepperoni, and Pepsis for the kids. Like they weren't hyper enough already. He couldn't help but think that Carla would have insisted they drink juice. He and Duncan had tap beer served in rime-rimmed glasses. The welcome lull in the incessant jabbering of the children while their mouths were stuffed with pizza didn't last nearly long enough, though. A visit from the big cheese himself took care of that: Chuck E., wearing a green and purple baseball cap over his enormous murine head; a purple jersey with a yellow C on the front over a long sleeve green undergarment; and green knee-length boxers over his furry mouse legs. He drew high fives all around and launched a new frenzy of chatter.

Looking back on things, the beer—at least the second one, which Ennis downed with Chuck and four Muppet-looking, animatronic characters perched onstage singing Happy Birthday to a mesmerized toddler, the Chuck E. Cheese Band blowing the roof off the place—might not have been such a good idea. He was fine until a gangly punk decked out in an oversized black jersey and black short pants that fell to his scrawny little calves shoved Luke aside and supplanted him at the Skee Ball table. Shoved him hard. Even then, he might have let it go if not for the awkward way Luke stumbled, the way he lurched sideways when his bad hip buckled.

Something broke loose inside him, something fierce and untethered. He rose from his chair and charged across the room with his cheeks aflame and his gut on fire. Crazed, completely insane. He grabbed the other boy by the elbow and spun him around and got in his grill, mere inches between them, a mama bear protecting her cub, the most ferocious beast in the animal kingdom about to rip his face off.

"If you touch him again, I'll pull your arm out of its socket, you little asshole."

He dialed up the pressure on the boy's arm, whose eyes grew big as fifty-cent pieces. His mouth fell open and he began to cry. And then he pissed his pants. Right there in front of his hoodlum friends, hot steamy piss streaming down his leg and onto the floor, a great big piece of humble pie crammed down his little hooligan throat.

"Take your hands off my son!"

Before Ennis could even turn his head, a pair of spring-loaded hands shot out and knocked him three feet away from Luke's oppressor. He righted himself and squared his shoulders to face his attacker, a human Brunswick bowling ball with a black handlebar moustache and shaved head and the same black jersey his son had on. The pants-pisser cowered behind his father, who balled his fists and flexed his muscles and twisted his face into a fearsome grimace. He moved to get at Ennis again, to do him harm, but Duncan inserted himself between them, his freckled, hairless face white with tension.

"I'm sure we can work this out," he said to Brunswick. "There must be some sort of misunderstanding here. Everything will be fine."

But everything wasn't fine. It wasn't close to fine. The boy had pissed his pants and disgraced his father. "Nobody touches my son except me. Get the fuck out of my way."

A crowd gathered, like in the alley after school, children and adults pressing and noisy, thirsting for blood. They were already taking sides, rooting, some for Brunswick, some for Ennis and Duncan, imploring them not to take Brunswick's shit. No one other than Duncan seemed all that interested in letting cooler heads prevail. Least of all Brunswick.

He pitched Duncan aside like a sack of trash and went for Ennis, but before he got there a pair of young guys with buzz-tops were all over him. Marines, maybe. And then

Brunswick's sympathizers were all over *them*. All hell broke loose, yelling and shouting and pushing and shoving, a real melee, with tables upended and chairs knocked over and two-dozen people straining and grabbing shirtfronts in front of the gaping and silent Chuck E. Cheese Band. It went on and on, snarling, red-faced adults surging back and forth across the room, the staff wanting no part of it. And not just men: foul-mouthed women, too. Where did these skanks come from? Ennis wondered. He stayed right there in the middle of it, never straying more than a few feet from Luke's side, his eye on Brunswick, who had forgotten about Ennis and was tangled up with one of the marines.

Finally a pair of police officers arrived. And then another and another, a whole squad of them, wearing stern, disgusted faces. They separated the combatants and huddled with the store manager before zeroing in on Ennis and Duncan and Brunswick. A female cop with a ponytail who was built like a gymnast tossed them all out, Ennis and Duncan first.

"I need you two to settle your bill and leave." She pointed across the room to Brunswick, whom two stout male officers with truncheons had calmed considerably. "He goes next, but I want you out of sight first. In your car and out of the parking lot in ten minutes. For your own good."

Ennis paid their bill while Duncan collected the children, Loni and Cassidy pale and mortified, Luke beside himself with guilt. "Please don't be mad at Ennis," he pleaded. "He was trying to help me. It wasn't his fault."

Duncan was having none of it. He paused outside beneath the smiling neon mouse and addressed Ennis with a stony face. "It's best if you don't see us for a while."

Ennis lowered his head. He was lucky Duncan didn't ask for Carla's organs back. What kind of fuck-up got kicked out of Chuck E. Cheese's, for Christ's sake? He understood why Duncan wanted him to stay away from the children, he really did. He would just have to deal with it.

But what he couldn't deal with was the flutter of panic inside him, a rising hysteria over the prospect of not seeing Luke again. Female hysteria.

A mother's hysteria.

The day of the Scottish Highland Games broke thick and gray, clinging to Windom Park like a cool, dank mist over Loch Lomond. Ennis arrived at eleven, his need to see Duncan and the children like a hunger pang. A week wasn't what Duncan had in mind when he told Ennis to lay off his family after the Chuck E. Cheese fiasco, so he came incognito, as Elaine. His brown curly wig, long sleeve boat neck top—a French sailor number right out of the fifties—beige women's chinos, and white canvas shoes were conservative, tasteful, and inconspicuous. Perfect for knocking around a Scottish fair. Perfect for a woman his age.

He checked his watch, a Michael Kors rose golden petite—the gals at the Clinique counter in Bloomie's again, who else? He had an hour to nose around before Duncan and his father Logan were scheduled to compete in caber toss, whatever that was. The children were sure to be there, too, a MacGregor family fix that would have to hold him until Duncan lifted the quarantine he imposed because of the brawl Ennis incited at Chuck E. Cheese's.

To transform Windom Park into a suitable Scottish venue, the basketball courts had been commandeered for a beer pavilion and entertainment stage, the baseball fields for the heavy athletic events, and the lush, rolling hillsides for sheep dog trials. At every turn, things Scottish assailed the senses: the mouth-watering, breakfast sausage smell of bangers; the alarming, fried-offal scent of haggis; the skirl of bagpipes; the flashing tartans of dozens of clans.

Ennis stopped by a general information booth to learn a little bit more about the Highland Games. A young brunette with sparkling blue eyes and a devilish smile, wearing a white peasant top and pleated plaid skirt and red ribbon in her hair, handed him a brochure. If she clocked him for a trannie, she didn't let on. The brochure said the Games began as part of an ancient custom called the *tainchel*—a gathering of rival Scottish clans that culminated in a cooperative hunt for red deer. The competitive nature of the clansmen led to running, jumping, and weight putting contests, which clan chieftains used to identify potential warriors. Piping and dancing contests came later.

Modern day Highland Games, he learned, were festivals of Scottish culture, featuring food, music, dance, and many of the original athletic competitions—including caber toss, the marquis event. About as strange an athletic contest as Ennis could imagine, heaving telephone poles end-over-end into the air, best he could tell. Caber toss, the pamphlet explained, began as a sixteenth century military exercise in which a tree trunk—or caber—of appropriate length was laid perpendicular across a stream. Such bridging exercises were crucial to an army's logistical success, so the peculiar knack of tossing a caber at right angles became an essential military skill. The cabers in use at the Highland Games, it said, were tapered logs that varied from fifty to one hundred thirty pounds in weight, and fourteen to twenty feet in length. He still had trouble picturing what the aim of caber toss was, what the contestants did and how they kept score, but he was getting hungry, so he thanked the Scottish lass in the booth and moved on.

He stopped by the food court and ordered a banger, his first ever—but not Carla's, he sensed. "So what exactly are bangers?" he asked.

A bald, overweight, wheezing vendor in a white twill chef's apron eyed his wig and lipstick and shrugged his shoulders. "Pork rump sausages, spiced sweet and savory. They're called bangers because they burst open with a loud bang if you fry 'em too long."

He served up a grayish-white, still crepitating sausage, about as long as a hot dog, but twice as thick, slit lengthwise on a warm French roll. Ennis took it with him to the beer pavilion and washed it down with a glass of Innis & Gunn, a bright amber pour of Scottish beer that tasted like whiskey with an oak finish. The banger was really good, and so was the entertainment, a group called Bad Haggis that played rock-and-blues laced with the mournful, majestic sound of the Scottish Highlands.

Next he paid a visit to the booth of Clan MacGregor. A lean, grizzled man in a Glengarry hat and kilt and tartan scarf directed him to a laminated poster of the Chief's Crest, a lion's head bearing a five-pointed crown encircled by the motto, *'S Rioghal Mo Dhream* — Royal is My Race. Beneath it was a paragraph on the history of the war cry of Clan MacGregor, *Ard Choille!* — the wooded height, coined in the early 16th century when Duncan Ladasach, the MacGregor of Ard Choille, was driven from his home by the hated Campbells, but refused to move on and instead waged a guerrilla war that immortalized him as Duncan the Bold.

So that's what all Duncan's piss and vinegar over Clan MacGregor and caber toss had been about. His forebears, his lineage, the royal line of the MacGregors — his genes. There would be three generations of them on the same caber toss field: Logan the Chief; his heir, Duncan the Bold; and little Lucas the Crippled, to bear witness to the greatness of the first two. Genes were, when you got right down to it, the main job of the species — any species. Passing them on to reproduce itself. But why was it that for the human species, believing in

God was part of the recipe? Look at Europe: empty pews, empty cradles. The only ones having babies over there were Muslims. And they were turning European churches into mosques faster than Detroit could crank out cars.

He arrived at the baseball field hosting the caber toss event with ten minutes to spare. A knot of males in kilts and sporrans and shirts displaying the logo of the Scottish American Athletic Association—the Scottish and American flags superimposed over a red rampant lion—warmed up beside a stack of cabers resembling freshly varnished telephone poles.

Ennis observed an athlete at the start of his move, a long caber upright on the ground in front of him. He squatted and grasped the pole and lifted it off the ground, then slid his hands beneath the tapered end and hoisted it into carrying position, balanced against his shoulder. He ran a short distance with his hands cupped beneath it before flinging it into the air. The tapered end flipped in mid-flight and fell away from him, with points deducted according to how far off twelve o'clock the narrow end landed. It didn't look like an especially riveting spectator sport—Ennis was partial to anything involving a ball or a puck—but there was no denying the strength and timing and balance required.

He squinted and found Duncan and his father at the edge of the field taking turns spotting each other. Duncan's children were nearby. Ennis made sure he stayed a good forty yards away. The last thing he needed was to be recognized in drag.

The snatches he caught of Duncan warming up suggested that a surprising amount of muscle hibernated beneath his kilt. He seemed to have no trouble cleaning and carrying the ponderous cabers, though his herky-jerky throwing motion left something to be desired. Logan, on the other hand—competing in the over-fifty Masters division, according to the program—was a caber-tossing machine, fluid and natural and remarkably precise with his landings.

The sun burned away the Scottish mist and warmed his shoulders like a shawl. The hairs of his wig tickled the nape of his neck, and he liked it. He smoothed his Chinos and reveled in their pleasing velvet texture. It felt good to be a woman. A woman supporting her family.

A muscular, square-jawed man in a kilt barked into a megaphone that the men's caber toss was about to begin. A tall adolescent stepped in front of Ennis and cut off his view. The boy realized what he had done and turned around, all pimples and hair and gangly limbs.

"Sorry, ma'am. I forget how tall I am."

He moved aside, so self-conscious he failed to notice that the odd-looking woman in the sailor shirt whose view he had blocked wasn't a woman at all, but a cross-dresser attempting to pass for a woman. Except that Ennis wasn't attempting to pass. Not really. He had finally come to accept the fact that he would never be mistaken for a genetic female, but the wonderful thing was that he no longer cared. Because the consequences of someone reading him were that there *were* no consequences. Beyond the occasional whisper behind the back of a hand or rare petty remark, no one gave a shit. More often than not, they gave a sly, knowing grin that said, "I'm onto you, pal, but it's okay." No one ridiculed him or threw garbage at him and no one assaulted him or refused him service in a restaurant. They didn't care. So eventually, he didn't care either. And guess what? Once he stopped caring, he didn't get clocked as often. He passed! Like with the introverted, acne-ridden, apologetic teen in front of him. He passed. And that was what gender accord felt like.

Duncan's first toss turned a fourteen-foot caber weighing eighty pounds, landing the tapered end at three o'clock. Ennis had to work hard—surprisingly hard—to suppress a cheer to add to the clapping and yelling of the MacGregor children, their little faces alive with pride and delight. Logan had little trouble landing a sixteen-footer weighing ninety pounds at one o'clock. And though the children cheered this too, Luke thumping his hands together and the girls jumping up and down, it left Ennis oddly unmoved.

For Duncan's second toss, he chose the same sixteen-footer Logan turned in the first round. He waved off his spotter, whom he'd used on the first toss to help stabilize his caber before making his run. Logan hadn't needed a spotter, so Duncan went without one, too.

He hoisted the big pole to vertical with a snatch and mighty thrust of his legs, but couldn't get it to stop wobbling. The top end looped from side to side, slowly increasing the radius of its arc while Duncan the Bold shuffled beneath it and moved his locked hands back and forth to try and settle the sway. One of his lunges overcompensated, causing the top to yaw sharply towards him. He yanked his hands in to straighten it, but not in time.

The varnished caber, its burnt-orange sheen gleaming in the midday sun, toppled into him like a giant redwood. The weight of it drove him under and slammed him against the ground.

Ennis looked to the children. They stood aghast, paralyzed with horror, like Ennis the day he watched his father's plane crash at the airfield. But it wasn't like that. Thank God, it wasn't like that. Duncan squirmed and pushed the caber off his chest and struggled to his feet. Dusted himself off and gave an embarrassed shrug. More than embarrassed. Humiliated.

Logan reached him first, with runnels of worry marking his face; Duncan's petrified children got there a moment later. They piled into him, hugging him and crying and laying their hands on him to assure themselves he was still in one piece. Logan patted Duncan on the shoulder and gave him a patronizing smile that launched Ennis like a torpedo from its tube, powered by a fissile force deep inside him. A feminine force.

He bolted onto the field and grabbed the front of Logan's shirt with both hands.

"A son can become a man by standing with his father or by standing against him. But a son who makes no stand will be a boy forever. I'm proud of Duncan, do you hear me? Proud as can be!"

Logan pushed him away—hard, his arms like pilings, his eyes accusing and cold. *You are too unstable to be around my son and grandchildren.* That's what he had told him the day Ennis lied his way into their lives, posing as something he wasn't. And now here he was in disguise again. He felt ridiculous, clocked for all to see, his wig a fright and his shoulders too big and his jaw too square and his hands, God, his hands, his thick male fingers and wrists.

But he wasn't in disguise. This is who he was. He pulled off his wig and spat on the ground. "That's right, it's me. Ennis Willoughby. I came to root for Duncan."

Luke glanced up from beneath his father's arm. "Ennis!" he called out. The girls recognized him, too. "Ennis, we missed you!"

Duncan looked repulsed, as if Eva Braun had claimed him as her son. Ennis realized Logan never told him the recipient of Carla's organs was a cross-dresser. And that threw him for a loop, because he knew what Logan thought of him, his condescending way and measured disdain. And yet Logan had refused to use Ennis's cross-dressing against him.

He left the field perplexed by Logan's restraint. But what really flabbergasted him—what sent him running to Becky's office the first open appointment she had—was the restraining order Duncan slapped him with the following day, a court order to stay away from his children.

Chapter 18

PRIVATE INVESTIGATORS SWAM IN the fetid slurry of life, and Ron Ely looked the part. He had heavily dyed black hair, a waxy face, a gangster yellow tie, and he stank of Old Spice. His office, though—a mile from the beach on the twelfth floor of a glass high-rise—had an altogether different feel to it: a black walnut presidential writing desk, fronted by two leather chairs of the same wood; a view to the shoreline through floor-to-ceiling windows; and built-in shelves filled with leather-bound volumes of law books that bespoke competence and professionalism. Despite his film noir gumshoe appearance, Ely turned out to be a former FBI agent with a master's degree in criminal justice.

Cullen had been referred there by Mark Puckett, a work-addicted cardiologist in his early forties with prematurely gray hair and bags under his eyes. Puckett paid a hefty retainer to an investigator chosen from the phone book to conduct a surveillance of his wife, whom he suspected of cheating on him during his long hours at work as director of Beach Park's cardiac cath lab. The PI told him his wife checked out clean—no hanky panky with the pool man, no trysts in local hotels, no secret love nest, but Puckett wasn't convinced. So he hired Ely, who promptly caught Puckett's wife *in flagrante delicto* with a tennis pro that on occasion substituted for the wife's regular female tennis instructor. The first PI had pocketed his retainer and then extracted another fee from Puckett's wife in exchange for attesting in his report to Puckett that she was pure as the driven snow. Puckett divorced her as a point of honor, but it was a pyrrhic victory: he landed in a one-bedroom apartment while she got the home *and* the tennis pro, who moved in with her a week after their divorce was final.

"That was a tough case all the way around," Ely said, when Cullen mentioned Puckett. He shook his head and sighed. "Sometimes people make bad choices. That's what makes us human, I guess. Vice is ascendant, Dr. Brodie, and virtue is in decline."

But Cullen wasn't there to bust a cheating wife. He was there to find his daughter, and Ely proved surprisingly tender about it. He wore a kind, sympathetic face and listened to his entire story without interrupting.

"Of course you want to find her," he said, after Cullen finished. "An only child you never knew you had? I'm sure she's all you've thought about since returning home: what type of person she is, what she looks like, if her adoptive parents treated her well, if she ever tried to find you, if she's healthy and happy and living a full life. But more than curiosity—and guilt and regret, which are perfectly natural in this situation—there's love you'd like to give her. Love you might never have known you were capable of giving." He smiled and winked. "And you're probably wondering if she's made you a grandfather yet."

It was true. She *was* all he thought about. He could almost see her, a fetching young woman of thirty-three, with long dark hair, a pretty, upturned nose, and a third generation of glittering green eyes. If only he could hold her and stroke her and tell her how sorry he was that he wasn't there for her when she was young. But it wasn't his fault. He never knew about her. *He never knew.* He would never have allowed her to be adopted if he did. And yes, he wondered about grandchildren.

"You must be very anxious to find her. California has a Mutual Consent Program. If the California Department of Social Services receives a signed consent from the adult adoptee and from one of the birth parents, their names and addresses can be released to one another. You should get your consent to them right away. Who knows? Maybe your daughter already signed one. It happens. Usually, though, these things take time. You'll need to be patient."

Ely twirled his wedding ring between his thumb and forefinger. "Suppose I find her, but she doesn't want to meet you? You need to know that I'll respect her wishes. I won't put you in contact with her unless she allows me to."

Cullen said he understood, though he didn't. How could a daughter not want to see her birth parent? But then again, how could a birth parent give a daughter away to begin with?

"It's also possible we won't be able to find her. You don't have a birth certificate and a lot of time has gone by. She might not even know she was adopted."

He knew what Ely was doing: obtaining informed consent. Patiently explaining all the things that could go wrong. Like he did when he told someone they needed dialysis. But things usually didn't go wrong. Dialysis usually went fine. He had no choice but to hope that things usually turned out fine for Ron Ely, too, that he was every bit the professional Cullen was.

Ely winced, as if recalling a case that had crushed even his hardened spirit. "The truth can be cruel. If you aren't prepared emotionally and psychologically to handle what I might find, you shouldn't hire me. Think it over. Talk about it with someone you really trust. I can recommend several good psychologists if you'd like."

Cullen smiled. "I'm dating a psychiatrist. At least I was before I left for the Cook Islands."

"Good. Make sure you talk to her about it. I've had several birth parents learn that the adoptee they were seeking had died. Some of them didn't handle it too well."

It wasn't often that Cullen felt ordinary in his Mercedes S-class, but he did that Saturday in the valet line at Neptune's Kitchen. A Maserati coupe squatted in front of him like a flexing penis, the *vroom vroom* of its engine a mating call to any female within shouting distance. An Aston Martin preened behind him, top down, vainglorious and gleaming in the spotlight of the midday sun. He was meeting Becky for lunch, their first date since he'd returned from Rarotonga, and he wanted to do it in style, high on a bluff overlooking the Mediterranean beauty of Pacific Shores and its golden curl of sand.

He had already apologized for standing her up that night, but they still had a lot to talk about. The erotic vapors of Rarotonga had made him love-drunk for Angie, like Gauguin succumbing to Tahiti, but his fever for her had finally broken. And the angrier he became at her for relinquishing their daughter, the stronger his love for Becky grew. His willingness to ditch her for a woman he hadn't seen in over thirty years had been insane. Becky had no baggage, no self-inflicted scars on her thighs: no secret pregnancy depriving him of his daughter.

She was perfect for him: kind, educated, intelligent—and younger. He liked that, landing a younger woman. It made *him* feel younger. And Becky could still have children. Maybe he'd get a boy this time, a son. The thought of it put a smile on his face that the long-legged blonde getting out of the passenger side of the Maserati mistook for flirting. Her sly return smile buoyed his spirits all the more.

Knowing he had a daughter changed everything—even the way he thought about women. Throughout his life, he had viewed the contraceptive revolution as an unmitigated good that freed women from the chains of pregnancy and gave them license to enjoy sex. But severing the link between sex and reproduction, he conceded, had consequences—like adolescent promiscuity. Not to mention the glorification of porn. Neither of which a father wanted for *his* girl. Having a daughter—even an adult one he never met—had caused him to consider women more deeply than before.

An older brunette with glossy red lips and bleached white teeth and a derm-abraded face wrung free of all emotion led him to a window table with a view of the coastline. The restaurant hummed and clattered, filled to the brim with winking crystal and shining cutlery and unabashed *joie de vivre*. He had a moment of regret over choosing it, the possibility of making Becky ill at ease amidst the St. Tropez glamour of the local habitués. No matter. He would tell her how lovely she looked and how much he missed her. How he was ready to settle down and commit. To her.

He sampled the Beaujolais Villages he ordered—one of her favorite reds—and took in the view while waiting for her. Bathers frolicked. The ocean glittered. Cliffs south of the beach rose up like ramparts, tawny and gouged.

From the moment she arrived—squired to their table by their blank-faced hostess—she evinced not a shred of self-consciousness. She wore her hair down and held her chin high and the one-shoulder, orange-and-white ruffle-neck dress she wore was a knockout, the hem landing mid-thigh. Cullen stood and kissed her and said she was beautiful. A handsome young Mexican server admired her tennis-star legs and pulled her chair out for her, his hair pomaded and thick, his lower lip pink and full. She favored him with a girlish smile. He bowed and turned away, the crease of his slacks as sharp as the *foie gras* with mustard seeds and green onions Cullen ordered for his hors d'oeuvre.

They talked first of Ennis, shop talk, neutral ground to ease into the thornier matter of their relationship, which had foundered ever since Angie's disturbing painting of Grady arrived. She said Ennis had been doing great until he somehow learned the identity of his donor and befriended the MacGregor family. She set her glass down and eyed him with the probing gaze of a wary psychiatrist.

Cullen shrugged. "I'm not surprised he found them. Ennis is pretty resourceful." He felt a stab of culpability over his role in things, but said nothing more.

She reached for her fork and dug into her *escargot bourguignonne*. "At first things went okay with the MacGregors," she said between mouthfuls, "but then—surprise, surprise—it all fell apart. He showed up en femme at a family event with the children present. Uninvited. Duncan overreacted and got a restraining order to keep him away from them. Ennis is convinced that Carla's soul refuses to move on to the next realm because she feels guilty over passing some sort of genetic condition to her son. A type of avascular necrosis of the hip, I think. I don't recall the name." She took a sip of wine and shook her head. "I'm extremely frustrated with him."

Cullen laughed. "A doctor frustrated by Ennis? I'm shocked."

They got around to each other when their entrées came, spinach-wrapped monkfish with Alaskan King Crab for him, squab with hearts of palm for her. Becky listened with a skeptical face to his bowdlerized version of what transpired in the Cook Islands—sans mention of his overnight with Angie—and how it brought closure to the deaths of Grady and Leslie.

"I'm glad for that. She's the only one that could have given it you, I suppose."

Her begrudging tone and the petulant look on her face gave him an anxious jolt. Did she suspect more had gone on with Angie than he let on? Or was she resentful that he hadn't asked her to go to Rarotonga with him? There was no way he could have, under the circumstances. She must realize that.

"There was a lot we needed to work through. I'm relieved that you understand."

He suffered fresh pangs of guilt over the black pearl necklace he had given to Angie instead of her—and of his desperate night-swim to Angie's home and the pent-up passion that followed. How understanding would Becky be about that? But that was before Angie told him about their daughter, the baby girl she gave away. Becky had nothing to fear from Angie now.

He smiled to put her at ease, but she fumbled her fork and gulped her wine. "Oh, I understand," she said. "More than you know." She trembled and appeared on the verge of crying. He reached across the table and took her hands. Engulfed them. She pulled away and spoke in a tense, earnest voice.

"What kind of doormat do you think I am? You're still in love with Angie. Do you think I can't tell? I read people for a living. It's all over your face. You love her, but you're settling for me. That's not okay." Her expression changed from emotionally anguished to fiercely determined, the look she got on a tennis court at match point. "I want to be the one you fly halfway around the world to see, not your consolation prize. And I *especially* resent being runner-up to a woman old enough to be my mother. I'm ending our relationship. Tonight. Now. I'm going back to Adam. I should never have left him in the first place. I'm sorry, Cullen. I did love you."

She tossed her napkin on the table and was gone, the hope and joy he had arrived with vacuumed from his heart. By Adam. Adam the barnacle-burner, the nerd in the photo. A swift and terrible despair threatened to suck him under. He fought it, but it was too much, first Angie and now Becky, tag-teaming him into submission. He gave in and let self-pity take him—until the Maserati girl capered by on her way to the restroom and gave a seductive wave. The perfect antidote for self-pity.

He grinned—a raw, vulnerable grin that froze her in her tracks—and winked with the poise of a spy resorting to plan B after his cover had been blown.

"I'm never taking a woman to dinner again," he told her.

The Burn Zone had fitness centers all across the county, including the two-story stand-alone near Nephrology Partners' business office. The sound system blasted a vexing mix of geezer rock and strident rap, as if a father in his fifties and his twenty-year-old son were vying for control of the dial. A long row of ellipticals and treadmills on the upper level looked down on the center's main floor, where exercise addicts with heaps of contoured muscle prowled silver Cybexes or pumped free weights. A concession counter near the locker room sold protein drinks spiked with enough caffeine to get your heart rate to eighty percent of maximal before you laced your cross trainers on.

Cullen glanced at the treadmill beside him, where Duncan MacGregor looked as though he might faint. Sweat poured off of him and his cheeks were as red as his hair. He grabbed the metal contact grips and hung on, appearing less interested in his heart rate than in keeping upright. Cullen checked the time elapsed indicator on his machine: twelve minutes. Maybe they should have skipped the gym and gone straight to Primo Pablo's for margaritas.

Duncan somehow made it to the twenty-minute mark. *GREAT WORKOUT!!!* the screen of his treadmill flashed. "One exclamation point would have been enough," he huffed. "Three is patronizing." He staggered off his machine and put his hands on his knees and sucked wind. His head lolled. Duncan was in the barf zone, not the burn zone.

Cullen shut down his treadmill and hopped off and looped his towel around his neck. "We don't have to hit the weights, you know. We can shower and head to the bar instead."

Duncan straightened up and gave him an envious look. "Something tells me you don't usually stop at twenty minutes."

"Actually I do, on account of my knee. I do most of my aerobic work in the water."

"The knee you blew out that kept you from playing college basketball?"

"Who told you about that?"

"That interior designer we hired to decorate our offices a while back. Tess. She told Carla all about you. I mean *all* about you."

Tess, of course—she and Carla would have been about the same age. Tess of the d'Urbervilles, talking about his shattered dreams and what he was like in bed. "No wonder Carla used to look at me like I was pathetic."

Duncan grinned. "More like in awe. Happy hour sounds good to me. I'll race you there."

Primo Pablo's was a gritty sports bar Cullen sometimes stopped at to watch Lakers games. The raucous, boisterous crowd got his pulse racing, the drunken hooting when Kobe Bryant flashed to the rim. They sat at a table that faced a big screen tuned to ESPN. A skinny bartender with a goatee and Packers cap passed Coronas and tequila shooters to a crowd closer in age to Duncan than Cullen. Music screeched overhead, bands Tess would have known, but that he did not. They ordered margaritas from a waitress with corn-fed cheeks and wide hips. The *tequila oro* went right to his head. He wasted no time in bringing up Ennis, which was why he had invited Duncan for a workout and drink in the first place.

"I'm sorry to hear about the trouble he caused. He gets a wild hair up his ass sometimes and does impulsive things."

Duncan took a sip of his drink. "It was the second public scene in a week he caused in front of my children. He should have told me he was transgender. It caught me off guard."

Cullen leaned forward. "He thinks a piece of Carla's soul came to him along with her organs."

Duncan's face lit up like a child's. "I believe in that sort of thing, spiritual energy and reincarnation. A lot has happened to him that connects to Carla."

"You mean like sushi and beets?"

"Other things, too. Like knowing her name. And liking jazz. I know it sounds crazy, but when he's around me, it feels like *she's* there."

Cullen had throughout his career encountered bereaved spouses who on occasion refused to let go. They coped with their grief by asking, in the words of his favorite poet, Richard Wilbur, *Is she now there, wherever there may be?* A few did more than wonder. They tried to make contact, tried to fling up the portcullis to another world and dialogue with the dead. It was not a new phenomenon: séances and mediums had been around forever. And though he did not believe in such ghosts, he understood the anguish that motivated those who did. It never failed to humble him.

"You must have loved her very much."

Duncan revealed how much during a second round of drinks and then a third, the kiss of the blue agave potent truth serum. Deeply potent.

"Carla had a difficult life when she was young. It left her damaged. Sometimes she took it out on me, ridiculed me because I worked for my father, things like that. It hurt my feelings, I guess, but I understood. There's nothing she could have said to make me stop loving her."

Cullen leaned forward. "I understand," he said, as gently as he could. "What kind of damage?"

"Carla was adopted," Duncan said, his eyes emotive and bright. "By a couple with two older sons. They wanted a daughter, too, but when they couldn't conceive one, they adopted instead. When Carla was fourteen, her twenty-three year old stepbrother—a charming, handsome alcoholic whom she had strong feelings for to begin with, and who still lived at home because he couldn't keep a job—came into her room one night and seduced her. She knew it was wrong, but he told her he loved her and that he would go to prison for life if she ever told anyone their secret. Carla and her brother slept upstairs; their parents' bedroom was downstairs. They never suspected a thing. The romantic and physical intensity of it was too much for her. She became addicted to it."

Cullen put a hand on his arm. "You don't have to tell me this."

"Yes, I do! I want to." Cullen shrugged and fell back in his chair.

"It went on for two years, until he drove his car into a ravine stone cold drunk and died. I don't think she ever got over him. She used to taunt me and call me Daddy's boy. I think she was trying to goad me into being physical with her, to take her by force to make sex more exciting for her. Like it was with him.

"I tried. I imagined that I was Duncan the Red, fresh from slaughtering Kings' men at the Battle of Glen Fruin, ravishing the wife of a vanquished foe in the castle keep. But I couldn't do it. Even though that's what she needed, I couldn't do it. I'm not convinced she ever had an orgasm with me, though she pretended she did."

He ran a finger around the rim of his glass and licked the salt off it, Duncan the Timorous, emasculated by his wife's incest with her dissolute stepbrother. Even with her dead and gone, he was tortured by it. No wonder he was willing to believe her soul lingered between this world and the next. It comforted him to think she stayed for him, that though she might not have loved him carnally, spiritually she did.

Cullen paraphrased Wilbur for him, though Wilbur's belief on the matter was not Cullen's. "One of America's Poet Laureates said the universe is full of glorious energy, an energy that tends to take pattern and shape, and that the ultimate character of things is comely and good."

Duncan looked up from his glass and smiled. "It's true. It has to be true, or what's the point of living?" It seemed to shake him from his funk. They talked of other things—sports, medicine, cars, even children—before their drunken rambling meandered back to Ennis.

"He thinks Carla can't move on," Cullen said, "because she feels guilty over a hip condition your son has. Ennis is convinced Carla gave him the gene that caused it and *knows* she gave it to him. He means well, Duncan, he really does. In his mind he's trying to help a mother relieve her guilt. What does your son have, if you don't mind my asking?"

"Legg-Calve-Perthes disease. Do you know much about it?"

"Only what little I remember from med school. Avascular necrosis of the hip. I have no idea what causes it."

Duncan's hands jabbed the air and he spoke in a professorial tone, a layperson schooling the doctor. "Some cases are associated with a genetic disorder that causes abnormal blood clotting—Factor V Leiden. If the veins around the hip are the ones that clot, it results in Legg-Perthes. Luke tested positive for Factor V Leiden. I tested negative. Ennis is right—Luke got the defective gene from Carla."

Cullen couldn't refrain from pointing out the obvious. "Except that Carla never knew she was a carrier, so how could Ennis?" He tried to keep his cynicism from creeping into his voice, but only partially succeeded.

Duncan appeared unfazed. "She didn't know she was a carrier while she was *alive*. What she knows in the afterlife is a different matter."

Utter nonsense. Pure dross. But if it helped get Ennis out of the MacGregor family doghouse, so be it. The real source of his emotional pain was his guilt over the enormous act of generosity Carla's organ donation constituted. "Then you must have some sympathy for what Ennis is going through because of it. He has an office visit with me next week. It would work wonders for his mental health if he knew he could see his donor's family again. I'd like you to think about removing the restraining order."

He motioned to the waitress to bring their bill. Duncan fumbled for his keys and shook his head. "I have to do what's best for my children."

Cullen awakened the next morning with a thrum behind his eyes. His head felt as if it were stuffed with straw. And thirsty? Nothing like *tequila con sal* to send you to the refrigerator with the singular focus of a camel at an oasis.

And breath to match. He vowed to quit drinking on school nights. He used to bounce out of bed the next day none the worse for wear, requiring only a shower and a cup of coffee to feel human, but no longer.

He slogged through hospital rounds tired and depressed, victim to the fitful sleep of the intoxicated — and the persistent sadness of being dumped twice in a month by women he loved. It was humiliating to lose Becky after assuming her desire to spend the rest of her life with him a forgone conclusion. He should never have been so arrogant. But she, at least, would leave no scars, whereas Angie... Angie was the queen of scars. On her legs and on his heart. Angie he would never get over. Nor forgive for relinquishing their daughter. Finding her was all that mattered now. Having a daughter gave his life meaning. And hope.

He finished up at the hospital and ploughed through his office schedule until the last patient before lunch, Mitchell Graves, a new consultation for chronic kidney disease. Graves was a genial, fleshy man with thin brown hair, a crooked smile, and an indentation that marred his forehead due to frontal bone malunion following a motor vehicle accident. He wore a white shirt and maroon tie and had his shirtsleeves rolled halfway up his forearms.

His case was straightforward, a forty-six-year-old diabetic with hypertension and a creatinine of 2.5. Cullen would need to explain that thirty-five per cent kidney function wasn't as dire as it sounded, that patients could live symptom-free with as little as twenty-five. His goal this first encounter would be to get Graves over the shock of being diagnosed with organ failure and to emphasize things he could do to preserve his residual renal function: avoid non-steroidal anti-inflammatory drugs and IV contrast dye, tighten up his blood pressure control, adhere to a protein-restricted diet, and take the ACE inhibitor Cullen would prescribe. All of which would reassure him that he was still in control. That's what patients feared, the loss of control, the notion that their disease would have its way with them with no hope of stopping it. Hope. They needed hope. Everyone did.

"What's your occupation?" he asked, in the soothing confines of his Tess-inspired office, safely removed from the stark, probing light of the exam room. He expected something mundane, an O-ring salesman or middle manager of a pet food distributorship. Graves unleashed a defiant smile.

"I'm a funeral director."

An unintended laugh escaped Cullen. "An undertaker named Graves?"

"You can imagine the ribbing I get."

"It isn't that strange, really. I know a bariatric surgeon named Pounds and an addiction medicine specialist named Crack. It happens. People have names related to their occupations."

He felt himself stiffen despite his attempt to put Graves at ease. Morticians were bottom feeders, scavengers picking at corpses. He resented them for it, plying their grisly trade after the battle to preserve life was lost. What kind of person would do it? What was the point? Keeping people alive was what mattered, not dressing them in costume after they were dead.

It wasn't really Graves's morbid métier he detested, though. It was death. He didn't even like to think about it. Whenever one of his patients died in his presence, he left the room as quickly as possible. Forced moments holding hands with a keening family over the ghastly doppelgänger that remained was agony for him. Death was defeat, shame: failure to prevail in the ultimate contest. He loathed dwelling even a minute in its leveling sorrow. Not once had he attended a patient's funeral, though he'd been invited a number of times.

The first and last wake he had ever witnessed was Todd Shemanski's, the summer before their senior year of high school. Todd had played point guard at Lourdes, a gifted playmaker who made everyone around him better. But he never made it to the state championship game against Adams. There would have been no need for ABA Left if he had, no miracle shot for Cullen to make. The game wouldn't have been that close. They would have beaten Adams by ten points if Todd had played.

He died in the Rapid City flood of '72, visiting relatives in the Black Hills. Over a foot of rain fell in six hours. A dam broke and sent a tidal wave of water raging down the city's flood plain. Two hundred and thirty-eight people died in the swirling, silt-laden waters that night. Todd's debris-battered face at the wake was purple and green and swollen, even through all the stage makeup they smeared on him. Cullen had hated funerals and morticians and death ever since. Because it forced him to think about what came next.

Nothing.

He suppressed the aversion he felt and led Graves into the exam room to give his corpulent body a thorough laying on of hands. He encountered no new findings. After stepping out of the room to give him time to pull his trousers on and button his shirt and fasten his tie, Cullen returned to wrap things up. Something in his demeanor must have registered the distaste he fought to disguise.

"You don't like morticians, do you?" The tone of Graves's voice signaled a challenge, not an observation.

Cullen sat on his doctor's stool with his forearms on his lap and his hands dangling between his legs. Graves perched above him on the exam table like a statue on a plinth, impassive and still.

Cullen cracked his knuckles. "My profession is devoted to life. Yours is devoted to death. How do you do it?"

"The living have an obligation to the dead. To prepare their souls for release to God. The body of a deceased person needs to be prepared for interment—or inurnment—in a special way. If not for that, I *couldn't* do what I do. It would be too bleak."

Cullen knew better than to argue with patients about religion—that was a good way to send them scurrying to find another doctor. But today the urge was too strong. "What if there's nothing to send them to? What if death is simply the end of life, and nothing more?"

Graves pointed his index finger down the barrel of an earnest gaze. "That's where we differ. At times I even envy the dead."

"Life is precious. Beyond precious." Cullen shook his head. "Why would you envy the loss of it?

"Oh, I don't envy their loss of life. I envy their death." The mortician pushed the sleeves of his shirt further up his arms. "Death is when we learn the truth about life. What it means."

Cullen rose up to his full height. "If we haven't figured out what life means by the time we die, I highly doubt death will do the job for us. Death is the end, not the beginning."

Graves slid off the exam table and moved closer. His eyes grew unnaturally bright. "If that were true, then life *would* have no meaning. But death doesn't end everything."

He beamed a gotcha smile and went on as if Cullen had asked him to explain. Which Cullen had *not*. "I know because of embalming. The formaldehyde and methanol we pump into their shrunken tissues to give them substance again. The dyes we inject into their collapsed veins to give color to their lifeless, porcelain faces. Embalming makes their souls visible. And their souls talk to me. They whisper of sorrow and joy and hope and despair and of the ultimate triumph of God's grace. And I wonder, 'Will I meet them in Heaven?'"

Cullen would normally have scoffed at such talk, discounting it as fanatical lunacy, but this time he didn't. The man's unexpectedly poignant, almost poetic, defense of the funeral parlor industry moved him, even if it didn't persuade him. Despite his skepticism, he sometimes fantasized about meeting Grady Nichols again in— wherever. To beg his forgiveness. He felt a flash of anger at God for allowing Grady to die, but then how could he be angry at something that didn't exist?

Graves pumped his hand and said he hoped there were no hard feelings between them. Cullen's anger ebbed. He regretted arguing with a patient. That was not the kind of doctor he was. "It isn't morticians I object to," he said, gripping Graves's hand. "It's death. I have my job to do and you have yours. And from what I can tell, you're damn good at it."

The minute Graves left, Cullen cancelled his afternoon schedule and signed out early to Ted Takagawa. He went home and swam in Emerald Cove to calm his agitation. He stayed until sunset, watching gulls carve swirls into the pearly sky amidst the wash of surf and smell of decomposing seaweed.

The following Sunday, the *Los Angeles Times* ran a brief story about a Catholic nun who was under consideration for canonization.

A Catholic nun who lived out her life tending to lepers on the island of Molokai appears headed for sainthood. Pope John Paul II first beatified

Mother Marianne Cope — who died of natural causes in 1918 — in 2004, after crediting her for the miraculous recovery of a fourteen-year-old girl dying from multiple organ failure. After a long, complex illness in 1993, the girl's attending physicians opined in her medical record that her case was futile. With death appearing imminent, the girl's family turned to Mother Marianne. A relic of the long-deceased nun was held against the dying girl's ravaged body and intercessory prayers to Mother Marianne were formally begun. Within two weeks, all of her organs were functioning normally. Her doctors offered no explanation for her astounding recovery, but Vatican physicians and theologians attributed it to the intercession of Mother Marianne. A second miracle — two are required for canonization, one for beatification — credited to Mother Marianne came a dozen years later, when a woman suffering from severe pancreatitis was told by her medical team that her condition was terminal. A nun from the woman's local parish began intercessory prayers to Mother Marianne and pinned some soil from the beatified nun's grave to the woman's gown. Inexplicably, her condition began to slowly improve. After nearly a year in the hospital, she made it home intact, completely cured. The Vatican Medical Board and cardinals of the Congregation for the Causes of Saints declared her mysterious recovery a miracle due to the intercession of Mother Marianne, whose anticipated canonization awaits final approval by Pope Benedict XVI.

Cullen read it in shorty pajamas over breakfast—a warm ham and Swiss croissant, a bruised, overripe banana, and a mug of Kona coffee. The ocean filled his kitchen window, vast and blue. "Miracles, huh," he said aloud. "We'll see about that."

He Googled the medical details of the cases cited. Neither struck him as extraordinary. Each had a run-of-the-mill critical illness and managed to survive. Such cases were hardly rare. He saw a handful each year. Who knew why some patients with prolonged shock-organ syndrome survived and others didn't? And yet the Church and families of the two women held their recoveries up as evidence of the supernatural, in the absence of any scientific verification to support their claims. It was completely illogical—though, on the other hand, how logical was it to expect the supernatural to be subject to scientific method?

He thought of Graves, the mortician he had seen a few days before. Perhaps miracles, like souls, existed in the eye of the beholder. Perhaps people of faith affirmed incidents like these as miracles because they believed in miracles. And skeptics rejected them because they did not believe in miracles. One man's miracle was another man's natural phenomenon. But then who were the dogmatists and who the objective observers?

What would it take, he wondered, to make *him* believe in miracles? More than a case of pancreatitis, that's for sure. Perhaps nothing could. He would simply attribute it to a previously undiscovered property of the natural world. Besides, there was no point in quibbling over something as insignificant as the purported intercession of Mother Marianne. That was small ball.

He gazed out the window at the ocean. Either it was *all* a miracle, or it all just happened on its own.

Chapter 19

ENNIS RETREATED TO THE sanctuary of his bathroom with a snifter of tequila the color of dark honey in one hand and a five-ounce packet of Vanilla Spice bath salts in the other. He turned the spigot and tore open the packet and dumped its yellow granules into the steaming water, a liniment for his aching bones. The aroma of freshly baked spice cake invested the room. He took a sip of tequila—El Jimador Añejo, aged for a year in a toasted white oak barrel that gave *añejo* tequila its amber color and oaky tinge. It went down smooth and slick, a slug of caramel and cinnamon and oak that warmed him from the inside out.

It used to be that Ennis took showers and Elaine took baths. But lately he found he could enjoy baths no matter who was in charge, Ennis or Elaine, his male or his female personality. One of the many benefits of gender accord, to use the preferred lingo of Becky's clinic. Without gender accord, there would have been no possible way to enjoy a bath *and* sip tequila; Ennis didn't do baths and Elaine didn't do tequila. But now, just like she promised, his male and female genders had become, what you might say, tolerant of one another. Not blended, mind you, but male and female at once. Piebald, not gray.

Gender accord made cross-dressing better, too. He felt more natural and relaxed about it, a calm satisfaction instead of adrenalin-powered dirtiness. Becky said that he was in charge of his cross-dressing, instead of cross-dressing being in charge of him. It was good to be in charge.

He set the snifter on the edge of the tub and climbed inside the bath. The warm water melted his buttocks and loosened his sack. He sank down until the waterline lapped his sternum. He traced the incision there, its long, rubbery ridge.

Carla was driving him nuts. He'd endured a non-stop barrage of extra-sensory instant messaging ever since the restraining order was issued. What he needed was a Center for Supernatural Accord, a place to learn how to gently encourage the ambivalent soul of his organ donor to get over it and move on. A little spiritual accord, that's all he asked.

He felt possessed, in need of an exorcism, but bath salts and booze would have to do. He let the sweet vanilla scent rise up his nose and a blissful wash of tequila sedate him. His muscles turned to gel. It was all he could do to lift his leg and grab the faucet with his bony, gnarled toes to turn the water off, before it spilled over the tub and onto the tessellated tile floor he laid himself before he became ill. After one Heineken too many, by the looks of the wavering grout line.

He soaked and sipped and sampled the perfumed air until his glass was empty and his bath tepid and gray. It almost did the trick, almost silenced her mystical nagging. Until his old nemesis guilt whispered in his ear. *Why are you sipping premium tequila in a scented bath while she can't even visit her children?* Guilt, the damning baritone of Denton Willoughby resurrected as the hectoring contralto of Carla MacGregor.

I want to see my son!

And she did have a contralto, he was sure of it. How though? He'd never heard her voice. Yet there it was, demanding things of him like they were married. Like she had a claim on him. But she did, didn't she? Her heart and kidney dwelling inside him: 'Til death do us part. He hauled himself out of the tub and looked at his raddled reflection in the mirror and shivered.

I want to see my baby boy!

Jesus, give some attention to the girls too, will ya? He had to shut her up, if only for tonight. He toweled off and put his robe on—the pistachio-colored one with the embroidered lace insets at the cuff—and drew the sash around him and set his jaw. More tequila, that's what he needed. A lot more. Enough to quiet the dead.

He padded into the living room and sat in front of the TV watching *Desperate Housewives*—Susan was such a slut—while he sipped his way through a second snifter and then a third of eighty proof, one hundred per cent blue agave tequila. But even the *añejo* and all the cleavage and horny-talking housewives of Wisteria Lane failed to silence Carla completely. She kept breaking through: insistent, stubborn, demanding.

I want to see him!

He stood with snifter in hand and his robe open, searching, half-expecting her to appear like a hologram at Disneyland. "It's a limp for Christ's sake. A goddamn limp! You didn't give it to him on purpose!"

He bent and filled his glass and sashed his robe and walked from room to room, gulping, not sipping. He went into the kitchen and swatted the air over his head. "Shut up! Shut up!" He slumped at the table with his head in his hands. "Please—shut—the fuck—up!"

I need to be with my son.

He hurled the snifter against the wall. It smashed with a pop and tinkle, scattering slivers and shards all over the travertine floor. He walked to the pantry to get a broom and dustpan. Barefoot. The blood trail he left forced him to consider the possibility that he was stinking drunk. Smashed, blitzed, plotzed: shit-faced. And that breaking an expensive brandy glass to make a dead person stop talking was not entirely rational. But that's how it was with tequila. That was how he once wound up hanging upside down at the Giggling Marlin in Cabo, suspended in midair, his ankles manacled to a rope and pulley system with a grinning, gold-toothed, black-mustachioed bartender squirting tequila into his mouth from a pouch. A lot of goofy-ass notions made sense after a bottle of tequila. Like purging Carla from his body, flushing her clean out of him. Exorcising her.

With bath salts.

The idea came to him while bending over to stanch the bleeding from the soles of his feet with a white dishtowel, a bolt of inspiration triggered by a box of Vanilla Sky bath salts on the counter—bought on impulse that very day, at the Las Brisas Qwik Mart. Not his usual brand, but the image on the box had looked so inviting, a pair of smooth-shaven female legs cavorting in a tub full of blue bubbles. How could he resist? It was enough to make a girl purr with anticipation. *Rrrrrroww.*

But he had something else in mind for the packet he extracted from the box. Something more extreme: a purge. He would flush Carla from inside him. And why not? If Epsom salts could do double duty as a bath salt and purgative, then why not sea salts? Other than a little magnesium, what was the difference? Catharsis, that's what he needed. Spiritual release—and if he shit up a symbolic storm in the process, so be it. Carla's organs could stay, but her spiritual residue, well, it was time for that to go.

He'd been more than accommodating, done everything he could do to be a good and grateful host: listened to the music she liked, ate the foods she favored, met her family, learned about her life. He had even tried to console her about passing her son a faulty gene. And how did she respond? By driving him insane with her endless handwringing over Luke's limp and constant cadging to see him. There were limits to what he could bear.

He filled a water glass from the tap and dumped the entire packet in and stirred it with a tablespoon until every last granule dissolved. He stuffed the empty package into the pocket of his robe and went into the living room and added a shot of El Jimador and chugged it down and sat on the couch to wait. For catharsis, relief: forced expulsion of the poltergeist inside him.

He sat up with a start thirty minutes later, as if he were a car and someone had turned over his engine. He felt like he'd been injected with a cup of coffee. Espresso. A double. Carla's heart banged against his ribs with such force that his head twitched with each contraction. His breath came fast and shallow and his palms grew damp. His vision turned 3-D, like wearing goggles at a movie.

His right calf flickered and then seized up in a powerful contraction that drove him to the floor in agony, an excruciating muscle cramp, like when he was on dialysis. He reached down and pulled his toes back the way the nurses used to.

"Ahhh! Ahhh! Ahhh!"

It went on for a minute before the painful knot of muscle gave way and relaxed. He felt hot, flushed, on fire, like the time he had pneumonia, only worse. He sat up grinding his teeth and smacking his lips. A power surge of wellbeing ripped through him. He was young, strong, invincible.

And brilliant.

He got to his feet apprehending the world with great clarity, the closely guarded strategies of hostile nations laid bare before him. The chinks, the ruskies, the ragheads: he saw all their plans. Poor bastards. For all their devious scheming, it was going to be another American Century. There were other revelations, too. He seemed on the verge of great inventions, an insight away from grasping the secrets of time travel and aging. The world of finance unraveled before him. Great riches awaited, shrewd investments only he would have the foresight and courage to make.

But danger lurked.

He turned off all the lights and peered out the window. A special-ops team had been dispatched to capture him this very night, a top-secret mission to prevent him from... from what? From bringing Carla to Luke, that's what. To keep her from telling him what he needed to know. That she gave him the gene.

He snatched his car keys from a hook on the wall and ran out the front door without locking it. What good would that do? If he left it open maybe they wouldn't blow it open with C4. He scuttered across the drive in his robe with his bloodied soles slapping the concrete and scrambled behind the wheel of his car.

His Impala squealed out of the driveway and into the winking, treacherous night.

⚜

Cullen groped his nightstand in search of the phone. It rang again, harsh, jangling, disruptive, the way it had for twenty-five years, telephonic torture depriving him of sleep. He grasped the receiver and clapped it to his ear.

"Hello."

"Answering service, Dr. Brodie." It was the perpetually hostile, doctor-resenting, over-caffeinated, two a.m. voice of Todd, their exchange's snarky gay telephone operator. "I have Beach Park ER on the line. Dr. Ralston. Shall I connect you?"

Why couldn't it have been a nurse asking for a laxative for a constipated inpatient? Something quick and simple, a ten-second interaction that allowed him to drift back asleep. But noooo, it had to be the ER. His only hope was for Ralston to be calling with a question on someone he intended to send home, asking for guidance on one of Cullen's dialysis patients.

"Yes, please."

The line clicked dead for an instant, then reinserted Todd into his ear. "Putting Dr. Ralston on the line." With a plosive p, a sibilant s, and a fricative th—the spiteful little jerk.

"Cullen, sorry to wake you. This is Ed. Got a sick one here."

He pictured Ralston sitting at the ER console, his white beard and nicotine-stained fingers, the whiskey-and-tobacco voice, his belly spilling over his worn cowboy belt. No one had actually seen him get up from his station and lay hands on a patient since Carter was president. *Got a sick one here.* What a wonderfully informative clinical summary. It told him absolutely nothing, only that he had to haul his ass out of bed to go in and manage some desperately ill patient.

"Talk to me, Ed. Some color commentary, yeah?" He braced himself for Ralston's usual farrago of physical findings and lab results. Wasn't the man's 401K fat enough to retire on yet?

"Sixty-three-year-old male who ran his car off the road. Had seizures and cardiovascular collapse in the field—beats the hell out of me why. Paramedics gave him Ativan and tubed him. Blood pressure's all over the place, on Nipride one minute and Levo the next. He's got a creatinine of 4 and a potassium of 7.8 and a bicarb of 5—and a blood alcohol level of 0.35. Head CT is negative. Got a medical bracelet on says he's a transplant patient and surgical scars over his sternum and groin."

The only groin Ralston had examined in the last ten years was his wife's—he must have read the nursing notes.

"He has a dialysis fistula in his right arm, but it's dead as a doornail. Clotted. Came in wearing nothing but a robe, by the way. A woman's robe."

Cullen's stomach sank. He had a visual of Ennis lying supine and drunk in the ER code room, his robe in ribbons beside him, cut away by the trauma team.

"What's his name?"

"Willoughby. Ennis Willoughby. He had a sine wave EKG when he hit the door, but I gave him an amp of bicarb, an amp of D50, and 10 units of IV insulin and got him into a junctional brady, with a repeat K pending. Oh, and an amp of calcium gluconate to keep him from arresting until you get here. And some Keppra for his seizure."

Funny thing about Ralston—he almost always got his patients stabilized, no matter how big a train wreck they were. And they didn't come any more wrecked than this.

"Nice work, Ed. I'm on my way."

He pulled on a pair of jeans and a cotton shirt and phoned the acute dialysis nurse on call from his Mercedes— Christy Millen. So far, so good. Having the right nurse was half the battle. There could be no fumbling of bloodlines, no time-consuming alarms triggered by sloppy machine preparation. She would need to be flawless. He told her to meet him in the ER. They would dialyze Ennis there. They risked a hyperkalemic arrest in the hallway if they tried to move him to ICU.

His potassium level had to be lowered as soon as possible. Once cardiac muscle was paralyzed by potassium, the muscular pumping chambers of the heart barely quivered. And nothing would start it up again — not epinephrine, not an electric shock, not even a pacemaker. Only restoring the patient's serum potassium to normal.

Next he dialed the ER and ordered a 20 cm, 13.5 French dialysis catheter to Ennis's treatment cubicle for femoral vein insertion — faster and less hazardous than the internal jugular approach he used with ambulatory patients. Ennis wouldn't be getting out of bed anytime soon, so having a catheter stuck in his groin — on the left, to avoid traumatizing his kidney transplant on the right — would be of no consequence. There would be no need for a catheter if his fistula were patent, but it wasn't. It must have clotted in the aftermath of his seizure. If everything came together, Christy would have a machine there with lines primed about the time he got the catheter in. There would be no margin for error on his part, either, no hunting and pecking for the vein, no mulligan for a kinked catheter. The calcium gluconate that Ralston gave would antagonize the potassium paralyzing Ennis's heart for only so long.

He punched the accelerator and opened his window to the damp, bracing air. A lot of things didn't add up. Ennis's potassium was high because his kidney transplant crapped out, but why? It was working beautifully at his last office visit. Was he rejecting it? Or had his transplant stopped working because of the seizures and shock? And why was he convulsing? He didn't have a seizure disorder. His erratic blood pressures were puzzling, too, hypotensive and in shock one minute, needing Nipride to bring it down the next. He shook his head. Driving drunk wearing only a woman's robe: maybe Becky had been right all along. They should never have transplanted him.

He hit the ER and hurried to cubicle B3, one of six in that section arrayed around a central physician's station. Ed Ralston hunched over Ennis's pallid, intubated body with the bell of his stethoscope pressed against Ennis's chest, which rose and fell with each gust of forced air from the respirator beside him. It would have been tweet-worthy, had Cullen known how to tweet, an event rarer than the coming of the Comet Kohoutek: a Ralston sighting at the bedside, with his polar bear whiskers and shock of white hair.

Cullen looked at the automated blood pressure cuff fastened to Ennis's arm: 86/52. A mean arterial pressure of about 60 mm Hg, he estimated, the minimum pressure required to perfuse vital organs. Below a MAP of sixty there wasn't enough of a pressure head to deliver blood to the brain — or a transplanted kidney. He glanced at the cardiac monitor above Ennis's gurney. He had a heart rate of forty-four, a wide QRS complex, peaked t-waves, and absent p-waves — the tracing of a heart succumbing to hyperkalemia.

Ralston noticed him at the foot of the gurney. He straightened up and removed the stethoscope from his ears and let it dangle around his thick red neck. "I'm glad you're here." He pointed to a pair of contact pads on Ennis's chest. "I've got the Zoll on him, but it's not capturing." The Zoll — their local metonym for an external pacemaker.

"It's not going to capture," Cullen said. He turned to a nurse next to Ralston, a short, fortyish brunette in green scrubs named Janelle. "Give him two more amps of bicarb and another liter of saline wide open. Where's the dialysis catheter I called for?"

She delegated the bicarb and saline order to another nurse and rolled a metal tray table toward Cullen. Her forearms were tautly muscled, with plump, prominent veins — a fitness center junkie, he guessed.

"I have your catheter and an insertion kit all set to go."

Cullen gave a tight smile to Ralston. "She's too good for you, Ed. You don't deserve her."

Ralston harrumphed. Janelle beamed. "What size gloves do you wear?" she asked.

He held his hands in the air with his long fingers extended. She raised her brow.

"Nines. Definitely nines. I'll be right back."

Ralston moved away from the gurney. "I'll turn his vent rate up to blow off a little more CO2 and buy you some time."

"Great, thank you."

His equanimity impressed Cullen. A higher vent rate— by compensating for Ennis's metabolic acidosis—would help. But what Ennis really needed was a functioning kidney: the body's chemist, carefully proportioning potassium and sodium concentrations and titrating acid-base balance to an optimal level. An elegant kidney.

Christy Millen arrived a few minutes later, a heavy-set woman in her fifties wearing a white lab coat and faded jeans. She pushed a portable dialysis machine alongside Ennis's gurney. "I should be ready to go in ten minutes."

Vintage Christy. No greeting, no small talk. All business. Perfect. "I'm putting the line in now. Then he's all yours."

Janelle taped the tubing of Ennis's Foley catheter to his right thigh and quickly shaved his left groin free of encroaching pubic hair. Not a drop of urine colored the bladder catheter's plastic tubing. Cullen donned a mask and gloves and prepped his left groin with Betadine, staining his skin the color of tobacco juice. He draped the area and probed for the femoral artery with the fingertips of his right hand. Its feeble pulse caused him to check the overhead monitor. Ennis's QRS complex had widened and his heart rate was down to thirty-six—barely twitching now.

He didn't bother with lidocaine. Ennis was comatose and every second was precious. He pinched an 18-gauge introducer needle in his left hand and, with the fingertips of his right, retracted Ennis's femoral artery laterally. The vein lay medial. He pierced the skin in one deft motion and advanced the needle at a forty-five-degree angle. A flash of dark venous blood came out the hub. He was in, the bevel of the needle safely nestled inside the vein.

He was about to reach for a guide wire when the artery beneath his fingers began to throb. Ennis suddenly had a bounding pulse. He checked the blood pressure cuff wrapped around his arm: 210/110, a 130-point leap in systolic pressure. He looked across the gurney at Janelle.

"What did his tox screen show?"

"Alcohol and benzos," she answered. "But he got Ativan in the field."

"Turn the Levophed off and cut his IV back to seventy-five an hour."

Blood pumped out the back of the needle as if from an artery rather than a vein. Cullen plucked the guide wire from the equipment tray beside him, but before he could thread it through the back of the needle, Ennis's body gave a disorganized jerk and lifted off the table. He convulsed, a full-blown tonic-clonic seizure that dislodged the introducer needle and spattered Cullen's shirt with blood.

He pressed his hand over the hole in Ennis's groin to stanch the torrent of blood spewing through it and gave a series of orders to Janelle. "Give him two milligrams of Ativan IV and a gram of Dilantin IV over twenty minutes. And turn up the Nipride."

He glanced over his shoulder. The roller pump of Christy's machine was spinning. She stood beside it with a bloodline in each hand, ready to go the moment he got the catheter in.

But he couldn't do a thing until Ennis stopped seizing. Janelle's thumb depressed the barrel of the syringe containing the Ativan. Ennis went flaccid a moment later. Cullen groped for his femoral artery again. Nothing. No pulse whatsoever now. He looked up at the monitor: sine wave. In a moment his tracing would degenerate into a chaotic ventricular rhythm they would be unable to shock him out of.

"Start CPR!"

A young male nurse began chest compressions. Ennis's frail, bony thorax collapsed beneath each piston thrust of his forearms. Cullen attached a syringe to the end of the introducer needle and advanced it through his original puncture site while pulling back on the syringe. Blood spurted into it. He removed the syringe from the back of the needle and retrieved the guide wire and fed it through the hub of the needle. It snaked up the vein without resistance. He withdrew the needle over the wire and discarded it, then threaded the tip of a dual-lumen dialysis catheter over the wire and through the puncture site. He popped the tip of the catheter into the vessel with a twisting motion of his hand — all with CPR in progress.

Ennis's body rocked with each compression. His skin grew mottled. Cullen ran the catheter up the femoral vein until the tip of the wire poked out the end of the catheter. He grasped it and withdrew the wire from inside the catheter and bled the remaining air out of each port.

Christy's hands flashed. Blood swirled through the PVC tubing and into the hollow fiber dialyzer suspended in the c-clamp. The dialyzer turned maroon. Christy set the blood pump at 300 ml/min. Within minutes a liter of filtered blood had passed through the artificial kidney and back into Ennis's ashen, lifeless body, bearing a fraction of the potassium it had before.

Cullen reached across the gurney and palpated his right groin. "Hold CPR," he commanded. Ennis's femoral artery tapped a steady beat against his fingertips. "He's got a strong pulse!" He checked the monitor—back in a narrow-complex rhythm. "Get a blood pressure."

"One-eighteen over fifty-eight!" someone cried out.

Cullen nodded. They called a kidney transplant the Gift of Life, but tonight the Gift of Life was a dialysis nurse with sure hands and a three hundred-blood flow. He looked at Christy and grinned.

"Dialysis nurses rock," he said.

It wasn't until the following morning, after an ICU nurse handed him the empty package of Vanilla Sky bath salts she found in Ennis's robe, that Cullen correctly diagnosed his puzzling clinical presentation. Psychoactive bath salts (PABS) were all the rage in Europe, and a growing fad in the U.S. They weren't bath salts at all, but rather designer drugs whose active ingredient was a potent reuptake inhibitor that gave rise to the worst features of LSD, PCP, cocaine, and crystal meth rolled into one: rapid heart rates, extremely high and fluctuating blood pressures, cardiac arrhythmias, hyperthermia, seizures, cardiovascular collapse and death. Ennis's car wreck and fit had perhaps spared him some of the more unseemly psychiatric effects: paranoia, hallucinations, violent behavior, self-mutilation and suicide. A lip-smacking, face-twitching, amped-up, wacked-out Freddy Krueger-with-a-Starbucks card was how one review article characterized the typical PABS user. Drug screens failed to detect them and treatment was supportive, with no antidote available. The white crystals inside the pleasing packages were indistinguishable from Epsom salts.

He walked into Ennis's room and stood at the foot of the bed, exhausted and pensive from spitting in Death's face the night before. Ennis lay still and peaceful from the white milk of Propofol. The urinary collection bag clipped to his bedrail remained empty and the FiO2 delivered by his ventilator was still at .70—seventy per cent oxygen, too high. He needed more fluid removed with his next dialysis.

Death had come for him the night before, but they turned the hooded ghoul away. *I looked, and there before me was a pale horse! Its rider's name was Death, and Hades followed close behind him.* Death: the final of the Four Horsemen of the Apocalypse, sent by God in preparation for the Last Judgment in the Book of Revelation.

God. Yahweh. Lord.

The Unknowable.

Chapter 20

THICK, MURKY LIGHT. A television with a dark screen suspended from a wall. Something in his throat. A mechanical whoosh beside him, the forced inflation of his chest.

A respirator. He was hooked up to a respirator, again!

He bucked against it, fought the choking sensation of the tube, even as a squall of air rushed into his lungs. He moved to yank it from his throat, but his wrists were lashed to the bed. He strained and tried to cough it out instead. A high-pitched alert sounded to his right. Terror seized him, full-blown panic at the horror of his predicament.

A hand on his chest: gentle, reassuring. A woman beside him, young and pretty and wearing a floral smock. He found her eyes, intelligent and bright.

Untie my hands!

"Mr. Willoughby, calm down. You're in Beach Park Hospital, in the intensive care unit. My name is Megan. I'm your nurse." Her reassuring face soothed him. He stopped struggling. "There's a tube in your lungs to help you breathe. The more you fight it, the worse it will feel. Relax. You'll get used to it."

She was right, he knew she was, but he couldn't help it. How would she like to be tied down and gagged? A new want seized his brain, a raw, animal craving more powerful even than his desire to be rid of the wretched tube in his throat: thirst. Insatiable, intolerable, unquenchable, drive-you-out-of-your-mind thirst. He wanted nothing—*nothing*—more than a glass of ice-cold lemonade. But what would it matter if a pitcher of it were sitting beside him? He couldn't drink it anyway. All it would do was torture him.

What happened? How had he landed in ICU *again*, like the bad old days before transplant? He remembered taking a bath and drinking tequila. Lots of tequila. A jumble of visions careened inside his head, fragments of scenes: throwing a glass against the wall, blood on the kitchen floor. Something he needed to do. Had to do. But what?

Nurse Megan reached for his leg. His left leg. Something was in it. He lifted his head off the pillow, inches at best, and craned to see what she was doing to his groin. There was tubing connected to it—blood-filled tubing. He felt violated, as if every cavity of his body had been invaded and instrumented by her probing hands. Maybe sweet Megan wasn't a nurse at all. Maybe aliens had abducted him and were experimenting on him in a spaceship.

"Ennis, it's okay. You have a dialysis catheter in your groin, in your femoral vein. You're on dialysis. The fistula in your arm clotted, so we had to use a catheter to do your treatment. Your kidney transplant stopped working, but your heart transplant is fine. Dr. Brodie is trying to get your kidney going again."

He went limp and turned his head to the left. There it was, beside her, the roller pump spinning, the plastic cartridge filled with blood: a sinister gray dialysis machine. His worst fear come true. He lifted his gaze to hers. *I wish I were dead.* Tears streamed down his cheeks. She took his hand and held it and wiped his face with a tissue.

He remembered drinking something besides tequila that night. Something nasty—bath salts, that was it! He'd swallowed a load of bath salts to purge Carla from inside him. To wash her loud, clamoring, transmigrated soul clean out of his body—because he was selfish, thinking only of his needs, not hers. He wanted her to move on, but leave her organs behind, thank you very much. And now look what he'd done. Killed her kidney in the process.

It came to him. What he'd been trying to do after he drank all that tequila. He squeezed Megan's warm, loving hand and smiled. If Dr. Brodie pulled him through—and he always did—he vowed he would do what Carla needed him to.

Becky showed up two days later, an hour after he finished dialysis, administered this time by a male nurse named Roy. Nothing against Roy, but he was, what you might say, a little challenged in the tenderness department. He hoped Megan would be back next time. If there had to be a next time.

No urine yet. Not even bladder sweat. Dr. Brodie said it was early, that his kidney transplant was probably hibernating from the shock it went through, but that soon it would wake up and he'd pee up a storm. Ennis wasn't so sure. Four days and not a drop of piss? That seemed like more than a hibernating kidney. That was a kidney that got stepped on, a kidney with the absolute crap kicked out of it. He tried not to dwell on it, the nightmare of dialysis again, but what else could he think about with that metal monster of a machine and somber-faced Roy staring at him for four hours? It was depressing. Real depressing. Open-a-vein, jump-off-a-bridge depressing. Figures his fistula would be clotted—Willoughby's Law: the worst possible thing at the worst possible time. But at least they had moved his catheter from his groin to his neck so he could move around when he wasn't tethered to the machine, and his heart transplant was fine. So there was that to be thankful for.

His breathing tube came out the day before—to swallow was heaven, especially anything cold and sweet—but he would gladly have put it back in to avoid facing Becky. She walked in and hugged him and told him how worried she'd been about him and how happy she was to see him doing so much better. The faint scent of fresh lemongrass rose off her neck. He was surprised at how warm her hug made him feel inside.

She sat at the end of the bed in one of her short black dresses, her nails lacquered and pink, the gold charm on her wrist elegant and dainty. A wisp of hair graced her forehead. He snuck a gander at her thigh, but failed to get a rise out of his shriveled pecker. He was in worse shape than he thought. He sincerely hoped Dr. Brodie was porking the bejeezus out of her. Someone needed to.

Her face went stern, the sympathy gone. "Did you try to kill yourself?"

"If one more doctor or nurse asks me that, I just might. No, I didn't. It was an accident."

She sat erect, mantled with concern. "Dr. Brodie told me you got drunk and ingested psychoactive bath salts."

He stared into the sheets. "I didn't *know* they were psychoactive. I bought 'em at a convenience store by mistake."

"If you thought they were Epsom Salts, why did you swallow them?"

He looked up and grinned. "I was constipated?"

She didn't laugh. She was circling like a hawk getting ready to swoop and sink her talons into him. Make him confess what he did not want to confess.

"You almost lost your life over this and might yet lose your kidney. Was it about your donor?"

She reminded him of his father, her condemning eyes boring into him. *Real men don't believe in ghosts.* There was no evading her now. She knew him too well.

He sank back in bed and pulled the covers to his chin. "She's driving me crazy. Her presence, I mean. Her spirit. I was trying to get rid of her. I drank too much tequila and saw the bath salts sitting there and tried to purge her from inside me. I had no idea they weren't really bath salts."

An unbecoming look of vindication crossed her face. She got off the bed and went over to a chair on his right and drew her knees together and folded her hands in her lap. He hated when she did that.

"This meets the criteria of a delusional disorder — thinking the soul of another person inhabits you and is influencing your personality. We treat delusional disorders resulting in self-harm with medication. Strong medication."

He threw the covers off and swung his legs over the edge of the bed. His bare feet slapped the floor. She stared at the dialysis catheter in his neck like it was an antenna coming out of his head. "That's what you think. You ain't turnin' me into no R. P. McMurphy. There's things that can't be medicated away, and souls are one of 'em. Sometimes I don't know what Dr. Brodie sees in you."

The muscles around her mouth twitched and her nostrils flared. He got her with that one, just like he intended. She composed herself and pasted her therapist mask back on.

"Dr. Brodie and I aren't seeing each other anymore — not that it's any business of yours."

A sense of abandonment seized him, like a child who learns his parents are getting a divorce. He wanted them together. He sensed she was to blame and resented her for it.

"I'm going to recommend that you be started on Zyprexa," she went on. "I think you're suffering from a delusional disorder triggered in part by feeling unworthy of your donor."

"Yeah, well maybe what I need is a second opinion from another psychiatrist. One who's not so rigid and close-minded."

She couldn't conceal her hurt. Good. She'd hurt him, too, by not believing that Carla's soul was inside him. She left without another word, which was just as well. She was right about one thing, though: he did feel unworthy of his donor.

But that was about to change.

The room they transferred him to came with a view of the front entrance of the hospital, with its looping drive and Technicolor lawn and gracefully flapping flag that made him think of his father. It came with a roommate, too—Marty Spanos, a wheezing, pain-in-the-ass Greek with a tangle of black curls and broad chest and thick moustache. Spanos had it in for the medical profession.

"Doctors aren't God, you know. They don't know everything. I read that hospital patients contract a quarter of a million bloodstream infections a year. Most of them from plastic catheters like the one you got stuck in your neck. Half the time they could get by without 'em, but their doctors forget to take 'em out. Do you really need that thing? Or is your doctor in too big a rush to get to the golf course each day to remember to remove it?"

Ennis sat at the edge of his bed over a tray of French toast and bacon and coffee—without cream, on account of the phosphorus restriction in his diet. His *renal* diet, kidney failure taking over his life again, even while he ate. He forked a piece of syrup-soaked French toast into his mouth and cast Spanos a look he kept in reserve for the DMV counter.

"Seeing as how my kidney transplant stopped working a week ago, and this here catheter is how I get dialysis to stay alive, I think maybe he knows it's there."

Spanos shrugged and got up and tied a flimsy striped robe around himself. "I'm gonna catch a shower." He turned around at the door and pointed his finger. "Don't let him forget about that thing."

Ennis waved him off in disgust, a man who was in the hospital for a COPD attack and yet continued to smoke. "I suppose that's your doctor's fault too," he muttered, after Spanos had shuffled out the door. "Probably forgets to call you each night to remind you to quit."

He finished his breakfast and had an aide bathe and shave him and help him to a bedside chair. He was weak as a kitten and his thighs were like jelly. But he was alive and out of ICU and eating French toast. Now, if only his kidney would give up some pee.

He put his reading glasses on and settled in with the paper to catch up on the latest political skullduggery while he waited for Dr. Brodie. His visit was the highpoint of Ennis's day, a daily status report from a professional who treated him with respect and gave him the straight poop. Dr. Brodie always had a plan, no matter what type of setback came Ennis's way. A plan he would patiently explain, in terms Ennis could understand. And he'd never once left him feeling bad about himself, even when he messed up—like this time, downing those PABS. How were they allowed to sell that shit? Where were the bureaucrats when you needed them? Asleep at the switch, that's where. Too busy worrying about what size Pepsi everybody drank or banning *foi gras* from restaurants. Who gave a shit if a few ducks were overfed for a week or two? They were going to be slaughtered anyway. They might actually save some *human* lives if they spent more time keeping sneaky-ass designer drugs off the shelves of filling stations instead of wringing their hands over whether a duck felt too full or not.

"That's more like it. Up in a chair and reading the want ads for a job."

Dr. Brodie stood grinning at the foot of his bed, his lab coat starched and white, his dark green tie knotted in a perfect Windsor.

"Morning, Doc. Figured I better get caught up on things, seeing as how I missed a week." He pushed off from the arms of the chair and thrust himself to his feet and pivoted onto the edge of the bed.

Dr. Brodie pulled his vacated chair across the floor and eased into it. He crossed his long legs and fiddled with the band of his watch. A patchwork of veins crossed the tendons of his enormous hands. Ennis detected a whiff of cologne, sharp and clean and woodsy.

"Your kidney's not coming around, Ennis. I can't tell if it's shock from the bath salts you got into or your immune system causing rejection. I suspect shock—acute tubular necrosis we call it, ATN—because your heart transplant from the same donor is doing fine. But the treatment for one is very different from the other. With your permission, I'd like to do a kidney biopsy to be certain."

So it was down to that. Damage from bath salts directly or rejection because bath salts screwed up his immune system. Self-inflicted either way. Wasn't it always with him?

He listened while Dr. Brodie recited the risks, benefits, and alternatives to renal biopsy, bleeding being the main risk of sinking a stiletto into a kidney transplant three or four times to snag a few hunks of tissue. After all the operations and procedures he'd been through, a little bleeding was about as threatening as taking a dump.

"Okay by me."

"Good. I'll set it up for tomorrow." Dr. Brodie stood to leave. "One other thing. That medication Dr. Winthrop recommended, Zyprexa. Are you still opposed to taking it?"

Ennis sighed. Becky had him cornered. It was hard to explain the feeling inside him *without* sounding delusional, but if it was a delusion, it was the most powerful, persistent, convincing one he could imagine. Becky didn't believe a piece of Carla's soul was inside him, but what made her belief rational and his delusional? She had no proof one way or the other. Beliefs weren't meant to be proved; that's what made them beliefs.

He shook his head. "Dr. Winthrop and I are at, what you might say, an impasse. I'm not going to take Zyprexa. Because I know what I know, and I know this: I was wrong about Carla giving her son Luke that condition he has, that Legg-Perthe disease. It wasn't her fault. And it's up to me to tell him."

Dr. Brodie frowned. "You mean it wasn't her fault because she didn't *know* she gave her son a defective gene, is that what you're saying?"

"No. I'm saying it wasn't her fault because she didn't give him the gene."

Chapter 21

CULLEN WAITED UNTIL THE last office patient had been seen and Bria had locked the front door behind her before he returned Ron Ely's phone call, which came in around three that same afternoon. He dialed Ely's direct number from the sleek white phone on his desk. His heart pumped violently. Had Ely found his daughter? Would joy unlike any other fill his heart? Or were his most tender hopes about to be crushed like an insect beneath the pitiless heel of a shoe?

"Ron Ely."

"Hello, Ron. Cullen Brodie returning your call."

A few fleeting moments of small talk, Ely's honeyed voice betraying neither triumph nor defeat. Then the moment of truth. The big reveal.

"I've been doing this long enough to know that if we haven't turned up anything by now, we aren't going to. I'm afraid we've come up empty. I'm calling an end to the investigation, Cullen. We can't find her. I'm sorry."

He mumbled something back. Ely's voice faded away. His hands shook so profoundly he could barely get the phone back in its cradle. Time telescoped. Sadness welled inside him, but something else smothered it. Something primal and vicious and unmistakably similar to his father's zeal and ferocity the day Chaz started it all.

He stood and swept every last item on his well-ordered birch wood desk onto the floor, including the phone, which hit the carpet with a clatter. He denounced Angie with all the fury he could muster. "You had no right to keep her from me!" He scooped a letter opener off the floor. It sang in his hands, a knife to twist and rent with. He hated her, despised her, loathed Angie Nichols the way his father loathed the abortionist Edward Nichols. He slashed the giclée of the Grand Canal that hung on his wall, cut it to ribbons like his father once shredded Angie's painting. Brodie's Tirade reprised, his father's hatred his hatred—because he was his father's son.

The defiling of the artwork drained him of his bile. His bloodlust. He cast the letter opener aside and slumped into the chair in front of his computer amidst the wreckage of his office. Anger gave way to sorrow and then something worse. A fear that had gnawed at him for years, an atrabilious anguish long repressed.

He despaired over the nothingness of it all, the oblivion that awaited everyone and everything. The certain fate of every speck of life that had ever been and would ever be. Within a generation or two, not a single patient he cared for would be alive to recall his altruism, his mission to relieve suffering and improve the human condition. And when the eternal darkness came for him, there would be no reward for his good deeds, or punishment for his transgressions. Because no one was keeping score. No one was there.

He used to think that life was its own reward, the sweetness of it, the emotional joys and physical pleasures. Folly. Pure folly. The most we could hope for was to be at peace with our nothingness, our meaninglessness, within the confines of a life that was pointless, because nothing endured. A life of contented nihilism, where hummingbirds and Shakespeare and Bach and the stars above were all random as a coin toss.

But he did not feel contented. The patina of vulgar satisfaction that coated his life had been peeled away like cheap paint by Ely's failure to locate his daughter. What had been the point of it? What was the point of any human life, if the planet we inhabited and every species on it were accidents that would one day be reduced forevermore to cosmic dust? Why care about anything or care to stay alive at all if we were destined for cold, dark nothingness, no matter what we did? Why bother to have children? For what — to condemn them to oblivion, too?

And yet, what if he were wrong? What if God was not an invention of man, but man an invention of God? It was his only chance to escape the existential horror that gripped him, the only solution to his crisis. For the first time in as long as he could remember, he looked for a sign that his life might not end in a black void. For a clue, no matter how ambiguous or tentative, that another realm might exist. Some shred of evidence that God might exist. God is all around us, the nuns used to say. God is everywhere, in everything we do. All you have to do is look for him.

The next morning, he called the pathologist who would be handling Ennis's biopsy and asked her to analyze an extra core of tissue for Factor V Leiden mutation.

Cullen's Mondays started at seven a.m., rounds at Beach Park Dialysis. He wheeled his black leather stool across the clinic with the jittery impatience of an alcoholic needing a drink or an addict needing a fix. The act of placing himself in the service of another human being felt good. Better than good: blissful. In attending to the needs of others, he embraced selflessness. And since dialysis was intermittent life support, he could feed his addiction to the virtue of selflessness by saving lives. Good stuff for a Monday morning. No wonder he craved it like a drug.

The first patient he saw was Carolina De Silva, a seventy-five-year-old woman who, despite her on-time of six a.m., always came to dialysis in lipstick and makeup and a dress she might have worn to Sunday mass. Her chromium helmet of hair gleamed and blood-filled tubing snaked over the arm of her chair, a scarlet column on its way to the plastic cartridge of her dialyzer, with its bundles of hollow fibers sieving off lethal toxins her native kidneys could no longer excrete. She rose at four a.m. to have time to dress and groom herself before coming. Carolina had been on dialysis for five years — four hours per treatment, three times a week, fifty-two weeks a year. It came out to 3,120 hours, the equivalent of 130 twenty-four-hour days of being hooked up to a machine to stay alive. Yet never once had he heard her complain.

As always, they spoke in Spanish, though her English was as good as his. She asked him, as she did at least once a month, if he knew what they said about the benefits of rising early? With a straight face, he denied that he did.

Her gray eyes danced. *"A quien madruga, Dios le ayuda!"* she said.

God helps early risers. That's what Carolina De Silva believed. That was why she got up at four a.m. and put her makeup on and did her hair and climbed into a freshly ironed dress, instead of showing up in pajamas or sweats like many of the younger patients did.

The call to his cell phone from Candace Hundley came a few minutes before eight, right before he left for the hospital. Her microscopic interpretation of Ennis's kidney biopsy five days earlier had showed acute tubular necrosis, meaning that his transplant stopped working because of shock, not rejection, as Cullen suspected. His kidney opened up two days later and he came off dialysis; today he was going home.

"Cullen? This is Candy. I'm calling about the Factor V Leiden test on Ennis Willoughby's kidney transplant."

He sat down at the nurse's station and drew a breath. He felt foolish for having ordered it. He did so in a moment of weakness, a selfish, childish, self-pitying reaction to Ron Ely's inability to locate his daughter. An aging, lonely man impulsively longing for an afterlife he did not believe in—it didn't get any more clichéd than that. Surrendering his logic in hopes of immortality. How very human of him. How very craven. And how utterly irrational to think she might be negative, in support of Ennis's claim of communing with her soul. Since Duncan tested negative, Carla *had* to be positive. And that meant Ennis was wrong, that she *did* pass the familial thrombophilia gene to Luke that caused his Legg-Perthes disease. It was all exactly as Becky the-psychiatrist-who-dumped-him said it was: Ennis suffered from a transmigration delusion, caused by the denial of his emerging transgender personality, and perpetuated by feeling unworthy of his organ donor.

Candy spoke in her bloodless pathologist's voice. "The tissue tested negative. The donor did not have Factor V Leiden mutation."

He clenched the phone: negative, with all it implied.

"Cullen? Are you there?"

"I'm here. That's not what I was expecting. Tell me— how often are new mutations the cause of this condition?"

"Not often at all. If ever. This is an old mutation. There's evidence it originated thirty thousand years ago in a common founder. Incident cases don't need to occur from de novo mutations—five percent of all Caucasians are carriers. Factor V Leiden is a widely prevalent inherited disorder."

He thanked her for calling and headed to the hospital with his mind in a spin.

He argued with himself all the way up the hill to the hospital. Was confirmation of Ennis's prediction that Carla was not a carrier of Factor V Leiden evidence of a connection with her soul? Or was it a lucky guess, another in a series of oddities concerning Ennis and his donor, but nothing more? The same odds as a coin flip, hardly a daunting statistical challenge: heads God exists, tails he doesn't.

And why had Duncan lied about testing negative for the gene? Perhaps he had his hands full raising three motherless children and didn't want to be blamed for Luke's Legg-Perthes disease along with everything else his children would blame him for over the next twenty years. Still, blaming his dead wife for transmitting the condition instead of owning up to it himself spoke volumes about his personal integrity. Duncan was a nebbish who depended on his father for all he had.

He found Ennis dressed and waiting and pacing the room, his face clean-shaven, his hair neat and combed. The striped dress shirt he wore looked two sizes too big for him and his tightly cinched belt gathered the front of his slacks. He had lost a lot of weight.

Cullen eyed his street clothes and gestured with his hand. "Not anxious to leave, are you?"

Ennis grinned and sat down on the edge of the bed and pointed to a nearby chair. "Have a seat, Doc. Then get me the hell outta here."

Cullen sat across from him in doubt over what to tell him. Ennis had no knowledge of the Factor V Leiden test ordered on his biopsy. Wasn't he entitled to know? Wasn't it unethical to withhold it from him? But Carla's Factor V Leiden status was irrelevant to his health, and telling him would only serve to reinforce his delusion that her spirit was communicating with him. Which was better for him—the truth, when the truth might harm him, or a benevolent withholding of truth for his own good?

He reached into the pocket of his lab coat and withdrew a prescription pad. "Your creatinine is back to baseline: 1.1. You can resume all your previous medications, with one addition—I want you to take the Zyprexa Dr. Winthrop recommended." He jabbed his pen in the air. "You could have lost your kidney or even your life from ingesting bath salts to flush a ghost out of you. I think you need to follow your psychiatrist's advice."

A look of raw hurt twisted Ennis's face. "Maybe I am delusional about Carla. Maybe a soul can't be in both this world and the next." He bowed his head and said in a wounded voice, "But she's real to me. So real."

He scribbled out the prescription: Zyprexa, 5 mg po daily, #30, with three refills. He signed it and tore it off the pad and thrust it at Ennis. Cullen glimpsed the sorrow and regret in his eyes: his doctor didn't believe him.

He pulled the prescription back and tore it in two. "There's something you need to know." He gave Ennis the Factor V Leiden result and apologized for not asking his permission to have it run.

Ennis showed his teeth and pumped his fist. "Yes! I told you, didn't I? I told you!"

After enduring hugs and backslaps and praise for being the best doctor a patient could have, a doctor who not only listened to his patients, but who actually believed them, Cullen excused himself and took an elevator down to main floor.

It was time to come clean with someone else.

They sat cloistered in Thomas Lawson's cramped office, facing each other over his pressed wood desk. The low-wattage overhead tube cast a thin pale light on Lawson's unkempt white hair and tense, ruddy face. Dandruff dusted the shoulders of his unbuttoned blazer like efflorescence on a cavern rock.

"I'm having second thoughts about God," Cullen told him.

The chaplain's relieved smile was beyond radiant—more like beatific. He gripped Cullen's hand. "I specialize in the spiritually challenged."

The pungent whiff of a half-consumed breakfast burrito sitting on his desk floated across the space between them. Cullen found himself hoping that Lawson wouldn't eat burritos every morning, that he would lose some weight and live a long life and not die of a coronary before he could retire and take his grandchildren to see the White House, or wherever it was grandparents took young children these days.

He told him about Ennis and his cross-dressing and his dual-organ transplant and peculiar aftermath, his startling knowledge of his donor's name. And the changes in personality he underwent, the specific new tastes in food and music he acquired—identical to those of his donor.

"He became convinced that her soul transmigrated into his body along with her organs. His psychiatrist thinks he's experiencing symptoms of gender dysfunction due to the emergence of his feminine personality, which he subconsciously conflated with his donor."

"What do you think?"

Cullen paused. "I think I believe my patient."

He offered Ennis's knowledge of Carla's negative Factor V Leiden status as evidence why. Not dispositive evidence, he conceded, but a preponderance of evidence.

Lawson leaned back and fiddled with a letter opener that had a crucifix for a hilt. His belly strained the buttons of his shirt. "Are you familiar with William James, the brother of the author?"

Cullen said he was not.

"William was a Harvard psychology professor and a founding member of the American Society for Psychical Research. He became enamored of a spiritual medium named Leonora Piper, who convinced him that she was able to channel the spirits of deceased human beings. It was on account of her that James advanced his white crow theory: 'To upset the conclusion that all crows are black... it is sufficient to produce one white crow.' What you have encountered, Doctor, is a white crow. And you are convinced, as was Professor James by his white crow, that you have observed empirical proof of the supernatural. Scientific evidence of a soul. Is that what you're saying?"

The words came easier than Cullen ever imagined they would. "That's exactly what I'm saying."

Lawson tossed the letter opener aside. The kind expression he wore grew stony, along with his voice. "If you came here expecting me to agree, you're going to be disappointed. Your experience with your patient has caused you to believe that you witnessed the physical tracks of a soul, tangible proof of the Divine. But you will quite likely see no more white crows in your lifetime. William James never did; he eventually quit looking for them. If you need scientific evidence of God to believe in Him, your belief will wither and die. Western culture has made a grave error in believing that God, if he exists at all, can be discovered through science. Reason describes how things work, but not what they mean. Reason is incapable of grasping spiritual truth. It takes faith to catch a glimpse of the Divine."

Droplets of sweat stippled his forehead. He returned Cullen's dubious gaze with a five-alarm fire in his eyes. "That was the brilliance of Christianity—what G. K. Chesterton called the paradox of Christianity. It acknowledged *both* reason *and* faith, not *either* reason *or* faith. Giving Christians access to both this world and the next."

Cullen gave a perplexed frown, not of disapproval, but of curiosity. "I attended Catholic grade school and high school and never once heard of Chesterton."

Lawson ran his pink fingers through his unruly hair. "Chesterton's *Orthodoxy* is the most reasoned defense of faith I ever studied. He devotes an entire chapter to the paradoxes of Christianity: 'turn the other cheek' and the Crusades, the nunnery and 'be fruitful and multiply,' the austerity of sackcloth and the extravagance of silk vestments. How could Christianity refuse to fight, yet constantly fight? How could it preach chastity, yet encourage sexual union? How could it be so severe, yet so lavish?"

He stood and waved both hands in the air like a lunatic—a beautiful, majestic lunatic, full of spiritual splendor, ordinary to look at, but magnificent in the Gospel he knew. Like an Apostle.

"Chesterton's answer is that Christianity accommodates both rationality and irrationality, because the flame of mankind is a passion that retains *both* the poetry of being humble *and* the poetry of being proud. Love and wrath, both burning. Can the lion lie down with the lamb and keep his ferocity? He can, and that is the miracle of Christianity, the reason why Christ is both man and God!"

He leaned over the desk, transfigured by the power inside him. His eyes bulged. His face glowed. Every word boomed his conviction. "Do not talk to me of white crows!

Your patient's transplant is evidence of the power of reason, not of a miracle. The miracle is that he is transgender, *both* man *and* woman. Because that is the nature of things: both/and, not either/or. That is how the universe is. That is how God is!"

His words scorched Cullen's face like the hot breath of Saint Michael burning the face of the Dragon, before casting him down from the verge.

He had no recollection of driving from the hospital to his office, so consumed was he by what Lawson had told him. He staggered through a side door down the hall from the main entryway and picked up the intercom to let Bria know he was there. There was a cancellation, she told him. He had thirty minutes before the first patient was due. He sat at his desk and buried his head in his hands to keep it from exploding.

Lawson had made him doubt the very thing that restored his willingness to give faith a second look. He went to him for spiritual guidance, to reconsider the existence of an afterlife—to reconsider God. All because of Ennis's brush with Carla MacGregor's soul. And what did Lawson do? Took Becky's side and chalked it all up to cross-dressing.

"Do not talk of white crows?" he said, as if Lawson were sitting in front of him. "That was the reason I *came* to you, you joyless Friar Tuck!"

He wanted his white crow back, but Lawson had robbed him of it. Stolen it from him. He punched the air with both hands. "Paul had his conversion! Why do you begrudge me mine?"

He shook his head. Perhaps an epiphany was too easy. Too convenient. Perhaps faith wasn't like that. Even Paul's conversion was the culmination of a journey. The nuns had taught that what really transpired on the Road to Damascus was the miracle of Divine grace, the love and mercy of God. Not because Paul did anything to deserve it, but because God wanted to give it. The power of sanctifying grace transformed the sinner and made him worthy of God's holiness. And wasn't that what he, Cullen, wanted? To be forgiven for the sin of Grady and made worthy again? He had been *dis*-graced long enough. Only the grace of God offered the promise of redemption, the means to partake in this world and the next.

Brodie's Tirade—his father's against Edward Nichols and his own against God—would stain his soul no more. He would expunge it by renewing his faith in what the nuns had taught him as a boy, but what he had rejected as a man: the duplex passion of Christianity, love and wrath both burning, the poetry of being proud in sweet repose with the poetry of being humble. He marveled at the wisdom of it, the binary nature of the universe, the duality of God—the Father *and* the Son.

All manner of dualities flooded his brain: war and peace, darkness and light, Heaven and Hell, man and woman, honor and shame. On and on and on they came, even dual images of Grady Nichols and Lucas MacGregor, wrapped in a paradox of innocence and corruption. But why? It made sense for Grady—his innocence and Cullen's corruption, the licentiousness that led to a child's drowning—but not for Luke. Luke was innocence and pity, not corruption, for what was more pitiful than a motherless child?

The answer came unbidden, an afflatus from another world. It wasn't about an innocent child losing his mother; it was about an innocent child having a limp. The corruption was in his limp.

He shut his office door and turned his computer on and entered a patient name into their electronic database, which contained the digital health records of all patients treated by Nephrology Partners. It was a patient who was followed by Jake Orr, the second most senior member of their group. The chart popped up. He stared at the identifying tab. A clarifying vision hit him with the force of a celestial body.

That of Logan MacGregor, rising from a chair and wincing, hobbled by a momentary limp that vanished as he hit his stride.

Chapter 22

LIKE DOCTORS IN MOST medical groups, the doctors of Nephrology Partners turned to each other for medical care. Cullen was no exception. His doctor was Ted Takagawa, his call partner in the group. And everyone knew it. Just like everyone knew that Jake Orr was MacGregor's doctor. Which meant that MacGregor's medical record was in Nephrology Partners' electronic database, which every nephrologist in the group had access to. Including Cullen.

Did he feel conflicted in opening it? He did. Was he in violation of federal privacy law, guilty of committing a HIPPA violation? He was. What he was doing was a betrayal of MacGregor, to whom he would always be grateful for giving him a job. As for the HIPPA violations— fines, crimes, and jail time, potentially. But none of it mattered. Not if what he suspected was true.

He gleaned from the record that MacGregor for the most part was remarkably healthy: normal cardiac stress tests, normal PSA levels, a normal colonoscopy. There was an appendectomy in the remote past and mild hypertension more recently. That was it. Save for a visit three years ago to an orthopedist.

For hip pain.

A series of x-rays, an MRI, and a bone scan had revealed degeneration of MacGregor's left hip, garden-variety osteoarthritis. The rest of his joints were pristine, no degeneration at all. The consulting orthopedist, upon inquiring about any trauma to the joint in question, had elicited from

MacGregor only a vaguely recalled history of a childhood episode of left sided knee pain that restricted him from running for a while, but that soon improved and had been fine ever since. He prescribed Celebrex as needed for pain and told MacGregor to come back if his symptoms worsened.

Cullen frowned. Childhood *knee* pain? It was MacGregor's hip that was arthritic and had caused him to limp, not his knee.

He closed MacGregor's chart, jumped on the Internet, and logged onto a subscription-only website for doctors, a compendium of the latest medical information across a variety of medical specialties. He entered Legg-Calve-Perthes disease into the search box and scrolled down the page that popped up. Typical symptoms of childhood LCP included a limp and pain in the hip or groin—or knee. The knee pain was referred in nature—originating from another source—and frequently misleading, in that it directed attention away from the offending joint, in this case the hip. Ten percent of LCP cases were familial, with some recent studies documenting an unusually high frequency of Factor V Leiden. The authors posited that the hypercoagulability caused by Factor V Leiden resulted in thrombosis of blood vessels supplying the joint, leading to avascular necrosis of the hip, the sine qua non of Legg-Calve-Perthes disease. While many patients had no sequelae, some suffered the onset of degenerative arthritis of the affected hip in their fifties or sixties.

Though MacGregor's orthopedist had failed to recognize it, childhood Legg-Calve-Perthes disease was the cause of his arthritic hip, Cullen was sure of it. And the Factor V Leiden disease that caused the disease in Luke had probably caused it in him, too. Meaning that if Duncan had told the truth about testing negative for the gene, then Logan was not Luke's grandfather.

He was his father.

It took him a week to decide what to do. He went back and forth, tussling with the choice he faced: do something or do nothing. He could go to Duncan with the evidence he had—Carla's negative Factor V Leiden test and MacGregor's bum hip and childhood orthopedic affliction, almost certainly Legg-Calve-Perthes disease—but he would look surpassingly foolish if it turned out that Duncan had for whatever reason lied about his test results. It remained a possibility that Logan had passed the Factor V Leiden mutation to Duncan, who in turn passed it to Luke.

Furthermore, was it really any of his business? Who was he to condemn sexual perfidy? MacGregor was a saint compared to him. MacGregor's degeneracy brought a life into the world; Cullen's extinguished one. And there were unintended consequences to consider. He had no way of knowing how Duncan and his father would react if he divulged MacGregor's secret. What if MacGregor killed himself rather than face Duncan? How would that help Luke? He would then be without a mother *and* a father, an orphan dependent on the goodwill of a half-brother who might well detest the sight of him. And what about Duncan? What if he failed to master the rage that would surely seize him when he learned the truth and wound up in prison for patricide? What of Luke then? What of his sisters? Or what if Duncan succumbed to the humiliation that followed his rage by committing suicide? Then Luke would have a father, but his sisters would not.

Yet to hold his tongue and say nothing seemed unthinkable. The harm that would accrue from remaining silent—the lie they would live, Duncan duped into raising the child of his father and unfaithful wife, MacGregor's shame festering like a cancer over betraying one son to sire another—would rot their lives from within. Like Cullen's had rotted after Angie pledged him to secrecy over Grady.

But most of all, there was Ennis, his patient, who was consumed with telling Luke his mother wasn't to blame for his limp. Ennis was possessed, and it made no difference whether it was a soul or a delusion that possessed him. Either way it was a possession, with only Cullen to free him from it.

He needed proof. Unassailable proof.

The swiftness of it took his breath away. Six to twelve weeks, Ely had estimated. And here they were in three, sitting across from each other at his black walnut desk, Ely's studied gravitas bolstered by the shelves of ponderous leather books behind him. Streaks of gray smudged his salon-dyed hair and room light glanced off the paraffin glaze of his chemically peeled cheeks like sunrays off a beach ball.

"The lab I use is called DNA Direct." He waved a manila folder in the air. "They analyzed the fragment of kidney you provided along with the samples we gathered. These are the results."

Cullen moistened his lips and swallowed. He had hoped to one day receive a letter from Ely revealing the name of his daughter. Instead he was there to receive a folder with the MacGregors' fate inside.

What he had learned in the preceding weeks was that human beings shed DNA like cats shed hair. Tiny bundles of it every day, in saliva, sweat, hair, skin, and blood. And it clung to all manner of things. Anything a person voluntarily discarded was up for grabs: gum they spit out; Kleenex they wiped their nose with; cigarette butts they flicked to the curb; glasses and utensils in restaurants; empty soft drink cans; water bottles at the gym; even razor blades and bandages in their garbage.

Surreptitious DNA collection had become ridiculously easy — and in ever increasing demand. The list of reasons for it was endless: a husband having a child tested because he suspected his wife of having an affair; a young woman having different boyfriends tested to determine which of them impregnated her; children having parents tested because they suspected they were adopted. But on Ely's end, it was the same drill every time. His operatives followed people around and collected their genetic refuse, which Ely then submitted to one of the many commercial DNA labs that had sprung up around the country. Paternity testing was cheap and fast: five hundred dollars to compare an alleged father's DNA with that of the child in question, and five working days to produce a courier-delivered envelope with the results.

Ely handed him the folder. "We got samples from Duncan and Luke at a movie theater. He took his whole family to see *The Princess and the Frog*. My operative sat three rows behind them. He slipped down the aisle and collected their empty popcorn containers, soft drink cups, straws, napkins, and hot dog remnants after the movie was over. The lab analyzed only Y chromosome material. Anything from Luke's sisters got discarded. We got Logan MacGregor's sample from a paper coffee cup at the Starbucks he has breakfast at each morning."

Cullen opened the folder and scanned a table listing the different alleles that had been examined. An analysis comparing Logan MacGregor's DNA to that of Lucas screamed out in bold red highlight at the bottom of the page.

Probability of Paternity = 99.99%.

The photo of Duncan and Carla and their children squatted on MacGregor's desk like state's evidence, a sad and tragic lie Cullen could not keep his eyes off. Her dainty collarbones and long, fetching neck, her enigmatic face concealing the awful truth she knew. It repulsed him, the thought of her lying beneath her father-in-law, a silverback taking advantage of troop primacy. Sexual privilege.

"That's a nice picture of them, don't you think?" MacGregor asked.

He smiled from across his desk, his sweep of silver hair, his stout chest and thick, confident face. Serene in his power. Cullen fiddled with the gold braiding of his chair and rested his hand atop the manila folder on his lap, serene in *its* power, the paternity test and disinterred family secret inside.

"Yes, it is. Carla especially. Her recipient has had a rough time of it, though. He insists that a piece of her soul came to him with her organs."

"I know. I've had the pleasure of meeting Mr. Willoughby. So have Duncan and the children. Duncan had to get a restraining order to keep him away."

"His psychiatrist thinks his delusions of the supernatural are symptoms of gender dysfunction caused by the emergence of his feminine personality, which he subconsciously merged with Carla. I thought so, too, until a few weeks ago."

MacGregor scowled. "We transplant organs, not souls."

"Maybe the souls are optional," Cullen said. "Maybe only a few special patients are capable of making that kind of spiritual connection. All I know is that he's awfully knowledgeable about Carla. Things he should have no way of knowing."

MacGregor wagged an index finger and smiled. "Ah, but he's transgender. Female intuition is a spooky thing."

"Female intuition is one thing. Clairvoyance is another. Take your grandson's Legg-Calve-Perthes disease and Factor V Leiden clotting disorder, for instance."

The color rinsed from MacGregor's face. "Duncan told you about that?"

Cullen nodded. "He told Ennis, too. Who in turn became obsessed with telling Luke that Carla wasn't to blame for his limp. Even after Duncan tested negative for Factor V Leiden."

MacGregor lowered his chin and spoke in a taut, subdued voice. "That's not possible. It proves he's delusional."

"It certainly seemed that way. Until I sent some extra tissue from his transplant biopsy for Factor V Leiden testing. I figured I could use the result to shatter his delusion by proving he was wrong, that Carla *did* pass the gene to her son."

MacGregor's jaw tensed. Cullen met his cold blue stare and went on.

"The test came back negative. Carla didn't have Factor V Leiden. Ennis was right. And since new mutations aren't a cause of incident cases due to the prevalence of the gene in the general population, and since Duncan tested negative, that opened up an entirely different can of worms."

His eyes narrowed and the corners of his mouth curled in defiance. "Are you suggesting that Luke isn't Duncan's son? That Carla became pregnant with another man's child and somehow managed to conceal it from him? That's preposterous. He looks just like Duncan."

Cullen squared his shoulders. "He looks just like you, too. I had an intuition of my own after the test results came back. You know how you wince and favor your leg for a few steps when you get up from a chair? It made me wonder. So I read your medical chart in our office EMR. There wasn't much there, really. Except for your visit to that orthopedist three years ago for hip pain. It's odd, don't you think, to have arthritis in only your hip, when every other joint is clean as a whistle on x-ray? Your hip didn't erode from old age; you had Legg-Perthes when you were a child. *You* gave Luke the Factor V Leiden gene. You're his father."

He opened the manila folder and readied the paternity test to confront the furious denial that surely would come. But it never did. MacGregor's shoulders slumped and anguish wracked his face, a wrenching sorrow that called to Cullen's mind a scene from *Gorillas in the Mist*, the face of a female who came upon the lifeless body of their troop's dominant silverback, the father of her offspring, murdered and mutilated by poachers. A look of such profound pathos he averted his gaze in sympathy — then and now.

"We were working late to prepare a Board of Directors report," MacGregor said, his voice flat and detached. "It had been building for months: glances held longer than they should have been; standing closer to one another than was necessary; supportive touching that had ceased to be innocent. I could almost smell the desire in her that night, like a cat in heat. I fell on her with a hunger that shames me still."

He slapped the surface of his desk twice with the palm of his hand. "Right here. On top of my desk. Forbidden sex.

"It never happened again. We blocked it out and resumed our lives. Even when she became pregnant, we never talked about it. I prayed he was Duncan's, but I knew he was mine. When he was diagnosed with the clotting disorder, I had myself tested for the Factor V Leiden mutation. It came back positive."

He sprang to his feet and crouched with his hands thrust in the air, like a salient silverback lunging at an invisible foe. "My passions got the best of me. You have no idea how lucky you are, to have avoided what was sent to destroy you. Something so despicable, so depraved, so wrong, that it clings to you for the rest of your life like the spray of a skunk, no matter how hard you try to wash it off. No matter how much good you do!"

Cullen stared at the folder in his lap. He stood and laid his hand on MacGregor's shoulder. "That same skunk sprayed me, too." He handed the folder to him. "You can keep this. I don't need it anymore."

He didn't know whether Carla's soul had transmigrated into Ennis or not. Maybe that's why she couldn't move on; she wanted Duncan to know. Or maybe it *was* all gender dysfunction and delusion and female intuition. Who was to say? How could anyone ever really know? But it didn't matter. The only thing that did was his patient.

"I don't care how you do it, but I want Luke to know that Carla didn't pass him the gene that caused his limp. And I want Ennis to be there when you tell him."

Souls were fickle things. Sometimes hers burned like white phosphorus, so hot it seemed like she might set him on fire. But more often her fifth dimension occupation of his innards was faint, subtle, like Tinker Bell, a few grains of Pixie Dust emitting the wispiest of photons. Not now, though. Now a veritable supernatural power surge jolted through him. This was her moment, what she'd been aiming for since he first awakened with her heart whumping inside him. A defining moment.

For all of them.

How could it not have been? Beginning with Duncan's phone call, informing him that the restraining order had been lifted and that he wanted to make amends by having him over to talk about things. An invitation Ennis eagerly accepted, only to arrive to this: Duncan and Luke and MacGregor tightly clumped on the posh white couch in the living room, the girls nowhere in sight; Luke clamped to Grandpa's lap, MacGregor's half-shut left eye purple and green and yellow; and Duncan drawn and sallow, ten pounds lighter at least.

Ennis dropped into the same mauve armchair he sat in the first time he passed beneath the front lintel of Duncan's fancy French Mediterranean. Dollars to donuts he got help from papa to afford it. Padre. El Jefe. Who probably hated Ennis's guts and was the one behind the restraining order in the first place. A lone citrine quartz centerpiece had replaced the previous porcelain clutter of the glass coffee table between them.

MacGregor looked unusually calm and at peace. About what? And how'd he get that shiner? He stroked Luke's head. Luke waved at Ennis. Ennis waved back.

He squirmed at the insistence of the force inside him, as strong now as it had ever been, as if Carla were about to crawl out of his belly and step onto the living room rug. He felt like he was about to deliver a ten-pound... soul. He wanted to be rid of her, to escape the intensity of it, the quickening.

"I'm grateful to you both for inviting me," he said. "I know I came on a little strong at Chuck E. Cheese's and the Highland Games, but like I told you before...." He glanced at Luke and caught himself. "I'm, what you might say, possessed. If you get my drift."

Duncan stiffened. He seemed to be carrying a great burden, summoning all his strength just to keep it from crushing him. "I know you believe Carla lives inside you. I do too." He dropped his gaze to Ennis's chest and fixed it there, right on his heart. "I forgive you. Don't worry about

Luke. My father and I will raise him—together. It will be alright."

Ennis wasn't sure who Duncan was forgiving, him or Carla. It was impossible to tell. MacGregor put his arm around Duncan with a look of compassion Ennis wouldn't have suspected he was capable of. Duncan slumped against the couch, spent. Luke crawled onto his lap and gave him a kiss. Duncan closed his eyes. Birdsong tweeted through an open window.

MacGregor nodded at Ennis to draw his attention, then turned to Luke. "Grandpa has something to tell you. Something important. You know that limp you have? It's because of something called a gene. A gene I gave you. It didn't come from your Daddy and it didn't come from your Mommy. It came from me. It skipped a generation. But it's going to get better, I promise, because I had the same thing when I was your age. That's the way life is. Sometimes we don't find out about things until we're big enough to understand them." His eyes found Ennis's. "When you're older, there will be other things you'll find out, too."

"You mean secrets, Grandpa?"

He turned back to Luke. "Yes, secrets. Sometimes secrets need to be kept until they don't matter anymore." He smiled: kind, grandfatherly, wise. "But there's one secret I can tell you right here and now, little Luke. One you don't need to be grown up to know."

He pumped his dimpled fists and bounced up and down on Duncan's knee. "Tell me, Grandpa, tell me!"

"Your mother loved your father. More than he knew."

"Oh, Grandpa, that's not a secret. Mama used to tell us every night when she tucked us into bed that she loved Daddy to the sky. Sometimes she cried when she told us. Do all grownups cry when they love somebody?"

The look of deliverance on Duncan's stricken face called to Ennis's mind a photo his father sometimes showed him when he'd been drinking, a famous photo of Eisenhower in a kepi with his hands clasped behind him while observing a pile of Jewish cadavers at Ohrduf, the first German-soil concentration camp liberated by Americans. The profound looks of salvation graven unto the faces of the wretched survivors as they stared at Eisenhower, amazed not only that goodness had endured in the hellish world that had engulfed them, but that a general with a German name was its embodiment.

The exquisite pressure inside Ennis eased, as if an invisible baffle had been opened. For the first time since hearing those miraculous words — *They have a donor for you* — he felt worthy of the woman whose precious gift he had been blessed to receive.

Becky would say that his quest for self-worth had been realized by a journey of self-acceptance, and that only through authentic self-expression had he overcome self-loathing. She would tell him, with her earnest face, that he had projected his shame over cross-dressing and his denial of being transgender onto his organ donor, deluding himself into believing that her female soul was causing havoc in his male body. His delusion ended, she would insist, because he finally came to terms with being transgender. Accepting his true inner woman Elaine had rid him of his imagined inner woman Carla.

Ennis winked at Luke. It was a perfectly reasonable explanation to give. Except that some things were, what you might say, beyond reason.

Chapter 23

CULLEN STARED OUT THE sandwiched Plexiglas of his cabin window at the bank of cumulus below. Mighty clouds of joy made luminous by yellow light from above. A natural phenomenon so precious, so breathtaking—so empyreal—it suggested the Divine. *Who made this infinite beauty, if not one who is infinitely beautiful?* Augustine's argument from beauty, a fifth-century case for belief. But not how Cullen had come to his.

Nor had he come to it by white crows. Ennis's eerie unmasking of MacGregor aside, Cullen did not believe that transplanted organs had the capacity to drag their donors' souls into unsuspecting recipients. He favored Becky's more prosaic theory instead: that Ennis's peculiar post-transplant sensations were caused by the emergence of his long-suppressed female personality. Denial of the shame he felt over cross-dressing gave rise to a vivid and powerful defense mechanism that blamed the transmigrated soul of his organ donor for his distress.

Cullen's newfound belief had come more from deducing God than discovering Him. Faith for him was not a warm glow in the belly born of instinctual conviction, but rather a conscious choice, an exercise of free will leading to the inevitable conclusion that skepticism was illogical. Atheism required an even bigger leap of faith than theism: it posited something from nothing twice, first the origin of matter and energy, then the origin of life. Not to mention the origin of the mind. Too many improbable origins for a series of unlikely accidents to account for, more than the doctrine of randomness could plausibly deliver.

So he had turned to God — to Christianity — to explain the origins of matter, life, and mind. Ever mindful that it was not a white crow that led him there, but a parrotfish, the Christian paradox of Ennis, *both* male *and* female, the most beautiful fish in the lagoon. But to be worthy of God, he had to first acknowledge that he was unworthy of God. Divine revelation required work, the embrace of religious ritual, active rather than passive worship. It would not be enough to be Catholic. He would have to be a practicing Catholic.

Which had made all the difference to the dozing woman beside him.

He turned from the window and clasped her hand. She smiled, but did not open her eyes. He feasted on her profile: the high-riding bones of her face; her finely tapered nose and chin; the fullness of her lips; the slash of raven hair draped like a bandoleer across her shoulder and breast.

The phone call that brought her to him came from the Mutual Consent Program of the Adoption Branch of the California Department of Social Services. The Consent for Contact form Cullen notarized and submitted months before at Ron Ely's behest had been matched by an astute social worker to a more recent posting by an adult adoptee in search of her birth mother. Carrie Snyder's form had stipulated that she was born in Laguna Beach to a woman named Angela Nichols. She did not know the name of her birth father; only that, like her birth mother, he had been living in Minneapolis at the time of her conception. In accordance with California law, Cullen's name and address and hers were disclosed to one another. Leading to this moment, he and Angie holding hands on a flight to Seattle to meet Carrie, their daughter, married with two young children of her own.

He leaned over and kissed her cheek and murmured that he loved her. And in that kiss, though they had not once spoken of it, he knew they would be married soon, and that at their nuptials their daughter and son-in-law would be matron of honor and best man, and that Tuti Okatai, Angie's Cook Island father, would walk her down the aisle in a traditional Cook Island wedding dress. And that there would be a single bridesmaid: Ennis Willoughby, in a pareu and lipstick, with a plumeria in his hair. Because that was the nature of things. That was how the universe was.

That was how God was.

Please continue reading for the
BOOK CLUB GUIDE
and the
INTERVIEW WITH THE AUTHOR.

Book Club Guide

1. Cullen Brodie saves the life of his patient, Ennis Willoughby. Does Ennis have an impact on Cullen's life? If so, how?

2. What is the meaning of the book's epigraph?

3. Which do you think the story suggests: that the soul of Ennis's organ donor, Carla MacGregor, inhabited him? Or that he confused his emerging transgender personality with Carla's imagined characteristics?

4. What is the book's cover symbolic of?

5. Which character do you feel the most sympathy for, and why?

6. Cullen and Angie react in opposite ways to the same tragic event of their youth. Compare and contrast their reactions and give an opinion as to why each reacted the way they did.

7. Which character changes most throughout the course of the story?

8. What did you learn from the story about the doctor-patient relationship?

9. What did you learn from the story about the nature of serious medical illness?

10. Discuss the role that art plays in the story. What is the significance in the story of the paintings *Olive Trees with Yellow Sky and Sun* by Van Gogh, and *Le Jeune Martyre* by Delaroche?

11. Most of the novel is set in the United States, but several chapters take place on the island of Rarotonga in the South Pacific. What is the island's significance to the story?

12. Discuss the dynamics of the relationship between Cullen and Angie.

13. The story suggests that cross-dressing and Christianity share a common essential truth. Describe what this might be.

14. What is the basis of the religious conversion that occurs in the story?

Interview with the Author

Tell us about the unusual title of your story.

The protagonist of the story, Cullen Brodie, is a doctor. His most unusual patient, Ennis Willoughby, is a cross-dresser — sometimes male and sometimes female. Parrotfish are hermaphrodites, spending part of their life cycle as males and part as female — like Ennis. Parrotfish are also brilliantly colored, sometimes in such a way that their color scheme is remarkably similar to the colors of the rainbow flag of the LGBT movement — like the parrotfish on the cover of the book. Cullen is the atheist in the title, and Ennis is the parrotfish.

You are a doctor — a kidney specialist — and a writer. What do the art of medicine and the art of fiction have in common?

More than you might think. I try to create complex characters that are three dimensional, so that they *seem* like real people. Patients *are* real people who need to be related to in three dimensions: physical, emotional, and spiritual. And each patient's illness is a story in which that patient is the lead character. It is not possible to provide effective care to a patient without knowing their story, and it is not possible to create believable characters without a story for them to act upon. In this way the roles of doctor and writer are the same: each must understand the central character and that character's story.

What was the most difficult aspect of writing *The Atheist and the Parrotfish*?

Writing from the point of view of a cross-dresser. It required a great amount of research to make the character Ennis Willoughby credible to readers. I not only had to understand Ennis's cross-dressing in a practical sense, to know what cross-dressers *do*, but also in an emotional sense, to know how cross-dressing *feels*.

Were any of the characters in your story inspired by real people?

Yes. The character of Ennis Willoughby is based on a man, long deceased, who was the most unusual patient I ever had. He was a gruff tradesman who came to my office one day wearing a dress and a bra and a female wig, at a time when public cross-dressing was rare. I asked him why he was dressed like a woman. He told me, "Because I like it, and that's all I want to say about it." I wondered ever since what exactly it was that he liked about wearing a dress. And now I finally know.

Very few readers will come to this story expecting to discover common ground between Christianity and cross-dressing. Explain what this surprising link means to the story.

There is an essential truth common to cross-dressing and Christianity—and to parrotfish. A brilliant paradox. Christianity accommodates multiple paradoxes; *both* the Crusades *and* turn-the-other-cheek; *both* the lion *and* the lamb; *both* the sinner *and* the saint. A cross-dresser accommodates *both* a male *and* a female personality. And the parrotfish, which is a sequential hermaphrodite, changes from female to male during its lifecycle, living as *both* male *and* female, not *either* female *or* male. Christianity, cross-dressing, and parrotfish are all *both/and* rather than *either/or*.

Why did you become a doctor, and why a writer?

I became a doctor to help other human beings and to engage with them in an intimate and meaningful way. Altruism is a basic human impulse—though often an irrational one: for example, Gentiles who risked their lives to protect Jews in the Holocaust, or soldiers who dive on grenades to protect their platoon mates. Patients allow me to satisfy my need for altruism. It is that way for most doctors that I know. I write for much the same reason; to seek meaning through storytelling and to touch other lives in an intimate way.

Acknowledgements

Many thanks to all who touched this book during its long journey, notably Mark Spencer and Caroline Upcher, early champions of this project who helped shape it.

I am deeply grateful to my publisher, Dave Lane, who plucked this story from the pile and launched it.

A hat tip to Dale Pease for creating the fabulous cover that captures so much in a single image.

Finally, special thanks to Eric Pinder, my editor at Evolved Pub, for his wisdom and skill. His many reads of the manuscript and careful attention to every detail improved it immeasurably.

About the Author

By day I'm a nephrologist, treating dialysis patients and kidney transplant recipients. By night I write fiction. I believe the two finest callings in life are doctor and writer, one ministering to the human condition, the other illuminating it, and each capable of transforming it.

I earned BA and MD degrees at the University of Minnesota and did my postgraduate training at Emory University in Atlanta and the University of California in San Diego. I live now in Orange County, CA.

I am a champion of the healing power of literature, and sometimes prescribe novels or short stories to patients to help them cope with illness. Fiction explores meaning in a way science cannot. Sometimes only fiction tells the truth.

For more, please visit Richard Barager online at:
Personal Website: www.RichardBarager.com
Publisher Website: www.EvolvedPub.com
Goodreads: Richard Barager
Twitter: @RichardBarager
Facebook: www.facebook.com/RichardBarager
LinkedIn: www.linkedin.com/in/RichardBarager

What's Next from Richard Barager?

RED CLAY, YELLOW GRASS:
A NOVEL OF THE 1960s
(Coming March 2018)

*Red clay and yellow grass, a battleground and a rock festival...
the senseless slaughter of Vietnam and the folly of utopian fantasy.*

David Noble is an orphan with a fondness for the novels of Walter Scott; Jackie Lundquist is a child of privilege, partial to J. D. Salinger and the importance of getting real. Their ill-fated college love affair implodes when David enlists to fight a war she opposes.

Angered by his choice—the marines instead of her—Jackie refuses to acknowledge his letters from Vietnam, where David is burrowed into the blood-red clay of Khe Sanh, one of six thousand marines entrapped by an army of North Vietnamese regulars. David survives the brutal siege, but returns home to find Jackie immersed in a counterculture world of drugs and militancy.

The two lovers find themselves fighting on opposite sides of the defining issue of their time, as the New Left and the New Right battle for a generation's political soul. To Jackie, the faltering war in Vietnam is a failure of national conscience; to David it is a failure of national honor. But neither her rise to fame as the antiwar movement's alluring

Radical Queen nor David's defiant counter-protest activities in support of the war can extinguish their passion for one another.

Both their conflicted affair and the Age of Aquarius itself careen toward the mellow-yellow grass of Altamont Speedway, site of the decade's last great rock festival: Altamont, the metaphoric Death of the Sixties, where honor and shame collide and tragedy awaits redemption.

More from Evolved Publishing

Just as we're certain you thoroughly enjoyed
The Atheist and the Parrtofish,
we're certain you're going to love
these remarkable books, too.

THE DAUGHTER OF THE SEA AND THE SKY
By David Litwack
www.EvolvedPub.com/David-Litwacks-Books

HANNAH'S VOICE
By Robb Grindstaff
www.EvolvedPub.com/RobbGrindstaffBooks

ENFOLD ME
By Steven Greenberg
www.EvolvedPub.com/StevenGreenbergBooks